KINMOUNT

Rod Carley

Library and Archives Canada Cataloguing in Publication

Title: Kinmount / Rod Carley.
Names: Carley, Rod, 1962- author.
Identifiers: Canadiana (print) 2020028116X | Canadiana (ebook) 20200281860 | ISBN 9781988989259
  (softcover) | ISBN 9781988989303 (EPUB)
Classification: LCC PS8605.A7547 K56 2020 | DDC C813/.6—dc23

Cover Design: Mitchell Gauvin and Kevin Hoffman
Author photo: Ed Regan

Published by:
Latitude 46 Publishing
info@latitude46publishing.com
Latitude46publishing.com

We acknowledge the financial support of the Ontario Arts Council in the production of this book.

ONTARIO ARTS COUNCIL
CONSEIL DES ARTS DE L'ONTARIO
an Ontario government agency
un organisme du gouvernement de l'Ontario

Printed and bound in Canada on 100% recycled paper.

KINMOUNT

Rod Carley

In memory of my parents,
for loving their alien son.

With apologies to the good people of Kinmount.

"I do not deny that what happened to us is a thing worth laughing at."

Miguel de Cervantes Saavedra, *Don Quixote*

PART ONE: MEETING

"Enter freely and of your own free will."

Bram Stoker, *Dracula*

ONE

"Come to Kinmount," the voice said.

It was Lola Whale.

Lola Whale was an aging Renaissance woman living in Ontario Highlands farm country. She was a home renovator, Raphael-inspired painter, and, in her latest incarnation, community theatre producer. Dave had worked for her six months earlier, hired on an outreach grant to direct an amateur production of Congreve's seventeenth-century Restoration comedy, *Love for Love*—his choice, a modern dress adaptation that was as bold an artistic statement as it was a financial flop.

Farmers left at intermission in droves to listen to a local entertainer cover Stompin' Tom in a dirt floor bar.

"You're joking," he said, turning down the radio.

Kinmount was the last place he wanted to revisit. The name alone said it all.

"The locals meet their future spouses at family reunions," he said.

"Very funny. Now put away that world weariness of yours and listen," she replied curtly.

"Their children are conceived at a red light. I don't think—"

Lola cut him off.

"Our town council has approved a three-day Summer in the Park Festival over the August long weekend."

"The mayor pays child support to his sister," Dave continued.

"I pitched them an outdoor Shakespeare for families," said

Lola, ignoring him.

The life of a hand-to-mouth freelance director was about as glamorous and lucrative as cleaning toilets, a summer job Dave had soldiered through during his second year at theatre school. Lola continued: "*Romeo and Juliet.* And they went for it. I want you to direct."

"Lola, no," Dave replied emphatically.

"You already know the local talent," she said.

"And look how well that went."

"We just have to educate them is all."

"No, Lola."

Dave watched with disgust as more and more shadflies landed on his mudroom window. To the children of Birch Lake, the shadfly was a national bird. This was not the case for the rest of the community. Shadfly season had officially started—a dead fish-smelling nuisance for the next two weeks. Millions of shads emerged from the shallow lake behind his tiny bungalow, overwhelming predators who were unable to eat them all. Those that survived carried out their egg-laying mission; it was a numbers game, the shadfly version of storming the beaches of Normandy.

"A full-time three-week rehearsal period," said Lola.

"They're amateurs. They all have jobs," Dave said, grabbing a broom. "And no teeth."

"So we juggle. After work and evenings. Weekends. Those that are free during the day, you work with."

Lola was as relentlessly optimistic as Dave was pessimistic.

"It would take six months," said Dave, sweeping dead shadfly corpses off his back porch and windows, his cell phone now on speaker, resting on the patio table.

"Now you're just being difficult."

"No, I'm not," he said. "Besides there is no one in Kinmount who could possibly play the leads."

"So you bring in a couple of theatre school grads who'll jump at the opportunity."

"They'll jump alright."

He brushed a pair of copulating shadflies off his t-shirt. A shadfly's adult life was simple. Find a partner and mate before starving to death (considering it had no mouth not a difficult task) or being eaten. Twenty-four hours to make it count. Just like a Birch Lake tavern on a Friday night.

"There's a budget to pay you, them, and build a set and make costumes," said Lola.

"The town is actually putting up money?" Dave turned on his water hose. It reared up like an angry garter snake.

"No, I am."

"No." He sprayed his mudroom windows, turning the mash of shadflies into mush.

"It's not a lot but I can pay you fifteen hundred, and Romeo and Juliet a thousand each. And you can all stay at my house. Free room and board."

"Uh-huh." He turned the hose off.

Lola lived in a five-bedroom Victorian home and rented out rooms to students during the school year.

"I don't think so," said Dave, returning to the kitchen.

"I'll get it all back at the performances. Donations."

"From all the farmers. Right. Unless I set it in a country bar you can kiss your money goodbye."

"No, I want it done as a period costume piece," she said.

He remained silent.

"Have a little faith. It'll be great."

"Faith is the least of my worries," he replied, unable to get the Congreve fiasco out of his mind.

"Think of the good it will do for the community," Lola said, appealing to Dave's higher altruistic self.

"And *Love for Love* tells you nothing?" Dave fired back, descending to his lower Darwinian self.

"This is Shakespeare, not some obscure long-wigged-and-winded Restoration hack. Everyone knows *Romeo and Juliet*. Besides, I'll have your back."

Despite her reservations, Lola had built the set, sold tickets, designed the poster, and made costumes for his Restoration "grunge" comedy. She'd even agreed to his decision to use

Nirvana for scene change music.

"Lola, I'm sorry, I'm just not up to it," he sighed heavily.

"You're making a big mistake."

"I'm used to it. What's one more?" His horribly miscalculated zombie adaptation of *Twelfth Night and the Living Dead*, two years earlier in Brockville, had left Loyalist audiences wanting to eat their own brains out.

"C'mon. You'll be brilliant. You know I make a mean Cornish hen." Lola could add gourmet chef to her list of accomplishments.

"Gluttony will get you nowhere."

"Stocked bar."

"Nice try."

The Rat Pack would have been envious of Lola's booze collection. Dave figured she'd punished her kids by refusing to put ice in their drinks.

"Local girls falling over a handsome director from out of town," she said.

"Kinmount is Canada's capital of unwed mothers under the age of twenty and you know it. Kids having kids. And the rest are grammatically challenged and wear spandex. And that's just the men. Sorry, Lola thanks for the offer. But I'm not interested. Really."

"You think about it and I'll call you in a couple of days."

"There is no 'thinking.' My answer is still no."

"Okay, okay, I get it. Suit yourself!"

She hung up.

He grabbed a cooler from the fridge and turned the radio up.

"A massive swarm of shadflies took over the Birch Lake municipal bridge last night," the CBC afternoon host explained to her listeners with the measured gravity of H.G. Wells. "Visibility was so bad that vehicles were unable to pass due to the swarm. The town will keep the lights turned off over the next few weeks in order to keep the bugs off the bridge."

He called Lola back.

TWO

Toronto was a city of ghosts.

He had trained there, struggled there, and moved away from there.

Now, back in its mid-day downtown clamour, Dave's senses were ambushed by his past on every street corner. And by rotting fumes from a garbage strike well into its second month.

He'd booked the auditions at his old alma mater, a rundown building on Queen Street East that was slated for demolition. Hopping off the streetcar two blocks before, Dave beat up on himself one more time for taking the job.

The applicants were recent graduates of the Lorne Greene Theatre School, thirty post-millennials with high hopes. Dave was an irregular director when it came to casting. First and foremost, he never sat behind a table. He detested that old British model of judgment and superiority. Rather, he sat beside the table, keeping openness with his actors to help calm their nerves and soften the power imbalance.

He gave actors specific direction after their monologues, three or four different scenarios to test their range and ability and, more importantly, promise. He was not some brush-off dictator.

Dave genuinely cared that actors did their best. He never humiliated or downgraded an applicant. He'd experienced that kind of old school bullying in his training and vowed he'd never behave that way. He'd kept his word for twenty-five years.

Most importantly, he never ate during an audition. Not

even Smarties.

Ten of the neophytes had no clue to how to handle classical text.

"And what are you doing today?" Dave asked a young actor.

"Portia from *The Merchant of Verona*," they replied.

"Venice," Dave gently corrected.

"Verona," was the irritated response. "Haven't you read Shakespeare?"

Four threw chairs and screamed their monologues in grandiose misapplications of the Method. Most were suited for film. The remaining seven he asked to stay. It was an exhausting eight-hour day. Mixing and matching chemistries to find the right fit for the star-crossed lovers was a delicate process, as difficult as creating a new perfume. He asked the young actors to read the balcony scene aloud, listening for a connected understanding of the language and clear diction. When asked to name the most famous scene from *Romeo and Juliet* most people would reply in unison, "The balcony scene." This is totally understandable because it's probably the most famous scene in English literature. The image of Juliet on her balcony with Romeo in the garden below is embedded in our culture, from stage productions to film adaptations to *The Simpsons*. It contains *Romeo and Juliet's* most quoted lines:

ROMEO: "What light through yonder window breaks?"
JULIET: "Romeo, Romeo, wherefore art thou Romeo?"

Dave himself climbed the balcony of a girlfriend in high school only to be met by her fuming father. The half-million visitors who flock to Verona each year can even act it out for themselves on a pseudo-balcony that was constructed by adding an old stone coffin to the exterior of a building, specifically to satisfy the hordes of tourists seeking an authentic *Romeo and Juliet* experience. At least if a hapless Romeo fell off the balcony, his funeral arrangements were taken care of. There is only one problem with this: there is no balcony scene in *Romeo and Juliet*. The word "balcony" never appears in the play. The only reference is to a window.

Even stranger, Shakespeare wouldn't even have known what a balcony was because there was no balcony at the time anywhere in the whole of England. The earliest use of the word "balcony" was in 1618, fifteen years after *Romeo and Juliet* was first performed. Dave read the play repeatedly, something most people haven't done since high school, to verify this strange fact. No balcony. Not even a mention. He determined that, in his particular case, it didn't really matter that Shakespeare never actually envisioned a balcony. Centuries of revision and retelling had made it precisely what audiences wanted. Dave could live with that.

He got his young actors up on their feet, putting the text viscerally into their bodies to assess their emotional access. Finally, he had them do the scene in their own words and then return to the original to see how their improvisations informed their acting choices. He was looking for intelligence and honesty.

All the rest he hoped he could bring out in rehearsal. A three-week pressure cooker to achieve the impossible. Theatre artists were masochists. All of them. Dave being the worst culprit of them all.

The role of Romeo could be a trap, dripping with syrupy romanticism and emotional angst. In short, Romeo is a player, a cock-driven Italian adolescent as fickle as the weather. His first unrequited infatuation, Rosaline, has sent his loins into a tailspin. He is playing Juliet at the Capulet ball, then stealing into her orchard and swearing his undying love beneath her non-existent balcony. Is Juliet an improvement over Rosaline or a replacement?

Romeo has all the right lines. The right lines that lesser girls might let him get to first "poperin pear" with.

Not Juliet.

She is a book girl and wiser than her coming-out party

years. She puts Romeo to the test, shutting down any declaration of love that smells of cheap romanticism. Romeo is knocked off his tights—his courtly love rulebook tossed to the night.

"What should I swear by?" he asks.

Juliet orders him not to swear by anything, especially the ever-changing moon, and just be himself.

Romeo thinks, "This girl has brains and balls."

She refuses to play the game of tease-and-pursue. He's met his match. This is the moment the player shifts. He brings unbridled action and she, cautious smarts.

B.J. Watts—the only male actor gifted with perfect diction that didn't seem forced—grasped the balcony text with muscularity, none of the false dreaminess to which so many actors fell victim. He was not overly handsome, but had the looks of a friendly dog with whom an audience could readily identify. He was an eccentric dresser, a juggler, and a ventriloquist (according to his resume), and his offbeat manner would bring a welcome quirkiness to the part.

By contrast, Miranda Murray was a petite blonde with a charming sweetness and refreshing, contemporary innocence. She attacked the text with intelligence and an authentic naturalness that marked a future in the theatre. Dave discovered she was the daughter of two university English professors, inheriting their love of language and wordplay.

Dave paper-clipped their headshots together.

His casting worries were temporarily put to rest.

THREE

Dave turned on the radio and listened to the town's mayor, Paul McGregor, shouting on a CBC call-in show. "I've heard of clearing a bridge because of ice ... or snow ... or an accident. But because of BUGS! That's a first. Forget about Sharknado. We had a sci-fi movie play out in front of us right here in Birch Lake. The god-damned bugs were piled up *knee-high* in front of our headlights! We had to get a snow plow, out of storage, to plow the little bastards off and then sand the bridge because it was so damn slippery." The Mayor was more flabbergasted than usual, the town having used up half of its annual snow-clearing budget by July. "I can tell you from a tourism industry perspective this is horrifying."

Dave had his Romeo and Juliet. It was the Kinmount casting that troubled him. The only thing Kinmount and Stratford had in common was the farm country in which their festivals were located.

Every production of Shakespeare involves countless acts of interpretation and revision, meaning cuts. The cut lines don't vanish but form a hidden subterranean text, an underworld of inference, inversion, mystery, and the subconscious mind. There is always the play that is read, the play that is imagined, the play that is created with collaborators, and the play that is presented. None are ideal. None are absolute. None are complete. The "cut" lines merely put aside for another director to restore.

Dave set about carefully cutting *Romeo and Juliet*. To hold an outdoor summer audience's attention, competing with a noisy midway, motorcycles, and mosquitoes (Shakespeare's actors competed with cock-fighting), he needed to get the running time down to a tight two hours, without an intermission, the length of a summer blockbuster. And, unfortunately, his audience was in Kinmount, which Dave likened to the toothless groundlings of Shakespeare's day who paid a penny to stand in front of the stage and heckle. The groundlings were the uneducated poor—easily distracted, loud, hot-tempered, drunk, averse to bathing, disorderly, and armed with fruits, vegetables, and the occasional inbred rodent to pelt at any actor who failed to entertain. They warmed up by watching a bear, chained to a stake, get torn apart by dogs.

In the Elizabethan age of sandglasses, sundials, and inaccurate clockwork, the prologue to *Romeo and Juliet* announces that the performance will last two hours, but it is a very different two hours than our modern sense of time. Shakespeare's society was an aural one, easily able to comprehend forty hits of wordplay per minute. Theatregoers gossiped of going to *hear* a play. Elizabethan actors spoke at lightning speed (faster than the hurling of a groundling's rotten tomato) and the entirety of *Romeo and Juliet* could most likely have been performed within "two hours traffic on the stage." A visually oriented modern audience, while accustomed to watching forty cinematic edits per minute, would be hard-pressed to keep up with the delivery of Shakespeare's players. Thus, contemporary actors had to speak slower to be understood.

Dave's task was to find a way for these two worlds to meet. An understandable uncut production of *Romeo and Juliet* ran three hours. Dave had to cut a third of the text. A daunting task. He altered and omitted passages, carefully trimming the language to get at the key images without sacrificing the nuances and subtleties of the original text. He called his process Shakespearean paleontology. He raised his mental pickaxe and broke down the difficult rock fragments of images no longer understood and those phrases whose meaning required two pages of footnotes. He picked and picked until he was left with a clean bone of language on which he could build a recognizable skeleton of the text.

"Ruffles? Where's my little dog?!"

He heard the frail voice sliding in through the porch screen door.

It was his ninety-three-year-old neighbour. Dottie was a fragile tiny widow still living on her own. Her son Roger had removed all her hidden stashes of gin (it was the sole condition of her being allowed to remain in the house). Dottie, now lost in the delusions of age and loneliness, weighed seventy pounds soaking wet but, in her day, had been the beauty queen of the Haliburton Highlands. Dave had seen the proof in the black and white framed photographs on her piano when he'd helped Roger install a used air conditioner a few weeks earlier.

He rushed out to assist.

"What's wrong, Dottie?" he asked. It was a familiar ritual.

"Where's Ruffles?" she implored, unsteady on her sandals.

He grabbed some dog biscuits, jumped over her fence and began the search.

Ruffles, a wiry fox terrier, was eating grass in the shadows at the far end of the yard. Dave lured him back to her porch with the stale biscuits. Ruffles crunched them down and proudly paraded up Dottie's back steps and into the house. Dave kept a stash of treats for these recurring emergencies.

"Oh, thank you, thank you," she whimpered, shaking his arm.

"All good, Dottie. False alarm," he reassured her, taking a bony hand in his and patting it gently.

He'd promised her he'd install a gate between their yards to help keep a better eye on Ruffles. Now the gate would have to wait. He'd be gone for three weeks.

"Dottie, I've got a directing job so I'm going to be away for a bit," he said slowly and carefully, not wanting to upset her further. "When I get back I will put in that gate. I promise."

"But Ruffles?"

"Clip him to his lead," he instructed. "I've attached it to your clothesline so he can run about the yard and not get tangled up."

It was an old school pulley affair identical to the one in his mother's backyard.

"Tug on this cord when you need to reel him in. I've counter balanced it so it will be as light as a feather," he explained carefully.

"I don't know." Her eyes were wide with worry.

"You'll be fine. It's only three weeks," he said evenly. "I'll let your son know I'm going to be away."

"Okay. He's *our* little dog," she said, giving him a needy hug.

He gently brushed a shadfly off her shoulder.

"Yes he is," he said, giving her a squeeze.

He returned to his kitchen. Dave wasn't abandoning Dottie so why did he feel guilty. Guilt and crackers were a staple of Dave's diet.

He called Dottie's son and set about packing.

He wouldn't need his camping gear. He had a Kinmount king-size bed waiting for him with an ensuite bathroom. He threw his sleeping bag back in the closet.

"LIST!"

"List yourself."

"LiiiiiiST!"

The voice of Hamlet's father echoed in his head.

It often did. Shortly after graduating, Dave got his first job with a children's touring company performing an embarrassing puppet mash-up of Dr. Seuss and Shakespeare, *Green Eggs and Hamlet*:

"To sleep, to dream, now there's the rub, I could drop a toaster in my tub."

The Dancing Llama Theatre Company operated under more than a dozen aliases as a result of lawsuits due to poor, non-union working conditions. Dancing Llama routinely enforced schedules that would be patently unacceptable by any standard. Dave was hired alongside five other recent theatre school graduates by company producer, Jimmy Minestrone, who treated his young charges like dirt, contractually obligating them to perform three shows daily in the remotest schools in Canada, then driving six hours to the next destination, at night, usually in the middle of winter. The wear and tear from here to there left the company exhausted.

After eighteen days of the third leg of their cross-country tour and operating on just six hours of sleep, the cast set off for a three-hundred-and-fifty-kilometre drive from Kelowna to Chilliwack. It was a cold January night and Dave's stage manager—a capable young technician named Becky—was behind the wheel of the company van as it climbed the mountains outside of Kelowna. Dave sat in the passenger seat, his eyes glued to the road. Dancing Llama was too cheap to outfit the van with proper winter tires. An avalanche had blocked sections of the highway earlier in the day. Snow was falling heavily.

"LIST!" a voice suddenly screamed in Dave's head.

"What?" said Dave confused.

"List," Old English for "listen."

"LIST!" the voice repeated, sounding remarkably like that of the actor playing Hamlet's father's ghost. But he was fast asleep in the back of the van along with the rest of the company.

Dave looked to his left. Becky had dozed off. The van veered off the highway.

"Becky!" Dave shouted, as he reached for the steering wheel.

Becky woke up to Dave screaming her name and, in a panic, slammed on the brakes. Under the fresh snow lurked black ice. The van began spinning out of control down the highway. To their right was a solid wall of Rockies. To their left, a two-hundred-foot plunge to certain death. Dave watched the rock encircle them, his brief life passing before his eyes: a recently failed relationship and the haunting ghosts of Christmases past. After what seemed an hour of donuts (fifteen seconds in reality) the van came to rest on a small patch of flat land beside the highway—the only patch for miles in either direction. The instant it came to a stop, a logging truck barrelled around the bend in the oncoming lane. Three seconds sooner and the cast of *Green Eggs and Hamlet* would've been an omelette.

After that, the Ghost of Hamlet's Father decided to stick around, the invisible embodiment of Dave's gut instinct.

"Hey, old man," Dave said aloud to his empty kitchen.

"LiiiiiiiiiiiiiiiiiST."

"I hear you. Enough already. I know it's crazy but I'm doing it."

He poured himself a bowl of cereal and packed his camping gear.

He knocked on his neighbour's door across the street, a real estate agent dabbling in long distance running like half the population on his street.

"You ready to sell?"

Before the door was open.

Skip had been asking him that question for months, trying to convince him he needed a bigger space. He knew Skip wanted his bungalow so his daughter and her new baby could live across the street.

"Not today, Skip," his conditioned response.

"You and your girlfriend free for a barbecue on Friday?"

Skip was fishing for information. Dave's latest relationship (Rosaline, the play an awkward reminder) had ended four months earlier, the same way they always did—a disillusioned girlfriend exiting stage left once realizing her romantic notions of dating a travelling theatre artist were a lost cause, and that she'd always come second to his art and be alone on her birthday. It was the cold hard cliché of Dave's life.

"No can do," said Dave. "I just got a gig and have to go out of town for a few weeks. I was wondering if you'd collect my mail and cut my lawn."

It was a familiar request.

"No problem. A variety six-pack of Irish ale is fine."

Skip's usual barter.

"Sure thing. Thanks."

He turned to go.

"Everything okay with you guys?"

"Sure. Why?"

Dave didn't want his neighbourhood to know his business.

"Haven't seen her car much."

"I just need some time to prep," said Dave, turning to leave again.

Even that was saying too much.

"Well, when you get back we'll have to have the two of you over," Skip shouted.

"Thanks, Skip," Dave said, giving him a thumbs up.

He returned to his driveway and noticed another pool of oil forming under his battered Tercel. He'd bought it used over fifteen years ago (Dave bought most things second-hand.) The new millennium had signalled the model's demise with the arrival of the sporty Platz, the sound made when driving over a shadfly and the unfortunate name of a Mennonite dessert.

Dave called his mother.

"You're going to end up a lonely, old man."

"Mom, please don't start—"

"You want that?"

"Of course not."

"Well?"

His mother wasn't exactly a shoulder to lean on, more like a linebacker who flattened him off the ball snap.

"I don't know what your problem is," she exclaimed.

"It's hard to pronounce," he fired back sarcastically. It was their bi-monthly argument.

"You have no financial stability, you're never home, and you are incapable of sustaining happiness."

"You forgot self-absorbed and suffering from low self-esteem. I wonder who caused that."

"Don't go blaming me because you can't stand being criticized. You chose your hopeless profession. A hobby, yes, I said, fine, but a living? You're a grown man who lives like a college student. To think what you could've been?"

"I know, I know, a lawyer." He delicately plucked a shadfly

by the wings off his fridge. There was no point in killing it, it would be dead in seven hours.

"Or a car salesman. You've got the gift of the gab. Your grandfather always said you could sell ice cream to Eskimos."

"They're called Inuit."

"Inuit *sminuit.*"

"I gotta go."

"Call me when you get back."

"I will."

"Drive safe and, for God's sake, don't get involved with some farmer's daughter."

"I won't."

"Sure."

"Mom?"

She'd hung up.

He tossed the shadfly out his front door.

He was selfish and always had been; the fall-out from pushing actors to make selfish character choices. And he was a coward. Still talking to his seventy-five-year-old mother like he had when he was in theatre school.

His mother wasn't exactly the poster girl for healthy relationships. Dave was only five when his father died. His mother remarried ten months later, to a younger man who'd lost everything betting against the Leafs in '67. His new stepfather immediately tried to get hold of Dave's small inheritance. His mother fought back. The legal battles, which began within weeks of the wedding, lasted sixteen years. By the time he turned twenty-one, every cent of Dave's inheritance was gone.

Dave's "Uncle" Thomas also had a difficult childhood, losing his father at the age of five and struggling to survive the social turmoil of Elizabethan England.

The two Middletons were born into mad, uncertain worlds, four centuries apart, a madness Thomas Middleton turned into art and Dave Middleton strived to make sense of today.

Nothing kept Thomas Middleton from writing. And nothing kept Dave from pursuing a career in the theatre, after researching his ancestry at the Kingston Public Library in high school and discovering Thomas Middleton was his great-great-great-great-great-great-great uncle. The chaos of Dave's home life drove him to embrace "the lickerish study of poetry and its unprofitable sweetness"—as his "uncle's" swanky blank verse put it.

"I've paid my dues," Dave had repeated to his mother in earlier phone conversations.

"And I've paid *my* cash and then some bailing you out," she'd responded. "I paid your car insurance. And then I couldn't pay your insurance because you had all those unpaid parking tickets."

Dave still had a wad of unpaid parking tickets on his kitchen table, the last chord of irresponsible adolescence.

There was a knock at the door.

Dave peered through the curtains and saw a hydro truck with a newly dented fender idling at the end of the driveway.

Now what?

He sized up the hydro worker instantly. A local. A Habs t-shirt under his coveralls. His French-Canadian heritage dating back to the first time Brulé slept with a Huron girl. A fisherman, probably at odds with the nearby reserve.

He wore his orange fluorescent safety vest with the authority of a border-crossing officer.

"Yes?" Dave asked.

"You see those wires?" the hydro worker asked.

Dave looked up and saw nothing but foliage.

"No," he said.

"Exactly," the hydro worker said bluntly. "Your wires go right through the branches. Very dangerous. The weight could bring the wires down. Start a fire. Electrocute a neighbour. Your tree has to come down."

"What?"

"Afraid so."

"By whose authority?"

"City."

"Can't you just trim it back?" Dave asked.

"No can do."

"Why not?"

"These Manitoba Maples grow like weeds. In six months it'd all be back."

"I'll prune them myself," Dave lied. He didn't own shears much less a rake. And he paid Skip to shovel his driveway in winter.

"Sorry, you're not insured. City property," the hydro worker said.

"Well, just chop off some branches then." A reasonable request figured Dave.

"The tree is coming down. City policy."

The same policy allowed for more potholes than a lunar landscape. Birch Lake's roads resembled a third world country, minus the hurricanes. It took twenty town employees to repair a pothole: one to repair it, two to hold SLOW traffic signs for oncoming traffic, and seventeen to drink coffee, smoke cigarettes, and lean against city pickup trucks.

"I refuse," said Dave.

"You don't have a say. I'm just telling you it's scheduled for Friday and to park your car on the street."

"It's murder," Dave declared dramatically. "That tree has been there since before we were born. Think of what it has seen."

The tree, in actual fact, had seen very little.

The hydro worker eyed him suspiciously.

"Anyhow, just make sure your car is off the driveway."

"I'll petition the neighbourhood."

"You can chain yourself naked to the trunk but it's still coming down."

Dave looked down the street and saw a large elm at the mercy of two city chainsaws.

"Have a nice day."

The worker laughed and wheeled away.

Once the tree came down the house would be totally exposed. Naked to the neighbourhood.

Dave felt alone and afraid.

"Drive me away," he said to his tired Tercel.

FOUR

Kin-mount.

A village of two thousand in the Eastern Ontario Highlands, an hour northwest of Peterborough, two and a half easy hours east of Toronto, and five hours of winding backroads south of Birch Lake. Named after Kinmount Willie, a sixteenth-century Scottish border warrior, Kinmount sadly lacked the ferocity of its namesake.

Like many rural communities, Kinmount got its start as a railway hub, with logging on the Burnt River soon to follow. Log-driving, pole-wielding lumberjacks, dubbed "shantymen," weathered harsh conditions and dangerous jobs by day. They spent their nights drinking, brawling, and impregnating local girls, then disappeared upriver. A trend set in motion.

Burnt to the ground three times, Kinmount now struggled as a farming hamlet. It hung limply onto its history while trying to survive in the train-less, log-less, electronic modern world and weeping for its fatherless children.

The sun was beating down on the banks of the Burnt River. It teemed with children and their teenage mothers. Dave drove past Kinmount's entrance sign, ignoring its dated claim of natural beauty. A weather-beaten billboard advertised the local golf course and its nine holes. He drove down the main drag, past the local diner and dollar store, turned left on Maple Avenue, and pulled into Lola's cobblestone driveway. Lola's house stood in manicured contrast to the bungalows that surrounded it in all directions like Scottish serfs serving a manor house.

She greeted him at the door wearing a Tilley hat, Australian slicker, construction boots, and a faded sundress that reflected her faded years. Her rubbery face framed by bangs. Dark brown eyes squinted under heavy lids. Her small upturned nose resembled a wine-soaked cork, her upper lip a fleshy caterpillar. A disconcerting sight as always.

He pulled his knapsack out of the backseat and struggled to remove his mountain bike.

"Cocktails are on," she grinned with her peculiar kindergarten-teacher-like voice that reminded him of an overly dramatic cruise director.

"Hey, Lola."

He wanted to turn around and drive home.

"Park your bike around back and I'll get your pack."

He wheeled his bike around the side of the house to the backyard and was greeted by a neo-classical nightmare. Lola's garden was a disturbing cluster of homemade phallic sculptures. An off-kilter fountain, adorned with misshapen cherubs pissing into the wind, served as the centrepiece.

Disturbing enough to cause Socrates to swallow hemlock prematurely.

Hedges were clipped into the shapes of centaurs. Flowers were arranged in small explosions of red as if blood were seeping out of the statues. He chained his bike to a small penis and walked back to the front door. Lola had left it open.

Framed prints of Renaissance maidens in varying stages of undress and an ornate gold mirror adorned the front hallway. He caught his tired reflection and reassured himself he was not the living dead, although the eyes staring back at him begged to differ.

He kicked off his sandals, feeling the unfamiliar coarseness of the multi-coloured Bohemian sisal carpets that ran throughout the house. The massive chandelier, carved out of deer antlers and hanging over the antique oak dining table, was already lit at five o'clock in the afternoon. The candles flickered in the sunlight. The heat they cast off was formidable. Lola didn't believe in fans or air conditioners, a violation of the natural world she would say. The candles had dripped wax on Dave's head during his Congreve stay.

He noted two formal table settings. He was feeling more like Jonathan Harker by the minute.

Lola reappeared with a tray of naan bread, figs, and cheeses that she set on the table. She returned with a pitcher of martinis, poured two tumblers close to overflowing, and offered him a glass.

"Sit, please. Dinner is simmering away. I put your things in your usual room."

"Please, Lola, don't go to any trouble on my account."

"No trouble at all. I must make our great director feel at home."

That was the last thing he felt.

She sat down at the head of the table, tossing her Tilley hat onto the sideboard. He sat down at the other setting on her right.

"A toast to young love," she declared, raising her glass with a small-calloused hand.

He self-consciously raised his glass, received her clink, and took a sip. His lips were instantly on fire.

"What is that?" he sputtered.

"Jalapeno. Cajun recipe."

She'd swallowed hers.

"Some kick."

"Keeps the girls in New Orleans clean," she laughed. "Better than penicillin."

"Peel the wallpaper off."

He'd have to pace himself.

"So, I've arranged auditions for tomorrow after church at the Legion."

"How many?"

"Fifteen."

"How many from *Love for Love?*"

"Most of them plus a few surprises."

"Surprises, eh?" he asked suspiciously.

"You'll see," she winked. "And two teenagers."

"High school kids? Really? They have the attention span of a gnat," he said. He was looking for an out.

"I've told them all to read the play. I made copies for everyone," she said, ignoring his sputtering.

"Lola, I'm working from the First Folio. I brought my script to photocopy."

"I'll make copies of your dead sea scroll when rehearsals start. Mine are fine to audition with. Don't want to scare them off out of the gate."

"Right." There was no point in arguing the virtues of the First Folio with her.

The First Folio, published in 1623, is a collection of thirty-six of Shakespeare's plays. Two of Shakespeare's colleagues, John Heminges and Henry Condell, prepared the original printings seven years after his death. Despite the volumes of books on Shakespeare that fill libraries around the globe, we actually know very little about the man himself. Only about twelve first-hand sources exist—Shakespeare's christening, a marriage certificate, death certificate, his children's birth and baptismal records, and a few court records. And that's it. The First Folio was the only way to try to discern what might've been the Bard's original intent. Unfortunately, the Folio fell into neglect in the early eighteenth century due to the passing of the Statute of Grammar. The Statute altered the original texts by conventionalizing Elizabethan orthography—the manner in which words were set down on paper. A committee of grammar geeks standardized the usage of capital letters and punctuation in order to set down clauses for easier reading comprehension. Plays that once were designed for acting became the stuff of bedside reading. Modern editors unwittingly eradicated the irregular punctuation clues in the original texts; clues that helped actors recognize the stepping-stones of a character's argument. Over the ensuing centuries, disciples of the First Folio secretly banded together, establishing an underground network of revolutionaries and academic outcasts. Returning to the First Folio remained Shakespeare's only hope, and Dave its stalwart droid.

"What about a stage manager?" he asked apprehensively, after stuffing his Folio copy back in his satchel.

"Ginny," proclaimed Lola, as if the name were on par with Oprah.

Ginny had stage-managed the Congreve. A middle-aged accountant by trade, she had fallen in love with the logic and mathematics of stage management, recording actor blocking patterns with different coloured highlighters and keeping her prompt copy as organized and pristine as a CRA tax return. He poured himself a second martini. Lola was polishing off her third.

Dinner consisted of chicken breast stuffed with Asiago cheese and asparagus, a mushroom risotto, and Greek salad. Dessert, crème brûlée. Lola had typed out two contracts outlining his fee and free room and board. She'd also offered to donate costumes from her private stock. He signed the contracts, pocketed one, and retired early. He needed to re-read the script keeping in mind the locals auditioning.

He climbed the stairs to the third floor, feeling the cherubs dancing on the canvasses that decorated the stairwell walls were watching him. He opened the door to his room and discovered all his things unpacked and put away. Even his toiletries were neatly arranged on the back of the sink.

He heard moaning coming from the second floor.

FIVE

Ginny was an amateur theatre enthusiast, sporting more come-dy-and-tragedy mask embroidered sweatshirts than Dave owned underwear. Her bearing reminded him of a Girl Scout leader, pleasantly efficient with a whistle at the ready. She was a natural multi-tasker loving the make-believe world of community the-atre, the cinnamon spice to her rice pudding life. Ginny's sofa spent more time on stage than in her living room. She passed out the scripts after carefully inserting them page by page in brightly coloured Duo-Tangs.

The first auditionee entered the Legion dining hall.

"Examine other beau-tie*th*," the thirty-year-old mom read aloud to an imaginary Romeo prior to crashing the Capulet ball. Dressed casually in black leggings and an athletic red tank top, she looked and sounded years younger due to her puckish energy and short-cropped black hair. Her line delivery, in her need for attention and validation from Romeo, was refreshingly self-referential. This Benvolio needed a hug, Dave thought.

She was deaf in one ear and had a pronounced lisp, a lisp that made her ripe for ridicule by the younger groundlings of Kinmount—the same Generation Z that got a kick out of flat-tening snakes on the backroads in their parents' pickup trucks. A figure skater in her glory days she had retained her figure despite having three sons. She was determined. No doubt the discipline of falling on ice repeatedly until mastering a spin.

Her career had come to an abrupt end at the age of twenty-one when she made headlines during a provincial short program competition by skating to an Amy Winehouse medley, and doing it in pants. More accurately, she did it in a bedazzled black unitard—Shakespeare was indirectly to blame. He first coined the word "bedazzled" in *The Taming of the Shrew,* along with three thousand other new words.

News outlets and social media viciously attacked her for being ugly and subversive and destroying the "beauty" of women's figure skating by refusing to wear a short skirt. She quit a few months later, furious with male judges who only wanted to see pretty, little figure skaters.

Benvolio, Romeo's cousin, would become Benvoli*a*. A lisping cross-dressing tomboy, in the tradition of Shakespeare's Viola and Rosalind, with a secret crush on Romeo.

ॠ

"REBELLIOUS SUBJECTS, ENEMIES TO PEACE!" the bearded long-haired singer roared. He was a throwback to a denim-on-denim Doobie Brothers album liner.

A 1970s acting school dropout, he was "better than the program," he impressed upon Dave three times. He had a command of the room due to his massive ego. "I could've been a rock star but it didn't work out." The biggest perch in the small pond of Kinmount, he and his vinyl collection lived in a rusty old travel trailer on the outskirts of town, the result of an ugly divorce in his mid-forties that left him homeless. He escaped the winter by busking on the beaches of Mexico and fancied himself quite the Romeo, his groove out of sync with the rest of the planet. Sixty was not the new twenty.

The Prince of Verona wants peace but can't restrain the violence between the Montagues and the Capulets. A small but crucial part with key monologues at the beginning, middle, and closing of the play, the singer in shades wouldn't be on stage long enough for him to become grating. Not exactly a prize or a prince, he did have volume and confidence, stilted delivery aside. Dave had him sing the Prologue to the tune of "Desolation Row," inspiring a glimmer of hope. But there would be no singing prince in Dave's adaptation of *Romeo and Juliet*. No guitar accompaniment. No channelling of Bob Dylan.

ॺ

Mercutio, Verona's witty skeptic, is the sum of all parts in *Romeo and Juliet* and Romeo's best friend and foil, mocking his idealized notion of romance. Mercurial in nature, he's at his hottest when cursing love, dreams, ambitions and, most notably, the Montagues and Capulets. At his coolest, he makes inappropriate sexual jokes, flirts with Juliet's Nurse, and tries to make his mates laugh. Mercutio is a showstopper. He's dirty, funny, and out of control. He is technically a minor character, but his personality has such a disproportionate impact that he has to die or he would take over the play. In fact, according to English poet John Dryden, Shakespeare himself admitted he had to kill Mercutio off by Act Three—or else, Mercutio would've killed him and renamed the play.

Baldwin McGregor had played the lead in the Congreve fiasco. He was twenty years old, full of sound and fury signifying many things. Tall and handsome, bearing a striking resemblance to a young Orson Welles (with the exception of a timber wolf armband tattoo), he, like Mercutio, masked his insecurity with wit and bravado. He was an only child, accidentally conceived at a Scorpions concert when his mother won a backstage pass, a one-night respite from her life as a chambermaid at The Cozy Cow. Baldwin lived in his mother's basement and planned his escape.

"Not bad, Baldwin," Dave said after Baldwin had finished the tricky Queen Mab speech, creating an entire imaginary fairy world and then destroying it—just to prove to Romeo that dreams and love are worthless. "Not bad at all."

It was clear Baldwin had worked on the piece.

"So who is Mercutio to you?"

"He's mad. Insane. Not sure why."

"Does he have a death wish?"

"He's certainly messed up."

"Can I ask you a personal question?"

"Sure," Baldwin replied without hesitation.

"You don't have to answer."

"Fire away."

"You ever felt betrayed in your life?"

"Oh, yeah. You remember that girl Rhonda I was seeing back in May?"

"The one with all those piercings?"

Rhonda made the grunge movement look like a tea party.

"Caught her tongue-dancing with my best friend Chuck when I went over to get back a *Black Adder* DVD and surprised them."

"What if she'd been secretly screwing Chuck for months and gave you AIDS as a result?" Dave asked.

"Fuck me," Baldwin exclaimed, eyes bulging.

A smile lifted the corner of Dave's mouth. "Fucked is right. So what if Mercutio is dying of syphilis because his betrothed cheated on him while he was off soldiering in Spain. She gives it to him on his return."

"He's screwed," said Baldwin.

"Exactly. Try the speech again and let that be your through line. Oh, and you've had three pitchers of draught at The Red Lion too. More Nine Inch Nails less Cohen."

Baldwin tore into the speech as if wielding a blowtorch. He found the misogyny and drowned himself in self-destructive mania.

"There you go. How'd that feel?"

"It rocked."

"It did rock."

"Thanks, man. Hey, I wanted to tell you I auditioned for the Lorne Greene School like you told me to and I just found out I got accepted for September."

"Congrats, Baldwin. We'll have some fun over the next few weeks."

"So I got the part?"

"You got it. Send in whoever's next."

ॐ

Surprise Number One.

Lord Capulet, Juliet's father, entered the Legion hall with a yachting breezy ease, dressed in summer whites, a resonant fake British accent politely in place. He was a Highlands District judge whose pear-shaped comportment suggested an appetitive man. His crimson complexion was no doubt due to a red meat and rum diet. He had electric blue eyes, resembling the glow of ionized gas after lightning. Clad in an untucked shirt, sleeves rolled up, and an effortlessly styled head of sandy-grey hair, he gave off a casual Kennedy look of aging refinement. He spent his free time in the summer lounging on the deck of his beloved cruiser-yacht, *The Court Ship*, escaping his mother-in-law, basking in the sun, entertaining guests, reading mystery novels, anchored deep in the sludge of the Burnt River.

He'd apparently loved the Congreve and wanted to audition.

At first, Lord Capulet in *Romeo and Juliet* seems like an okay dad. When Paris comes sniffing around for thirteen-year-old Juliet's hand in marriage, Lord Capulet puts him off, citing Juliet's young age and even suggesting that he'd prefer his daughter to marry for love. But he doesn't play the good father for long once Paris wears him down.

"Try this speech."

Dave had the Judge read Act Three, Scene Five. Lord Capulet isn't too happy when Juliet refuses to marry Paris, her now legitimate suitor.

"His response to Juliet's disobedience is so violently harsh I begin to see him as a bit of a tyrant," said the Judge.

"Bingo," replied Dave.

Capulet understood the text and accessed an inner rage, so much so that he turned even redder, if that was possible. Dave wanted to know what was behind his considerable reservoir of anger. A torturous trial, perhaps? Or just the day-to-day monotony of manning the bench and having to deal with mankind's stupidity.

Two days earlier, a Kinmount groundling had sat before Judge Capulet in court. He was a disrespectful wise ass.

"State your name, occupation, and the charge," said Capulet.

The defendant said, "I'm Sparks, I'm an electrician, charged with battery."

Capulet winced and said, "Bailiff, put this man in a dry cell."

The Judge then ordered a recess and convened court after a long lunch. The first case involved a chicken farmer charged with drunk driving who claimed it simply wasn't true. "I'm as sober as a Judge," the man claimed. Capulet replied, "Clerk, please enter a guilty plea. The defendant is sentenced to thirty days."

At any rate, Capulet was a rare find. If he could survive the rehearsal process.

આ

A tragedy needs comic relief, and who better than Juliet's bawdy Nurse—the town bicycle of Verona. It's Shakespearean comic gold: a lower-class woman, inherently funny; and she's a nurse, meaning all she can talk about are bodies—bodies having sex, bodies having babies, bodies having sex, bodies nursing babies, bodies having sex. Not to mention, she has a way with dirty jokes that rivals Mercutio. Joan Gallagher was the town bicycle of Kinmount. A hairdresser by trade she operated her own tiny salon, *From Hair to Eternity,* on the main drag, sandwiched between two vacant storefronts. She was a free-speaking spitfire, forty-five years old, with the voice of a raucous crow, her horsey facial features housed in a bony frame. In an earlier era, she'd be best described as a gold-digging coquette. Enough said.

ॐ

Tybalt, Juliet's short-tempered first cousin, was the pride of Kinmount. A farmer's son, he was a poster boy of healthy living, tanned, fit with classic features: high cheekbones, a prominent lower jaw and chin, dark brown eyes and even darker brows, full symmetrical lips, essentially Michelangelo's David in blue jeans. Alpha males walk with a swagger (Shakespeare's idea—he invented the word "swagger"). Kinmount Tybalt was different. He walked with pep in his step. He didn't walk like the average man. He walked with meaning. He worked for his family's fencing business (not the rapier variety) and was positioned to inherit it. He was the opposite of his fictional counterpart, a content level-headed twenty-five year old, loving and protecting everything about his little village. *And* he got the girl. Engaged to his adolescent sweetheart, he was responsible on all fronts, yet possessing a refreshingly dark sense of humour. He was a modern day shantyman to the county girls who fawned over him. Tragically, Tybalt's "pole" was spoken for.

ॐ

Friar Lawrence, the real villain of the play, has no business marrying Juliet to Romeo knowing she is betrothed to Paris. It's a bad decision followed by more bad decisions that make matters worse (giving a coma-inducing potion to a teenage girl). The road to the title characters' untimely deaths is paved with his good intentions—no, not paved, *potholed*. Friar Lawrence was book smart and knew a lot, but most of it was useless in the real world. He had no street smarts. How could he when he spent his days walking around reciting poetry and collecting herbs.

Kinmount's Friar lived in his head, too busy devouring graphic novels to have a foothold on reality. He worked at a used record store and was the oft-cuckolded boyfriend of the Nurse. He was a short, thirty-something dreamy-eyed fried-food eating teddy bear who gobbled up science fiction just as readily. He possessed an odd drawbridge mouth, which served as a frown most of the time.

A hybrid of the Pillsbury Doughboy and Beaker, the woebegone assistant of Dr. Benson Honeydew, Dave wrote on his audition form. The Friar's hair was its own fright show—untamed and shockingly orange.

Sadly, cloud watching, good-natured, overly naïve personalities are often blindsided. Therein lies the reason why modern-day priests and ministers have difficulties getting a bank loan. Kinmount's Friar would never pay off his student loan much less get a bank loan.

ॐ

Surprise Number Two.

She entered the room with a radiance that caused the Legion to glow. Bright flashing green eyes, long auburn hair (the kind Anne Shirley coveted), and a pastoral sweetness Dave hadn't encountered before. All tucked into leather riding boots.

"Hey," she said, in a voice so quiet he had to lean in to hear.

"How nice to meet you," he said back, finishing her near silent greeting.

"I'll be straight with you. I've never acted before but my sister said what a good time she had working with you." Her voice was scarcely a whisper. Only her articulation made her words intelligible. Her sister had played Angelica in the Congreve, a quick-witted farm girl with a flair for put-downs. Lady Capulet appeared to be the demure petite counterpoint.

He noticed her engagement ring. Her fiancée had to be a mime.

"No problem," he said. "Let's read the first mother-daughter scene."

Lady Capulet shifted uncomfortably.

"Like many other mothers of teens, Lady Capulet in the play has her hands full with Juliet," Dave explained. "She does make an effort to reach out to her daughter now that she's of an age to be married, but it's obvious that Juliet's closest bond is with the Nurse; Lady Capulet never even comes close to challenging that. As a result, she doesn't come across as a particularly great mom.

"But why?" she whispered back.

"It seems likely that she herself had an arranged marriage with Juliet's father and went along with it obediently," said Dave, enjoying playing the role of all-knowing director. It was how theatre artists flirted. "So, when Juliet rebels against her planned marriage with Paris, she's rebelling against her mother's way of life, and against the kind of marriage that Lady Capulet learned to suffer through. In general, moms don't like that—either in the twenty-first century or the sixteenth century."

Her reading was quiet and needed work. How could he possibly get her to project outdoors when he was straining to hear from only five feet away?

"Very nice," he lied. "So what do you do in the wilds of Kinmount?"

"I used to be the public librarian until our illiterate council closed it."

She was as quiet as a library at midnight.

Dave could pick out two words: "librarian" and "closed."

That explains her voice, he scrawled on his director's notepad. The occupational hazard of years of imposed silence.

"Now, I run a day care," she continued.

"A bay chair?" he teased.

"Day-care."

"A day care!? How could she possibly command a room full of fatherless three year olds?" Dave didn't share that thought.

"And I ride on weekends."

"You ride on weak bends?" Dave asked. "Motorcycle?" He raised his volume, hoping she'd take the hint.

"I ride my horse on week-ends."

She didn't.

He stood up and sat on the edge of the table. "I'm sorry, your house?"

"My horse," she repeated.

Dave's eyes brightened. Bogart and Bacall's famous race-track exchange in *The Big Sleep* was his favourite snippet of film dialogue. He tried to concentrate.

"Very nice," he smiled. "I think with a little work we can get you there. How does that sound?"

She nodded and left with a script and he daydreamed momentarily of a different life that included horseback riding lessons and hearing aids. He gave his head a shake. Her invisible voice would eventually turn any Bogey and Bacall fantasies into a silent movie nightmare.

২

For the roles of County Paris, Juliet's legitimate suitor, and Peter, the Nurse's long-suffering servant, he cast a playful student couple home for the summer from Trent University. Their relationship appeared to have a carefree spirit about it. Paris—tall, trim, and preppy, sporting fashionable tortoiseshell eyeglasses and studying International Development—was clearly the wife in the relationship. He could be molded into a strait-laced young lord, while Peter—majoring in ancient history, physically nimble and charmingly odd, dressed in 1940s linen summer attire, replete with straw fedora and silver cigarette case (filled with vintage Popeye candy sticks Dave would discover)—would be a workable clown.

ॐ

Two stoned teenagers rounded out the casting as servants.

In Shakespeare's day, a boy was trained in the art of rhetoric, the tools to win an argument, from the age of four, and by the time he reached adolescence, could out-debate a contemporary lawyer. The stoners could barely cobble ten words together much less utter an intelligible coherent thought. They were on the rural fringes of Generation Z, variously known as Zedders, Post-Millennials, and Generation Snowflake ("snowflake", the derogatory slang of frustrated Boomers trying to label the likes of Baldwin, Peter, Paris, and the stoners, implying they had an inflated sense of uniqueness and an unwarranted sense of entitlement).

The Zedders of Kinmount, unlike the rest of their urban counterparts, weren't raised in the sensory-inundated environment of digital technology and mass media. For one reason only—the village didn't have an internet connection.

Pot replaced gaming.

SIX

The garbage strike was unbearable.

Entering its third month, the stench of ripped open bags was magnified by the heat. Bags were baking in the sun, stacked by the hundreds, spilling open in city parks, falling out of dumpsters, overflowing from city containers onto the streets; a rubbish pandemic with no end in sight. The raccoons had taken over and Toronto was at their mercy.

Angry citizens dumped bags of garbage onto the Don Valley Parkway in protest. One of the bags exploded off the roof of Dave's car as he drove under the Bloor Viaduct. His Toyota Tercel looked like it had been hit by a coffee grain and rotting vegetable piñata.

He flicked on his wipers. This only made matters worse. He took the off-ramp, struggling to reach out his window to scrape the eggshells out of the blades. He put on his hazards and managed to take the Richmond Street exit. He pulled into the first gas station he saw.

He got out and began wiping the wet decay off the roof and window with his t-shirt. He gagged at the smell.

He got back in the Tercel, took a right on Parliament followed by another right, and weaved his way along Queen Street towards East Chinatown. Fruits and vegetables spilled everywhere during the day giving the neighbourhood an organic, messy, market vibe, offensive to the City of Toronto's desire for control and sterile order. But East Chinatown had changed since his theatre school days, reflecting the cultural make up of its inhabitants and the new gentrification of Toronto. It was no longer a Chinese majority and the remaining Chinese element in the area was very old. His favourite bakery was now an architecture firm, his old apartment torn down for a new condo development. No more cheap dim sum.

Since the Don Jail had closed, the neighbourhood was safer. When he was attending Lorne Greene, it was a common sight to see drunks, released at noon wandering the streets, hanging around the jail parkette and harassing seniors, who didn't speak a lick of English, for cigarettes.

After negotiating a confusing maze of one-way streets, he pulled up in front of B.J.'s rundown second floor apartment overlooking the Riverdale library.

"Ready to go?" he asked as the paint-cracked door opened. The smell of boiling turnips accosted his nostrils.

"One sec, okay?" said B.J. good-naturedly. "I have to cool these babies off before I pack them. You like turnips?"

Dave detested turnips. As a boy, he'd secretly fed the foul-smelling vegetable to the family lab under the table. Two months after their beloved "Bark Twain" had died, Dave still tossed his turnips under the table.

"We're not doing *As You Like It*, B.J.," he coughed, covering his nose. Audrey, the country wench in Shakespeare's back-to-nature comedy, was infamous in Elizabethan times for entering with a turnip, an early dildo that kept the groundlings in stitches.

"What?" asked B.J., missing the reference.

"Never mind. Let them cool," Dave frowned. He blew out his breath in a short discontented snort.

Stale weed mixed with the turnips to create a further vegan odour. He hoped B.J. wasn't a pothead. Dave avoided weed on all fronts because it left him in a paranoiac state. The last time he'd smoked up it took him twenty minutes to figure out how to pick up his wine glass.

"We can load the rest of your stuff," he said, trying unsuccessfully to mask his impatience.

B.J. stuffed a knapsack and duffel bag into the Tercel's small hatch. He returned with a rack filled with potted herbs and a hand puppet.

The puppet—a purple peg-leg parrot with a bright orange beak, happy lazy eyes (lids half-shut), and a generous white underbelly—suggested a Jimmy Buffett "Parrot-head." Parrot-head being the nickname for Buffett's legion of eternal Margaritaville beach-bum stoner hammock-dwelling fans, living in fleabag shacks bunched up together in beach bars facing the empty sea.

Was B.J. a closet Parrot-head? Turnips, weed, and a parrot puppet—just what Dave needed.

"These will ride on my lap. And, don't worry, my bike comes apart."

B.J. noticed Dave was not impressed with his purple friend.

"This is Chickpea," he said, sliding his right hand inside the puppet.

"Chickpea," Dave repeated skeptically, unsure of what to make of it. He'd developed an uneasiness around puppets after surviving the ill-fated *Green Eggs and Hamlet* children's tour.

"I help him learn his lines," squawked Chickpea in a high-pitched vibrato, B.J. throwing his voice to Dave's surprise. He hadn't lied on his resume after all.

"Nice to meet you, Chickpea," said Dave, awkwardly forcing himself to play along. Chickpea reached out a furry feather. Dave gave B.J. a quizzical glance and shook Chickpea's wing tip.

"Let's a get a move on, Chickpea," Dave said, abruptly ending playtime.

The three of them took the wheels and handlebars off B.J.'s ancient mountain bike and crammed it into the hatch.

The turnips, wrapped in two layers of tin foil and newspaper, were carefully stuffed in the last remaining corner alongside Chickpea.

They hopped in and headed north.

"Forget using your cell phone. Kinmount's a dead zone. No

cell towers," Dave updated B.J. while negotiating a series of one-way backstreets.

Miranda Murray's parents lived in Rosedale, an affluent district formerly the estate of William Botsford Jarvis and named by his granddaughter for the wild roses that grew there in abundance. It was the oldest and wealthiest suburb in Toronto and even though it was located in the middle of the city, virtually no cars could be heard due to the scores of trees, with the exception of Dave's dying muffler that announced his arrival two minutes ahead of his parking brake.

Miranda's parents were waiting on the front lawn.

Her father dubiously sized him up and Dave spent ten minutes reassuring Professor Murray that his daughter would be safe. He gave his word. He didn't mention the dead zone. He was only two years younger than her father yet Professor Murray's pretentious authority made Dave feel like he was an inept child, that Dave's craft was somehow lacking. It gave credence to the old joke: a young boy tells his mother he wants to be a theatre artist when he grows up. His mother answers, "Oh honey, you know you can't be both."

Five pieces of luggage and one touring bike later they were headed towards the 401, a cubist sculpture of auto discomfort.

SEVEN

They pulled into Lola's driveway at three p.m.

She greeted them in a floral one-piece jumpsuit that would've given Ertha Kitt pause.

"Hey kids!" she gushed, wobbling down her cobblestones. "Come on in. Cocktails are on."

"Lola, we're tired. Let's get them unpacked first," said Dave.

"Nonsense," she insisted, ushering the pair up her front steps.

He pulled B.J.'s bike out of the hatch and left it on the lawn to be assembled. He then wheeled Miranda's bike around back, prudishly leaning it against the fountain (Professor Murray wouldn't be thrilled knowing that his daughter's bike was chained to a penis.) He lugged her suitcases to the front foyer and heard laughter emanating from the dining room.

"Fifty drunken goat-clad priests dancing around a giant phallus, can you imagine it?" Lola was saying.

Plop went the jalapeño peppers for emphasis.

"You telling your choric dithyramb stories again," Dave said, entering the candlelit room. More wax dripping than usual. Lola had regaled him with her colourful account of Greek mythology during his last stay. The choric dithyramb was the orgiastic ascendant of car key swapping sugar bowl parties in the 1970s. In ancient Greece, fifty drunken goat-skin priests danced around a giant phallus chanting odes to Dionysus, the God of Swingers.

"I'm enlightening our young thespians on the backyard."

"I think you've enlightened this room enough. Can we not blow out a few candles? It's stifling in here."

"Do you two mind them?" she asked, refilling her drink and pouring him a martini.

"House rules," B.J. said diplomatically, wiping a bead of sweat off his brow.

"They're lovely. So romantic," Miranda gushed.

"B.J., can you do something with your turnips, please? Bury them in the backyard or something," Dave said while exiting to the kitchen to pour his drink down the sink.

"You can put them in the fridge in the basement, B.J.," Lola offered.

"Thanks."

"Through that door," she gestured. "Switch is at the top of the stairs."

B.J. and Chickpea grabbed his turnip bundle and disappeared.

"So, my sweet little thing, tell me about your father," Lola grinned, refilling Miranda's glass.

"Lola, she just got here. Easy on the third degree," Dave jumped in, returning from the kitchen.

"Nonsense. Is he handsome? A Byron I bet." Lola's eyes lit up.

"He's more of a Somerset Maugham. It's his favourite author. His specialty at U of T. He's obsessed with our inability to control our emotions. He says it constitutes bondage." Miranda answered with a detectable strain in her voice that Dave picked up on.

"Ah, I see. 'It is an illusion that youth is happy,'" said Lola, quoting *Of Human Bondage*. "You concur?"

"I'm happy most of the time," Miranda replied, twiddling the pepper in her glass.

"Of course you are and so you should be—such a pretty little thing. I could eat you with jam."

"Lola!" Dave exploded.

"What? We're just getting acquainted aren't we, dear?"

"Yes. Is there a washroom I can use?" asked Miranda.

"Up the stairs, my dear. The lavender door. Cranberry towel set is for you."

"Oh, that's so nice. Thank you." And she left the room.

"Don't look at me that way."

"Lola, please go a little easy until they get to know you. Miranda is not one of your student boarders." God knows what went on there, he thought. "I don't want her calling her father and telling him she danced naked around a hedge cock on her first night."

"Your first reading isn't until three tomorrow. Let them have some fun tonight." She picked out a bottle of scotch from behind the bar.

"*Your* idea of fun and the rest of humanity's are very different," he replied matter-of-factly.

"If you're going to be like that, why don't you just go to your room and mope."

"I want them working on their scripts tonight and rested for tomorrow. Please, set an example," he said, taking the bottle from her.

"Fine," she snorted and stormed out of the room. He heard her clumping up the stairs, slamming her bedroom door.

"Shit," he muttered to himself.

"Have you been down there?" B.J. asked, dusting himself off as he emerged from the cellar.

"No. I have a thing about basements."

"Fifty heads hanging on the wall. A wild boar, a black bear, a huge moose."

"She used to hunt. With a crossbow."

"That's messed up."

"Uh-huh."

"Even a cougar with a pair of boxers in its mouth!" exclaimed Chickpea, back in action.

"Fitting." Dave thought of the Nurse on the prowl on a Saturday night. "The Hemingway suite she calls it. Lola's a little on the eccentric side. In case you hadn't noticed."

"Ah, she's harmless," Chickpea squawked.

"Yeah, she's harmless," Dave repeated the phrase, chewing on an ice cube.

B.J. sat down and rolled a joint with Chickpea.

"You might want to take that outside."

"Right," said B.J. and Chickpea together. Dave wondered how that was even possible.

The trio retired to the backyard.

"Where's Miranda?" asked B.J.

"Washroom."

"Don't worry. I only toke at night," B.J. volunteered, sensing Dave's uneasiness.

"Good. I didn't want to have to ask," Dave said. He quickly changed the subject. "Not exactly a garden that fosters tea and scones."

"Only if Oscar Wilde were a guest," Chickpea joked while B.J. inspected his herbs.

"Yeah, don't bring that up. Lola will want to have a séance."

They shared a laugh.

"Hey, guys."

Miranda joined them, pulling her hair away from her mouth.

"This place is so cool. Do you know there's a mobile with cherubs copulating hanging in the bathroom?"

"At least there isn't lipstick scrawled on the mirror," Dave said.

"Oh, but there is."

"What?"

"A greeting. 'Welcome thespians. May love blossom in these rooms.'"

"Great," Dave said hotly, opening the back-screen door and entering the kitchen.

"Please don't fret. I think she's lovely," Miranda shouted after him.

"She's just eccentric," Chickpea offered up, flapping his wings. He passed the joint to Miranda who didn't decline.

The sound of a bell ringing and getting closer pierced the evening quiet.

A gunshot rang out from the front yard, followed by a boy's scream.

The trio raced to the driveway only to see Lola brandishing a pellet gun and screaming at a terrified Dickie Dee ice cream boy cringing on the sidewalk. His front tire was shot out. Other neighbours were opening their front doors.

"I've warned you three times. Don't ring that fucking bell in front of my house!" Lola wailed.

EIGHT

The summer rain on the tired building's tin roof sounded like popping corn. The company sat assembled around a long table in the Legion dining hall, Dave at one end and Ginny at the other.

"Please remove all ball caps," Ginny said good-naturedly to the pair of stoner teenagers and the Friar.

"No way. It's a free country," the taller stoner replied.

"And it's only a free country because of the men and women of this Legion," said Capulet striking a judicial tone. "So, no matter how old-fashioned you may think it is, please show some respect young man and remove your cap." Capulet leaned in, yachting cap in hand, "Unless you want to buy the house a round of drinks."

"What?!" the shorter stoner sputtered.

"Lose the hat or buy the table a round. It's that simple," said Ginny, removing the Friar's sweaty ball cap as she did so, in a key no doubt employed when ordering her teenage sons to clean their rooms.

The two stoners hastily obliged.

"Thank you, gentlemen," said Capulet. "That wasn't so hard was it?"

Dave sighed, debating in his mind which was worse, shadfly season in Birch Lake or a first reading in Kinmount—it was a close race. He slowly stood up. He had to address the cast, set the tone for the rehearsal process, and inspire the company. He really wanted to sneak out the back door. He cleared his throat and found himself looking at B.J. who nodded back in support.

"Shakespeare was a natural adaptor," Dave began. How many times he had said that before. "It was in his bones, much like how we as Canadians have to adapt to the winter each year."

The current heat wave made shovelling snow seem like light years away.

"I've never adapted yet," the Nurse shouted out.

"Frozen pentameter," Dave quipped. He needed a better joke to break the ice. "Two wealthy historians live a few blocks from each other in downtown London. They both claim to live in the original lodging where Shakespeare wrote *Romeo and Juliet*. They should put a *plaque* on both their houses."

Capulet laughed. Miranda, Baldwin, and B.J. groaned. No one else got the joke. Inwardly Dave cringed, he felt like the opening act at Yuks Yuk's on amateur night.

He began again, skipping the jokes: "The original story was not Shakespeare's own. He borrowed his plots from other plays, history, and myth—he was a theatrical starling of sorts, stealing the nests of other writers."

"Owls do that too," said the Friar, watching the Nurse listen to Dave.

"One of my ex-boyfriends sounds like an owl," said Peter.

"Who?" said Paris.

The company laughed.

"When Shakespeare wrote *Romeo and Juliet* in about 1594," Dave soldiered on, "he was adapting it from an Italian novella and a long tradition of tragic romances before it. It's a play that is structured around opposites, contradictions, and contrasts at every level." He spoke slowly, emphasizing each word, observing that the migraine of actors assembled before him were a ragtag bunch of similar opposites, contradictions, and contrasts.

"Oh, hoo-hoo," laughed the taller stoner. "I get it."

Those who laugh last think slowest, Dave thought, but caught himself before saying it aloud. Instead: "Shakespeare compresses the action of the play into five feverish days in the middle of July, set in a city gripped by a heatwave and riven with factional feuding."

"Sounds familiar," said Baldwin, wiping the back of his neck. The company laughed.

"Factional?" asked the taller stoner.

"Dissenting," said Dave.

"English," said the shorter stoner.

"Allow me," said Capulet. He addressed the taller stoner. "Young man, a moment earlier, you and your friend didn't want to take off your ball caps."

"And the Friar," added the taller stoner.

"And the Friar," repeated Capulet. "Ginny and I told you to take them off."

"And we did," said the shorter stoner.

"Yes, you did," said Capulet, ever patient. "Now, that brief encounter was a factional feud. It involved an argument between two or more small groups within a larger group."

Dave thought of himself and Lola.

"Just like dinnertime at my folks," said the taller stoner.

"And mine," echoed the shorter stoner. Pot-induced munchies and social assistance were a deadly combo.

"Please continue, David," said Capulet graciously. Dave caught a whiff of the Judge's cologne; Polo, the smell of golf, yachts, and expensive sweaters. He plowed on. "His protagonists are not mythic, noble men driven by lofty motives. Like all of us here, Capulet and Montague are two average, flawed men jockeying for position in a small town."

"Sounds like the Mayor and Lola during the last election," laughed the Nurse. "Remember?" She mimed pulling her t-shirt off to a chorus of laughter from the locals.

Dave didn't want to know. "They allow and encourage their households to transform a minor slight, like the removing of ball caps, into a major vendetta."

"Try every weekend in Kinmount," Baldwin smirked.

"There are no villains, only victims in the play," said Dave. "All of the characters are motivated by complex ambitions, desires, fears, dreams. Most mean for the best—some are driven to the worst."

The company listened, exchanging looks. It was clear who wanted the best for Kinmount—Capulet and Tybalt. That was easy. But who could be driven to the worst?

"We are not doing a dusty museum piece," said Dave, holding up his script for emphasis. "I do not subscribe to false bardolatry. We are pulling Shakespeare off his pedestal kicking and screaming, and getting him back on the rehearsal floor, or grass in our case, where he belongs. Shakespeare wrote both soaring poetry for the aristocracy and the language of the street for the common folk."

Peter mimed knocking the Bard onto the legion floor. "Et tu, David," he groaned, imitating a bewildered Shakespeare. The stoners laughed.

"*Romeo and Juliet* was the *first* play to be produced in London after the infamous Black Death of 1592 to 1594 wiped out close to a third of the population," Dave explained. "All the theatres were shut down for three years. Images and references to the plague permeate the play such that the plague itself becomes a character—much the way Caesar's ghost haunts and dominates *Julius Caesar*. The plague struck and killed people with terrible speed. Usually by the fourth day you were dead. The time frame of *Romeo and Juliet* moves with a similar deadly speed, from the lovers' first meeting to their deaths."

"I can't imagine waking up on Saturday and being dead by Tuesday," said Miranda.

"The plague underscores all that happens, mirroring the fear and desperation of the characters' individual worlds," said Dave, adopting a sombre tone. "I'm pretty sure most of us have lost someone to cancer." The company nodded uncomfortably. "We can only imagine the dreadful immediacy of *Romeo and Juliet* when it was first performed for an audience who had each lost family and friends to the plague. Here was a play referencing that very loss and terror." Dave circled his troops; his director's passion, despite himself, as infectious as the plague he was referencing. "What a gutsy and attention-getting backdrop for the love story that unfolds! In the wake of Ebola, the opioid epidemic, Lyme disease, HIV, not to mention the scourge of cancer, we know what this fear is like." Dave had hit a nerve.

"By using the original setting and its plague components," Dave explained, "our production will serve as an analogy for today. We will play the humour of the first three acts to its fullest until the "plague" of deaths begins. We will explore the passion and exuberance of youth, the need to live every day as if it was your last, because it very well could be. Your life expectancy is thirty."

"Whoa," said the taller stoner. "Like I'm already middle-aged. That sucks, dude."

"It does," said Dave. "You have no idea what will happen when you start your day. You could be killed in a duel, run over by horse-drawn cart, be accidentally hit on the head by a falling chamber pot, or drink water from an outdoor fountain, toxic with bacteria boiling in the summer heat, and catch the plague."

"Like the fountain at the marina," said the shorter stoner, making a face. "Tastes like goose piss."

"How would you know?" said Baldwin, grinning at B.J.

Dave went on: "If you want to perform Shakespeare, then you need a roadmap for making interpretive choices; you have to delve into the text and find not just understanding and comprehension but the human experience as well. You have to make it yours. Thankfully Shakespeare gave us a map: the First Folio." He held up his Folio. "Shakespeare is telling us something when the verse rhymes, when the rhythm falters, when words repeat, or when alliteration shows up. Every punctuation mark is a clue, an invitation to a choice, a change in tone. Shakespeare's actors didn't get many rehearsals and he didn't write stage directions, but they didn't need them. He handed it to them in the text. The text is a road and the punctuation is road signs. Full stops are highway exits, commas are speed limit signs, semi-colons are yield, stoplights, one-way signs, and colons, green lights, and passing lanes."

The company scribbled down notes. More accurately, B.J., Miranda, Baldwin, Capulet, Lady Capulet, and Tybalt took notes. The stoner teenagers imagined a six-cylinder brand new Shakespeare Folio with tinted windows. The rest were still wrestling with Dave's cancer analogy. Wasn't doing a play supposed to be fun?

"Now, we will use this reading to test the waters," Dave concluded, sitting back down in his uncomfortable metal chair, "to explore your road map and test the punctuation signs. Begin."

"TWO HOUSEHOLDS BOTH ALIKE IN DIGNITY—" the Prince roared, ignoring Dave's direction. Dave almost fell off his chair. A child's baseball smashing through the window would've been less disruptive.

First readings were like a trip to the dentist. He'd forgotten that. And he was in a legion hall without air-conditioning. with the actors of the corn, not the Stratford Festival main stage rehearsal hall. At Stratford, the actors would've applauded him on day one. Had any of his big speech landed? He suspected not. For Dave, directing a play was like dating, going from casual chilling to a serious relationship within a matter of weeks. And now he was on the worst blind date of his life. Kinmount, where hope sprained its ankle.

"Don't shout it. Don't act it. Just say the words. And please slow down," Dave implored.

"The inherent stage direction is 'two hours traffic on our stage,'" said the Prince, sitting back on his chair, arms folded across his chest, initiating a power struggle on day one.

"I know. But that was Shakespeare's day," explained Dave, wishing he were anywhere but Kinmount. "His was an aural society so they spoke faster. We are a visual society so we have to slow it down. Please continue."

"We are violating the author's intent. Besides, our audience won't last two hours," the Prince declared, making eye contact with the rest of the company.

Dave's molar was beginning to throb and it was only the first line of the play.

"On second thought we are going to cut the chorus. Get right down to the action," he said.

"So that's how it's going to be. An actor disagrees with you and you cut their lines." The Prince tossed his script on the floor for dramatic affect.

The room became a rabble.

"No," said Dave. "I'm saying we don't need it. The opening fight between the servants will grab our audience's attention right away."

"Shakespeare's estate will sue. You want a lawsuit up your bony ass?" threatened the Prince.

"No one will sue. The play is in the public domain." Dave scribbled the word "thickwad" on his script.

"And you are in the public domain of Kinmount," said the Prince. "And the mayor is a regular of mine at karaoke night."

"Good. Hopefully, he'll buy a ticket," Dave said, not hiding his irritation. "Moving on." A half hour had passed and he'd managed to get through only the first fourteen lines of dialogue.

"What's a buckler?" asked the shorter stoner.

"A small shield," said Dave.

"How small?"

"Size of sauce pan lid."

"Spaghetti sauce 'cause we're in Vernona, right?"

Dave's root canal throbbed back to life.

"*Coals* leads to *colliers* to *choler* to *collar*. You have to the follow the wordplay. It's a wit match like a tennis game," Dave explained.

"Don't play tennis," said the shorter stoner.

"Ping pong then."

"Nope."

"Okay, it's like I say, 'Today is too hot' and you say back 'Don't be haughty.'"

"Or Juliet is a real hottie," said the taller stoner.

"Let's stick to the script, okay," said Dave, trying to restore order.

"I am. It's called Romeo and JULIET. You may think I'm a hick but I got a big stick. I should be Romeo."

B.J. glanced at Dave. The Capulet servants were well cast.

Too well cast.

"You are cast in the role that suits you. There are no small parts only small actors," Dave explained.

"I'm not small anything," fired back the taller stoner. "You wanna see, Miranda?"

"That's enough," said Dave.

"Show her your poperin pear, Weed."

"Don't you start, Baldwin," Dave warned.

"Hey, I'm just being Mercutio. You have to live it to be it. You told me that. You said acting is not a moral act. It's what people do, not what they should do," argued Baldwin, already reeking of poor Elizabethan hygiene and three days' worth of beard scruff.

"Yes, I did. But only within the context of the scene the actor as the character finds themself in," said Dave. Gum disease was forming beneath his molar.

"That's what I'm doing," said Baldwin, splashing water on his face from a thermos in an attempt to get the right "syphilitic" look.

Dave hoped he didn't have another Shia LaBeouf on his hands.

"Right. Okay," he said. "But we can do without the misogynistic comments. Stick to the page. Moving on."

A director was a universal juggler.

"Here were the *th*ervan*th* of your adver*th*ary,
And your*th*, clo*th*e fighting ere I did approach."

The rabble snickered.

"Fuck off," Benvolia hissed.

Dave did the math. There had to be two thousand *s*'s in Benvolio's text.

"Maybe we can change '*th*ervant*th* of your adver*th*ary' to 'duet of your enemy,'" Baldwin suggested sarcastically.

"Tha*th* a human righ*th* violation!" screeched Benvolia.

"We're not changing anything. It's part of Benvolia's character." Dave held his ground.

"*Th*ure, Dave," laughed Weed, the taller stoner.

Was it a bad filling?

"But Montague is bound as well as I,
In penalty alike; and 'tis not hard, I think,
For men so old as we to keep the peace."

Capulet's voice boomed off the walls of the Legion. Ginny looked up and took a break from drawing and colouring tiny drama masks on the cover of her Duo-Tang.

"Lovely. But lose the British accent," Dave said diplomatically.

"It's Shakespeare," said Capulet.

"And we're in Canada," said Dave. "Next."

"Nurse, where's my daughter? Call her forth to me."

The table leaned in to hear Lady Capulet.

"A little louder," Dave coached.

"Nurse, where's my daughter? Call her forth to me."

"Much better." Dave smiled encouragingly.

The stoners and Baldwin shared a look.

Inwardly, Dave groaned at his impossible task. "Continue, please." His molar was about to crack.

The Nurse attacked her lines with a raunchy sunburned gusto:

"Thou wilt fall backward when thou hast more wit;
Wilt thou not, Jule?' and, by my holidame,
The pretty wretch left crying and said 'Ay.'
To see, now, how a jest shall come about!"

"You should know, eh, Joan?"

Baldwin again.

The Friar stared at his untied sneakers.

"Still trying to find that toothpick of yours, Baldwin? I got a pair of tweezers you can borrow."

The Nurse didn't miss a beat.

"Rise above," Dave said to himself.

"What's that?" the Nurse asked.

"Keep your text in the air. Rise above," Dave said, stabbing a pencil into the palm of his hand under the table.

B.J. and Miranda read the balcony scene.
You could hear a toothpick drop.
Dave was spared dental surgery. For the moment.

NINE

Dave parked at the Visitor's Centre about eight miles south of town to breathe in the summer constellations and escape the dead zone.

He listened to CBC Northern Ontario on his iPhone:

"Because of its short life span, the shadfly reminds us we're responsible for our lives and we must be mindful," Backwoods Bart, an eccentric Northern Ontario naturalist, was waxing poetic to the familiar science journal host. "The fact that it lives a day is a crucial lesson for us. The shadfly's wings are sensitive to the slightest breeze. We are reminded to be careful when the wind blows. Any creature that emerges from the water is symbolic of the subconscious mind."

Any creature emerging from the Burnt River would be symbolic of a 1950s Japanese horror film.

Dave didn't want any wind blowing in Kinmount.

He trimmed Benvolia's text and pondered replacing the Prince with B.J.'s puppet.

TEN

Some directors ran a tight ship. Dave was running a pirate ship. There was some swearing, some drinking, and a good vowel movement to start the morning.

It was the second Tuesday of July, the second morning of rehearsal, a lazy summer day shaping up like any other, and Dave was drilling the company in pairs, teaching them to fence with Shakespeare's language and duel with their words, to break the lazy Canadian habit of speaking like a birthday balloon slowly losing air.

"Lift those phrases up," he instructed the local actors. B.J. and Miranda were back at Lola's doing text work—Romeo and Juliet didn't appear in the opening fight scene. "Shakespearean thoughts are not complete until they reach an end stop: a period, a question mark, or exclamation point. In some cases, a twenty-line speech contains only a single end stop, though it has lots of other punctuation that enables you to breathe and build along the way. Arc your lines rhetorically towards the end stop. It will help defy our Canadian tendency to drift off the line and lose energy. We find many arcs in nature. A rainbow, a palm tree bending in the wind, the curve of a wave just before it crashes against the shore. Waves always get to shore, and you must be just as committed to reaching your ultimate destination. Each line, each thought is a wave heading for land."

The Burnt River begged to differ.

"Rhythm changes always illustrate character development, a shift to a new thought or a new permutation of an idea," Dave stressed emphatically. Lola had the rhythm of a strobe light; the thought flashed across his mind and was gone.

"The importance of the end stop is that it indicates where such a gearshift must occur. Like driving standard, you have to switch gears for emotional change, a physical change, or both." Dave knew he was working in a bardophobic community. "We must treat the audience to an experience of startling variety. Surprise them and they will buy in."

"And not throw fruit," tossed in Baldwin.

Tongue twisters were next on the agenda. "We are lazy speakers because we are lazy with our consonants," Dave demonstrated. "We find the emotional meaning of a word in its vowel sound, its intellectual meaning in the consonants. Clip the consonants around the vowel and you understand it."

Sadly, there wasn't a tongue twister in existence that could help remedy Benvolia's lisp.

The Prince fancied himself a self-appointed expert. Unfazed by his lack of an official directorial role, he abruptly stood up while everyone else was doing breathing exercises and shared his genius: "Some of the younger actors may not be familiar with what Shakespeare's rhythm should sound like ..." At this point, he extended his arm masterfully and clicked his thumb and fingers rhythmically, chanting: "Ka-KA-ka-KA-ka-KA-ka-KA-ka-KA!"

The company broke out in hysterics. The Prince sounded like a cross between a broken castanet and an upstart crow. Marlon Brando had a pithy definition of an actor: "A guy who, if you ain't talking about him, ain't listening." Baldwin finessed it: "And if you ain't 'ka-KA-ing' with him, you ain't acting."

Stupidity was a car heading towards a brick wall and everyone argued over where they were going to sit. Dave wished he was the hood ornament.

At the old Curtain Theatre—the venue for which *Romeo and Juliet* was originally written—a simple, uncluttered thrust stage allowed for swift, fluid action and concentration on language. A curtained area upstage provided useful concealment for characters overhearing conversations. Parts of the polygonal-shaped theatre's walls were discovered in 2012 by a team of London archeologists, beautifully preserved, better than any of Shakespeare's other theatres. There was no sign of a balcony.

By contrast, rehearsals in Kinmount were held outside on a large patch of dried grass adjacent to an old musty sawmill, the crumbling architecture a sign of the town's better days. Yet its two-tiered roof was still sound, the first of which could be accessed by a second storey window—Juliet's improvised balcony. A balcony, even one covered in pigeon shit, did what a window cannot. It functioned not as an enclosure but as a form of exposure. Once the English introduced balconies, they quickly became a space of sexual display for English women. A dutiful daughter remained secure within her father's house, but the young woman who stepped onto the balcony exposed her desirability, and her own desires. The window may have let light in, but the balcony let Juliet out, even as it invited Romeo in. Indeed, it became a trope in stage and film versions to have Romeo climb up to Juliet's balcony, an architectural mounting that foreshadowed their sexual mounting and climaxed in both characters' deaths. Ginny filled a bucket with soap and water, mounted a ladder, and set about scrubbing the shit off the neo-romantic roof.

Fight director Pete O'Neill hailed from Pickering. Apparently having a nuclear power plant in his backyard didn't rank as a concern. Recently, the Ministry of Health had mailed a bottle of iodine pills to all residents living in the area to be used in the event of a radiation leak. Pete kept the pills in his glove compartment. Dave had met him at a youth workshop and liked his easy amiability. Plus he brought his own rapiers. Together, they choreographed the opening fight scene that afternoon.

Tybalt brought in a case of bottled water. The midday sun was a scorcher. The Burnt River was far too polluted to permit an afternoon dip.

Sweat dripping, the servants drilled their moves. Tybalt did not perspire. He was indeed a rural god.

Dave conceded that the Prince could make his first entrance

riding in on a horse. He gave him his shining moment and the cut chorus speech was soon forgotten. The motley stallion belonged to Tybalt's farm and he good-naturedly offered to truck the horse to and from rehearsal as required. The spectacle would distract the audience from noticing the Prince's wooden acting—a time-honoured director's sleight-of-hand trick.

Tybalt was a natural with the blade. Benvolia's figure-skating athleticism served her well. Dave was pleased, although the Capulet servants' endless teasing of her li*th*p could lead to an unscripted death.

A play's first day on its feet dictated how the rest of rehearsals would go. It was an old theatre superstition.

By the time the sun began to set, the opening scene was staged. Dave crossed it off his rehearsal schedule—another director ritual.

The company retired to the Red Lion pub, located on the edge of town, to down a pint. Four centuries earlier, Shakespeare's men raised pints at their favourite watering hole, the George Inn in the south end of London. Taverns were forbidden in central London for reasons of morality and social respectability. "A Puritan walks into a bar," said no one ever.

Large and small stones made up most of the Red Lion's outer structure. It was difficult to see through its small stained glass windows, but the animation from within could be felt outside. Entering the Red Lion through its old wooden door, regulars were welcomed by the smell of alcohol and sound of country music. The busy bartender managed a welcome wink.

The Prince set up his equipment on a small stage in the back corner and performed a CCR cover set.

The Nurse danced with the Friar while stealing looks at Tybalt.

Tybalt drank soda water while playing darts with Baldwin. Was he also Kinmount's ultimate DD? Was there anything remiss with his personality? An inner demon waiting to pounce?

Apparently not.

Capulet had to be in court the next day.

Lady Capulet had gone home to her fiancée.

The servants shot pool, their fake ID rammed into their back pockets.

Dave sat at a table with Miranda and B.J. sharing a pitcher, studying Kate, the bartender and waitress. Dave had become a regular during his Congreve stint.

Kate Quinn had knowing eyes. Knowing, of all things: fixing a drainpipe, understanding the truth in someone's eyes, raising a teenage daughter on her own. Her forty-something figure was lean and trim, in torn jeans, a tight t-shirt, and no-nonsense cowboy boots. Her boyish haircut framed her surprisingly delicate features. The years had been kind to her despite the cigarette lines.

When she brought over their pitcher, she touched Dave's shoulder.

"Back in the *low* countries I see," she said with a smirk.

"*Count*ry matters," Dave quipped back without a trace of Hamlet's disdain.

She frowned and returned to the bar.

Had he pushed it too far? Hamlet directs the line as an unpleasant sexual jest at Ophelia. Dave hadn't.

"How was the day?" asked B.J.

"A good start," replied Dave, his eyes still following Kate. "Yours?"

"B.J. and Chickpea made turnip stew for lunch. Delicious," Miranda grinned.

"Sorry I missed it," Dave said wryly.

They shared a laugh.

"And Lola?" Dave asked.

"Don't know," replied B.J. "She was gone when we got up. But she did leave a box of corn flakes and Grand Marnier on the sideboard."

"Of course she did," said Dave.

"We read over the balcony scene. I can't wait to get started tomorrow," Miranda gushed.

"Did you notice anything interesting in the Folio?" Dave

asked, reaching into his canvas satchel and pulling out his director's script. "Compared to the modern text?"

"Juliet's mind moves faster in the Folio," replied Miranda. "The punctuation really keeps her ideas hopping. Hardly a period in sight."

"Indeed," Dave grinned, finding a much-needed moment of textual refuge.

"Romeo has a wicked verse line," said B.J., digging into his knapsack for his script.

"Nice 'murse,' buddy," cracked a local while carrying a pitcher of draft back to his table. He reeked of pig shit.

"It's called a satchel, moron," said Dave under his breath, pinching his nose. He turned to Miranda and B.J., "Did you know in Shakespeare's day men wore satchels? Small pouches called 'sweat bags,' suspended by a belt. They were designed to hold spices and herbs to fight body odour. Elizabethan deodorant. Ham-let over there should try it."

"Raiders of the Lost Spice," laughed B.J.

They opened their scripts to Act Two, Scene Two, and the "balcony" scene, Miranda sliding closer to B.J. to read off his copy.

"So, what did you find?" asked Dave.

B.J. leaned in. "In the Folio, when Romeo first sees Juliet on her balcony, he utters a long verse line of sixteen syllables: 'It is my Lady, O it is my Love, O that she knew she were.'"

"And?" said Dave.

"In the modern text, it's been altered."

"How so?"

"It's split it into two lines:
'It is my lady, O, it is my love!
O that she knew she were!'"

"And how does this affect you as an actor?" asked Dave.

"The long verse line is messier. It's a more human moment," reasoned B.J., glowing with the excitement of his first Folio discovery. Dave loved watching good actors interpret an irregular verse line. It was his brave new world. B.J. continued: "Romeo can't contain himself. He's cramming a sixteen syllable line into the space of a normal ten syllable line. He has to speak faster. The line comes exploding out of him. It's the lust of a horny teenager. The modern text completely changes his speaking style."

"The modern editors reshaped it by being tidy," said Dave. "Nicely done, young Skywalker." He was pleased.

The trio cycled back to Lola's. Surprisingly the house was in darkness. After locking their bikes, they cautiously unlocked the front door feeling like Nancy Drew and the Hardy Boys and the Case of the Eccentric Landlady.

"Lola?"

No response.

They turned on the foyer light and dining room lights.

"Wonder where she is?" asked B.J.

"Probably working late," said Dave.

None of them believed it.

Dave imagined her leading a meeting with a secret coven of witches in a farmer's field.

They called it a night.

Dave fell asleep thinking of Kate.

ELEVEN

Lola didn't reappear for three days.

On the morning of the fourth day she appeared in the dining room doorway. They were eating breakfast and didn't hear the key in the front door.

She was a sight—a torn cherub's costume slipping off one shoulder covered in grass and mud stains, black makeup smeared down her cheeks, bruised knees, a long red wig hanging limply in her left hand.

"Lola! Are you okay?" asked Dave, dropping his spoon with a clatter.

She turned to look at them with a glare.

Silence.

She slowly climbed the stairs until they heard her door slam.

No one said a word cycling to rehearsal.

The first half of *Romeo and Juliet* is a comedy. After the deaths of Tybalt and Mercutio, everything changes.

Dave was working on the former, the Nurse-Mercutio Lenten pie chase sequence, and peals of raucous laughter echoed off the banks of the river. Mercutio and Romeo were engaging in one of their favourite pastimes, talking trash and telling some of the dirtiest jokes in Western literature. Two bros chillin' together.

As planned, the Nurse showed up to meet Romeo. She looked ridiculous fanning herself in the heat. Mercutio couldn't resist mocking her: first telling her the fan she was flapping like a hummingbird to cool herself should be used to cover her face since it was far more attractive than she was; then, when the

Nurse questioned him about the time of day, he managed to turn a description of the clock striking noon into a graphic portrayal of masturbation, his innuendoes simultaneously insulting and titillating the Nurse.

The Nurse and Baldwin's flirtatious chemistry was informed by late nights at the Red Lion, and, no doubt, a few post-tavern sessions. Fortunately, the Friar wasn't scheduled for rehearsal. Dave felt sorry for him. It was no wonder he buried himself in comic books. Lois Lane never cheated on Superman.

"A bad day in rehearsal is better than a good day at the beach," read B.J.'s t-shirt. The sun blazed down daily, tanning and burning the company, challenging the veracity of that slogan.

But Dave's biggest challenge was the goose shit that covered the grass. Wawa's noble statue did not reflect the horror of Kinmount's resident geese. They were not the V-formation autumn migrating variety. They were *townies*—white trash birds littering the ground with cigar-butt-sized turds. They were loud, aggressive, and annoying, but worst of all their shit was everywhere—a messy problem vexing rehearsals as actors slipped and slid on their slick green deposits. B.J. and Miranda were forced to keep their eyes on the ground and dance around the little green cylinders.

The geese further polluted the Burnt River.

"Did you know an adult goose shits a pound a day," said Baldwin, wiping a particularly nasty bit off his boot.

"Good, goose, bite not," laughed B.J., playfully referencing the scene they had just rehearsed.

"We've got to stop them from fouling up the grass," Dave said.

"Under control," said Tybalt.

The next morning he brought in two of his family's border collies, Wayne and Shuster, to get rid of the geese. The geese nervously regarded the dogs as coyotes in the wild. The collies, using their herding instincts, scared the birds away but didn't harm them. Wayne and Shuster attended rehearsals daily from that point on.

ত

A multiple choice question. What does the sound "mmmme eeeeeeeeeeeeeeeeeeeeeeeeeeeeeeeeeeeooooooooooooooooowwww" signify?

A) A chainsaw
B) An amplified mosquito
C) A cat in a woodchopper
D) King George

If one lived in Kinmount, the correct answer would be D) King George.

Not the British monarch, but a six-month-old micro pig who made that odd sound while having his butt rubbed.

King George lived in a pen beside a small outbuilding that served as Lola's workshop on the outskirts of Kinmount. He was Lola's pet pig. The size of a miniature poodle, jet-black with four little white hooves that resembled Edwardian spats.

Miranda fell in love with him. "He's adorable," she said as she knelt down to scratch his ears and tickle his chin. King George rolled over on his back and stuck his bright pink tongue out inviting any worshipper to rub his belly. He snorted in piggish delight. B.J laughed as Chickpea imitated the snorts and joined in on the scratching.

"Mmmmm, bacon," Dave teased.

"That's not funny." Miranda scrunched up her nose.

"Swine," scolded Chickpea good-parrotedly.

"King George is a royal ham," announced Lola, carrying a crate of power tools from her black Ram pickup truck. It was the first time Dave had seen her dressed in suitable clothing: denim work overalls, Kodiak boots, trucker hat, and carpenter's belt.

"His father was King Hamlet and his mother a Duchess. A royal porker," said Lola proudly. "During the school year children come on field trips to visit him. He loves the attention. I make wooden pig whistles for them to take home as souvenirs."

She pulled a small wooden object out of her tool belt and blew into it. King George reacted with giddy delight, sputtering up to Lola. She appeared to be his adopted mother.

"I used to make train whistles and miniature paddles for the ecology centre to sell to tourists before it burned down," Lola said.

"How did it burn down?" asked Miranda.

"No one knows for sure. Arson is suspected. A visitor's centre and nine guest cabins went up in smoke." Lola rested the crate of tools on her knee. "One fatality. Police couldn't find enough evidence to lay charges."

"A park ranger, right?" Dave asked, remembering a CBC news story from a few summers back. "Something about his burnt remains found in a bathtub?"

"Tied to a bedframe with piano wire is more like it," said Lola. "Some strange goings on at that centre. Someone should have blown the pig whistle there long before that fire." Lola's look hardened.

"How so?" asked Dave.

Lola grunted and carried her tools into the workshop. Dave and B.J. shared a quick look, and Dave followed Lola into the outbuilding.

Wooden shelves lined the walls. Each shelf was divided into a smaller containing unit, and each unit was labelled. Various tools were neatly organized and categorized alphabetically within the units. Mason jars labelled and filled with screws and nails and other hardware lined the upper shelves. A lathe and massive table saw stood waiting in one corner. Above the lathe, more shelving with lumber stacked according to length and width. A wooden library ladder on wheels was hooked to the shelving, allowing easy access to the upper shelves. A large work bench dominated the middle of the shop. In another corner, paint and painting supplies were carefully arranged. Leaning by the door were a collection of brooms and a shop vac. There wasn't a speck of sawdust on its cement floor. Nor an itinerant nail or screw to be seen. In short, the order of Lola's workshop was the polar opposite to the chaos of her house.

"A giant joiner's compass," is how Dave's "Uncle" Thomas probably would've described it. It was sound in every direction. Its symmetry was perfect. It was indeed the kind of shop worthy of sixteenth-century tall-ship building.

"If a ship shape ship shop sells six ship shape ship shop ships ..." Dave ran the tongue twister quietly over his tongue. It had been years since he'd been forced to memorize it for speech class.

"Nice shop, Lola."

"It is my oasis. My holy temple of expensive sawdust," she said, rolling the ladder around the room to the lumber shelves.

"And no candles," he grinned.

"Why would there be candles in a workshop?" Lola exclaimed. "Wax all over the floor. Not enough light to work by. Very impractical. Really, David."

He bit his tongue. Just when he was sure he was beginning to get a bead on Lola she took a left turn.

She busied herself laying out planks on the worktable.

"Hold this, will you?" She handed him the end of a measuring tape. She pencilled off the different lengths.

"Lola, the other morning ..." Dave hesitated.

"What about it?" she asked, without looking up.

"It's just ... you were gone for three days. And when we saw you at breakfast ..." he stopped mid-sentence. "Everything okay?"

"You are familiar with *The Bacchae* I imagine," she said.

"It's been a while, but yes. All those old Greeks—Euripides, Sophocles, Aristophanes, Antihistamine, Syphilis," he joked.

"You remember what happens to Pentheus?" she asked.

"Ah, yeah," Dave said with a trace of unease. "King Pentheus is furious in Euripides' play, *The Bacchae*, because all the women of Thebes, including his own mother, are out in the bush doing crazy rituals in honour of the God, Dionysus."

"And who is Dionysus?" Lola asked.

"You know exactly who he is," Dave said. "Don't play coy with me. He's the God of sex, fertility, and wine."

"Continue," she said with the stern command of a school-mistress, rapping his knuckles with the extension of her tape measure.

"Ouch!" he winced.

"That did not hurt. I barely touched you."

"It hurt," he whined.

"Continue," she repeated.

Dave rubbed his knuckles, shook his head, and did as instructed.

"Pentheus arrests a stranger, a guy he believes to be head of the Dionysian cult. Bad luck for Pentheus, the stranger really is Dionysus in disguise. Dionysus convinces Pentheus to go spy on the women. But the strait-laced King must do this in disguise, wearing women's clothing. Then things get grisly. Pentheus's mother, possessed by Dionysus, rips her son's body apart with her bare hands after she catches him, dressed in drag, spying on her and her friends. Because of the spell she is under, she thinks Pentheus is a lion. Slowly she comes to her senses and realizes she's really holding the head of her son."

"My three days," Lola said bluntly.

Dave felt uncomfortable again. Is that what Lola had been up to? He shuddered at the image.

Lola changed the subject and began to cut wood. "How are rehearsals going?"

"Good. All things considered. Got rid of the geese," Dave shouted over the noise of the table saw.

Lola raised a disapproving eyebrow.

"The geese are fine. Tybalt's dogs chase them away each morning," he said.

"And our young lovers?" she asked.

"B.J. and Miranda have terrific chemistry. And Baldwin is on fire."

"She's a peach of a girl. Luscious. Count Vlad would wait centuries for that one."

"Can you please stop it with the vampire talk? Miranda is a fine young actor. Period. Leave it at that. I've warned you before. She is not to be a topic of your delusional fantasy life."

At that precise moment, the piece of wood Dave was holding jerked dangerously close to the saw blade. He jumped back startled.

"Jesus, Lola," he cursed.

"Careful. Wouldn't want to lose a finger," she grinned, turning off the table saw.

Dave stormed outside.

B.J. and Miranda were running lines on a weathered bench beside King George's pen.

"Let's go," said Dave, abruptly. "The collies will be there by now."

"Is Lola all right?" asked Miranda.

"No," Dave snapped. "The fruits in her cake are more toxic than usual this morning."

The sound of Lola's power drill punctuated the early morning breeze. By noon, the day would be stifling.

The trio cycled to the rehearsal site, Miranda pretending all the while that King George was riding in her basket carrier, and that her bike could fly. "King George, the Extra-Pig-estrial," she shouted in delight. "Whee!"

The four Elizabethan benches, freshly painted, arrived a few hours later. Lola had changed into a yellow strapless '50s summer cocktail dress. A big yellow bow, platinum blonde wig, and black patent leather pedal pushers completed her latest ensemble.

She reminded Dave of a drag queen, Lana Lust, he'd seen at a "Lads an' Lashes" charity fundraiser in Toronto years ago.

Tybalt's fiancée, a raven-haired lass of twenty-two, was attempting to choreograph a dance for the Capulet ball. She volunteered teaching gymnastics to children and Zumba to seniors at the Kinmount Community Centre. However, as much as she tried, Elizabethan dance was not her forte. Nor was it the forte of the acting company. They huffed and puffed with uncoordinated left feet. Only Miranda, B.J., Lady Capulet, and Tybalt had anything resembling rhythm. Mercutio and Benvolia got to sit the dance out. "It's a zombie attack in slow motion," Baldwin whispered to Dave.

Lola interrupted the choreography.

"Stop, please stop. You are butchering the English court," she declared. "That, young lady, is not a *pavane*."

"I'm sorry. I'm trying, I just don't know how ..." Tybalt's fiancée trailed off. She was equally frustrated.

"She's trying her best," Tybalt jumped in, protecting his vulnerable spouse-to-be. He was indeed a modern-day courtier.

"I know you are, dear. And you are to be applauded for your courage. But a pavane is unique to Queen Elizabeth's court. Gather around, my darlings." Lola was in her element.

"Here we go," Dave whispered to B.J.

"Sssshhh!" Lola hushed back.

The company sat in a semi-circle in front of Lola.

"Do you know that the Queen used dance as part of her daily exercise?" asked Lola of her groundlings. "She was educated in dancing. In the morning, she would perform as many as seven galliards, one of the most demanding and energetic of all the Elizabethan dances. She continued this regimen until her late fifties. She expected all her courtiers to be proficient in dancing. So, listen up, Baldwin."

Baldwin plunked himself down on the grass.

"The pavane was a stately processional dance where Elizabethan couples paraded around a hall, lightly touching fingers," Lola instructed.

"Oooooo! Touching fingers. Intense, man," sneered one of the stoner teenagers.

"Intense is right, young peasant," Lola said, not missing a downbeat. "Pavane means peacock, and the name of the dance is derived from the sight of the trains of the women's gowns trailing across the floor like a peacock's tail or, in our case, the bonny grass of Kinmount."

Lola demonstrated with a stately swish and spin, the grass her runway. "It is comprised of a pattern of five basic steps. Okay, everyone up on your feet. Join your partner. Our fearless young director will dance with me."

Lola moved her pickup truck closer to the acting space. She opened her glove compartment and a jumble of cassette tapes spilled onto the passenger seat. She rifled through her collection until she found what she was rummaging for—a mixed tape of Elizabethan greatest hits.

She inserted the tape in the battered player and, after a few seconds of dead tape, a violin and a flute began to play, followed by a lute and, lastly, a viol—all in perfect harmony. Shakespeare's world came to life. The musical consort soared and sparkled. The dance music cast a spell.

Wayne and Shuster howled their approval.

Lola hopped out of her truck, grabbed Dave, and instructed the troupe. She drilled the five steps repeatedly adjusting bad postures and limp limbs. Rhythms relaxed and, after two hours, the Kinmount acting company—better suited for such Elizabethan country-dances as *The Friar and the Nun, Punk's Delight*, or *Cuckolds All in A Row*—had transformed their awkward beginnings into an elegant courtly affair.

Lola could add Dancing Master to her list of special skills.

TWELVE

"Who wants to go first?" Lola asked as she placed her wine glass upside down in the centre of the dining room table. She was dressed as a dotty Madame Arcati from *Blithe Spirit,* in a frilly, feathery, floaty orange gown. A matching orange wig tucked under a maroon turban completed the Noël Coward fright sight.

"This is not a good idea," Dave protested. He'd played ouija during his theatre school days, and it had gotten out of control. A classmate had jumped out of her residence room window as a result. Hasbro should have been sued and shut down.

"We could go UFO watching instead," he said drily.

"Oh, pish," Lola replied. "All in good fun. Miranda wants to play, don't you dear?"

Miranda smiled, returning from the upstairs washroom, "I've never done it before. But I don't see why not. Maybe we can talk to Shakespeare."

"B.J.?" asked Lola.

"My aunt had one of those Hasbro spirit boards. We'd play it as kids. Spook ourselves," said B.J. Having just finished a post-dessert joint on the porch, he was in no shape to protest.

"Then it's settled. Let's try and bring the Bard of Avon here for a visit." Lola opened the top drawer of the sideboard and pulled out a stack of small cards wrapped in a red elastic band.

"What are those for?" Dave asked.

"That silly parlour game is for kids, "Lola said. "We are doing the real thing. Hungarian ouija. To bring the dead in contact with the living."

She began to separate the cards. "Miranda, be a dear and

clear off the rest of the dishes. We need a bare surface."

Miranda carried the key lime pie plates into the kitchen.

"On these cards are the letters of the alphabet, the numbers zero to nine, the words 'yes' and 'no.' The table becomes our talking board. B.J., please arrange the letters alphabetically around the circumference of the table. Keep even spaces," Lola instructed.

B.J. did as he was told.

Lola placed the numeric cards in a row at one end of the table. The word, "yes," she carefully placed on the corner closest to the window, the word, "no," diagonally on the opposite corner.

Miranda returned from the kitchen. "I want to know if Shakespeare slept with Marlowe," she giggled, smirking at B.J.

Dave rolled his eyes. Rumours of Shakespeare and Christopher "Kit" Marlowe indulging in covert "beast with two backs" escapades in London's West End inns had titillated sexually frustrated academics for centuries. Not to mention Marlowe's supposed authorship of the bard's works (his death was faked, according to Marlowe scholars) or that Shakespeare murdered Marlowe in a jealous rage over Marlowe's superior artistry.

"Sweetie, could you light the candles in the candelabra? Matches are in the top drawer of the sideboard," Lola asked.

Miranda stood on a chair and attempted to light the candles. The matches kept blowing out.

"We don't need the candles," said Dave.

"But of course we do. What kind of mood-maker are you?" said Lola.

"The theatre kind. And right now I am an uptight stage director worried about his cast playing with fire when they should be prepping for tomorrow." Dave's responsibility for Miranda was weighing on him. Dr. Murray would have his head on one of Lola's platters.

"Nonsense. Lots of time for that," Lola said breezily. "Besides, I'm the producer. And you are under my roof."

Dave's molar began to throb again.

B.J. handed Miranda his lighter and she lit the candles.

"Only six wicks may burn, my dear. Blow out that last one," Lola said. "B.J., can you get me another glass of wine, please."

"Certainly. Would you like an ice cube?" he asked.

"No, love, this wine must be served at room temperature," Lola replied.

"Then you better cook it a couple of hours," Dave shot back. Six candles on a July evening without air conditioning. Already the dining room was a furnace.

"Do something useful and stack the chairs in the hallway," Lola ordered.

Dave begrudgingly dragged the chairs into the entranceway. He was outnumbered.

"Now, all we do is wait for sundown," Lola said to B.J. and Miranda. "So, until then, let's share ghost stories."

"Oh, please," Dave piped in from the hallway.

"Does this house have any ghosts?" Miranda asked.

"You're looking at her," shouted Dave from the living room.

"Oh, my yes," said Lola, ignoring Dave. "B.J., be a love and turn off the lights."

B.J. did as instructed, flicking off the switches in the kitchen and entranceway.

The candlelight cast strange projections in the room. Their shadows crept up the ceiling. They took on the haunting shapes of keening gargoyles and glided about the room.

Lola continued her tale, whispering hoarsely: "This house was built in the late 1890s by a doctor who took up residence here in the growing village of Kinmount. Unfortunately his stay didn't last long as he had an affair with a nurse (who was rumoured to be married) and was run out of town."

"*Lola* should have been run out of town years ago," Dave muttered, catching his image in the hall mirror. He needed sleep.

"And the doctor haunts this house?" Miranda asked wide-eyed.

"Footsteps on the basement stairs, faucets turning on in the middle of the night, strange sounds from the second floor," Lola said quietly and ominously.

"Oh, c'mon, Lola. You're the only one haunting this place," Dave shouted from the hallway.

"Either join us or remove yourself. Eavesdropping is not polite," Lola reprimanded him.

Dave sighed and joined them in the dining room. He gestured to the window. The sun was disappearing on the horizon line.

"Can we please get this over with? I want to go to bed," he yawned.

"Okay, grumpy-pants. Now, we each need to stand around the table. Equal distance from each other." Lola ushered them to their places.

"We have to employ the proper magical invocation in order to get the spirit we want to enter our circle," Lola instructed.

"Please, Lola. Enough," said Dave.

"Ignore Mister Doubty-pants," said Lola. "Let us all hold hands and hum the word 'omi.'"

Dave broke the chain and parked himself in the entrance way in case he wanted to bid a hasty retreat.

"I'll observe," he said, crossing his arms in defiance.

"Suit yourself. Alright on the count of three. One. Two. Three. Oh-meeee."

"Oh-meeeeeee," chanted the trio minus Dave.

"Oh, beloved Bard of Avon, you wordsmith of all time, William Shakespeare, we welcome you here tonight with love and safety," Lola said as a third-dimension cantor. "Everyone place your index finger lightly on the stem of the wine glass and bid William to join us."

The three gently air brushed the bottom of the wine glass with their index fingers. They closed their eyes and attempted to conjure the Bard of Avon into the dining room. The wine glass jerked forward and paused before slowly circling the table. Gaining momentum, it became a blur of figure eight patterns as B.J., Miranda, and Lola barely managed to keep a finger touch.

"White water rafting of the occult," Dave mumbled bitterly

to himself. "Here we go."

"Oh, William, are you are here with us tonight?" Lola intoned.

The wine glass swept about the table top coming to rest on the "yes" card.

"Oh, welcome, dear bard. We are honoured to have you in our presence," said Lola, bowing her head.

"May we ask you some questions?" Miranda asked timidly.

The wine glass moved towards Miranda and then circled back to stop at the "yes" card again.

"Oh, joy! Oh, bliss!" squealed Miranda.

"Oh joy, oh, bliss," muttered Dave.

"Did you love Anne Hathaway?" she asked.

"Yes," answered the glass.

"Did you have a relationship with the Earl of Southampton?" she continued.

"No," answered the glass.

"Christopher Marlowe?"

The glass ignored the question.

"Are you the true author of the plays attributed to William Shakespeare?" asked B.J.

The glass reared up on its stem and blasted toward B.J., almost sliding off the table. It reversed and then raced helter-skelter about the table at a frenetic speed. The trio did their best to hang on. The glass made for the "yes" card and repeatedly ran over it for emphasis.

"B.J., you have offended our illustrious guest. Apologize at once," Lola scolded.

"I'm sorry, good Sir. No offence intended I assure you," apologized B.J. wiping his brow. The pot wasn't helping.

The glass came to a stop.

"Are you enjoying rehearsals?" Dave asked sarcastically, arms folded.

The glass slowly moved towards him and then veered to the left. "Yes."

"Any suggestions?" Dave asked.

"Enough of your sarcasm. Ignore him, William. Do you have a message for any of us?" Lola said.

The glass glided towards the window making small circular patterns before stopping in front of Lola. After a brief pause, it moved towards the alphabetical letters.

"Hurry, Miranda. Grab the pad and pencil by the phone. I need to write this down," said Lola impatiently.

Miranda scurried into the kitchen and returned just as the wine glass was stopping at the first letter: "M."

"M for Miranda?" she asked, holding her breath.

The glass moved from letter to letter. Lola shouted each letter out. Miranda performed secretarial duties.

M-A-N-Y-A-G-O-O-D-H-A-N-G-I-N-G-P-R-E-V-E-N-T-S-A-B-A-D-M-A-R-R-I-A-G-E

"Many a good hanging prevents a bad marriage," translated Dave.

He looked directly at Lola.

"Feste the Fool says it in *Twelfth Night,*" he said wryly.

There was an uncomfortable silence. Lola avoided Dave's stare. Dead husbands were not on her agenda.

The glass jerked itself up and down.

"It looks like it's laughing," observed B.J.

"Like a dolphin," Miranda cooed.

"Very clever. Any other messages, you quillish rogue?" asked Lola, attempting to shift the focus away from herself for once.

The glass parked itself in front of Dave.

Then four clean strokes and the message was delivered.

L-I-S-T

"Got it," said Dave quickly.

The glass spelt out the word again.

"LIST."

"I heard you the first time." Dave found himself talking to the glass. He was not going to share that Hamlet's father's ghost was haunting him. Or, more specifically, the author of Hamlet's father's ghost.

"List? What does that mean?" asked Miranda.

"Nothing," said Dave. "We're finished. Put the cards away, Lola."

"Does our famous director not take direction well?" Lola teased.

"It's not real. None of it," Dave said emphatically. "The glass is being guided by our unconscious muscular exertions. It's an illusion that the glass is moving under its own control. You are deceiving yourselves. Convincing yourselves that Shakespeare's spirit is truly at work. It's what psychologists call a 'dissociative state.' Your consciousness is somehow divided or cut off from some aspects of your normal cognitive function."

"There goes the party pooper again." Lola reached down to pick up the wine glass.

At that instant, the glass started to vibrate. It toppled over and began bouncing on the table.

"Earthquake?" shouted B.J. looking around the dining room.

"Nothing else is shaking," cried Miranda, further spooking the room.

The glass stopped moving.

Silence.

Suddenly the candles blew out, the only light now coming from the moon shining in the window.

"I'm scared." Miranda was trembling in her Birkenstocks.

"Lola! Put that glass away! NOW!" Dave ordered.

As Lola reached for the glass, it moved away from her touch and started racing around the table. Fingerless.

"Dissociative state, my third nipple," said Lola to Dave, not taking her eye off the erratic movement of the glass.

"Have we upset you, William?" she asked.

"I don't think that's William," said B.J.

"Are you William Shakespeare?" demanded Lola.

The glass tore across the table knocking the "No" card onto the floor.

"That was rude of Mr. Shakespeare. Not the manners God gave a goat. He could have said goodbye," Lola scolded the glass.

"I don't think the glass cares," said Dave, rushing to the wall switch. The dining room light refused to come on.

"Who are you?" asked Miranda, resisting the urge to run out of the room.

The glass changed gears and headed for the letters, jerking back and forth between the "h" and "a".

H-A-H-A-H-A-H-A

"Great. Our spirit has a sense of humour," said Dave. He headed for the hallway to flip on the entrance wall switch. Nothing.

"Who are you and what do you want?" demanded B.J., moving to Miranda to protect her.

The glass attacked the letters, spelling out:

L-O-R-E-T-T-A

"Loretta?! Is that you, dear sister?" asked Lola, reaching for the glass to no avail.

The glass charged back to the letters.

"No."

"Who do you want to speak to?" demanded B.J.

The glass attacked the cards. The dining room was dropping in temperature

M-Y-G-R-A-N-D-D-A-U-G-H-T-E-R

"Your granddaughter!?" exclaimed Dave.

"Miranda, is this your grandmother?" gushed Lola, jumping up. "How exciting!"

Miranda ground her teeth and tore at her hair. "Oh my God!" she wailed. "My grandmother! My father's mother, Loretta! She died of a stroke in April." B.J. put his hands on her shaking shoulders.

"We are stopping this right now." Dave reached for the glass but was blocked by an energy force that propelled him backwards, flattening him against the wall.

"What do you want?" cried out Miranda.

H-O-W-D-A-R-E-Y-O-U-H-O-W-D-A-R-E-Y-O-U-H-O-W-D-A-R-E-Y-O-U

The glass would not stop spelling out the phrase.

"How dare you what?" Lola shouted at Miranda. "What did you do to your grandmother?"

"I'M SORRY!" screamed Miranda, bursting into sobs. "I'm sorry, Grandma. So sorry. Please, stop. I'll practice again. I will, I promise. Please stop, please stop, please stop ..."

The glass glided across the table toward Miranda. Gaining speed. The Waterford crystal version of the shark in *Jaws*. It slid off the table shattering at Miranda's feet. Miranda ran out of the room wailing up the stairs, B.J. in alarmed pursuit.

The lights came back on.

The chill left the room.

Tropical room temperature returned.

Dave peeled himself off the wall. He steadied his nerves and glared at Lola.

"Oh, shut up," she said. "Help me clean up this mess."

Lola poured them each a double gin and tonic. Dave did not refuse. He swept up the broken glass. Lola gathered up the cards. Dave snatched them from her and threw them in the trash. They could hear Miranda crying on the third floor. It was going to be a long night.

THIRTEEN

Mozart filled the house. Not a ghost. It was Miranda. She was up at the first streak of dawn, practicing on the parlour piano.

B.J. was making breakfast in the kitchen when Dave poked his head in.

"Everything, okay?" he asked, referencing the music wafting in from down the hall.

"She'll be alright. Quite the scare. Her grandmother was her piano teacher from the age of eight. Miranda hated the piano but she had to take lessons to please her father. She quit playing after her grandmother died," B.J. explained, handing Dave a bowl of berries and yogurt.

They sat down at the table to eat. Dave turned on the radio. CBC Toronto crackled to life.

"You don't actually believe those were spirits last night, do you?" asked Dave.

"I don't, but it sure was convincing," B.J. said, popping two slices of rye bread in the toaster.

"There is a logical explanation. We all know we are only using ten percent of our brain's capacity. The rest remains a mystery. A mystery I don't think we should mess with. Think about it. Our collective focus last night. So the glass moved. It had to be the power of that focus. Not a spirit. They were dangerous, unknown waters we were treading. And even more dangerous to call those 'waters' spirits from the other side. Especially with a bunch of actors with over-active imaginations susceptible to the power of suggestion. We conjured up our worst memories. Look at me thinking I was pinned to the wall. Ridiculous, but still frightening," Dave theorized.

"What do you make of Shakespeare and Miranda's grandmother?" asked B.J., buttering toast.

"All thoughts and questions we had about Shakespeare already in our minds. Our focus allowed our unconscious to become conscious. Nothing more," Dave continued.

"Like opening a box of Freud," said B.J.

"Exactly. Why I'm against it. We don't know what we have locked away in our heads. Drawers that should remain shut. Leave it for the head doctors not some ghost game. Look what Miranda's unexamined guilt over her grandmother manifested. Unnerving stuff."

"And the lights?"

"I don't know. Power surge? We *are* in a dead zone. Pun intended. Maybe there is a correlation to the lack of cell towers and the electricity. Or maybe it's faulty wiring. Look at this place. Coincidence, but not the hand of a demented dead grandmother," Dave reasoned.

He poured himself a coffee. Mozart switched to Vivaldi.

"At least it's cheerful," Dave remarked.

"What do you think of giving her the day off?" asked B.J. "Let her get some rest."

"Yes," agreed Dave. "Get the piano guilt out of her system."

The familiar CBC news chords chimed in. Dave went to the kitchen to turn up the volume.

The cold war between North Korea and the United States of America had heated up yet another notch. The President had said at three in the morning that North Korea would force all white Americans to pinch their eyelids with clothespins. The Doomsday clock was ticking faster than the metronome in the parlour.

"We'll all be swallowing Pete O'Neill's iodine pills soon enough," Dave joked grimly.

The announcer moved on to regional weather. The Kinmount heat wave would continue.

Dave turned off the radio. Miranda stopped playing.

"Any sign of Lola yet?" asked B.J.

"Not yet. She's probably sulking. Or channelling Isadora Duncan," Dave said flatly.

Miranda entered the dining room. It was hard to imagine swollen patches under the eyes of a young twenty-something, but Miranda sported them like puffy tea bags. Her exhausted eyes were dark and bloodshot. Lower lids hung down revealing two lines of tired pink.

"You okay?" Dave asked, masking his concern. He hoped she hadn't called her father.

"I will be," she said, wiping a strand of hair away from her mouth.

"Quite the night. I did try to warn you all," he said, sipping his coffee. "You didn't call your father, did you?" He knew the expression on his face looked stupid.

Miranda stared down at him and did not respond.

"You do know that wasn't your grandmother," he reasoned, as if talking to one of Lady Capulet's three-year-old day-care kids. His tone was low and consciously patient.

"Whatever," she replied, leaving the room to rummage through the fridge, returning with a slice of watermelon.

She munched in silence. Dave and B.J. shared a concerned look.

"Good morning, my lovelies," announced Lola from the hall entrance way. Her lips were redder than usual. Her wine-stained teeth managed to glisten despite their lack of whiteness. She was dressed in a faded pink kimono. Fluttery false eyelashes glued in place resembled dancing spiders' legs. Sky-blue eyeshadow completed the unsettling picture. "What beauteous, dulcet tones to greet the day with. It's been far too long since the sound of that piano has gifted the parlour. Thank you, my dear. Your grandmother would be proud."

Lola stretched in the doorway. Her yoga posture, balancing on one leg, was akin to a flamingo during a heavy wind, a lawn ornament gone astray.

"Ummmmmmm," she chanted.

Dave poured himself another coffee and retreated to the porch.

Lola joined him, scotch in hand.

"And how is our fearless director this morning?" she said coyly, deliberately avoiding the night's proceedings. Or was she oblivious? The jury was out on that one.

"Oh, please, Lola. Don't start," Dave warned. "I've had just about enough of you and your manipulative freak show—"

She broke in, smiling confidently: "You really should try meditation, David. Get rid of that controlling attitude. It doesn't serve you,"

"And you know all about that, Ms. Ghandi," he fired back. "Don't you think it's a little early for scotch?"

"It's always happy hour somewhere in the world." She raised her glass and took a long sip.

"The sun never sets on the Lola Whale Empire, is that it?"

"But of course," she grinned.

Dave and Lola were a funny breed. They both needed to be in control, although neither would admit it. Each had a childhood with little contact with other children, constructing their own realities by necessity. They had created worlds where they felt safe, to protect and hide their vulnerabilities. And continued to do so into adulthood, Dave as a director and Lola as—no one was quite sure.

A bird began chirping loudly. Dave scanned the backyard for the source of the sound, his eyes coming to rest on a fat, red cardinal sitting on top of the head of the giant phallus.

"Oh, be quiet, Horton," Lola said to the bird.

"Horton?"

"My second husband. He annoyingly still comes for visits in the morning," Lola replied. "Don't you check up on me, you fat, red bastard!" she shouted at the cardinal.

"Maybe he takes issue with your breakfast cocktails," said Dave.

"He took issue with everything," said Lola. "Most uptight

man I ever met. No *joi de vivre*." She gestured towards the cardinal. "And thick as that cement penis. Light a match to find a gas leak."

"So, why did you marry him?" Dave asked, wondering the reverse, why on earth Horton would want to marry Lola.

"You men are all the same. Put on your best Sunday suit when you come a-courting and then reveal your true troll selves once the deed is done."

Dave didn't take the bait. "You're one to talk about 'controlling natures,'" he fired back. "Pot meet kettle."

(Surprisingly, Shakespeare did not coin the term, "pot calling the kettle black." Credit must go to Miguel de Cervantes, the phrase first appearing in his seventeenth-century Spanish novel, *Don Quixote*).

"Oh, would you like some tea?" Lola asked, throwing her empty glass at the cardinal. The bird flew away before the glass struck the statue, shattered, and splashed its contents and glittering fragments over the penis and ground.

"Your insular bubble is truly something to behold. You have blinders that would've given Secretariat pause," Dave laughed darkly.

"Piffle. I just know how things are to be done. I don't mind if you disagree with me so long as you do what I say."

"Lola, I am not your monkey helper."

"Now, come and look at some costumes unless you want to stay out here talking to that wastrel Harold."

Lola turned and left the porch. Dave sighed and followed her in. Two more weeks and he'd be out of Kinmount for good.

Lola led him up to the third floor, into a small room that reeked of moth balls and lavender. Standing against the wall, furthest across the cramped makeshift dressing room, was a large intimidating wardrobe. A well-oiled padlock protected its contents. She lifted a loop of skeleton keys off a wall hook and chose the largest one.

"This belonged to my great-grandmother," she said. "Solid oak. Made by her Mennonite husband for her as a wedding gift."

She unlocked the heavy door and the wardrobe creaked open. Mothball fumes filled the room causing Dave to choke. In an instant, he was in another world. Many worlds to be exact. And none of them Narnia. The wardrobe's contents ranged from mid-eighteenth-century jackets, waistcoats, and riding breeches to late Victorian dresses. Men's period shirts hung in a tight row on wooden hangers. All in mint condition. Perfectly pressed. Treasured artifacts. As well preserved as the day they were first sewn and embroidered.

Lola handed Dave a small roll of green painter's tape and a marker.

"Mark which ever ones you want. Label them by character. I will take measurements today and start on modifications and alterations," she instructed. "Shakespeare won't know the difference by the time I'm finished."

Dave was still staring at her collection in awe.

"Thank you, Lola. Wow! They're ..." He meant it sincerely.

"Yes, they are the real McCoy. Passed down through my family. I am their final keeper."

"These should be in a museum," he said.

"Nonsense. To gather up dust and be gawked at? No, they are meant to breathe and have life. And that is your responsibility and privilege," she said.

"Are you sure?" Dave asked. "These are antiques. What if a dress rips or a pair of breeches gets torn?"

"Then they served the theatre bravely," she said. "Get on it with it. I have things to do."

"I don't know what to say. Thank you. And, Lola ..." Dave hesitated, "your pavane is beautiful."

"But of course, kind sir," she curtsied and blushed.

She left the room quickly.

Was she tearing up?

Lola Whale was an enigma inside of an enigma.

He slowly began to tear off pieces of tape.

Beethoven pounded up the stairs.

FOURTEEN

Dave stayed on geese-less game and one week later, the company was ready for their first stumble-through. Lola was in attendance. Sporting a peasant skirt, summer parasol perched above her bonneted head, notebook in hand, she sat in a folding lawn chair beside Dave.

The actors found their way through the scenes, calling out to Ginny for lines as needed, and, with Dave's practical cuts, the run came in just under two hours.

It was a particularly hot July, both in Kinmount and in Verona: tempers flared more quickly; the relentless heat made it hard to sleep, which in turn caused rational minds to make rash decisions; and irrational minds to push themselves to the brink of madness.

Dave's plague context boiled in the blistering heat, the horror of dead bodies and images of graves coming to life. In the winter, the plague seemed to disappear, only because fleas (which were a major culprit in spreading the disease) were dormant. In the summer, the plague attacked again. During plague outbreaks, bodies were left to rot in empty houses and there was no one to give them a proper burial. As there was no cure for the plague, superstitions abounded regarding its cause: the stars, climate, drinking, gluttony, the night, foreigners. Verona was a paranoid and suspicious society. The slightest sign of sickness would lead to the terrifying conclusion that the plague was back—did Juliet's artificial death announce the return of the plague to the Capulet family? Dave thought so. The plague was responsible for the Friar's letter not getting delivered to Romeo in time, directly causing Juliet's and his death.

"A plague o' both your houses!" Mercutio screams in Romeo's arms, his parting words after being stabbed by Tybalt and realizing he is going to die. He'd joked and laughed about the cut until it was too late. It is the famous curse on the Capulet and Montague families, and foreshadows the unpitying hands of fate that punish children for the sins of their fathers, much like the Kennedys. Baldwin had become a raging, blistering cold sore in the role, his syphilitic death-wish clear from the moment of his first entrance, needling Romeo about not wanting to dance, and advising him that the best way to cure a broken heart was to get laid.

Under Dave's direction, Baldwin put a dark psychological spin on Mercutio's strange imaginative rants. His big speech in his first scene started off as a stream of consciousness stand-up routine about the mythological fairy Queen Mab, and ended up fuming about (of course) sex. Dave provided him with a playable back story. Episodes of sleep paralysis in Elizabethan England were often explained as a demon or succubus sitting on the sufferer's chest—and possibly having sex with them. Young women were "hag-ridden" by Mab. She'd seductively lead them down a weed-infested garden path into the arms of sweet-talking men, losing their virginity and becoming pregnant in the process, their dowry and lives ruined. It's little wonder that "Mab" was groundling slang for "slut."

Making Benvolio a girl paid off, as did her secret crush on her cousin Romeo. There lurked a deeper swampier truth beneath the sewers of Verona in having a young woman cross-dress as a boy to protect herself from Queen Mab and the misogyny of the wolf packs of Italian young men. In Dave's staging, Mercutio, when he is sober (which is seldom) treats Benvolia like one of the boys. In the scene following the Capulet ball the pair is drunkenly searching for Romeo. Dave was insistent that only Mercutio be hammered. Benvolia tries unsuccessfully to get her self-destructive friend home to bed, an Elizabethan DD of sorts.

Mercutio shakes her off and starts crudely objectifying Rosaline, describing her various body parts in a disgusting yet menacing exhibition while, at the same time, sloppily trying to get into Benvolia's breeches—in a modern context, trying to fuck his best friend's kid sister.

Dave's interpretation infused this dirty little scene of "poperin pears" and "open arses" with an uncomfortable awkwardness. It was the polar opposite of the balcony scene, which followed. Miranda and B.J. brought such honesty and conviction to their encounter that Ginny remarked to Dave, "If I didn't know it was the sun beating down, I'd swear it was the moon."

Dave had chosen his star-crossed lovers wisely; their chemistry was an apothecary's dream.

All Dave's directorial choices were based on careful examination of the original Folio text. One particular oddity is the language and punctuation used by Lady Capulet in the wake of her nephew Tybalt's death. Tybalt kills Mercutio, Romeo kills Tybalt in revenge, Romeo runs away, and the Montague and Capulet families rush to the town square only to discover the bodies. Lady Capulet's behaviour is strange and over-the-top. It is almost embarrassing. Her words are not those of a grieving aunt, but those of a lover:

"Tybalt, my Cozin? O my Brothers Child,
O Prince, O Cozin, Husband, O the blood is spild
Of my deare kinsman!"

Is Lady Capulet a good, obedient wife going along with her husband's wants, or is she carrying on a secret affair with her fiery young nephew? Dave opted for the latter. Lady Capulet is much younger than her husband, since she married him when she was only about twelve years old. Talk about robbing the cradle blind. In Dave's mind, the age difference had to cause tension in their marriage, hence her pursuing an affair with her nephew. "Too soon marred are those so early made [wives]," Capulet tells Paris, clearly referencing his own wife.

The skeletons in the Capulet closet exploded under Dave's ever-watchful eye. The only problem was no one in Kinmount would hear Lady Capulet's grief beyond the first row. Her wailing was pathetic.

"She looks like a fucking mime," Dave whispered to Ginny during the run, while writing "louder" for the umpteenth time in his notes.

"At least she knows her lines," whispered back Ginny. "I'd never be able to hear her call line if she didn't."

"How can you tell?" said Dave glumly. He wracked his brain to fix the play's weakest link.

Lord Capulet is the embodiment of a nouveau-riche mafia godfather. Dave pushed the physicality of the role. Capulet's aggression is most prominent in the big, confrontational scene with his daughter over whether or not she would marry Paris. He was a man prone to physical domestic violence against the Nurse, his wife, and now his daughter. Capulet slapped Juliet hard across the cheek. It looked real enough to those company members watching.

But it wasn't.

Capulet missed her face by a good six inches. Miranda actually "napped" the slap, creating the sound of impact by clapping her hands in front of her face, out of view of the audience.

The rapier and dagger fights were as deadly as the plague itself.

A fight has to look just real enough. Audience trust is shattered when a fight gets too real for comfort. Pete O'Neill knew his stuff. His fight choreography was visceral, but completely devoid of actual danger, creating beautiful tableaus of carnage. Throughout rehearsals, Dave kept adjusting the angles of the naps to make sure the audience was fooled by the illusion.

The stage violence began with the opening scene. Dave achieved the schoolyard brawl he wanted, even if the stoner servants couldn't remember their lines.

Old Sally still had a whinny or two left in her old bones. For a brief moment she became "Mustang Sally" again, a young mare full of horsepower. The Prince mounted her and rode in from the back parking lot. The badlands became the highlands, a brief spaghetti western on the streets of Verona. The kids would love it.

Romeo is not out on the streets fighting like all the other young men. He's off doing what he does best: daydreaming of a girl. Later, when Tybalt wants to rumble, Romeo flat out refuses because he doesn't want to hurt his new bride. After Tybalt kills Mercutio, Romeo's BFF, Romeo feels responsible. He's ashamed of himself for not fighting Tybalt in the first place. He blames it all on his love for Juliet. Many Elizabethans believed that love between a man and woman could turn a man into a milksop. Being "effeminate" didn't mean you were acting like a woman; it meant you liked women a little too much. The pressure to be a "man" got to Romeo and he sought vengeance.

In Dave's version, Romeo didn't just kill Tybalt; he butchered him, gutting him like a pig. It was savage. It was awful. It was perfect.

Dave gave encouraging notes to his troupe. "We're in a good shape, exactly where we need to be at this stage."

"Where's Lola?" asked Miranda.

She and her lawn chair were gone.

"Anyone see when she left?" asked Dave.

"Halfway through the Prince's final speech," said Baldwin.

"Was she okay?" asked B.J.

"She looked fine to me," said the Nurse.

"She was mumbling to herself," observed Capulet.

"Nothing new there. So be it," replied Dave. "Okay, gang, finish getting off book and we'll pick up with the first five scenes tomorrow afternoon."

The company dispersed. Miranda and B.J. cycled off together to find a beach. Dave was in need of a reward for getting the play blocked. He went in search of Kate Quinn.

FIFTEEN

He found her stacking empties.

"Hey, need a hand?" he said, leaning in the open doorway.

"Hey. No, I'm just about finished. Good way to spend a day off, eh?" she laughed.

"Hear you," he nodded in agreement.

"Where's your posse?" she smiled, looking around him.

"Just finished a run through. I sent them home to work on lines," he said, boyish smile engaged.

"How did it go?" she asked, wiping her hands on a dishrag.

"I think it's going to be okay," he replied, turning off his director's brain and turning on the charm.

"So you get to relax for a minute?" She began cleaning tables.

"You free?" he asked as casually as possible, masking his nervousness.

Kate stopped cleaning. She looked at him and tossed him the rag.

"I can be. What did you have in mind Mr. Shakespeare?" she asked.

"How about we grab a baguette, some cheese, and you surprise me," he grinned.

"Grab a stool and I'll be done shortly." She gestured towards the beer taps. "Help yourself." She returned to cleaning the last table, fully aware Dave was watching her. His endorphins began to slow dance with his loins. He poured himself a Keith's and sat at the bar. The floor beneath his stool was covered in the previous night's peanut shells. He scanned the tavern interior, a combination of warm honey-coloured wood and mottled brick-work. The walls were littered with memorabilia. Whether they were collected or donated, Dave couldn't tell. A barn-board sign was nailed to a support post beside the cash register. Its upper-case letters were sloppily painted with a white latex primer. It read, "Hungry? We'll feed you. Thirsty? We'll get you drunk? Lonely? We'll get you drunk."

Haphazardly arranged on the wall behind the old bar were rows of faded framed Pee Wee hockey teams, dating back to the early '70s, smiling like toothless ghosts—The Red Lion Rockets. How many of the padded children grew up to be padded stool regulars?

"The odds of an actor making it in Hollywood are as slim as a kid making it to 'the show,'" Dave's favourite acting instructor, Ron Freeman, had informed his first-year class. "Last year, there were ten-thousand ten-year-olds playing hockey in Ontario. Of these players, only one-hundred-and-ten made it to the OHL. Of those, only seven made it to the NHL. Seven out of ten thousand. Only point-zero-zero-seven percent. Subtract five and you have the odds of making it in Hollywood. So, if you want to be Tom Cruise, get out now."

Dave had missed his chance.

Beside the Rockets hung a yellowed, black-and-white photo of Stompin' Tom in a cheap dollar store frame. Beside it, an autographed stompin' board.

"You think you are directin',
But both those masks are frownin',
You'll be askin' for direction,
On a Kinmount Saturday night."

Dave heard Tom pounding out the revised lyrics on the worn hardwood of the Red Lion. Was it dehydration messing with his brain? He already had to contend with Hamlet's father's ghost's listing. Did he now have to deal with the voice of a dead singer in a black cowboy hat too? He pushed the hallucination away.

He examined Tom's stomping board more closely. "You think he really signed it?" he asked Kate, who was washing her hands in the bar utility sink.

"Before my time, but I do know Old Tom and Jimmy's families were related back across the pond or something," she said.

Jimmy O'Connor had owned the Red Lion since before the invention of the fax machine. He was the eldest of twelve children, each christened Jimmy. His father was a Jimmy as was his father, and his father before that. In fact, the first Jimmy O'Connor could be traced back to the twelfth century in Connacht, Ireland—the patriarch of a family of hound-loving Catholic nobles. Red Lion Jimmy would never rule the world.

Dave noted a black mourning bow wired to the picture frame. Tom had given his last stomp years earlier.

"How's Jimmy doing?" he asked, referencing the frame.

"Still moping about, wearing that bloody black armband," she said, drying her hands.

"You know, in Shakespeare's day they didn't wear mourning bands," Dave said, between sips.

"No, eh?" she said in the manner of one making polite conversation. She counted the previous night's take.

"They stuck sprigs of rosemary in their hatbands instead. It was a symbol of remembrance."

"Where'd you learn that?" she asked, concentrating on her coinage.

"Did a production of *Hamlet* a few years back. I had my Laertes make a wreath out of a rosemary bush to place on his sister Ophelia's grave."

"And here I thought rosemary was for seasoning chicken," Kate joked, separating her loonies from her toonies.

"Earlier in the play, Ophelia goes mad after Hamlet accidentally kills her father. She throws sprigs of rosemary at the other characters."

"A lot of rosemary in that play of yours," Kate remarked casually, taping a torn five-dollar bill back together.

"Never was there a tale sadder than that of Hamlet and his

spooky dad," Dave wise-cracked, poking fun at the final couplet of *Romeo and Juliet.* "Rosemary was also associated with love and fidelity," he added flirtatiously, polishing off his Keith's.

"That explains why you can't find it in men's kitchens," Kate said drily, taking Dave's empty glass and washing it in the sink.

"And it was supposedly planted around houses to ward off witches."

Kate's ears perked up. "Witches?"

"A lot of hocus pocus, in my opinion," said Dave. "A convenient way for men to persecute midwives. And for Lola Whale to play games with the occult and scare my actors."

Kate stopped doing what she was doing. "There are a few folks around here who think Lola came out of the broom closet," she said. "Jimmy for one. He calls it 'bitch-craft.' Claims Lola made his kegs run dry."

"Lola may be odder than a Greek myth, but she's no witch."

"He was drunk and forgot to put the beer order in is all," Kate said drily.

"My point exactly. There's always a reasonable explanation." Dave didn't mention his bizarre relationship with the ghost of Hamlet's father. "I have an ancestor, a playwright, who was into the occult. He helped Shakespeare write the witches spells in *Macbeth.*"

"Isn't it supposed to be bad luck to say that?" Kate asked. "Even I know that."

"Only if you say it in a theatre and believe in evil spirits. Nothing but silly actor superstition."

Kate bent down to lock a drawer. Dave spun around three times on his bar stool and spit over his left shoulder. Despite his bravado, he wasn't taking any chances after the strange ouija incident.

ॐ

Half an hour later, they were sitting on Kate's roof sharing a bottle of tequila, smoking her Du Mauriers, and listening to a vinyl recording of Jeff Buckley on her grandfather's portable Seabreeze record player through her open bedroom window.

Dave was mid-sentence: "Shakespeare wrote to put money in his pocket, food on the table, and fire in the bellies of his audiences."

Kate had asked about his odd fascination with Shakespeare. He'd jumped at the chance to impress her, missing the point.

"And strike fear into modern teenagers," she added wryly.

"That's only because of bad high-school English teachers who don't understand him. Besides, most of Shakespeare's audiences were illiterate."

"He'd feel right at home in Kinmount," she sighed.

"They have bear-baiting on Main Street?" Dave joked, wanting to hold Kate's wit in the palm of his hand.

"So how can an audience understand him?" she said, leaning in through the window to flip the record.

"His words were chosen to be spoken and heard," replied Dave, raising his voice, "not to be read and deadened at a desk. They wither when performance is removed."

"Wither?" She reappeared. "Look at you, Mr. Scholar," she teased.

"I'm no scholar. By choice. Academia is about as useful to a director as a cat is to a mouse."

She lit another smoke. "Go on."

He took another shot of tequila and continued: "He was practically forgotten in the one hundred and fifty years following his death, except for when he was briefly revived during the Restoration; the story of *Romeo and Juliet* was changed to give it a happy Hallmark ending."

"Juliet woke up in time?"

"Yup. Same thing with *King Lear*. Cordelia lived and married Edgar, the boy next door."

"So, what happened?" Kate seemed genuinely interested. Or was it the tequila talking. She poured them each another shot. Dave shifted easily into entertainer mode. He'd shared this story before, but never on a rooftop: "There was a famous actor, David Garrick. He was the young Ian McKellen of his day, before Gandalf—athletic, handsome, with a brilliant understanding of the text. He was the first to promote realistic acting and make theatre respectable."

"Ian McKellen?"

"Garrick."

"Right."

"In 1769, Garrick turned the Shakespearean dial from 'so-so writer' to 'god.' He single-handedly kick-started the Stratford tourist treadmill and made Shakespeare famous. At the same time, a bunch of cloud-gazing silly leftovers of the Romantic Movement started preaching the tale of the rural boy-genius from Stratford."

"And the Romantics were?"

"The eighteenth-century version of anti-establishment hippies. Shakespeare became their idol, their poster boy of romance and poetry; a blank-verse Elvis of sorts."

"Did Shakespeare wear blue suede tights?"

"So, the clouds looked down on the Romantic Movement's leader and said, 'Hey, he's shaped like an idiot.'"

"Nice," Kate laughed.

"Not long after, the anti-romantic Realist Movement rose up in retaliation."

"No more Hallmark?" She butted her dart in the eaves trough.

"Happy endings be damned," Dave pronounced, waving his arms, causing him to momentarily lose his balance and nearly fall off the roof. Kate grabbed his arm. He hid his embarrassment and recovered quickly: "The Realists accepted a situation for what it was and didn't believe in something that wasn't true. They refused to sugarcoat the truth and believed in things they could see, touch, hear, et cetera. A belief in God was impossible because there was no physical evidence of his existence."

"Guess I'm a realist," said Kate.

"Oh, I know you are," said Dave. "Anyhow, fuelled by Darwin's theory of survival of the fittest, the Realists led an assault on the church, forcing the Victorian upper classes to search for another way to civilize the masses."

"Charming," said Kate.

"And so Shakespeare was elected to the executive board of English Literature, the new academic subject devised to do just that."

"And now?" she asked, inhaling deeply.

"If he were alive today, he'd be writing for Hollywood and Netflix—slasher films, rom-coms, epics," Dave shrugged. "It's ironic that he was writing screenplays three hundred years before the invention of film."

Dave didn't want to share with Kate that Shakespeare was out of his depth in the modern world of sexual, gender, religious, and racial equality. Racialized and religious minorities weren't the only ones that had been chained to the stake in Elizabethan England. Women certainly had been almost completely disempowered. At the close of a comedy, most female characters were essentially auctioned off to anyone who expressed an interest (in the tragedies, they died). In *Much Ado About Nothing*, Hero took back her fiancé despite having had to fake her own death to thwart his jealous rage.

Was asking talented female actors to abase themselves before the violent misogyny of a former age too much? Dave was exploring that issue in *Romeo and Juliet*. Could Shakespeare still be a beacon of the future? Or did he strictly belong to the past—and if so, did Dave too?

"And you?" Kate asked him.

"And me what?" he replied, hoping her question had to do more with his availability than the Bard.

"How do you direct a dead guy whose work is four hundred years old?" she asked.

Nope. Her question failed to match his desire. But at least he could impress her by sharing how his process worked. His previous girlfriends had all loved his work in the beginning stages of their relationship.

"Whenever I work on a text, a new adaptation," he explained, moving closer, "I try to imagine that I've just received a blank manila envelope at my front door, and inside it is a work by Shakespeare. But his name isn't anywhere on it. All I have is his words and the story. So, I'm not going to be influenced by academic research. I only have the original text. I have to dive in, let it speak to me, find out how it relates to me, and how can I make it relevant to a new audience. Take *Romeo and Juliet*. I thought I was directing a story of young love rising above the misogyny and violence of society. Now, I'm not so sure. The tragedy looks more and more to me to be about Romeo giving into the pressure to be a man."

"Men." She exhaled in disgust, recognizing the symptoms. "From my experience, bad male behaviour is like the lure of pepperoni and cheese when dieting. Only a matter of time."

Dave chose to sidestep her comment. Gutsy Kate, in *The Taming of the Shrew*, had to capitulate to a form of mental abuse. Had Kate Quinn as well, Dave wondered. He suspected an ex had treated her badly.

"I prefer all-dressed," he joked lamely.

"What's the weirdest Shakespeare you've ever seen?" She fixed her eyes on him. That wasn't the question he was anticipating. Weirdest Shakespearean production he'd seen? Dave had seen a lot.

"Well, not including my own," he sallied, and they shared a laugh, "there's a full translation of *Hamlet* in Klingon. There's a Popeye *Romeo and Juliet*. He eats his spinach to climb Olive Oyl's balcony."

"Romeo, the sailor-man," Kate sang while lighting up another smoke. Her raspy voice reminded Dave of Melissa Etheridge.

"A woman in England adapted *King Lear* almost entirely staged with sheep," he said, straight-faced."

"No way. I don't believe you," she coughed.

"Lear gives his final monologue cradling a black ewe in his arms."

They both broke into laughter.

"Baaaaaad Baaaaa-rd," Kate riffed.

"Whoa! Hot dip-thong," he flirted.

"Dip-thong? Is that some weird director thing, dipping panties in fondue?"

"It's a gliiiiding vowel," he demonstrated, overdoing it. "It's a combination of two adjacent vowel sounds." His innuendo was clear.

"Real women prefer *briefs*," Kate fired back, deliberately ignoring his mutual orgasm pun.

"And *brevity* is the soul of wit," said Dave, finishing the rally. "You should've auditioned. You'd have made a bang-up Nurse to Juliet."

"Not on your life," she replied, both flattered and apprehensive. "Even if I was interested, which I'm not, my job at the Red Lion makes it impossible."

There was a strange unwritten rule among theatre directors. Never talk about your day job. A director had to give the impression that they floated around, with no visible means of support. Dave had been fired from his last in-between-directing-gigs job the week before he got the call from Lola. Filling in for a receptionist on maternity leave at the Birch Lake Regional Health Centre, he was unable to decipher the doctors' scrawls and invented his own diagnoses. The Urology Department medical records read like a who's who of the Cretaceous Period.

"Do you mind if I bum another—" he asked, feeling the weight of his other life. Authors suffered a similar fate. Did Shakespeare ever have to wash dishes in a tavern?

Kate lit a cigarette and handed it to him. "So, here you are back in town, drinking tequila with me on my roof. What is that monkey brain of yours thinking?"

"My life is like a book."

"A book?" The corners of her mouth tightened ever so slightly.

"Hear me out," Dave said. "My life is still mid-chapter, spine a little bent; pages dog-eared but intact, the glue's still holding. I'm a dust jacket whose summary has yet to be completed.

Maybe you can help brush off some of the 'dust.'"

He smiled at her.

"Words, words, words," she grimaced. "Do you know what humanity really needs?"

"I'm all ears," he said.

"Global warming of the heart. No one takes responsibility anymore. They slip out the back door without leaving a note."

Or a text, Dave thought.

They sat in silence. But not an uncomfortable silence. He felt more at home in that moment than he had in a long time.

"I wish I lived in Ireland," he said, decidedly changing the topic and opening up.

"Why?" she asked, brushing an ash off her lap.

"Sadness is celebrated in Ireland," he sighed. Dave also envied Irish artists for more practical reasons—free post-secondary education and no income tax.

"And you want to be sad?" said Kate.

"Life is sad. We have all this pressure in North America to be happy. One big McHappy meal. But in Ireland, sadness is accepted. I like that."

"So being sad makes you happy," she quipped.

"Very funny. There's more to it. Ireland. And it's not just Bono. It's Yeats and Synge and Wilde and Beckett. It's literacy. Literacy is the way out, a coinage," Dave explained. "Plays and books have a strange force. They can actually liberate. And that's a power in a country that doesn't have many other things. Where jumping into oblivion is encouraged." Dave took a smoke from her pack.

"You're free to jump off my roof anytime you want," she volunteered.

"You know what I mean."

"Actually I do. But don't most artsies feel that way?" she asked.

"I am not an *artsy*," he snapped. "Artsy is to artist what jock is to athlete. An artist is an athlete of the soul.

"Sorry. Sensitive aren't we?" Theatre types were a strange

breed, Kate reasoned. "The fact that no one understands you doesn't mean you're an artist." She laughed easily.

"Doesn't matter, Kate." He sulked.

"I'm kidding." She punched his shoulder. "Can't you take a joke? Get out of that head of yours. The universe doesn't revolve around you."

They smoked in silence breathing in the stars.

"The planet Uranus has twenty-seven moons," said Dave. "Most of which are named for Shakespearean characters. Juliet, Queen Mab ..." trailing into silence.

He turned and looked at her.

"I'm nothing but a guest at the feast of artists," he said.

"Explain, please." She was trying to follow his chopped logic.

"I was raised in a broken home. I was an only child. I had a very sad childhood."

"So, who didn't?"

"Let me finish. But I wasn't raised by alcoholics or drug addicts. I wasn't beaten or abused."

"So, unless you're damaged you can't be an artist." Kate raised an eyebrow.

"Pretty much. Growing up, my curfew was when the streetlights came on. How boring."

"That's actually comforting. Most kids today aren't so lucky."

"I despised its blatant normality."

"That's your greatest fear."

"What is?"

"That you're ordinary. Like the rest of us."

Dave let out a heavy sigh—a sigh that had been building for decades.

"You admit it?"

He nodded reluctantly. It was true.

They each fired back another tequila shot, relaxing into the night.

"Do you think Romeo and Juliet would've made it?" she asked.

"They don't."

"I know, but if they'd lived, do you think their marriage would've survived?"

"I doubt it. Society was stacked against them. It was a relationship founded on lies. They only knew each other for five days. It wasn't love at first sight. They were obsessed, infatuated, out of control, and irrational."

"Sounds like lust to me."

"Yup." Dave was already thinking that Kate's roof would be a serviceable balcony, if the tequila and stars aligned.

"Where does the love go?" she mused.

"Songs have been written for centuries to try and solve that riddle," Dave observed. "Even Shakespeare couldn't."

"Jeff Buckley would have found the answer," she said, curling into him, the tequila softening her, "had he lived."

"I doubt it," he said, gently stroking her hair.

Dave was in his second year of theatre school when the news broke of the singer's accidental drowning. What a tragic waste. "The Forever Young Club." Privately, he envied the Club. All dead before the age of thirty, never having to compromise their gifts, grow bitter, or direct a show in Kinmount.

"My mother says love goes directly to God and he tosses it back," he said.

"I beg to differ," she said, her body tensing and pulling away. "God's aim is as reliable as bowling. God throws gutter balls."

He'd accidentally struck a nerve, a hint of fury beneath the surface.

"Fates and Furies," he whispered to himself. "Men are ruled by Fate," his favourite theatre history teacher, Professor Schlosser, had said when discussing Greek tragedy. She was a tall, commanding, stylish Gertrude Stein who lectured without notes. Professor Schlosser believed the male view of things was naively victorious, ultimately resigned, and complacent. Women were ruled by fury: they were secretive, damaged, repressed, less happy (due to men), and, accordingly, much less complacent. "The angrier woman modifies the easier male," she'd explained to a lecture hall of twenty-year-old acting students. "She forces him to see the truth with corrective revelation. We are all sentenced by fate and charged with fury; the man belongs to the Fates, the woman to the Furies; if it was the man's fate to be with a Fury, it is the woman's fate to be a Fury." Professor Schlosser was ahead of her time, trying to reach her young, self-absorbed charges in a world dominated by old boy conservatism. But her words had struck and stayed with Dave. If fate had brought him to Kinmount, was Kate now his secret Fury? He erased the thought from his mind. Too much tequila.

They drank in silence again. The constellations started to move.

"How's Elspeth?" he asked, avoiding the topic of God altogether.

"Do you really want to know?" she asked.

"Yes, I do," he assured her.

"She's at a summer riding camp. Lauren's teaching her."

"Lauren?"

"Lauren. You know, your Lady Capulet?"

"Riiiight. The horse whisperer."

"Elspeth is horse crazy. It's all she ever thinks about. Which isn't a bad thing. No boy troubles. Yet. Says she wants to be a ferrier."

"A *whattier*?"

"Making old-school horseshoes. Sort of like a blacksmith."

"That's different."

"That's my daughter." She paused before broaching the subject. "You never had any kids?"

"None that I know of," he laughed, a rote response.

"I'm serious. You ever want to have children?"

"I have enough trouble parenting myself," he said, stretching his back. "Don't get me wrong. I like kids, especially those precocious ten year olds who can carry on a conversation better than their betters can. As if lifted from the pages of Salinger."

"Like you?" she said, polishing off the tequila.

"I always wished I grew up in the Glass family. Living in a

massive New York brownstone apartment. With unorthodox siblings. Endless brilliant bantering. Smoking in the bathtub while arguing with my mother. So, what's Elspeth like?"

"A precocious twelve year old who can carry on a conversation better than her mother."

A gentle bah-bump-bah. Even the stars appeared to laugh.

"That I'd like to see," he said. "What about you?"

"What about me what?" She wasn't sure where he was headed.

"What's something you suck at?" he said.

"I can't garden," she said. "And my bathtub floor requires a chisel."

"I'll bring my flip flops next time."

"Next time?"

"I'm sorry, I—"

Had he jumped the gun?

"Relax. Just kidding." Kate reassured him he hadn't. "I was going to ask if you wanted to stay over."

"I should get back," he said stupidly. It was a conditioned response. "Another long day tomorrow," he said. "Rain check?"

The responsibility of the *work* always took precedence. Therefore, no vacations, no weekend getaways, no long-term relationships. His was a demanding muse.

"You sure?"

Dave shrugged.

"No, I'm not sure."

He leaned in to kiss her. She tasted of lime, nicotine, tequila, and connection.

They made out on the roof and passed out in her bed.

PART TWO: MADNESS

"When you keep your head when every one about you is losing theirs, maybe you don't understand the situation."

Bob Rigley, *Chicago Tribune*

ONE

"LIST!"

Dave woke with a start.

"LIST!"

"SSshhh. Not now," he whispered hoarsely.

"LIST!"

"Okay, okay."

Kate stirred beside him.

"Who are you talking to?"

"Sorry. Voice in my head. Go back to sleep."

"What time is it?" she asked groggily.

The sun was just beginning to dance on the curtains, weaving tree branch shadows into a dawn mosaic.

She reached for her alarm clock.

"Five thirty. Are you always up this early?"

"Afraid so."

"Can you get back to sleep?"

"Doubt it."

"Were you having a bad dream?"

"You could say that."

"What then?"

There was no way he could tell her he was being haunted by a fictional character. She'd think he was madder than Hamlet.

"I should get going."

Dave's morning-after guilt settled in—a guilt that, in his younger years, caused him to cut off his own paw rather than risk being late for or not prepared for a rehearsal.

"Okay," she said. "Do you regret staying over?" she asked.

"It's not you. Trust me," he tried to reassure her.

"You want me to make you a coffee?"

"No, I'm good. Last night was great. Can I see you again?"

"Let's see what the week brings."

"Okay," he said.

Her wind had left his sails.

She registered his disappointment. "I'm not saying no," she said.

"Great," he said, forcing the moment. Why did mornings have to be so awkward? He should have accepted the coffee.

He crawled out of bed onto the floor. The room started to spin like a cheap midway ride. After three failed attempts, he managed to pull on his shorts and t-shirt. He stumbled into his sandals and slowly made his way downstairs, gripping the railing tighter with each unsteady step.

Cycling back to Lola's was a challenge. His hangover had settled in and the sun fried his brain.

He dropped his bike on the front lawn, vomited into a bush, and queasily climbed Lola's front porch steps.

He fumbled with the key in the lock, the door creaked open, kicked off his sandals, and headed to the kitchen to put on a pot of coffee.

He stopped in his hungover tracks.

Lola was sitting in her accustomed spot wearing a satin purple kimono nursing a scotch. Her pellet gun rested on the sideboard.

"Where were you?" she growled.

"Lola, you are not my mother," he sighed and began searching for the coffee in the pantry.

"Sit down. We need to talk," she said.

"Okay," he said, returning with a small bag of stale Arabian blend. He poured a carafe of tap water into the coffee maker.

"Now."

He plunked himself down on the counter beside the coffee maker.

"Yes?" He was in no mood for her dramatics. All he wanted was his coffee, two aspirins and another hour of sleep. He should have drunk a gallon of water before he and Kate had fallen asleep. Lola's voice was irritating at the best of times but now it sounded like a screeching violin in surround sound.

"I want to discuss yesterday," she declared.

"Can't it wait until tonight?"

"No, it cannot."

"Okay, okay." He poured the coffee into a ceramic mug and sat down at the table.

"How do you think the run through went?" she asked.

"You know what, I'm surprisingly pleased. We're in pretty good shape."

"You think so."

"Yes, what, you don't?"

Lola removed a notebook from her kimono pocket and began flipping through it. "There are some changes I want made."

"Changes" he repeated carefully.

"Changes. *Romeo and Juliet* is a love story."

"Yeees," he said, stretching out the vowel into a tripthong.

"What I saw yesterday was not a love story."

"No, it wasn't," Dave said matter-of-factly. "And I don't think it is a love story."

"You don't think it's a love story," Lola repeated carefully.

"No, I don't."

"You don't."

"No."

"What is it then?" she said tersely.

"It's a tragedy. Romeo and Juliet were never in love. It was lust. There is no way two people could fall so deeply in love that they would die for each other in three days."

"In your cynical mind."

"No, facts are facts. It's really the tragedy of a young man caving into the machismo rules of his society and setting off an irreversible chain of events."

"Oh, I saw all your machismo misogyny and violence, trust me."

"And your point is?" Dave asked impatiently. He needed those aspirin.

"Fighting. Bloodshed," Lola continued.

"Shocking," he said, rubbing his temples in an attempt to kick-start his brain.

"There is no need for sarcasm. How many characters died in this macho 'tragedy' of yours?"

"It's not *my* tragedy, Lola. Not including Romeo and Juliet, there are three other deaths—Tybalt, Mercutio, and Paris. Oh, and Romeo's mother dies offstage."

"In your twisted version."

"My what?" She'd rear-ended him. "Lola, when's the last time you read the play? High school?"

"I had a perfectly divine experience in eighth grade in Miss Maple's class for girls," she said.

"Eighth grade," he repeated critically. "Then you've most likely forgotten the nasty bits," he theorized. "Memory is tricky that way. You're not alone. I do it all the time." A thought struck him. "Maybe your teacher omitted the ugly bits on purpose. Teachers did that, do that, they're afraid of the material, not understanding what's really going on in the text. Maybe, Lola, you've never been exposed to the actual play. It was censored. Have you ever thought about that?

"I'm sure Miss Maple did no such thing," Lola replied, her voice quivering. Memories were stirring up, memories of loss perhaps. A tear snuck out and rolled down her cheek. She quickly wiped it away and secured the lock on her past. "She took her teaching responsibilities very seriously and gave us girls some semblance of order and refinement. She lit a pathway for us—the classics, Jane Austen, the Brontes. She gave us romance and hope."

"Exactly my point," said Dave gently. "She was well-meaning and trying to protect you from the truth of the play. And over the past four hundred years, for reasons similar to her whitewashing, *Romeo and Juliet* has mistakenly become *the* love story, the 'proverbial' love story of all time. But it's not."

"It's not," she repeated drily.

"Yes, no," Dave was tired. "The phrase 'Romeo and Juliet' is used to connote young love, but that doesn't make the play a love story."

"You are wrong, David. Now, enough of this whitewashing babble. Whether or not Shakespeare intended for all the deaths is immaterial. *I* want you to remove them. Others have made these changes before, have they not?"

"Sure, Nahum Tate in the seventeenth century. He gave all Shakespeare's tragedies happy endings and destroyed them. But he was a parasitical, boot-licking sycophant trying to win the favour of Charles the Second."

"No, he preserved them for audiences who worked hard and needed something to hope for, not death and misery."

Dave rested his elbows on the table and screwed up his eyes on Lola.

"Lola, the deaths are part of Shakespeare's story," he explained slowly. "Romeo and Juliet fall in love within a violent society. Their 'love' raises them above those around them. But they end up paying for it with their deaths."

"Not in Kinmount they won't. We are presenting a love story for families, families who want a happy ending. So you will cut down on the violence, lose the sword-fighting, and take out the deaths."

He choked on his coffee. "You're joking."

"Do I look like I'm joking?" she warned. "Furthermore, all the dirty little jokes you felt you needed to add for some strange reason, you are cutting."

"I didn't add anything. It's all Shakespeare," Dave protested, pushing his coffee back.

"No, it is not. It's your filthy mind pretending to be him. So you are cutting all of that unnecessary crudeness and behaviour."

"Lola?" he said with alarm building in his voice. He realized she was deadly serious. His molar began to throb. "Look, I'll show you," he said quickly, hauling two dog-eared scripts out of his satchel: the Folio and a modern edition.

"There's no need to argue," she said.

"I'm not arguing, I'm explaining." He quickly opened both texts, a harried chef trying to prepare two separate dishes simultaneously.

"It's all in the Folio," he said. Sweat dripped off his upper lip.

"You and that bloody First Folio of yours, playing God."

"Just look!" A drop fell on the modern page.

Lola reluctantly followed his shaking index finger.

"Here," he said, "Mercutio's Queen Mab speech. Act One, Scene Five, before the Capulet party. In the modern edition, his speech is in blank verse, but in the original, it's in prose. He's speaking in the voice of an everyday groundling. The modern version has 'prettified' it, changing prose to blank verse. Mercutio is describing the components of Mab's fairy coach. In the modern text he describes Mab's coach as being pulled by a '*team* of atomies.' The image is comforting, conjuring up a sleigh being pulled by a team of horses or reindeer. In the Folio, it's quite the opposite. Her chariot is being drawn by a '*teeme* of atomies.' A swirling mass of bugs, like an invasion of shadflies coming out of a swamp. Or a plague of locusts. And they're not pulling anyone I'd want coming down my chimney or entering my dreams."

"Bugs, smugs," Lola retorted.

"Now, here's the biggie, the gravest change of all," Dave was hell bent. "Mercutio is describing the lash at the end of Mab's whip. In the modern edition, he says the tip is made from 'the lash of film,' film being a light layer of dew. But look what it says in the Folio, in the original text."

Lola followed his finger to the Folio, adjusted her reading glasses, and squinted until she found the phrase halfway down the page.

"Read it aloud," Dave instructed.

She didn't say a word.

"Read it."

"The lash of Philome." Her voice was quiet and hoarse. She choked on the pronunciation of Philome.

"Short for Philomela," said Dave. "And who was she?"

"Enough of this nonsense."

"Come on, you're the big expert on Greek mythology, Lola. You know damn well who Philomela was. She was a princess of Athens and the younger of two daughters to Pandion, King of Athens. What happened to her?"

"Stop it."

"You know, don't you?"

"Stop it, right now."

"She was raped and mutilated by her sister's husband. He cut out her tongue so she couldn't identify him."

"Enough!"

"That's quite a difference. A lash made from morning dew as opposed to a rape victim's tongue? The modern editors censored the play. And do you know what the horrible thing about censorship is? To avoid falling afoul of a censor, we question ourselves and censor ourselves. But we're not the ones who are in the wrong. The Folio gives us Shakespeare's intent. It's night and day. It is the only way to approach the character of Mercutio and the world of the play. Now do you see?"

He was out of breath.

"All I see is misogyny," she fired back.

"Yes, that is the society we are dealing with here, the backdrop to the action," Dave explained urgently.

"This production will not talk about or treat women in such a disgusting manner. You make the Nurse a salacious slut. Juliet's father slaps his own daughter."

"Yes, exactly as Shakespeare wrote it, so that Romeo and Juliet's romance shines so bright by contrast." He stressed the word 'romance.' "All the adults eventually let them down." Dave was adamant.

"Not this adult," declared Lola. "And Shakespeare did not write all that. I know some of it is yours. And now, when you return to rehearsal this afternoon, you will take out all the violence, death, obscenity, and misogyny. I specifically hired you to direct a *Romeo and Juliet* for the families of my community. Families, you understand?! And that is exactly what you are going to do."

"I'm not your servant." He measured each word with authority. "I'm not going to tell your story of *Romeo and Juliet,* because it stopped being your story the moment you engaged me. Theatre is a collaborative medium, Lola. It is also the actors' story. They bring who they are to their characters. And we all serve the playwright." He attempted to reassure her: "You're working with a director who knows his stuff, so you, as producer, can relax and tamp down on those controlling tendencies of yours. I'm telling a Shakespearean story the way Shakespeare would have presented the material at the Globe Theatre. You asked for a 'period' production and you're getting it. Besides, you haven't attended a single rehearsal until yesterday's run-through. It's a little too late to suggest changes."

"Because I thought I had a responsible director working for me that I could trust, one who understood this was a family show, not some ego-driven maniac serving only himself. I should never have let you direct *Love for Love,*" Lola fired back with the fury of a gunpowder plot.

Her marksmanship was keen, it was a palpable hit, and she hit a nerve.

"Lola, can we please not bring that up," Dave squirmed uncomfortably. "It was a great adaptation but for the wrong audience. I admit I missed the mark on that one."

"You're not in Toronto, David. I fell under your spell once before and it isn't going to happen again."

"Lola, you've hired me to direct a play you don't actually know. You have to trust me. My approach holds true to the populist spirit of the Bard."

"Populist spirit? Trust you? Rubbish. I know *Romeo and Juliet* is still the most beautiful love story ever told. And I will not have children watching violence and listening to profanity. They get enough of it in their daily lives. Teen suicide is on the rise in this community. Why on earth would I want to help encourage it?"

"Maybe you should have chosen a different play. *A Midsummer Night's Dream*, perhaps? *The Comedy of Errors*?"

"It's a bit late for that now," she said testily.

"Didn't your ouija-Shakespeare say he liked how the show was going?" he added. "You heard it straight from the dead Bard's mouth." It was worth a try.

"Don't bring up those cheap theatrics. Fix it."

She tore two pages out of her notebook and handed them to him. "Here is a list of all the offending passages. Since you are forcing me to pull rank, I am. I'm the producer, I run the show, I call the shots, and I hired you, so make the cuts."

She rose out of her chair and headed for the dining room.

"No."

There was a terrible silence.

"What did you say?"

"I won't do it."

"You most certainly will."

"No, I won't."

"Clean it up, now!"

His "Uncle" Thomas had been a purveyor of inconvenient truths about sex, poverty, disease, political corruption, religious hypocrisy, and sectarian hatred. From the beginning, certain people had tried to shut him up. His second play was publicly burned. Censors cut passages from his promptbooks. And, with the greatest success of his career, he was rewarded with imprisonment. How could Dave possibly back down?

At that moment, B.J. appeared in the kitchen, his plaid bathrobe hanging open over a pair of grey sweatpants.

"Morning," he chimed in, pouring himself a coffee. He sensed trouble. "What's up?" he asked, treading lightly.

"Lola wants me to cut the deaths of Romeo, Juliet, Mercutio, Tybalt, and Paris. And give the play a happy ending," Dave whispered hoarsely, not taking his eyes off her.

"That's a good one," laughed B.J., sitting down at the table.

"For a moment I thought you were serious."

"I am serious, B.J.," Dave said grimly.

B.J. looked over to Lola.

"You and Miranda will live happily ever after," proclaimed Lola, crossing her arms and pushing up her cleavage, revealing a strange-looking mythological tattoo on her left breast.

"Can you try and talk some sense into her?" Dave implored, taken aback by Lola's disconcerting tattoo. Was it a Fury?

B.J. shifted awkwardly in his chair. He avoided conflict whenever possible. He cleared his throat, trying to find the right words. "With all due respect, Lola," he began, his voice strained. "The play is a tragedy—"

"Don't you start too," Lola hissed, stepping back into the kitchen to confront him. "Mr. Middleton has brainwashed you."

"Lola, I'm not changing a thing," Dave shot back. He slid back his chair and crossed his arms defiantly.

"You will, or you can drive back to Birch Lake this instant," she warned.

He scowled at her. "Fine then, I quit." He stood up and advanced towards her.

"You can't quit," she ordered, blocking the hall entranceway.

"What's it going to be, Lola?" he said, not backing down.

"You will make the necessary changes." They had arrived at a stalemate.

"Lola, all I have in my life is my artistic integrity," Dave explained, trying to reason with her. "I carry it everywhere I go. It's the one thing I like about myself. I'm a Knight Templar for Shakespeare, an underdog warrior in a war for culture. I cannot make your changes. They are a violation of the original intent of his text. And that intent is sacrosanct. I'm sorry; you give me no choice but to resign."

"Artistic integrity? Bullshit. All you have is an ego the size of my first husband's," she fired back.

"What?" Dave blurted out in an unexpected peal of disdainful laughter.

B.J. sat stunned and helpless, watching the drama unfold

"Find yourself another director. I'm done," Dave said in disgust. "Sorry, B.J."

"Oh, no you are not," she bore down.

"Oh yes I am."

"If Dave goes, I'm afraid I go," B.J. jumped in, as much as he was capable of jumping in.

"MEN!" screamed Lola. "You all stick together. Like a pack of lying, two-timing jackals!"

Dave tore up the list.

"How dare you! Get out of my kitchen!" Lola roared. "NOW!"

"Clean *that* up!" Dave said, tossing the bits of paper in the air. "And one more thing. You're a hypocrite, Lola. Shooting that boy's tires out and claiming to want to protect children from violence? You're insane!"

"Insane!? Don't you use that tone of voice with me, Mr. Middleton. My first husband tried that and he found an early grave."

For a control freak, love and desire to control others was synonymous. Once Lola lost control over Dave, the object of her desire, hostility took over in full force. She grabbed the pellet gun from the sideboard and aimed it at Dave's heart. "Get out, both of you!"

"Lola!" shouted B.J.

At that moment, Miranda entered the kitchen. She froze in the doorway.

"Lola?" she said, quivering in disbelief.

"Go back to your room." Lola's voice was as tense as her trigger finger.

"What are you doing!?" Miranda exclaimed, looking at B.J. in terror.

"These men refuse to alter the play. They'd rather have you die."

"But Juliet does die," said Miranda confused.

"She doesn't in Kinmount," Lola said firmly, cocking the pellet gun.

"But Shakespeare wrote it that way. It's a tragedy," Miranda tried to explain.

"Ssshhh!" whispered B.J., concerned for Miranda's safety. "It's not worth it."

"My dear, these men have poisoned your mind. What would your father think?"

"He would argue it's a tragedy too," Miranda persisted.

"Men—they're all scum-sucking satyrs. Don't listen to them." Lola's eyes darted wildly.

"But it's the play. Please, Lola, put that gun down. You're scaring me," Miranda pleaded.

"Make up your mind, girl. Either Juliet lives, or she dies," Lola threatened, recklessly waving the barrel of the pellet gun.

"Juliet dies." Miranda said it.

Lola whirled the pellet gun on her.

"Over there. Now!" she ordered, gesturing with the barrel for Miranda to join Dave and B.J.

Miranda scurried over to the pair, standing next to B.J.

"I'm giving you one minute to get your things and get out. You aren't quitting, David, you're fired. And I'm pulling out my money. The production is cancelled," Lola said, tightening her grip on the pellet gun.

"Now move!" she screamed.

Hell had no fury like a Lola scorned.

The trio raced out of the kitchen to their bedrooms.

"Fuck, fuck, fuck," Dave cursed, as he threw his belongings into his knapsack.

One minute later Lola was ushering them out the front door at gunpoint.

"Our bikes?" demanded Dave.

"Get in your car and drive. Now!" she screamed.

"Lola, be reasonable. We need our bikes."

"Now!" She fired a warning shot above their heads.

Dave's Tercel screeched out of the driveway.

TWO

The company was assembled on the grass beside the muddy banks of the Burnt River as the morning sun beat down. Some sitting, a few standing, Capulet with his legs stretched out in Bermuda shorts in his accustomed Adirondack chair. Wayne and Shuster lying in the shade.

Dave stood before them, his fingers stroking his goatee in an attempt to mask his anxiety.

"Okay, gang. We have ourselves a little problem. Lola has pulled out as our producer."

The company reacted instantly.

"What?" That was Baldwin.

"Oh boy," said Peter.

"When?" Then the Nurse.

"This morning," said Dave.

"Why?" asked Tybalt.

"What did you do?" demanded the Prince.

"Explain please, David," said Capulet, ever the reasonable one.

"She demanded that I cut all the violence and give the play a happy ending. I refused," Dave explained.

"That makes absolutely no sense," said Capulet.

"I quite agree," said Dave. "But it's true."

"She's nuts," argued Baldwin.

"True too," said Dave. "So?"

"We've been rehearsing for two weeks. We do the show," insisted Tybalt. "Besides she's bluffing. Her moods change on the hour."

"Not with this," said B.J.

"We now have no money. Do we forge ahead despite Lola?" Dave asked the company. "Take a moment. And know what you are committing to if you say 'yes.'"

Dave shared a look with B.J. and Miranda.

"A show of hands?" he asked. "Who's still on board?"

A chorus of digits stabbed the blue sky.

"Alright," said Dave, relieved for the moment. "Now, the next order of business. Miranda needs a place to stay. Anyone willing to help?"

"I have a guest room," offered up Lady Capulet.

"Sorry, I can't hear you," Dave snapped.

"She has a guest room. Clean the wax out of year ears, dude." It was the shorter stoner who apparently had the auditory perception of a bat.

"Great. Thank you."

"What about you and B.J.?" asked Capulet.

"We've got to figure that one out," Dave said.

"I would gladly help you lads out. but my mother-in-law is staying with us for the summer and I'm up to my ears in colonial debate," said Capulet.

"I live with my parents but you'd be welcome to crash in our barn," offered Tybalt.

Dave looked to B.J. No. They'd probably get infected with mad cow disease.

"I live in my mom's basement. Sorry dudes," Baldwin chimed in.

"I've only got a bachelor," echoed the Nurse and the Friar.

"I'm full up," said the Prince with a creepy wink. "Don't want you cramping my trail-feathers." Trail-feathers? Did the Prince's trailer have a revolving screen door? Dave cringed at the thought.

"The '70s called and want their lava lamp back," jeered Baldwin.

"If my trailer is a rockin'," the Prince sang raunchily, "don't come a—"

"I get it," Dave interrupted. Hell wasn't just other people; it was other people living in Kinmount.

"*Tho*rry. Three *th*creeching kids," said Benvolia.

"Full house," said Ginny. "Sorry."

"You can sleep in our bathtub," said the taller stoner.

"It's okay, gang. I'll figure something out."

He set about rehearsing the first act, tightening up blocking. and highlighting key relationship moments. The sun was unbearable by three o'clock. so he broke rehearsal early and went to the Red Lion.

"Hey Kate," he said, sidling up to the bar.

"You're early."

"The heat. Sweatus pentameter."

"Want a pint?"

"Please." The air conditioning provided welcome relief. "I'm changing rehearsals from three to nine to beat the sun." He sat on a stool and cleared his throat. "I, uh, I just want to say last night was ..."

She handed him the Keith's. "Don't go getting all Meg Ryan on me. It was a nice time. Let's leave it at that."

Kate was all business. Dave was confused.

"Okay."

He coughed and started.

"I've got a bit of a problem." He swallowed hard. "Lola has pulled out of the show."

"What?"

"Yup." He picked up a pretzel from the bar snack bowl and began to knead it between his fingers.

"I should have warned you about that. She's unstable. She ran for town council on a platform to open a nudist beach beside the fairgrounds."

"There's an image." The pretzel snapped in two.

"So, now what?" she asked.

"The cast voted in favour of going ahead."

"Are you a glutton for punishment?"

"Salad bar and all. Anyhow, B.J. and I are stuck for accommodation."

"Elspeth is with me. And although I like you, there is no way I'm ready for you to crash at my place. Sorry."

"I'm not asking that. I get your situation."

Kate registered his understanding. "I appreciate that. So what *do* you want?" she said.

"Lola pulled out all her financing. Any ideas where we night be able to stay. For free. B.J. and I both have sleeping bags."

Kate rubbed her forehead. Give a man an inch and he'll take your house key. "I can lend you some camping equipment. I've got a small tent and some supplies. I haven't used them since I split with Steve."

"Thank you! You're a peach," Dave exclaimed, kissing her on the cheek and bounding out the door.

"A *peach*?" He'd called her a peach. Who still used words like that? "Where did you park your carriage?!" she shouted after him. But he was gone. She picked up the pretzel halves and shook her head.

א

Dave had hope. And hope was one step closer to disappointment in his pessimistic mind.

He and B.J. clumsily surveyed their new digs like the city boys they were. They set up camp on the shore of the geese-polluted river beside the rehearsal site under an aging elm tree. Ample shade for the heat of the afternoon.

A marina volunteer locked the public facilities at midnight. With no washroom access, Dave stealthily snuck off to pee in the bile of the river. A bile that had yet to infest Birch Lake. His whizzing stream danced under the moonlight on the brown murkiness of the river in step with one of Lola's deranged pissing cherub statues.

Some people counted sheep; others counted their blessings. Dave lay awake with a litany of every mistake and poor choice he'd made running through his head, from the silly to the stupendous. The repetitious hammering of a broken lullaby, an insomniac's endless catalogue of Dr, Seuss:

"I ask to be, or not to be.
That is the question, I ask of me.
This sullied life, it makes me shudder.
My stepfather's boffing my dear, sweet mother.
Would I, could I take my life?
Could I, should I, end this strife?
Should I jump out of a plane?
Or throw myself before a train?
Should I from a cliff just leap?
Could I put myself to sleep?
Shoot myself? Or take some poison?
Maybe try self-immolation?
To shuffle off this mortal coil,
I could stab myself with a fencing foil.
Slash my wrists while in the bath?
Would it end Lola's angst and wrath?"

Eventually exhaustion took over, and his troubled thoughts of Lola gave way to a restless sleep.

It poured rain for the first time in weeks. Dave and B.J. woke to find themselves floating in their sleeping bags. The canvas tent leaked. Drenched to the bone, they dragged their belongings out to dry after a miserable, sleepless night. Chickpea was a soggy mess.

The company arrived in drips and drabs. Tybalt presented a freshly cut key to Dave.

"I borrowed it from a parks and recreation dude I know. You have access to the public washroom and showers twenty-four seven. Wear your flip flops."

Dave thought of Kate's bathtub.

"Thanks, man," he replied, trying to mask his less than masculine discomfort and trepidation. Dave was a glamper.

The company looked to him for guidance.

He postured himself with a forced ease he'd learned from watching Paul Newman lean in doorways.

"Okay. So today, we start with our Act Two. Capulet, Lady Capulet, Juliet, the Nurse."

He'd skip the stoner servants until clean up. He was waiting for Wayne and Shuster to clear the playing field when the Nurse came sirening across the grass.

"Oh my God," she wailed. "Robert's had a heart attack. He's in the hospital!"

Capulet was out of commission.

"What? Oh my God." That was Miranda.

"When?" asked Dave.

"How?" asked B.J.

"Holy shit." That was Baldwin.

"He sprained his heart?" asked Weed, the taller stoner.

"Is he going to be okay?" Dave asked the Nurse, ignoring the taller stoner.

"I don't know." The Nurse rifled through her knapsack to find a painkiller to calm her nerves.

"How did you find out?" asked Baldwin.

"A friend of mine is a porter. He called me," the Nurse panted.

"What do we do, Dave?" asked Miranda.

Dave had no idea at that moment. The straw was plummeting toward the camel's back.

"You have to play Capulet," said Ginny, nervously fingering the reading glasses that hung from her neck.

"Ginny, no can do. I can't direct and act," Dave sputtered.

"That's a brilliant idea," Baldwin jumped in. "Direct and act."

"Yes," agreed Tybalt.

You're the only one who can do it," echoed B.J.

The company erupted in agreement.

"Alright, alright. I'll do it," Dave groaned reluctantly. He blamed himself. He shouldn't have pushed Capulet so hard in rehearsal. But this was no time for self-flagellation. "Okay, so a change of schedule," he said decisively, pulling out his notebook. "We are now going to review all of Capulet's scenes in Act One before the dinner break. Set up for the first scene."

Tybalt, as was his accustomed fashion, quickly moved two benches into place.

Dave settled into the role with iambic necessity. He'd created the blocking and character subtext so the challenge would be stuffing the lines into his exhausted brain. Baldwin agreed to be his stand-in so Dave could both act and still clean up the scenes Capulet was in. Mercutio and Capulet did not share any stage time. The roles were originally double cast, a necessity within Shakespeare's small acting company. Most of his plays were designed to be done with sixteen to eighteen actors playing all the roles. Actors fell into particular archetypes and played similar characters—"the old man," "the mother," "the young hero," "the best friend," etc. Shakespeare's actors were comparable to porn stars today; many were popular and "fun" to watch, but no one wanted to bring them home to meet Dave's mother.

In Shakespeare's day, women were not allowed to perform on stage—not only was it unthinkable, it was illegal.

Boys were the best substitutes for playing female parts. A male pre-pubescent teenager who still had smooth skin and whose voice hadn't changed would've played Juliet. Unfortunately, the white makeup used by the boy players was lead-based and highly poisonous.

At least Dave didn't have to worry about lead poisoning in Kinmount, although swimming in the Burnt River did cause its own kind of pox.

The men in the company who played the older women roles had to shave in order to hide their true gender. With so many men cross-dressing as women, Elizabethan theatre was a bizarre drag queen spectacle.

Male heroines lasted until 1661, when an unknown named Margaret Hughes played Desdemona one night at an illegal theatre, and, instead of stopping the show, the ever-game Charles the Second changed the law to allow women to act. By the stroke of a pen, the king's own mistress, Nell Gwyn, became a star. And, four hundred years later, Miranda Murray could play Juliet without giving it a second thought.

THREE

On the dinner break, Dave went to visit Kate.

"A heart attack?" She poured him a Keith's.

"Yup. He's going to be okay but he's had to back out of the show."

"So who's replacing him?" she asked, sorting cutlery.

Dave frowned. "You're looking at him."

She stopped mid-fork.

"Can you handle it?"

"Do I have a choice?" he sighed. Dave had the market cornered on sighing. "I was wondering if you could my run lines with me after rehearsal."

"Do *I* have a choice?"

"Only if you can spare the time, I mean."

"I'll ask my sister to babysit for a few more hours after my shift. We can do it here. How's that sound?"

"Great. I really appreciate it. You're a—"

"Don't call me a peach again. It makes me feel like I'm eighty."

"Life-saver," he finished his sentence.

"Any sign of Lola?"

"Nope. But I'm sure she's not finished yet. I keep expecting a shot to the back of the head."

"She is that unstable."

Perhaps if Kate could look into Lola's eyes she would catch a glimpse of the truth, maybe a clue to understanding the First Folio of Lola Whale, what was behind the irrational thoughts, emotional inconsistencies, and odd punctuation of her life.

"B.J. and I are going to take shifts in the tent to make sure there are no surprises," said Dave.

"Good plan. If anything happens, call me."

She was back behind the bar before Dave could respond.

ॐ

Back at the rehearsal site, Dave was working on the explosive final scene of Act Three—Capulet losing his temper and threatening his daughter with banishment unless she agreed to marry Paris. The scene probably caused his heart attack. A handful of seniors from a nursing home on the adjacent bank of the river were sitting in lawn chairs enjoying the proceedings—the company's own private fan club. Dave drilled his moves in the scene again and again, carefully mapping out the physical violence. And the lines were sticking. By sundown he and Miranda were ready to go at it full throttle.

SIRENS!

Kinmount's two police cars came blaring onto the rehearsal site. Flashing lights bathed the river in red. Four doors opened and slammed simultaneously.

Dave had just faked a stage slap across Miranda's face.

"Police! Don't move!" shouted a burly officer.

Dave froze.

Miranda screamed.

Lady Capulet fainted.

B.J. swallowed his joint.

A tall officer grabbed Dave and pinned him to the hood of a squad car. His chin smashed down hard. Handcuffs scraped his wrists.

The Nurse rushed the burly officer. He tried to restrain her.

"What's going on, Frank?" she demanded.

"Cool it, Gallagher!" the burly officer ordered, getting her into a bear hug.

"It's a play," Dave stammered repeatedly as the tall officer tried to ram him into a back seat. "Hey!" he yelled. "I didn't do anything!"

"Be quiet," ordered the tall officer, accidentally slamming the door into Dave's head.

"Are you alright, ma'am?" a third officer asked Miranda.

"Stop it! Stop it! I'm fine." She recoiled into B.J.'s arms. "Let our director go. He didn't do anything."

"Let go of me, Frank, you inbred hick," the Nurse bellowed, elbowing the burly cop and breaking free. "Are you out of your mind? Did that sister of yours finally bite you and give you rabies?"

"You want a ride in the backseat too, Gallagher?" Frank warned, bending over to catch his breath.

"What? With you? For a little poke and diddle, Frank? Want me to tell your wife about last Labour Day at the pig roast?"

"Okay, calm down, calm down. Enough of the pig roast talk," Frank muttered.

A fourth officer was giving Lady Capulet mouth-to-mouth until she came to and slapped him.

The third officer stepped in.

"Are you okay, ma'am?" he asked Miranda again.

"She's not a 'ma'am,' John. Try joining the twenty-first century, you dork."

"Please, Joan, I'm trying to ascertain what's going on. And your lip is not appreciated," said Officer John, the third officer.

"Officers, I think there's been a huge misunderstanding," said B.J., keeping his breath at arm's length.

"And you are?" Frank said, turning on B.J.

"B.J. Watts."

Frank looked him over, rolling his eyes at the sight of B.J.'s baggy pantaloons.

"You're not from here," he said. It was a statement not a question.

"No, officer, I'm not. I'm an actor. I'm from Toronto."

Being an actor and hailing from Toronto were the two things Frank did not want to hear.

"Look, Officer, we are rehearsing *Romeo and Juliet* and you just hand-cuffed our director."

That was Ginny.

Officer John piped up.

"*Romeo and Juliet*? My brother is in that. And Old Sally."

"And Wayne and Shuster scare the geese away," said Ginny.

"Why didn't you say something?" Frank stammered.

"Because you didn't give us a chance," argued the Nurse. "You just started busting heads like you always do." She turned to Officer John. "That's right, your brother is playing Tybalt and Old Sally opens the show. We were just rehearsing a scene when you came plowing in. What gives? Horny Tim's close early?"

"We got a phone call that someone was being attacked down by the old mill."

"Oh my God!" Miranda said, tight in B.J.'s embrace.

"From who?" B.J. asked.

"I'm sorry, we can't disclose that information," said Officer John.

"Lola?" said the Nurse.

"Again, I can't say," Officer John nodded.

"Can't you arrest her for mischief or something?" asked B.J.

"Or stick her in a padded cell for life," added the Nurse.

"I need to ask you some questions, young lady," Frank said, ignoring the Nurse and addressing Miranda. He pulled out his notebook. "Your name?"

"Will my parents find out?" asked Miranda, sharing a concerned look with B.J.

"Not unless they read *The Kinmount Crier*."

"Miranda Murray," she said quietly.

"And you're from Toronto too?"

"Yes, sir."

"Does that really matter?" Ginny asked.

"Not unless she's got a warrant out on her," Frank laughed.

"Oh, please, Frank," jabbed the Nurse.

"Alright, alright," said Frank. "Now, Miranda, what's the case?"

"Dave's my director. We were rehearsing a stage slap and push."

"Frank, you half-wit, look across the river." The Nurse pointed across the bile. "You see those seniors. They watch us rehearse every night. Do they look alarmed to you?"

Frank looked across the bank to the seniors' home. The residents leapt to their feet booing him.

"You better un-cuff our director pronto or I'm pretty sure he'll sue your damn ass off, Frank," said the Nurse. "You're the one who should be locked in the amoeba."

"Amoeba?" said B.J.

"The town jail only has one cell," the Nurse scoffed.

Frank was starting to sweat. Officer John hurried back to the squad car.

"Let him go, Leo. False alarm." The tall officer quickly took the cuffs off. "I'm sorry, sir, for any inconvenience," said Officer John to Dave. "I'm afraid my partner's a bit old school."

"What? Too much *Dragnet* as a kid?" said Dave, attempting to get out of the squad car. He winced in pain and sat back down. The squad car interior began to spin. "Oh, my head is killing me."

"Do you think you need an ambulance?" asked Officer John.

"No ambulance." Riding in an ambulance was not on Dave's bucket list.

"Okay, but you should have that looked at," said Officer John. "Hang tight." He returned to the group. "I'm sorry for the misunderstanding, folks. Your director is a little dizzy so I'm going to take him to Emergency."

"Is he okay?" asked Miranda.

"I'm sure he'll be fine."

"Good night officers," B.J. said quickly.

Frank turned to go but stopped. He sniffed the air and turned back to B.J.

"Do I smell pot on you, boy?"

"Boiled turnip, I assure you."

"Turnip!? Takes all kinds," Frank blustered. He shook his head and walked back to his car. "Torontonians. Ain't got the sense the Lord gave a duck."

B.J.'s improvisation training had paid off.

"You folks have a nice night. See you at the show," said Officer John with a wave. He closed his passenger door and plunked himself down beside Frank.

They drove off debating whether weed and cooked turnips smelled alike. John assured Frank they did. He was a chip off his younger brother's block.

Dave rubbed his head while staring at Kinmount's nightlife passing by him through the right back-seat window—teenagers getting drunk and looking for fights. A night on the town lasted about eleven minutes. Being able to hit a road sign with a beer bottle, while driving, was considered a necessary skill.

He pressed his forehead against the glass. It was cool to the touch and strangely soothing. At least he could scratch "riding in the back seat of a police car" off the list. Still, more pressing, was what Lola had next up her kimono sleeve. He closed his eyes and sank into the leather upholstery.

FOUR

Word of Dave's riverside escapade with the police spread through the Highlands faster than the Nurse cuckolding the Friar on a Kinmount Saturday night.

The morning headline in *The Kinmount Crier* read "Local producer quits summer show: director's immorality to blame."

Dave read the article as he sat in Emergency waiting to get his head examined. He needed his head examined for staying in Kinmount.

Officer John, concerned Dave might have a concussion, had dropped him off hours earlier. Fifteen people had gone in ahead of him, even though when he arrived there were only four in the waiting room. One was a teenage mother with a colicky baby. The other was an intoxicated young local with a washcloth, wet with blood, pressed up against his right eye. Two drunken buddies sat laughing on either side of him.

The admitting nurse repeatedly barked at them to keep it down.

Dave recognized the sputtering laugh of the taller of the buddies as that of one of his stoner servants. He saw Dave.

"Hey, bro, what you doin' here?"

"Possible concussion. Not sure Weed, you?" he asked.

"Playing a game of Lights Out in Bobcat's basement and he took one in the eye."

"Lights Out?" asked Dave, not really wanting to know the answer.

"You haven't played before? Ah, man, you don't know what you're missing. What you do is you sit in Bobcat's basement with all the lights out. And each player gets three darts. And you throw them where you think someone is sitting. And it's totally dark, right. So you gotta use ESP to sense where someone is. Total zen. I got Bobcat in the eye on my first dart."

Dave sighed. This from a servant who couldn't place a bench properly if he had a map. Dave looked to Bobcat who nodded and grinned. He was missing a few teeth.

"He's a fucking warrior, man," Weed grinned. He put an arm around his bleeding one-eyed champion.

If Dave didn't have a concussion from the police cruiser door he certainly had one now.

"Bobcat Kelly?" The voice of the admitting nurse blasted over the loudspeaker.

This was not the first visit for Bobcat and his misfit band. The admitting nurse waved her clipboard in frustration at the waste of the Ontario taxpayers' money.

"Yo," replied Bobcat. Getting up and promptly falling down. The stoner and the other buddy dragged him through the emergency doors.

Dave continued to be ignored.

The sun was streaming in through the large glass windows.

"Dave Middleton," bellowed the change-of-shift admitting nurse.

Dave awoke from an uncomfortable slumber, curled up in a fetal position on the institutional furniture.

"Coming," he yawned.

An hour later, he was released.

The on-call intern wasn't sure if Dave had a concussion but, to be on the safe side, "Make sure someone stays with you and wakes you every two hours."

"That won't be difficult," Dave said, thinking of his current sleeping arrangements.

He followed the fluorescent paw prints to the main reception.

"Cardiac unit. Third floor. Private room. Not sure if he is receiving visitors. Ask at the desk."

When he entered the room, Capulet was awake, his wife sitting beside him peeling an apple.

"Hello, David," Capulet smiled despite his obvious discomfort. He was as pale as his hospital bracelet.

"Hi, Robert, how are you doing, old sport?"

"That eighteenth hole is a killer."

"That's why I stick to miniature golf." Dave had good memories of playing drunken mini-putt with his mates in his twenties. It was his generation's equivalent to a drive-in movie.

Capulet attempted a laugh but couldn't. He gripped his wife's hand.

"Joanne, could you give David and me a moment. Maybe grab me the morning paper?"

"Certainly, honey. Please don't agitate him, Mr. Middleton."

"I assure you I won't," said Dave.

She kissed her husband gently on the forehead and left the room with a warning look back at Dave.

"Want a slice?" asked Capulet, offering Dave a piece of apple.

"No thanks. The way things are going I'm afraid I'll end up naked wearing a fig leaf."

"You think this is paradise?" Capulet riposted, gesturing to the monitor and leads on his chest. "Sorry about having to leave the show."

"Don't give it another thought. So, what happened?"

Dave pulled up the only chair.

"Joanne's mother is a battle-axe on toast."

"She's visiting right?" Dave said. "That's why B.J. and I couldn't stay with you."

"Visiting? Try invading. It's the *blitz* all over again."

"I thought she was British?" Dave said.

"By birth only, I assure you. In truth, she is a Wagnerian Valkyrie. Every dinner an argument," explained Capulet. "She always begins with Britain's mistake in giving Canada its independence. 'Sticking a maple leaf flag on an outhouse doesn't change the fact that it's an outhouse,' she's fond of saying.

'Canada should have been Britain's dumping ground for her convicts, not Australia,' she repeats ad nauseam. 'Australia has kangaroos and koala bears, while Canada is nothing but a land of hooligans—'"

"Hooligans? Has she ever been to Australia?"

"'A colony of murderers, thieves, and whores with hearts as cold as your frozen winter.' *And*, as a Judge, all I do, apparently, is 'stir the scum porridge.' To Joanne's mother, civilization is tea at dawn and G and T's at three."

"What century is she living in?"

Capulet adopted an imperious British accent, imitating his mother-in-law: "The colonial model worked well in Africa for centuries until that Mandela came along. If he'd been born in Britain none of this civil rights nonsense would have happened. People know their place. Prime Minister Thatcher knew what she was doing. Iron Lady with an iron fist. The sun never set on the British Empire on her watch. And now you inbred heathen want to abolish the monarchy. What's next? Cancel *Coronation Street*? It's absolutely disgraceful."

Capulet moaned.

"Is she for real?" Dave asked.

"Sadly she is as real as her pull-up knee hose."

"How do you put up with her?" Dave asked.

"Obviously not very well," Capulet sighed, referencing his hospital bed. "Last night after dinner she started in on Canada's First Nations."

His imperious British voice again:

"'And what did the Indians ever do for Canada? Invent lacrosse. I don't know anybody who plays lacrosse.' Her words, not mine. That was it. The dam finally burst. 'You insufferable cow,' I screamed at her." Capulet's monitor began to beep. "And then my heart burst."

"Want me to get the nurse?" asked Dave, alarmed by the monitor.

"Give it a second."

The beeping stopped.

And I thought *my* mother was tough," said Dave, checking the monitor.

"You can't reason with Joanne's mother. Believe me I've tried."

"And she has to visit?" Dave said.

"She makes Joanne feel so guilty for moving to Canada that it's now our annual penance to endure her summer visit. And all she does is try to convince Joanne to move back to Somerset to look after her. To leave this cesspool and me behind faster than you can say 'Rule Britannia.' She should have died years ago."

Capulet closed his eyes and rubbed his forehead.

"She doesn't sound frail to me," said Dave.

Capulet opened one eye.

"She's eighty-five and suffers from diabetes. And she's addicted to sweets. Like a sow at an English toffee trough. Her walker bends under the weight of her. Creaking, groaning, and knocking Joanne's vases helter skelter. What the *Titanic* probably sounded like just before it sank."

"I'm surprised you lasted as long as you did," said Dave.

"Sometimes patience is a curse hiding a screaming kettle." They sat in reflective silence. Capulet chewed on an apple slice. It had already turned brown "How are you holding up?" he asked.

"We'll see if I survive Kinmount." Dave let out a defeated sigh.

"You will. Despite yourself, I see the missionary in you." Capulet's cobalt-blue eyes and tone brightened slightly.

"More like Missionary Impossible." Dave felt a headache coming on. Maybe it was brain cancer and not a concussion.

"Don't give up, David. At least you don't have a psychotic mother-in-law bunkering down with you," said Capulet, taking a bite.

"There *is* Lola."

Lola. Her very name gave him the shakes.

"There will always be Lolas," reasoned Capulet after swallowing a seed.

"And shadflies, spandex, and karaoke. Your mother and Lola should get together. The Doomsday Clock would bust a spring. We'd all end up on Pete O'Neill's iodine pills." Dave wasn't kidding.

"Well, it's nitro for me now," said Capulet. "My blood pressure went through the roof. They're putting in stents. No more rum and red meat. Can you see me as a vegetarian?" Capulet dropped the remainder of the apple on the bedside table beside his new medications.

"Last week I went into the Kinmount Restaurant and ordered the lunch special. Waitress asks me if I wanted the meat or the veterinarian lasagna. I kid you not," Dave grimaced.

"I don't doubt it," said Capulet. "I see it and hear it in my court room every day. And it offends my ears. The system is broken. We need to educate."

"And Kinmount is the front line?" Dave replied, feeling like he was talking to a recruiting officer. He'd dropped out of cadets in high school after one too many push-ups.

"That's why I'm here," Capulet explained. "Well, not *here* exactly." He gave his hospital gown a disapproving look.

"You're a braver man than me, Gunga Din," Dave quipped.

"No, just stubbornly Quixotic. There's a nobility in chasing windmills, you know?"

"Well, I'm chasing a wood chopper. Shakespeare ground up limb by limb until all that's left is his mouth screaming, 'Once more unto the breach.'" Dave stared at a ceiling tile and groaned. "Lola tried to have me arrested last night."

"Oh dear. What now?"

"Police raided the rehearsal site. They got a call saying a young woman was being assaulted."

"And you're positive it was Lola?" Capulet briefly slipped into his Judge voice.

"Who else?" Dave sighed wearily.

"She *is* relentless."

"What's her story?" Dave asked. The question had been burning inside him for weeks.

Capulet rubbed his wrist and stared out the room window. He sat up and motioned for Dave to lean in. He checked the door and then spoke quietly:

"I moved to Kinmount thirty years ago. Lola had arrived about ten years before. She was married to a schoolteacher, so the story goes. There's a daughter somewhere in the mix. The husband disappeared unexpectedly. Rumours surfaced that Lola had killed him and buried him in her basement to get his life insurance money and pension. Only rumours. She was definitely different. She opened her own contracting business. I hired her to build an addition on the house. Her workmanship was immaculate. She handled a power tool better than any local did. And that created resentment. She loved Greek mythology and would recite Aeschylus on her breaks."

"Aeschylus," Dave repeated uncomfortably. "Oh, boy."

In drama circles, Aeschylus was regarded as the "father of tragedy," but he wasn't the garden-variety soccer-dad-of-tragedy—he was a motorcycle-riding, leather-jacketed rebel *with* a cause. Before Aeschylus came along, Greek tragedies only featured one actor and a chorus (boring stuff); Aeschylus added a second actor, thereby inventing dramatic dialogue, making him the originator of all subsequent theatre, most notably the works of Shakespeare, and, two thousand years later, movies and television. Not too shabby for a guy who, when he wasn't writing, was busy being a war hero.

"Lola gave Joanne the willies but I found her refreshingly eccentric," explained Capulet. "She liked to discuss famous British sodomy trials. They fascinated her. Oscar Wilde. All of it."

"How nice," said Dave, wishing he'd never asked the question in the first place.

"But she got stranger after that. She began dressing even more oddly. The years go by. There are a few more husbands. And a few more divorces. The first time I saw her in my courtroom was a few years later. A dispute with a neighbour over some backyard sculptures she was making. The neighbour accused Lola of spray-painting the words 'BEWARE THE

FURIES!' on his garage door. But he couldn't prove it and Lola denied it with all the put-on Southern charm of a plantation governess."

Dave had seen that "charm" first-hand and experienced its explosive rage.

Old Aeschylus knew a thing or two about explosive rage. By the time he was an established playwright, a young upstart named Sophocles gave him a run for his money. Sophocles brought to the game a new secret weapon: a third actor. Aeschylus knew a good thing when he saw it and, in no time, he was working three-actor scenes into his own tragedies, including his masterwork, the *Oresteia* trilogy. It was a cycle of revenge within three generations of a single family, climaxing with the arrival of the Furies in *The Eumenides*, the third instalment of his blockbuster saga. It was the *Return of the Jedi* of his day, except the crowds that lined up outside the theatre to see the premiere of *The Eumenides* were toga-wearing Ancient Greeks pumped to see the Furies in action.

The Furies were a trio of mythological old women seeking vengeance. By all accounts, the Furies were visually terrifying. The audience would've gasped and jumped out of their cement seats, watching the hags torture and kill their male victims in a variety of gruesome ways. Shakespeare based his Weird Sisters in *Macbeth* on the Furies.

Another image for Dave to try to swipe left.

"She disappeared for the winters," Capulet continued. "In the summer, more rumours. Neighbours saw women coming and going at all hours. They talked of strange ceremonies in her backyard. She last appeared in my courtroom over a labour dispute with a disgruntled farmer who claimed she put a curse on a barn she built for him. All his milking cows dried up. Again, how can you prove that in court? We're not seventeenth-century Salem. I tossed it out. She's tried unsuccessfully to run for town council twice. Two years ago, the ecology centre burned down and the talk around here was that she did it. But that's the village rumour mill. No legal proof. There was nothing concrete."

"I heard about that fire on CBC. I asked her about it. She told me the burnt remains of the park ranger were actually found tied to a bed with piano wire." Dave repeated the grisly details. "Do you think she might have done it?" he asked.

"Like I said, there were only rumours. But, again, not enough evidence. Some folks think she's a local hero." Capulet readjusted his pillow.

"A hero?" Dave was puzzled.

"The ranger was a suspected child molester. No hard proof but ..." he trailed off. He was growing tired.

Was Lola a crazed vigilante? Could Dave add that to the list? Nothing made sense.

"And then she got into producing community theatre," said Capulet. "And here we are."

"Until two days ago," said Dave. His stomach began to growl. He was famished. He hadn't eaten in twenty-four hours. *And* he had no money for food. He'd forgotten that little item.

Capulet reached for his pain medication.

"I bet that daughter of hers could tell a story or two," Dave said, pouring a glass of water and handing it to him.

"No one knows where the daughter lives," shrugged Capulet, swallowing his pills. "She left Kinmount when she was a teenager. It was all before my time."

"She's probably buried in the basement too." Dave shuddered.

"Have you seen this, Mr. Middleton?" Joanne said urgently, entering the room, morning paper in hand.

She eyed Dave uneasily the way people do when they know someone is innocent of a crime yet the very fact they're accused of it in the first place somehow taints that innocence. Like a scarlet letter.

"Yes," he said, not meeting her stare.

"Look at this, Robert. The woman's insane," she said.

Capulet skimmed the article. He managed a wry laugh. His wife scolded him.

"There's nothing funny about it, Robert. Mr. Middleton, you need to put an end to the show. Quit while you still can. Nothing good can come of this." She tossed the newspaper in the garbage bag attached to the bed.

Dave looked to Capulet and bit his lip.

"No can do. I have to chase the windmill."

He gave Capulet a pat on the shoulder. "See you later in the week. Rest, old sport."

Capulet's voice stopped him in the doorway.

"The press will come after you looking for a response. 'No comment' is my advice. Don't stoop to her level. Show dignity in the face of adversity. Don Quixote humbled himself by riding a donkey."

"An ass," Dave said self-deprecatingly. He disappeared into the hallway.

Dave didn't think he had anything in common with Don Quixote, Miguel de Cervantes' dreamy idealist and title character in the world's first novel. Dave was a weary pessimist while Don Quixote was a ridiculous buffoon pursuing an impossible dream. Dave was enduring an impossible nightmare.

Cervantes was Spain's answer to the English Bard. Interestingly enough, he and Shakespeare lived at the same time. Despite the geographic distance and their dissimilar biographies, both focussed on the discrepancy between reality and imagination. Cervantes wrote *Don Quixote* at the same time Shakespeare was wrestling with Hamlet's Father's ghost. Both died on the same calendar day and year—April 23, 1616—although Cervantes was born about seventeen years earlier.

It's unknown if the two men ever crossed paths, but it is possible. After twins were born to Shakespeare and his wife, Anne Hathaway, in 1585, seven lost years of his life unfolded for which no records exist. Although most speculation assumes he spent his time in London perfecting his craft, a few die-hards of the bardolator crowd speculated that Shakespeare travelled to Madrid and became personally acquainted with Cervantes. Vivid imaginations even speculated that Shakespeare arrived shortly before the defeat of the Armada to spy for the British crown.

It is common knowledge that Shakespeare's last play was *Henry VIII*. During a performance on June 29, 1613, a cannon set off during the opening performance misfired, igniting the wooden beams and thatching. The Globe Theatre went up in flames, the proverbial thatch that broke Shakespeare's back. He retired from the theatre, no doubt utterly spent. But, in actual fact, *Henry VIII* was not his last play. In between rehearsals, Shakespeare was putting the finishing touches on his last play, *The History of Cardenio*, stealing one of Cervantes' characters from *Don Quixote*, possibly with the help of Dave's "Uncle" Thomas. After the Globe Theatre burned down, Shakespeare's *Cardenio* went unpublished and un-revived in any form until the early eighteenth century. The manuscript supposedly wound up later in the Covent Garden Museum. The world will never know, because in 1818, Covent Garden burned down too. It remains a literary mystery on par with the lost gospel of Mary Magdalene, albeit no hotshot American author has taken the Shakespeare-Cervantes bait.

A few conspiracy theorists even proposed that Shakespeare was the author of Cervantes' works and/or vice versa. Critical interpretation is a mug's game, doomed as any misbegotten fan's attempt to corral Cervantes and Shakespeare into the same frame.

Dave imagined what might've happened had the two titans tried to meet up somehow for a beer. Have you heard the one about the two dead European guys with beards who walk into a bar at the turn of the seventeenth century? So the first one says, "Let's you and me have a drink and invent modern literature."

The second one answers, "Ok, but the better writer's buying."

First one says, "How do you know which one of us is better?"

And the second one says, "I've heard only the good die young. Whoever dies first is better."

BAH-BUMP-BAH.

In any event, Dave felt he had more in common with Wile E. Coyote than Don Quixote, with Lola repeatedly "meep-meeping" him off a cliff into oblivion.

The walk back to the rehearsal site was arduous to say the least. His head ached. He was hungry, tired, and emotionally exhausted.

And he wanted his bike back.

FIVE

The Kinmount Crier

"Local producer quits summer show:
director's immorality to blame."

By Elizabeth Mackenzie

KINMOUNT—The producer of an open-air production of
William Shakespeare's *Romeo and Juliet* has withdrawn all support from the production.

Lola Whale distanced herself from the production in a letter
to *The Kinmount Crier* yesterday. The play is being presented
outdoors behind the sawmill over the August long weekend as
part of the community's Summer in the Park Festival.

In the letter, Ms. Whale said she withdrew her support from the
show because of "extreme artistic differences" between her and
the show's director, David Middleton. Specifically, she said the
production includes violence to women, abuse, coarseness, and
vulgarity.

Ms. Whale said she wished to have her name removed from the
production.

Mr. Middleton, who is a graduate of the Lorne Greene Theatre School, and spent five seasons directing at the Dominion DeVere Drama Festival, could not be reached for comment on Wednesday.

Performances are scheduled for August 4, 5, and 6.

SIX

Dave sat at the picnic table under the large elm tree. Initials of teen lust were carved into its sun-bleached benches—an unofficial tally of Kinmount's abandoned mothers. Where were the fathers? Was Tybalt the only responsible young man in the county?

Baldwin flanked him on his right. Miranda and B.J. sat on the opposite side.

"A midnight raid. Tonight." Dave rallied his musketeers. Musk being the operative word. He needed a shower and a change of clothes. "To rescue our bikes from Lola's backyard."

"In." That was B.J. and Chickpea.

"Yes." Miranda rang in.

"Baldwin?" asked Dave.

"Hey, man, what would Mercutio do?" Baldwin flourished his rapier with the newly trained zest of a Highlands Zorro. Pete O'Neill, their intrepid fight director, had more than earned his pints.

"We'll meet up at the Red Lion at ten to hatch our plan," Dave quickly concluded as the rest of the company arrived. Tybalt and the stoner teenagers unloaded four bales of hay, a Hibachi, briquettes, and a bag of groceries from the back of Tybalt's pickup. "For you and B.J. to put your sleeping bags on to keep you high and dry. And some burger and tofu dog action."

"Thanks, man. You're the best," said Dave, rubbing his growling stomach.

"Very cool, my blade brother," said B.J.

"Gracias," chirped Chickpea.

"How's your head?" the Nurse asked Dave.

"Still sore." He did not want to have a concussion discussion.

"You should sue the ass off that idiot," advised the Nurse.

"And he's legally allowed to carry a gun?" Miranda asked.

"Frank Willow. Kinmount's finest," replied Baldwin. "Proof that evolution can go in reverse."

"I just want to forget the whole thing," grumbled Dave.

"Good thing my brother was there, eh?" added Tybalt.

"John's cool. He was a big help," said B.J.

Benvolia remained quiet. She was fed up with yet another day of lisping jokes.

"Does your entire family have its own secret super-hero identities?" Dave asked Tybalt.

"The Kinmount Crusaders," pronounced Tybalt in an exaggerated baritone. "Yeah, we kind of look out for the township. Someone's got to, right?"

"Want to help me nab a shoplifter at the record store?" inquired the Friar. "My inventory is dwindling."

"Stop taking afternoon naps in the storeroom, you lazy loon," jabbed the Nurse.

Familiarity did indeed breed contempt.

"I can do security for ya," said the shorter stoner.

"Alright, let's start at the top of Act One. Minus Old Sally. Places, please."

Dave had to get the day underway before the sun won. The heat was too much for the old mare to rehearse. Dave clapped his hands to get his troupe moving.

"And how am I supposed to make my entrance?" demanded the Prince.

"Stop whingeing and get on with it," said Dave.

Baldwin broke a limb off the elm tree and handed it to the Prince. "Endow it, dude."

Peter the clown grabbed the branch, transforming it into a makeshift hobbyhorse, and galloped about, whooping and hollering. Tybalt grabbed another branch and followed suit.

Then B.J., riding on Baldwin's shoulders. They circled the Prince, neighing and whinnying. The remainder of the company cracked up, a cloudburst of jocular rain, as Wayne and Shuster attempted to herd them.

"We needed that laughter to break up the monogamy," Dave joked.

"That statement is beyond my apprehension," said B.J., not missing a beat.

The infectious laughter of the actors bounced off the banks of the river, all the way to Circle Lake, some sixty kilometres south. With two notable exceptions: (a) the Prince, who stormed off to his trailer (he'd parked his tent trailer onsite to retire to when not rehearsing—which was ninety percent of the time); and (b) Benvolia, who remained silent and unnoticed.

"We are looking for David Middleton," said an unfamiliar voice.

Wayne and Shuster began to growl.

A trio of middle-aged business owners approached the troupe. The voice was that of a man with bad skin, dressed in beige slacks and a yellow golf shirt. White socks and sandals completed the fashion crime. He was skinny, except for a fried-food paunch. He clutched a Tiger Tail ice cream cone that was dripping down his wrist. The sun burned into his widow's peak.

The second was a doughy fellow in grey polyester pants, a plaid short-sleeve shirt, and loosely knotted tie.

The third was a woman dressed in an ill-fitting summer dress, her hem too high and her cleavage too low.

"A rare daylight cougar sighting," murmured the taller stoner to the shorter stoner.

"I'm Dave Middleton," answered Dave carefully.

"We need to talk," announced the second man.

"How are rehearsals going?" asked the woman, distracted by Tybalt's glistening biceps.

"Fine," said Dave. "Who wants to know?"

"We represent the town council and we have some concerns," began the second man.

The first man interrupted him.

"We have been informed that your play might be unsuitable for families."

The Nurse jumped in indignantly. "And why is that, Booger?"

"Do you know everyone in Kinmount?" Dave snapped at the Nurse. He was in no mood for more games. "Who informed you?"

"A concerned citizen," said the woman.

"And was that concerned citizen Lola Whale?" he asked.

"We are not at liberty to say," Booger responded, just as his ice cream plopped onto his big toe.

"Way to go dad," jabbed the Friar. He turned to Dave and whispered, "The wheel's spinning, but the hamster's dead."

"This guy's your father?" asked Dave.

"Tom Lacey," the first man introduced himself.

"Booger," repeated the Nurse.

"I'm a municipal alderman and you will show me some respect."

"He runs the hardware store. My dad's a tool," said the Friar.

"Enough," said the second man. "Back to the matter at hand. We have been advised that you are adding modern vulgarities to Shakespeare. We are a good God-fearing town, and such blasphemous licence will not be tolerated. There are children to think of."

"Whoa," said Dave. He did not want a repeat of Lola's kitchen. "I assure you I have not tampered with *Romeo and Juliet*. I give you my word."

"Your word isn't worth spit. I saw today's paper. You are treading on precarious terrain, Mr. Middleton." That was the second man crossing his arms, taking on the appearance of a beach inflatable about to burst.

"You want me to prove it?" Dave said.

"You give us no choice," said the woman.

"When does your council meet next?" Dave asked.

"Thursday," she replied.

"Two nights from now?"

"Yes, this Thursday night. At seven sharp."

"Put me on the agenda," Dave said firmly.

"I'm not sure with such short notice, we can—"

"Put me on the agenda," he demanded.

"Be there at seven. And no funny business," said the second man.

"Oh, I will be," assured Dave. "With bells on."

The second man and the woman left arguing with Booger, who wanted to replace his ice cream. The woman stole a look back at Tybalt.

"Just great," said Dave. "Does it ever end?"

"At least the helicopters haven't turned around," piped in Baldwin, referencing Coppola's agony while filming *Apocalypse Now*. The military helicopters he'd hired at great expense, for his epic twelve-minute centrepiece chopper assault, turned around and left to put down a local guerrilla uprising at the precise moment Coppola yelled "Action."

"Give them time," replied Dave grimly. "The Burnt River is beginning to smell like napalm."

"So you're really doing it?" asked B.J.

"No choice." Dave began to feel dizzy. Addressing the rural council would be akin to trying to explain what artistic vision is to a room full of accountants. Only, in the case of Kinmount, the accountants couldn't add.

"The slings and arrows of outrageous censors." It was Ginny, her expression mirroring the mask of tragedy on her t-shirt.

"Right," said Dave, sitting on one of Tybalt's bales of hay to steady himself. He began to sneeze. A summer cold he did not need.

"I'll come too," said Lady Capulet. Dave leaned in to listen. "I can make photocopies of whatever excerpts of the play you want to use. They shut down my library. You need to win this."

"No pressure," sighed Dave. "Could someone fetch the Princess from his trailer?"

Peter galloped off.

"Shakespeare is rolling in his grave," Miranda said.

"Grave or no grave, we have to get down to work." Dave sneezed. On second thought, maybe he was allergic to hay? Great, another insult to add to the injury of his aching head.

After rehearsal, Dave walked Kinmount's main drag to pick up the show posters at the local copy shop/laundromat/vacuum cleaner outlet. Paris had designed the graphics and image: a bright red rose on a thorny stem, subtly dripping blood. Some of the drops deliberately resembled small hearts. Dave had approved the expressionistic design, in Lola's absence, two days earlier on the eve of the big bang kitchen blow-out.

He passed the Kinmount Restaurant on Main Street, advertising its daily special in the window:

Desert and a Coffee: $5.00.

A sign beside it read:

"Sorry, WE DON'T HAVE WI-FI. You will have to talk to each other. Pretend it's 1995."

He peered through the hardware store window and saw Booger at the counter, his shirt now covered in ice cream, bagging some fireworks for the taller stoner—Weed the dart thrower. He passed the Dollar Store (now selling eveningwear), the Friar's vinyl shop, and the Kinmount Credit Union, arriving at Fay's Laundry-Copy. He could feel the heat from the dryers outside on the sidewalk.

He opened the door, and the broken overhead bell signalled his arrival. The laundromat was filled to the diaper with teenage mothers and their whining babies strapped in strollers.

He walked up to the counter, taking note of the flyers pinned to its veneer facade: a fishing derby in August, a plowing match on the Labour Day weekend, and a poster for the Summer in the Park festivities. The events included a petting zoo, children's face painting, an antique car show, fireworks and ... *Romeo and Juliet* crossed out with a black magic marker.

Dave felt a wave of paranoia wash over him. He rang the bell on the counter and steadied his nerves. A tall woman with a frizzy perm, wearing a conservative blouse and floral skirt, emerged from the back room.

"Can I help you?" she asked.

"Hi. Are you Flo?" Dave asked.

"Been that way for fifty-five years. What can I do you for?"

"I'm here to pick up the *Romeo and Juliet* posters."

"And you are?"

"Dave. Dave Middleton."

"You're that director aren't you?"

"I sure am," Dave answered, hoping for a congratulatory response, or the request for an autograph.

"Get out," she barked and grabbed a coat hanger from a drawer beneath the cash register.

"Excuse me?" Dave was caught off guard.

"I said get out," Flo warned, menacingly raising the coat hanger. "Lola Whale dropped by to warn me about you. *And* I read the paper. You are not welcome here, Mr. Big-City Director. Corrupting the morals of our children. How dare you have the nerve to show your face in my shop? You have some gall, mister. There are NO posters. Now, get out before I call the police."

Flo reached for her phone.

"Wait, please," Dave pleaded. "There's been a huge misunderstanding. I am not and never have been a misogynist. The police made a mistake. We were rehearsing and—"

"I don't call slapping a girl rehearsing, Mr. Middleton. I call it assault." She began to dial.

Dave reached over the counter and pressed the receiver down.

"Please, listen to me," he implored. "You don't understand. Lola is insane. She's poisoning your mind with lies."

"You're the poison. Move your hand before I charge *you* with assault." Flo meant business. She whacked the counter with the hanger.

Dave backed away. His chest began to throb. Would he be joining Capulet in the cardiac ward? Then it dawned on him.

Lola had crossed out the show on the festival poster. Had she done that to all the posters?

The overhead bells rang.

"Excuse me, are you Dave Middleton?" asked a young woman in denim shorts and white t-shirt in the doorway.

"I don't know anymore," Dave said, gripping his chest.

"I'm Elizabeth Mackenzie. I'm a summer student with *The Kinmount Crier*. Can I ask you some questions?" she asked, notebook and pencil at the ready.

Dave heard Capulet's voice in his head.

"No comment," he blurted out.

"What do you have say to about the assault at the sawmill last night?"

"No comment," he wheezed.

"I want to hear your side of things," she pressed.

"NO COMMENT!"

He raced out the door and collapsed on a public bench on the sidewalk.

"Get a grip," he repeated to himself as he struggled to breathe. He managed to right himself and soldiered on down the main drag. The stores were a blur. All he saw were Summer in the Park posters with *Romeo and Juliet* crossed out by Lola's magic marker.

Kate was serving chicken fingers and fries to a regular at the bar when Dave stumbled in.

"What's happened now?" she said, ushering him to a back table beside the dartboard. "You look worse than the corner store beside my house."

Dave fell into a chair and slowly got his breathing under control.

She poured him a Keith's and sat down across from him. They sat in silence for what seemed hours.

Kate waited for him to speak.

"You can't write this stuff," he finally exclaimed, downing his pint. "How has she not been institutionalized?"

"Your guess is as good as mine."

"You read the paper?" Dave stared into the bottom of his glass.

"Oh yeah." She paused and then, "Are you sure you don't want to pack it in?"

"I can't," he said reluctantly.

"You can't," she repeated. The absurdity of his pronouncement was clear.

"I gave my word to Robert."

"You what?" she asked. Dave's monkey brain was beyond analysis.

"I visited him after I got out of Emerg-"

"You were in Emergency and didn't call me?"

She was clearly upset.

"Sorry, I didn't want to wake you. Cop slammed my head with his squad car door. I went to see if I had a concussion."

"And do you?"

"I don't know."

"You don't know. How have you survived into your forties? Follow my finger."

She examined the speed of his eye movements.

"You look okay."

"Thanks, nurse. Anyhow, I visited Robert after I was released. And he's convinced me to hang in. Chase the windmill is how he put it."

"And look what happened to him." She returned to the bar to cash out her regular.

"That was his mother-in-law, not Lola."

"And your point is?"

"Could you imagine if Lola were your mother-in-law?" piped in the regular as he wobbled towards the door. He put a finger to his head. "BANG!" And he was gone.

"I can ride this out. I don't know how, but I can." Dave downed the rest of his Keith's.

"Not if Lola has her way. Besides, Don Quixote tilted at windmills, didn't he? He didn't chase them. And you're chasing a tornado."

"Don't I know it. She's got to Flo at the copy shop. She won't print our posters. And Lola's crossed out the show title on every festival poster in town."

She brought him another Keith's.

"So what are you going to do if you aren't using common sense like any normal adult and quitting?"

"I'm normal?" He managed a self-effacing laugh. "Well, one thing I'm doing is getting my bike back. We're planning a covert raid tonight after midnight."

Kate stifled a wince and sat back down beside him. "And things aren't bad enough."

"We have to. I've got to do something to get my balls back. She's had them in a vice for two weeks now."

"Your balls back," she reiterated. "What are you, sixteen? You're worse than Romeo. Who is this *we*?"

"B.J., Baldwin, and Miranda. Want to join us?"

"You're joking, right?"

"Half serious." He smiled meekly.

"It's a bike, Dave. Cut your losses and quit."

"It's *all* our bikes. And we're doing it. We're meeting here at ten to plan our attack. Think on it."

"There's nothing to think on." She stood up, returning his empty glass to the bar.

"I'd sure love to see you again," he blurted out.

"You've got enough on your plate without adding some inane notion of a small-town romance with the local barmaid."

This time she avoided *his* eyes.

"I'm serious," he said. He crossed up to a barstool to get closer to her.

"I know you think you are." She retreated to find a dishtowel.

He lay his head down on the bar: "I'm beat."

"You need a nap. There's a pillow and air mattress in the store room. I crash there sometimes between my split shifts."

"You sure?"

"I'm the only the one here. Now get before I give my head a shake."

Dave managed a grin. She moved the cases of empties into a corner. He plopped down on the mattress and was asleep in seconds.

She sat down on a milk crate and let out a deep sigh. Boys never grow up; they just get bigger.

SEVEN

Baldwin leaned against a support beam in the darkest corner of the Red Lion. He'd transformed into a World War II French resistance fighter, dressed head-to-toe in black, with black army boots and a black beret, having shaved and sketched in a black pencil moustache with an eyeliner stick. He raised a pint to the mission.

He cleared his throat and rhymed:

"We'll ride into battle pledging our souls to thee,
To unlock and release and soon make free,
Thou two-wheeled chariots that number three,
Fighting in the gardens of night's cherub pee."

B.J. chimed in:

"Nor fox nor hound nor harpy-croaked Whale,
Shall stop us on our quest for the grease-chained Grail."

He too was dressed in black: a spandex unitard, sneakers, and toque, a cross between Jacques Cousteau and a modern dance student.

Followed by Miranda in a black singlet, black torn jeans tucked into a pair of Lady Capulet's black riding boots and a black baseball cap:

"With courage in our loins we shall not fail,
Until our three noble steeds ... land us in jail."

The table gave her a look.

"Sorry," she said. "Bad rhyme. Nerves."

"... lead us to ale," Dave concluded.

Other than the addition of a black bandana, he was in the

same jeans, sandals, and rumpled black shirt he'd been wearing since his false arrest.

"You both have the keys to your bike locks?"

B.J. gestured to the keys hanging off the chain around his neck.

"Miranda, you'll keep watch hidden in the front yard. If you see or hear anything suspicious blow on this," Baldwin instructed. "Capisce?" He handed her a wooden duck call.

"A duck call?" asked Dave. "Seriously?"

"That's an Echo Wood special," explained Baldwin. "It lets off one helluva quack. I borrowed it from my grandfather's hunting kit. He won't need it until October."

"Works for me," said B.J.

"A whistle is too obvious," added Baldwin.

"Alright, then. Miranda, you blow two Daffy Ducks to warn us," said Dave, wondering how he'd got himself into yet another mess. He should have listened to his mother and gone to law school. Became an adult with grown-up responsibilities. Had a future.

Baldwin checked his watch.

"It's the midnight hour, freedom fighters," he said. "Operation Bike-kirk begins."

They got to their feet. Baldwin motioned with a military hand signal for them to follow him out the back door.

"Hold it one second."

It was Kate. She emerged from behind the bar.

"Are you joining us?" asked Dave.

"A civilian?" inquired Baldwin, accidentally rubbing off his moustache. "Shit."

"No, I am not. What the four of you are doing is asinine. My daughter's friends have more sense. But, I'm also not going to let you get shot or end up in jail. So, against my better judgment, I'm giving you one of these," she schooled, handing Dave a walkie-talkie. "If something goes wrong, *when* something goes wrong, buzz me. Push the button down to talk"

"You sure?" asked Dave, clipping the walkie-talkie to his belt.

"No, I'm not sure. But if things go off the rails you will need all the help you can get. I can call the police. But, right now, I'm going home to sit on my roof."

She started turning off the lights.

Dave wished he was joining her.

"Closing time, folks," she said to a couple of Red Lion baseball players licking their wounds at a table beside the front door. "Time to pay up."

Once in the parking lot they squeezed into Dave's Tercel. Baldwin rode shotgun. He looked in the rear view mirror and reapplied his moustache.

Dave parked two blocks down from Lola's house on a side street. A large hedgerow blocked the car from view. As they opened the doors, Miranda whispered for them to pay attention.

"Use this," she said passing around a small jar of black make-up. "Smudge your faces. It'll help disguise us."

One minute later and they looked like a band of crazed miners. B.J. lit up a joint and inhaled deeply.

"I'd go easy on that stuff," said Dave. His dark brown eyes registered their disapproval. "It's anything can happen night."

"Righto." B.J. took another deep drag, pinched the tip, and pocketed it.

The night sky was overcast. Not a star visible. B.J. attached a night light to his toque. Baldwin pulled a pair of lock cutters out of his knapsack. Miranda gripped the duck call.

"Ready?" Dave whispered.

A nodding of heads.

They slowly approached the house. The street was quiet. No cars at one a.m. on a Monday morning.

"Down!" whispered Baldwin. He dropped to his stomach and began crawling along the sidewalk.

The others followed suit. Dave felt ridiculous.

When they reached the driveway, Baldwin motioned for

Miranda to hide in the shrubbery by the front porch.

"We'll cover you."

"With what?" Dave whispered.

"With these little babies." Baldwin reached into his pocket and pulled out half a dozen pub darts he'd stolen from the Red Lion. He handed Dave and B.J. two darts each.

"Are you crazy? You think this is a game of Lights Out?" Dave's vein on his temple was throbbing. He was thinking of Bobcat's missing eye.

"I didn't know you played. Cool, dude." Baldwin was impressed.

"I don't play. Someone's going to lose an—"

"Move!" Baldwin interrupted Dave's protestations, gesturing for Miranda to crawl to the shrubbery. B.J. flipped on his headlight to "low" to illuminate a path for her. Once she was safely tucked in the shrub, she gave a thumbs-up.

Baldwin motioned for B.J. to take the lead. They slowly crept along the side of the house stopping at the backyard entrance gate. Light shone through the cracks. They peered over the top of the gate.

Four Tiki bamboo torches were lit around the largest phallus in the centre of the yard. Red dripping candles were spread about on any level surface available. Fireflies blinked like mini-flashlights in the dark, silently darting about, magical and ethereal.

"They're beautiful," whispered B.J., buzzing from the weed. He turned off his headlight. The bugs grew even more restless. "They blink because they're mating. They're trying to attract each other."

"That's a whole lotta lovin' goin' on," Baldwin whispered. "There must be fifty of them! Even the bugs have orgies in Lola's backyard."

B.J. was entranced.

"Some cultures believe that fireflies are the souls of the dead." Dave got goosebumps as B.J. said it.

"That's a lot of dead people coming to visit. Wonder how

many of them are buried in her basement?" said Baldwin, his French Resistance posturing slipping.

"Be careful. Or we could be next."

Dave's words hung in the summer air.

The night smelled of their adrenalin.

"It's now or never," Dave whispered. "Come on."

He carefully unlatched the fence. They crawled in, one after the other, taking cover behind the cherub closest to them.

"Miranda locked her bike by the big fountain," said B.J., training his headlight on the fountain in the middle of the yard.

"Go for it," said Baldwin, pointing to it.

B.J. crawled towards the fountain. Red food dye had changed the colour of the water to blood. At least B.J. hoped it was food dye. He found Miranda's pink touring bike exactly as she'd left it when they'd returned from the beach after the first stumble through.

B.J. slipped the lock off and lifted Miranda's bike over his head and quickly carried it to the gate. Baldwin's darts were poised and ready.

"One down," whispered B.J.

He crawled to the far corner and found his bike locked to a birch tree—exactly where he'd left it. His mind wandered. Miranda's image returned to massage his pot-baked brain. He revelled in his beach memories. Miranda had tasted of honey and immortality. Fifty fireflies could not hold a candle to her shimmering, unearthly beauty.

Revelling a little too much in his thoughts as he carried his bike to the gate, he accidentally slammed his big toe into the base of a cherub.

"Ouch!" he winced. "I broke my toe."

"Ssshhhhhh!"

He hobbled the rest of the way lifting his bike over the fence and collapsing behind the cherub. His big toe was indeed broken.

A third storey light went on.

"Sorry, guys," he apologized.

"Oh shit," said Dave. "We've been spotted!"

"Hurry man! We don't have much time" Baldwin pushed Dave into the garden. "Go! We've got your back."

Dave crawled towards the back steps. He'd locked his bike on one of the railing posts.

No bike.

Dave looked frantically about.

No bike.

He approached the giant phallus glowing in the Tiki torch-light. He stopped in his toe-careful tracks.

There.

Strapped to the head of the phallus.

His handlebars.

Like a morbid mountain bike/antler hybrid.

Lola had sacrificed his bike.

QUACK! QUACK!

Miranda's duck call sounded the alarm.

Lights on the second floor switched on.

B.J. hopped the fence, stumbling into Miranda.

"Dave! C'mon!" Baldwin shouted.

"She's destroyed my bike!" screamed Dave.

"She's crazy! C'mon!" yelled Baldwin.

Lights on the first floor switched on.

Baldwin ran to grab Dave.

B.J. and Miranda came around the corner and tried to mount their bikes. Lola had let the air out of the tires.

The back door burst open.

The world froze.

Only for an instant.

And then ...

Four half-naked women exploded onto the deck.

They were draped in loose-fitting, tattered black togas, sporting giant insect wings made from bent coat hangers and old furnace filters. Their arms were stained with strange mythological symbols. Cascading red wigs, entwined with thick-clustered rubber snakes, perched above metallic masquerade half-masks splattered with red paint. Each clutched a goblet of red wine in one hand and wielded a misshapen trident in the other.

"RAAAAAAAA!"

Their wild paralytic screams would make a mandrake jealous. The fireflies flashed faster, natural strobe lights, bouncing off the four women.

Dave and Baldwin strained their eyes trying to decipher who was who.

"Over the beast, doomed to the fire, this is our *fury*, man-pigs!" chanted the shortest woman stepping out in front of the others. A rubber snake was wrapped around her waist.

"Over the beast, doomed to the fire, this is our *fury*, man-pigs!" she repeated, pointing her trident at Dave. That had to be Lola. The others followed suit chanting along with her.

"Over the beast, doomed to the fire, this is our *fury*, man-pigs!" the chorus of women wailed.

Aeschylus was now officially applauding in his grave.

It was at that moment that Dave realized the tridents were made from pieces of his bike: pedals, spokes, sprockets, frame, fenders, and all.

"ENOUGH!" he bellowed. "Lola, what have you done to my bike?!"

"Mortal, how dare you address me in such a manner. I am Tisiphone, Goddess of Vengeance, Daughter of the Night," bellowed Lola.

She threw her goblet to the ground and gripped her trident with both hands slashing the air in Dave's direction, his pedals spinning madly like a weathervane in a hurricane.

"You are trespassing on sacred ground. Leave now or pay the price, man-pig," she warned.

"Lola, stop it. This has gone too far."

The rest of the women turned to face him.

"Lola, why are you doing this?" cried Miranda from the safety of B.J.'s arms.

"Ah, there you are, my Daughter of Light. I knew you'd come back to me." Lola grinned lustily, her teeth gnashing and flashing in the glow of the fireflies.

"Join us," said two of the women in unison, beckoning Miranda towards them with Dave's bike corpse.

"Join u*th*," echoed the fourth woman out of sync.

"Benvolia?" Dave stammered. His brain was short-circuiting. "What are you—"

"Over the bea*tht*, doomed to the fire, thi*th* i*th* our fury, man-pig*th*!" Benvolia chanted.

Dave quickly calculated the events of the past two weeks. Benvolia had to be the company mole; how else could Lola have known what was going on in rehearsal? Had she been Lola's spy from the beginning?

"Why?" asked Dave. The betrayal stung. "I treated you fairly. How could you?"

"Man *th*cum," she hissed.

"*Th*it for brain*th*," Baldwin fired back, preparing his darts.

"Men scum deserve no pity," Lola decreed. "The Furies will destroy you all. Come, Megaera and Alecto."

The women slowly advanced down the porch steps.

"Your little charade is done, Lola. You can keep your traitor. I want full payment for my bike. Now." Dave stood his ground.

"Never." Lola raised her trident over her head. "Attack!"

The women charged down the steps.

"Get to the car! Now! I've got this!" Baldwin shouted to his comrades at the gate.

B.J. and Miranda grabbed their bikes and ran to the car. Well, Miranda ran. B.J. hopped.

Tridents filled the air like spears. Baldwin and Dave's darts filled the air like arrows. The battle was on.

Dave reached for Kate's walkie-talkie, unclipping it from his belt. He held it up to his face and pushed the button to talk, turning off the receiver and turning on the transmitter. He shouted into the microphone: "Kate, call the police, now!" A trident narrowly missed his head.

Baldwin ripped a Tiki torch out of the ground and waved

the flame at Benvolia and the taller Fury, keeping them both at bay.

Rudyard Kipling was laughing in *his* grave. Unless he was one of the fireflies.

Dave scrambled about the yard gathering up the fallen tridents with Lola in drunken pursuit.

A shot rang out.

Everyone looked towards the gate.

There stood the Dickee Dee ice cream boy with an air rifle trained on Lola.

"Back inside. Now!" the boy shouted at the chorus of women.

"I'll take it from here, son," boomed a deep, resonant voice.

A large man stepped out of the shadows and stood behind the boy, hands on hips, in full Canadian military commando gear. He was cool and collected, watching Lola and her mad harem very, very closely. "Ladies, stand down."

The women refused.

"How dare you, man-pig!" Lola bellowed, slurring her words. She was having a hard time standing. Benvolia rushed to her assistance, her trident, the last one not in the hands of the enemy, trained on the large man. The two other women each picked up a rock.

"Now!" the large man ordered. He meant business.

"Die man-pig!" Lola screamed.

"Stand down!" he commanded.

"Fire!" Lola screeched.

Benvolia's trident flew through the air. The large man leapt up with a judo kick and blocked it, knocking it to the ground. Dave scrambled to retrieve it.

The taller women threw her rock with the coordination of a drunken pitcher. The large man ducked effortlessly and the stone fell harmlessly onto the lawn behind him. The second rock came right for his chest. He stepped out of the way while at the same time catching it in his beefy hands, a twenty-first-century Hercules in action.

"She picked the wrong neighbourhood kid to pick on," whispered Baldwin to Dave.

"This guy's ready to rumble," Dave whispered back. "He could take on a herd of bulls by the horns."

The low wail of a siren. A next-door neighbour had called the station.

"The road of life, Ms. Whale, is paved with flat squirrels that couldn't make a decision. I'm making yours for you," warned the large man. "You don't charge these folks with trespassing," he instructed firmly, "and I don't charge you with assault for shooting out my son's tire."

The siren was getting louder, a few blocks away.

"Man-pig!" Lola wailed.

"Lola!" Benvolia yelled. "It's the poli*the*. *Th*top!"

Lola rushed the large man. The taller woman tackled her in time and the two fell to the ground like a flailing squid.

The siren cut out as the squad car pulled up out front, its whirling red light bathing the side of the house.

"As is if there isn't enough blood imagery," said Dave to Baldwin.

Slamming car doors pierced the night.

The popcorn patter of a pair of footsteps racing down the driveway, well, one pair racing, the other pair wheezing in second place.

"Police! Don't move!" shouted the first officer. It was the voice of Officer John. Which meant the second officer had to be Frank, just what Dave needed.

On seeing Dave, Frank blurted out in disgust, "Oh, you again." The last thing Dave wanted was another backseat lift to emergency.

"What's going on here?" said Officer John, taking charge. "It's one in the morning. We got a call there was a loud house party, and a fight broke out on the back lawn."

"All that happened tonight, Officer," said the large man, calm and assured, "was a barbecue that got a little out of hand."

"You having a costume party?" said Frank, sizing up the

bizarre fright show in front of him.

"Man-pig," hissed Lola, slowly getting up with the assistance of the taller woman.

"What did you say?" growled Frank.

"Shut up," whispered the taller woman hoarsely, kicking Lola in the shin. "Nothing, Officer. She was talking about the barbecue. She loves her pork. Big fan of pig. Fan-pig."

"Right," said Frank, not buying it.

"Is that correct, Ms. Whale?" said Officer John, recognizing Lola under the makeup. It wasn't the first time he'd dealt with her or seen her in some crazy get-up. A year ago, he had to arrest a ghost. Lola had drunkenly called the station at the two in the morning saying the ghost of her dead husband had broken into her house and wouldn't leave. So Officer John fake arrested it and carted it out of the house so he could get some peace.

"Is what correct?" Lola said tersely.

"You were having a barbecue and everyone had a little too much to drink?" said Officer John, repeating the large man's statement.

"Yes," volunteered the taller woman. "Too much red wine. But we're all fine. Just a toga party that got a bit out of control. Time for bed, right?"

"Not so fast," said Frank. "How come you guys ain't in costume?"

"We changed," said Dave. "After dinner."

"We were just heading out when you arrived, Frank," shouted Baldwin from the far reaches of the backyard. He was about to take a piss in a bush. His nerves and bladder had taken a beating.

"Hold it right there, actor-boy," ordered Frank, shining his flashlight on him. "You want me to charge you with indecent exposure? You'll end up on a sex offender list. Your life will be ruined."

"For pissing in a bush? What the fuck, Frank?" said Baldwin, zipping up too quickly. "Fuck me!"

"Language. There are ladies present." Frank shone his

flashlight across Lola's backyard. "How come I don't see no barbecue?"

"I wheeled it home," the large man lied. "After it cooled down."

"Can I see it?" said Frank.

"Sure. Two doors down. Back of the car port."

"That won't be necessary," said Officer John. "We'll call it a night. I'm letting you all off with a warning. The new noise bylaw goes into effect at eleven p.m. In the future, if you're carrying on after that time, you will be arrested and fined. Understood?"

"Affirmative," said the large man. Dave and Baldwin nodded, as did the taller woman, lighting up a smoke.

"Watch that wig, ma'am," said Officer John. "It's flammable."

The taller woman sneered at him. The shorter woman said nothing. Benvolia sat cowering on the porch steps. Lola glared at Dave.

"Is that understood, Ms. Whale?" Officer John repeated.

"Perfectly," she said, not taking her eyes off her prey.

"Good then. Well, good night," said Officer John.

"Stay out of trouble," warned Frank.

"Trouble can't even find me," Baldwin shouted as the two officers returned to the patrol car. They sat and waited and watched.

Dave turned to go. Lola spit on his sandal.

"I'm not finished with you, David," she hissed.

The taller woman butted her dart, grabbed Lola by the arm, and tugged. "C'mon inside, honey. We'll get the man-pigs later."

Dave hoped it was an empty threat.

The women withdrew.

Lola stopped with a jerk on the porch and turned back, raising her arms in invocation, a high priestess wasted on cheap red wine. "Beware the Furies," she growled and stumbled into the kitchen.

"Thanks, man," Baldwin said to the large man with a sigh of relief.

"You missed a bit," replied the large man. Baldwin sheepishly wiped off the remains of his fake moustache.

Dave had seen enough action to last a lifetime. He offered his hand to the boy's father as they walked down the driveway. "Hi, I'm Dave Middleton. Thanks for being our cavalry, sir."

"Don't call me 'Sir.' The name's Gord, Sergeant Gord Ryan," said the man, shaking Dave's hand firmly. "Glad to meet you. I just got back from Mali."

"Mali? That must've been hot," said Dave, trying to remember where Mali was. Indonesia?

"Sweltering. Desert wind turned our entire base into an orange dust ball. You heard of Operation Presence?"

"No, I haven't, Sergeant," Dave replied, thinking how the large man would be perfect casting for the Prince. Was it too late to arrange a trailer fire?

"Peacekeeping for the U.N.," shared the Sergeant without a lick of false modesty.

"The pen is mightier than the sword," pronounced Baldwin with a flourish. He was now a "smudged" Resistance Fighter.

The Sergeant gave him a look. "A semi-automatic weapon would beg to differ."

"Well," said Dave, "I sure am relieved to have you on our side, Sergeant. We're working on a Shakespeare play for Summer in the Park. Lola stole our bikes and we were trying to get them back," he explained.

"Lola is a live one. Successful mission?" asked the Sergeant, scanning the back yard.

"We rescued two out of the three," Dave reported back. "Mine was destroyed. See those tridents on the ground ..."An idea struck him. "Listen, Sergeant Ryan, with the way things are, you wouldn't be interested in helping us out with security by any chance, would you, sir?"

"Could we, dad?" The boy was pumped.

"Two doors down. Small stone house. Come at oh-eight-hundred." The Sergeant didn't waste a syllable. "And don't call me 'Sir.'"

Just as quickly as they'd arrived the boy and his father vanished from the battlefield and back into the neighbourhood.

"Give me a hand," Dave said.

Baldwin carried what was left of Dave's bike to the Tercel.

"Why did you blow the duck call?" he asked Miranda, while stacking the tridents on the dashboard.

"A raccoon jumped into the hedge and startled me," said Miranda. "Sorry." Underneath the black makeup she was as pale as the ghost of Lola's dead husband(s).

"Not your fault. It was a crazy night." B.J. reassured her, giving her a hug.

They jumbled into the car, Miranda and B.J.'s bikes safely stowed in the hatch.

"Next time, we use a Trojan penis," said Baldwin.

Dave cradled his bicycle seat and pressed his face against the steering wheel. The helicopters had turned around.

"Drive me away," he whispered.

EIGHT

For nearly four thousand years, theatre had survived religious persecution, war, plague, the rise of television, AIDS, *CATS*, funding cuts, and electronic media. But could it survive Lola Whale?

Dave had his doubts.

B.J. rolled a doobie and passed Dave a beer. The tent reeked of sun-baked canvas. They sat in silence on their respective sleeping bags, perched on the four bales of hay. An industrial Coleman flashlight, courtesy of Kate, illuminated their cramped surroundings. The Tercel was parked in the marina parking lot in an unlit corner. B.J.'s bike was still in the hatch. Dave's bike was impossible to salvage. The tridents rested on the grass outside the tent.

"Lola called herself Tisiphone," said Dave mid-sip. "And the other two she addressed as Megaera and Alecto." He took another swallow. "Benvolia must've been their brainwashed apprentice."

"The Furies?" said B.J., carefully lighting the tip of the joint while slowly rotating the rolling paper in his fingers to achieve a red-hot cherry.

"Fright wigs and all," Dave continued. "Did you notice that strange tattoo of Lola's?"

"Oh, yeah."

It'd creeped them both out.

There was a reason why people didn't want to make the Furies mad. If there was a criminal lurking about who hadn't been punished, the furious, snake-haired, bloody-eyed Greek goddesses flapped their wings and rose up from the black pit of Tartarus to seek vengeance. Their favourite methods of punishment included driving people insane by repeatedly singing Alanis Morissette's *You Oughta Know*, blighting big stretches of countryside, and blasting whole cities with plague—they could have done a real number on Verona. Back in the day, rumour had it there was a flock of Furies wreaking havoc, but later, Greek farmers admitted they were spreading fake news and that there were in fact only three. Whatever their number, the "Sinister Supreme Sisters" of vengeance—Alecto, Tisiphone, and Megaera—didn't mess around. They righted wrongs, tortured the guilty, and drove criminals insane, particularly men who killed their children, wives, or parents. Not necessarily in that order. Aeschylus brought them to life in *The Oresteia*. In their theatrical debut, the Furies hunt down Orestes, the son of Agamemnon, for killing his mother, because she murdered Orestes' dad. The Furies were more than a little miffed when Orestes got away with it too. They also hated Apollo, the brainy sun god who told Orestes to kill his mom in the first place. Worshipped for being the multi-god of sun, light, music, truth, healing, poetry, and prophesy, Apollo was also a silent patron of the Greek plague—an embarrassing fact he tried to keep to Zeus and himself.

Apollo and the goddess Athena hammer out the proper punishment for Orestes, marking the invention of courtroom drama. The Furies advocate for Tarantino-style justice, an eye-for-an-eye kind of thing, and are enraged when Athena decides to introduce democracy to Athens. She puts the matter to a fair trial, engaging mere mortals for the jury. The Furies would rather tear people to pieces than piece together legal arguments. As it turns out, the jury is split, but Athena's vote is the tiebreaker, and she sets Orestes free.

The Furies are less than pleased with the outcome, but after a lot of persuasion, Athena convinces them to accept the verdict and stay in Athens as goddesses in charge of helping good people and punishing bad people (instead of just punishing). From then on, instead of being "Furies," the goddesses were known as "The Kindly Ones," a.k.a. the Eumenides. Thanks to Athena's clever thinking, a trio of horrifying monsters, whose only purpose was to torture their victims, became a trio of worshipped goddesses, working together to ensure the health of a ground-breaking legal system and proper conflict management. They also became the misapplied manifestation of Lola's rage.

Lola's fury went a long way in shaping both hers and Dave's fate. If it was Dave's fate to have Lola come into his life, what caused her to *become* a Fury? Like Dave, there had to be tragedy in her past. But just what was the real deal with her dead ex-husbands he wondered. Domestic abuse? And what really happened to her daughter? Was her father a pedophile? Was Lola's first marriage similar to the Capulet marriage? Was she younger and forced into it? Could she have been pregnant? Shakespeare knocked up Anne Hathaway, and her brothers forced him into wedlock. Did Lola's husband stifle her and their daughter? Control freaks often begot control freaks. Her ensuing husbands seemed to be variations on the same broken theme. Replacements rather than authentic love.

Lola never did find her Romeo. The whitewashed version of *Romeo and Juliet* she studied as a girl in Miss Maple's girls' class gave her a false sense of hope, a dream of a romantic love that didn't exist in the real world. It was a fairy-tale teenage love story that she never got to experience, and had longed to her entire life. Had she projected her fantasy onto Dave? Was he her substitute Romeo? Things were fine until he changed the outcome of her version of the plot, triggering her wrath. It was a story Shakespeare could channel via Lola's ouija board to Stephen King, and become the best-selling novel about an obsessed psychotic fan holding an author captive and forcing him to write her stories.

Whatever the fallout of Lola's past, it set her on a path of vengeance, unnervingly steady at times, and crazy as a soup sandwich at others. The Furies eventually shifted, becoming a kindly healing force. Was it too late for Lola to heal? Was her damage beyond repair? Athena's jury was split. Lola would have to decide or society would do it for her.

"Since when is standing up for Shakespeare considered a crime?" said Dave, slamming back his beer.

B.J.'s cherry was off to a strong even start. The joint burned slowly. He was pleased. He inhaled long and slow, causing his voice to slide up a register: "Thank God Lola can't fly."

Dave attempted to crack open another beer. The twist-off cap shredded his hand. "Fuck me! These caps are lethal!"

B.J. exhaled slowly and handed Dave a rag before inserting his hand inside his parrot-friend. "What happened to make her so damaged?" B.J. asked.

"She's got enough baggage to fill the Grand Canyon," replied Chickpea, joining the conversation.

"But why did she have to unpack it on me?" said Dave, wrapping his palm.

"She certainly has your number," said Chickpea.

"I'm afraid she'll be tormenting me until the end of the world, Chickpea." Dave cracked open another beer. He used an opener.

"B.J.'s dad says that come the end of the world, the only survivors will be the cockroaches. He's an atomologist," said Chickpea

"A *what*-ologist?" said Dave.

"Entomologist," said B.J., correcting Chickpea gently.

"He studies insects," explained Chickpea. "Cockroaches have been around for five hundred million years he says."

"Three hundred million," said B.J.

"Three hundred million years," said Chickpea, "so they've outlasted the dinosaurs by about one hundred and fifty million years. Right, B.J.?"

"Correct," smiled B.J., scratching Chickpea's beak.

"Tough little creatures," Dave said, pondering his fate.

"They can even survive on cellu-light," said Chickpea eagerly.

"Cellulose," said B.J.

"Cell-u-lose," Chickpea repeated and continued. "And, in a pinch, they eat each other to survive!" He hopped up and down with excitement.

"I didn't know cockroaches were cannibals," said Dave.

"They can even soldier on without a head for a week or two," added B.J. grimly.

"Like Lola." Dave downed the rest of his beer. "And probably Sergeant Ryan." Given a choice, he'd take a headless soldier over a headless Fury any day of the apocalypse.

"And they're fiendishly fast," B.J. took over, while trying to shotgun with Chickpea. "As Chickpea and I've discovered opening my apartment door and turning on a light." B.J. exhaled smoke into his parrot-friend's beak. Chickpea struggled to inhale. "They have the reputation for being survivors—living through anything from steaming hot water to nuclear holocaust ... and if and when they do survive Armageddon, they will probably be performing theatre. There is something of the scrappy cockroach in every actor that hammers out a living." B.J. toasted the air with his beer.

"It's going to work," insisted Chickpea.

"How? We have no Benvolio," muttered Dave.

"I don't know," said B.J. "Quantum physics, Universal Law of energies ..."

"Yogi Berra," added Chickpea

Dave gave the parrot a puzzled look.

"You know," squawked Chickpea. "It ain't over till the fat parakeet sings."

An idea suddenly struck B.J. "What about Chickpea?"

"What about Chickpea?" Dave said sullenly.

"He could play Benvolio."

"You're kidding, right?"

"No, he's a great little actor."

"I could have the lines down by tomorrow," chirped Chickpea, flapping his wings.

"Be serious," said Dave. "Benvolio is in three scenes that

don't include Romeo. You may be able to throw your voice but you can't split yourself in two."

The trio sat in dejected silence.

"I'm sorry I dragged you into this. If I'd known—" Dave began.

"It's okay. It's been a..." B.J. paused, trying to find the right word.

"Adventure," volunteered Chickpea.

"That's one way of putting it. More like a Conrad odyssey. " Humour cut through Dave's miserable luck.

"How's your toe?" Dave felt guilty about that too.

"Taped it to the others with duct tape. The weed is helping. Sure you don't want a toke? Take the edge off?" B.J. passed the joint to Dave.

"What the hell," said Dave, against his better judgment, reaching out his right thumb and index finger. He took a long drag and coughed.

"Finish it," said B.J., handing Dave a roach clip. "Only a few hits left."

Dave inhaled and choked on the smoke as it curled down the back of his throat. He felt like Martin Sheen in Coppola's Vietnam epic. Was Lola Brando? "The horror! The horror!" Conrad put it best.

"I'll take first watch. Wake you at three," coughed Dave between drags. "Better dreams."

Dave unzipped the entrance, parted the flap, and stepped outside. The clouds had cleared and stars filled the sky like sleeping fireflies. He plonked himself down in one of Kate's lawn chairs, a trident resting on his lap.

He breathed in the constellations. His mind wandered back to Shakespeare, Cervantes, and Aeschylus. So, the two dead European guys with beards are sitting in a bar in Madrid. A third dead guy, with a grey beard and toga, walks in.

The first one says, "Hey, old man, you're a week early."

The second one says, "Toga party isn't until next week. Who are you?"

And the third one answers, "I'm the greatest writer who ever lived."

The first two share a look and laugh.

The first one asks, "So what did you write?"

The third one says, "I invented the Furies."

And the second one asks, "You mean the Greek Furies?"

The third one says, "Yup."

The first two share another look.

The first one says, "I gotta see a man about a mule."

And the second one says, "I think my carriage is double-parked."

BAH-BUMP-BAH.

The weed slowly blurred his consciousness.

He began to sing quietly the opening lyrics to "Bobcaygeon." The Hip was his favourite band. Bobcaygeon was only twenty minutes south of Kinmount.

"It was in Kinmount, I saw the constellations,
reveal themselves, one star at a time."

Never would have worked. What would Gord Downie have done in Dave's situation? Written a protest song?

"So, I went to Lola's house at midnight,
and cherubs cried 'til dawn,
Lightning flashes mourned the fireflies,
the Burnt River's soul was gone."

The nine stars of Leo the Lion began to whirl clockwise, then counter-clockwise, changing positions, and transforming into letters, spelling out K-A-T-E Q-U-I-N-N. In front of Dave, a nostalgic band shell appeared. Jars of fireflies served as patio lanterns. And there stood Kate swaying to the music of the Hip. She was radiant in a 1940s strapless summer white party dress. Dave rose from his lawn chair. He walked up the steps of the band shell into Kate's waiting arms. She smelled of lilacs and sandalwood. They began to slow dance. It was a private concert for two. Dave gently pulled back her hair to kiss his Kate when—

Gasp!

She morphed into Lola—only her body had become a giant cockroach with wings, her hair a nest of writhing snakes, dressed in wellies and a faded sundress. Just as Dave was about to scream, the ghost screamed in his head:

"LIST!"

"What?" wheezed Dave in a daze, waking up.

"LIST!"

He turned and saw two headlights bearing down on the tent, coming at reckless speed.

"B.J.!" he screamed.

B.J. woke with a start.

"Get out!" Dave screamed again. He stumbled into the tent, grabbed B.J. hard and pulled him out of his dreams. They dove out of the tent landing hard on the ground next to the flap opening.

The headlights ploughed into the tent crushing the aluminium frame and sped off into the night. Shouts could be heard from partying boaters docked overnight at the marina.

"You okay?" panted Dave, checking himself for broken bones. He was still quasi-stoned.

"I think so," B.J. said, quasi-stoned as well.

They surveyed the damage. Kate's tent was flattened. The cooler crushed. Some of their belongings were floating in the river. Hay everywhere. Dave began to sneeze.

"You allergic?" asked B.J.

"Am now," said Dave. He waited for the sky to rain blood. "Any sign of the rest of the Furies?"

"Give it a minute," B.J. replied.

They listened for flapping wings and hissing snakes.

Nothing but silence—save for the classic rock tunes drifting over from the marina.

Suddenly, B.J. screamed:

"CHICKPEA!"

He searched desperately for his little friend.

"You guys okay?" said a boater, American from his accent, shining a flashlight on Dave.

"Barely," said Dave, trying to get his bearings. "Did you see anything?"

"Looked like a large pickup. By the size of her I'd say a Ram. Driver had to have been drunk and lost control. Real erratic. Must have been doing seventy at least. A wonder they didn't end up in the river."

"If only," Dave wished.

Lola the Fury wasn't finished.

PART THREE: METHOD

"Though this be madness, yet there is method in't."

William Shakespeare, *Hamlet*

ONE

Dawn and the early morning mist cast an eerie light over the wreckage.

The mangled tent frame remnants resembled the aftermath of a suicide bomber attack. Tattered pieces of canvas flapped in the breeze. Battered bales of hay and loose straw littered the ground. The Styrofoam cooler was crushed beyond recognition, its contents mashed into the dirt. An exploded ketchup bottle bled over the straw. The hibachi had landed in the River, its grill barely visible above the muck. Clothing was strewn about; it was as if a family of campers had been vaporized. Pages of script were scattered everywhere.

The remnants of Chickpea were spread out like hummus. It was a pita-ful sight.

Noisy geese and scavenging crows were arriving to peck out a breakfast.

Officer John and Officer Frank were trying to salvage a tire print.

Dave and B.J. sat on the picnic table under the elm tree. They had draped what was left of B.J.'s sleeping bag over their shoulders.

Neither spoke.

The weed had worn off. Dave was quietly going into shock. He shivered under the heat of the rising sun.

The theatre had always been for Dave about the rekindling of the soul and discovering what made the world human.

What could possibly make Lola human?

Theatre was the touchstone of his humanity. This morning

that touchstone felt crushed and broken. The pantheon of his beliefs had collapsed. The pyramids of his faith shattered. The statues of his heroes defaced.

Theatre was supposed to make him feel less alone. Yet, Dave never felt more alone in his life.

Off in the distance came the familiar sound of a pickup pulling a horse trailer. The sound of barking border collies eager to start their day filled the air.

Tybalt came to a stop. He hopped out and opened the passenger door. Wayne and Shuster raced to the disaster site. The angry crows flew up to the overhead branches of the elm tree and rained down a string of curses on the dogs. The geese retreated to the seniors home.

Tybalt carried a tray of Tim Horton's coffees for the three of them, a morning arrival ritual now firmly in place: Dave, a "double double"; B.J., no sugar; and a decaf with milk for himself. He stopped walking towards them when he saw the carnage.

"Oh boy. You okay?"

B.J. nodded glumly.

"Lola?" Tybalt asked.

B.J. nodded again.

"You sure?" asked Tybalt.

B.J. shrugged his shoulders.

"Any witnesses?"

"A boater over in the marina saw a black pickup," said B.J.

Tybalt looked down at Dave. He was pale and clammy. His eyes were staring at the river but not seeing.

"How are you doing?" Tybalt asked with concern.

Dave looked away. His shoulders were still shaking under the sleeping bag.

Tybalt turned back to B.J. who shook his head sadly. "Chickpea is dead," he said. A piece of stuffing fell from his grieving fingers.

"I can't do it," Dave suddenly blurted out, unable to look at them. "It's all too much. She's won. You can't argue with insanity. She kicks us out of her house, Robert has a heart attack, and she tries to get me arrested. Then she slanders my name all over town. I'm sure the whole Canadian theatre community knows by now. She destroys my bike. Miranda will be in therapy for years. I promised her father I'd look after her. I gave him my word. Look how well that's worked out. Kate's tent and walkie-talkie are destroyed, your hibachi—"

"And Chickpea," choked B.J.

"And Chickpea," reiterated Dave bitterly. "We have no money. We have no costumes. We have no posters. B.J. and I have no place to stay. And, now, we have no Benvolio. And we open in one week. Even Don Quixote couldn't beat those odds. I'll let the company know this morning. Then drive B.J. and Miranda home. I'm sorry, guys, for what I've gotten you into. And worst of all, she's killed my love of theatre. She's murdered it in the first degree. No one will hire me now. To the world, I'm an evil misogynist corrupting the morals of children. You got a shotgun in that pickup of yours. Take me out behind the mill and put me out of my misery, will you? You'd be doing me a favour."

"Go easy on yourself, man. This is not your fault. No one could have predicted this mess," said B.J., looking to Tybalt for backup.

"I have a solution," said Tybalt.

Dave lurched off the picnic table and grabbed Tybalt by the shoulders.

"There is no fucking solution!" he screamed. "While I appreciate your irritating positivity even you can't turn water into wine. If you could, I'd drink a barrelful right now. And walking on the Burnt River doesn't count. It's so polluted even your barbecue won't sink. So, thank you for your *solution*, but face facts, there is no show!"

Dave's head was throbbing. The site began to spin. His knees buckled and down he went.

B.J. and Tybalt leapt to his aid, picking him up and sitting him down on the picnic table.

"Put your head between your knees and breath," instructed B.J. "Long deep breaths to the count of ten."

Dave slowly began to inhale and exhale.

"There is a solution," Tybalt said gently. "When you are able to listen to reason, I will tell you. It's all going to be okay."

Tybalt's soothing manner could convince world leaders to come to an agreement that morning—championing bicycles and making cars extinct, stopping global warming and oil wars, ending racism and gender inequality, and bringing about the return of drive-in movies.

Dave sat up, rubbing his temples. Wayne and Shuster were lying at his feet. He gave them each an ear scratch before speaking. "I owe you both an apology for the 'Dr. Director and Mr. Hyde' routine. But, seriously, I am done."

"No worries," said Tybalt, reaching into his jeans' pocket. "Here, take this."

He handed Dave an unmarked business envelope. It was stuffed to the point of bursting its seal.

"What's this?"

"Open it," Tybalt instructed.

Dave tore open the envelope. A wad of twenty-dollar bills spilled out.

Dave stopped.

"Three thousand dollars," said Tybalt. "That should cover our show costs. Costumes, posters, whatever we need. Rent a motel room for you and B.J. for the week."

"Where did this come from?" asked B.J.

"It's my savings," said Tybalt.

"I can't accept this," said Dave. "I feel awful enough as it is."

"It's a loan," said Tybalt. "I believe in this show. It's important for the community. I have faith I will make it all back at the gate. And your fees too."

"And if we don't?" asked Dave.

"Call it an investment in arts education. Now, let's do the show the way you want to," Tybalt grinned, putting out his hand in a gesture of old-school solidarity.

Dave gripped Tybalt's outstretched hand and squeezed. Then hugged the stuffing out of him.

"I don't know what to say."

"You don't have to say a thing. I'm glad I can help," said Tybalt. "Just one request."

"Anything," said Dave.

"I want you to speak at our family's church service Sunday morning about the transformative power of theatre. Okay?"

"Yes, of course," mumbled Dave, still in a daze.

"Good. Now what's the plan?" asked Tybalt.

And, just like that, Dave's old director-self returned. Almost like riding a bike, if he still had one.

"I'm going to arrange on-site security, and find B.J. and myself a place to stay. Then visit Robert to discuss a replacement Benvolio. I have a hunch he'll have an idea. You two meet with the troupe, run lines, and review the fights until I get back. Take everyone's measurements. I'll be up bright and early tomorrow to go and rent some costumes."

"I'm going to see how my brother's making out. Carpe diem, boys!" Tybalt slapped Dave and B.J.'s backs and walked over to the accident site.

"What a guy. Can you believe that?" said Dave, sipping his coffee.

"Providence comes in mysterious forms," observed B.J., sipping his coffee. "Just don't lose the cash."

"Roger that," said Dave. "I'll deposit it as soon as the bank opens."

He started for the marina parking lot, stopped, and turned back.

"And, B.J...I'm sorry about Chickpea."

"Me too," said B.J. with a sniffle. "He was a great little parrot."

"That he was," said Dave, reflecting on his own abandonment issues. Bark Twain had helped keep him safe as a boy. Chickpea had served a similar function for B.J.

"Now, get going before one of Lola's Valkyries jumps you," B.J. said, holding back his pain.

Dave left B.J. gathering up the stuffing remains of his friend.

TWO

The Ram pickup was nowhere in sight.

Shutters covered the windows.

Lola had barricaded the front of her house for whatever storm she was brewing. Dave drove by slowly, hunched down over his steering wheel to avoid detection. His muffler rattled and choked up blue exhaust. He parked on a side street, a few houses down, behind a large camper van.

He quickly made his way down the side street and slunk onto Maple Avenue.

The small non-descript bungalow, two doors down from Lola's, was neat and compact. Grey fieldstone framed with black soffits and eaves troughs gave the appearance of a Victorian cottage. A tiny, perfect front lawn unrolled to meet the house like a putting green. The smell of freshly cut grass. Like gasoline, cut grass was one of those odd, pungent smells that calmed Dave, probably because it was linked to warm weather and his only happy childhood memory—summer camp away from his stepfather. A sign erected next to the driveway read "IF YOU ATE TODAY, THANK A FARMER. IF YOU ATE IN PEACE TODAY, THANK A VET."

Dave noticed a large rosemary bush growing in a bountiful garden in front of an enclosed porch. Scarlet snapdragons, perennial beds of roses, and daisies splashed the house with inviting colour.

"Too bad that bush wasn't planted in Lola's backyard," he said aloud to a garden gnome perched beside the porch steps. He thought of the Scottish play. The allied soldiers each cut a branch off a tree to hold in front of them while they marched towards Macbeth's castle in hopes that he would somehow think they were trees and not an army. It was the stuff of Monty Python. Yet, somehow, it worked. Maybe he and his team should have disguised themselves with rosemary branches when rescuing their bikes. "Just how would the power of rosemary stack up against an insane bunch of Furies?" he wondered.

Above the porch, a Canadian flag waved proudly. A silver Ford pickup was parked under a makeshift, portable garage shelter.

A peeling bumper sticker greeted Dave: "Heroes don't wear capes. Heroes wear DOG TAGS."

Dave knocked on the front door.

The boy answered.

"Hi," said Dave. "I'm Dave, from last night."

"I'm Johnny. I'll get my dad," the boy said, opening the door wider for Dave to enter. "Please take off your sandals."

The hall vestibule was orderly—only a doormat, boot rack, and three jacket hooks.

"You had breakfast yet?" came the Sergeant's voice from the back of the house.

"No, sir," said Dave. "But don't go to any trouble. I can come back later."

"Come, join us," shouted the Sergeant.

Dave removed his sandals and followed the smell of bacon and the sound of the Sergeant's rich baritone voice. He passed a masculine-looking living room. Framed paintings of World War II aircraft, geometrically arranged on the walls. Beneath a Spitfire oil painting that Dave knew was famous, a dark leather couch and trunk that served as a coffee table. A leather armchair and ottoman in one corner, and a floor-to-ceiling bookshelf stocked with hardcover military fiction.

He entered the kitchen. It reminded him of Kevin Costner's yellow-wallpapered domestic sanctuary in *The Untouchables*. A contrast to the living room: fresh flowers on the Formica table, family photos on the fridge, spotless appliances and counters, clean, organized, and ready for use.

The Sergeant was sitting at the head of the table. He was dressed casually in cargo shorts and a khaki t-shirt. Its slogan read, "Only you can prevent friendly fire."

"Catchy," said Dave.

The Sergeant's wife, a robust, attractive woman with bright hazel eyes and a welcoming demeanour, was serving up breakfast.

"Pull up a chair for our guest, son," the Sergeant commanded without a trace of the gruffness Dave expected. He was a role model for sure. And clearly a man who looked after his platoon and brought them home alive.

Johnny fetched a chair from beside the wall telephone (the Sergeant still had one, long yellow cord and all) and placed it at the table.

"Sit down, Dave," he gestured. Dave was sure the Sergeant protected the entire neighbourhood.

"Thank you, sir." Dave did as he was instructed.

"I told you not to call me that." The Sergeant corrected him. "I'm no officer. What's the most dangerous thing in the military?"

"What?" Dave said.

"An officer with a map and compass."

Dave laughed politely.

The boy joined the conversation: "My dad says being in the army is like being in my Wolf Cub pack, except that the Wolf Cubs have adult supervision."

Dave smiled at the boy.

"This is my wife Marjorie," the Sergeant said proudly.

"Pleased to meet you," she said, serving Dave a plate of hash browns with onions, crisp bacon, scrambled eggs, and buttered toast.

Dave was waiting for the Beaver and Wally to join them.

"Dig in," said the Sergeant once his wife had sat down.

The foursome's cutlery clinked and clanked.

Between mouthfuls, the Sergeant asked Dave, "So, you want

me and Johnny to do security for this play of yours?"

"Ah, yes, please," mumbled Dave, his mouth full of eggs.

"Finish your eggs," instructed the Sergeant, licking his fingers.

"We don't talk with our mouths full," volunteered Johnny. "It's impolite." The boy was a model soldier.

"Lola is a serious problem," said Dave, wiping his mouth with a paper towel.

"So I gather," said the Sergeant. "She *is* a nuisance."

"That woman can chew nails and spit rust," Marjorie said, refilling her husband's and Dave's coffees. "Nutty as my Christmas fruitcake. She spray-painted graffiti on our neighbour's garage door. And she's getting worse. Shooting out Johnny's tire. Can you imagine?"

"I've seen more combat since I got home," laughed the Sergeant. "But I think I set her straight last night."

"Afraid to say she's gotten worse," said Dave. "She tried to run B.J. and me over in the middle of the night."

"On the street?" asked the Sergeant.

"No, in our tent. We're camped by the old sawmill," said Dave.

"You sure it was her?"

"Pretty sure. Lucky I was awake. Police are investigating," said Dave, accidentally catching a whiff of himself. He wondered if the Sergeant could also smell B.J.'s stale pot from the night before.

"I hope they arrest that crazy woman," said Marjorie.

"And, until then, I was hoping you could guard our rehearsal site overnight," Dave explained.

"Can we, Dad?" Johnny pleaded.

"One second, son. For how long?" the Sergeant asked.

"One week," said Dave. "I can pay you an honorarium."

"That won't be necessary," said the Sergeant. "I'd like to see her try and run over *my* tent. She won't know what hit her. You've got your security. Johnny and I will set up our base camp after supper."

"Thank you, Sergeant. You don't know what that means to us," Dave said, greatly relieved.

"Call me Sarge," grinned the Sergeant, patting his well-fed stomach.

"Sarge," Dave repeated.

Johnny was beaming at the prospect of his father-and-son adventure.

"Can I wear my Wolf Cub uniform?" he asked his father.

"Yes son. Marjorie, you think you can prepare some rations for us."

"A banana loaf, perhaps," she smiled, knowing her husband's weakness.

"Ten four," the Sarge winked, leaning over and kissing her cheek.

"Thank you for breakfast, Mrs. Ryan," said Dave.

"Our pleasure," she said. "Let me put together a care package for you and B.J. You like roast turkey sandwiches?"

"Yes, ma'am," Dave said.

"Where are you boys staying now?" asked the Sarge.

"I'm going to book us into a motel," Dave replied.

The Sarge and his wife shared a look.

"Check into the Twin Pines Motel. A few miles south on the County Road. My brother Reilly runs it. I'll give him a ring now. Get you a discounted rate," the Sarge said, getting up from the table.

"You are too kind, Sarge," said Dave. "I really appreciate it."

"My brother had hopes of being an actor once. But it wasn't in the cards. I know how tough that livelihood is. It takes guts. Now, you put on this Shakespeare of yours and make us proud," said the Sarge.

"I will, Sarge." Dave found himself saluting.

The Sarge playfully saluted back.

Dave walked quickly to the Tercel. A picnic hamper of turkey sandwiches and banana bread in hand. No slashed tires.

Things were looking up.

THREE

The three thousand dollars safely deposited in his bank account, Dave stepped off the elevator onto the cardiac ward.

Capulet was sitting up in bed, reading Louise Penny's latest Inspector Gamache mystery when Dave knocked on the open door.

"Enter," said Capulet breezily. He was in good spirits and looking much better. His colour had returned.

"Hey, old sport," said Dave. "How are you feeling?"

"Much better, David. A day or two at most. Doctors are trying to figure out the right dosage of blood pressure medication," Capulet smiled.

"That's great news," said Dave, sitting down in the guest chair.

"What's the news from the court?" asked Capulet.

"Invasion. The Lola Armada. Scandal. Spies. Courtier's gifts. Attempted assassination. Military defence tactics," said Dave.

"Oh, my. In only two days! Do share," said Capulet.

"Last night we attempted to free our bikes from Lola's backyard. We rescued B.J.'s and Miranda's, but mine was destroyed, its parts welded together into tridents by Lola and her cult."

"Tridents? Is she worshipping Neptune now?"

"God knows," said Dave. "But she was dressed as one of the Furies."

"Oh dear," sighed Capulet.

"Cursing me and wanting vengeance. A neighbour, G.I. Joe, put a stop to things just in time."

"Maybe there is some unpunished crime in Lola's past," Capulet ruminated. "Perhaps a wicked act of some sort was inflicted on her. She sought revenge and, sadly, still seeks it all these years later. No matter how misplaced that revenge may be. And you triggered it somehow."

"Or maybe she was just born psycho, one sandwich short of a picnic."

"No, there's more to it than that," said Capulet, tapping his food tray for emphasis. "There has to be. Hmmmm. Maybe there's something about the missing daughter. But just what it is, I don't know."

"She probably had sense enough to get out of town early when she realized her mother was nuts."

"You could be right. But maybe her mother wasn't the reason she left."

"If I grew up here, I'd want out of Kinmount." Dave looked out the window and noticed a group of children playing tag in a park across the street. They were innocent and carefree, oblivious to the vengeance of gods and community theatre producers. The gods purportedly made people do things in Greek tragedy. In reality, it was the subconscious minds of the characters.

"The subconscious was just referred to as 'gods,'" Professor Schlosser was fond of repeating. "The Greeks knew that somehow. Human problems needed human solutions. We had to figure things out, or we'd destroy ourselves," she had said during a tutorial. "And aren't we doing well? The Holocaust. Hiroshima. JFK. In movies, whenever the earth is attacked by aliens, or is threatened by an asteroid, humanity bands together as one to save the planet. In reality, we aren't even able to plant a bunch of trees."

Dave had no idea what the solution to Lola was.

"What about that park ranger?" he asked.

"Too recent," Capulet replied. "Whatever happened to Lola happened a long time ago."

"You've been reading too many Inspector Gamache mysteries. Now, here's something for you: Benvolia was serving as Lola's spy all along."

"What?"

"Can you believe it?"

"Oh dear."

"She's out. So, we need a new actor."

"Sadly, victims of abuse often turn to false prophets. Her lisp was nothing to laugh at," said Capulet.

"Tell that to the teenagers," sighed Dave. "It gets better. I have to defend my director's vision at a town council meeting tomorrow night. Last night, Lola tried to run B.J. and me down in our tent with her truck. We're lucky to be alive."

"Madness has surely taken over." Capulet shook his head sadly. "That is a serious offence. A charge of criminal negligence at the very least. Fourteen years maximum prison term. Maybe even attempted murder if the police can prove it was her and have evidence her actions were premeditated."

"They are investigating," said Dave. "Tybalt's brother, John."

"He's a good man: professional, humane, and not lacking in common sense. He's a stalwart presence in my courtroom," said Capulet. "His family are good people."

"You're telling me! Tybalt gave me three thousand dollars to save the show."

"Why, that is indeed fortuitous!" Capulet's eyes lit up at the news. "Your windmill is within reach, young knight." He studied Dave for a moment. "Kinmount is different, isn't it?"

"With an intellect rivalled only by a garden tool."

"Seriously," Capulet rumbled.

"Alright, alright, the members of the company are growing on me," Dave admitted.

"I sense that. So, I'd refer to him as Justin from now on in respect of his generosity. And maybe the others too," Capulet said.

"I'll think about it," said Dave. He felt miscast as Capulet's emissary of goodwill, like hiring the wrong Carradine brother for *Kung Fu*. "So, the Benvolio recasting issue, any ideas?"

"Have you asked any of your cast mates?" asked Robert.

"No. My instincts are to ask you."

"Good instincts," Robert laughed.

"Well?"

"You remember our earlier visionary conversation?"

"I think so."

"There's a young lad I know that lives in the village of Literal."

"Literal?"

"No word of a lie. His name is Ziggy, Ziggy Brewster. His family situation is, well, complicated. Only nineteen but I think he has got something. He was in my courtroom last month. He was charged with arson. It was clearly an accident. I gave him a suspended sentence and probation. He needs community service hours and a break," stated Robert.

"What happened?" asked Dave.

"I'll let him tell you that."

"You think he can handle Shakespeare?"

"Possibly," Robert said. "He's creative and has the makings of a good writer. I've read a few of his poems. He also makes his own no-budget small movies.

"How do I find him?" asked Dave.

Robert picked up the phone on his bedside table and dialled.

The phone on the other end of the line rang five times.

"Good morning, Monika! Is that you? Ah, Wyatt, sorry. It must be my connection. It's Robert Wyld calling ... yes, Judge Wyld. Is Ziggy about?"

He covered the receiver.

"His grandfather is going to get him," Robert whispered to Dave.

The phone crackled back to life. "How's it hangin', Judge?" said the voice on the other end.

"Know what I put in my rum and Cokes?" said Robert.

"Just ice," replied the voice, loud enough that Dave could hear the punch line.

"How goes your summer, Ziggy?" said Robert, "... oh, really? Yes, I'd love to read them." He covered the receiver. "His new poems." Dave nodded. Robert returned to Ziggy, "I have someone here that would like to talk to you. No, you're not in trouble."

Robert passed the phone to Dave.

"Ah, hi Ziggy, it's nice to meet you. My name is Dave Middleton ... ah, that's right ... the director guy ... Robert has told me all about you ... yes, all good," Dave said, catching Robert's eye. "Anyhow, I'm directing *Romeo and Juliet* here in Kinmount for their Summer in the Park Festival and ... oh, you read about it ... yes, it is all quite ridiculous ... false accusations ... I bet you do ... at any rate, the reason I'm calling is, I've lost one of my actors ... no, not literally, but it wouldn't surprise me ... Robert thought you might be interested in auditioning ... the part? Benvolio ... right, Romeo's cousin ... we open in a week ... so, what do you think? ... that's terrific ... in two hours? Great ... no, all good, Robert can give me directions ... okay, here he is."

Dave passed the phone back to Robert.

"Yes, you can trust David ... he knows his stuff ... I'm feeling much better, thanks. Doctors say I should be out in a day or two ... yes, I'd love to come down for a barbecue soon." Robert looked at Dave and shook his head, "no."

"I'll give David directions and he'll be there around noon ... hope it all works out."

Robert hung up the phone.

"All set," said Robert.

"So, what's the scoop, why no barbecue?" Dave was intrigued.

"Ziggy's father and grandfather are both taxidermists. You never know what might end up on their grill," laughed Robert.

"Roadkill recycling," Dave said, having no interest in grilled raccoon.

"Something like that. The old Brewster home is an hour's drive from here. Head south on the County Road, turn left on Circle Lake Road, and you'll come to the village of Literal. Ziggy's is the seventh mailbox on your right. You can't miss it."

"Righto, well, I better get going," said Dave. "I have to find a clean copy of the script. Mine's at the bottom of the river."

"Here," said Robert, reaching under his pillow. "Take mine. I've been reading it between mystery chapters. Phantom limb of sorts," he said, handing Dave his script.

"Robert not only chases windmills but repairs them as well," Dave thought to himself as the elevator door closed. "But windmills need wind."

A patient from a different wing stood beside him. Dave stared at his sandals to avoid conversation.

"We are reminded to be careful when the wind blows," said the patient.

The words were Backwoods Bart's from his CBC shadfly radio interview. Had the patient listened to the same interview? Or was he delusional.

"A shadfly ate my sister," the patient said.

It was the latter. The elevator door opened and Dave escaped.

The heat was stifling as he unlocked the Tercel. Not even a breeze.

FOUR

Dave's cell phone lit up like an air traffic control tower on 9/11.

Five miles outside the Kinmount town limits the dead zone ended.

He pulled over and parked on the gravel shoulder. He checked his voicemail. There were messages from his mother, the Town of Birch Lake, and journalists hungry for a story.

He'd call his mother back later.

The Twin Pines Motel was built on the outskirts of Kinmount in the 1950s. Not much had changed about its homogenized appearance. It was a standard, single-storey motor hotel consisting of a single L-shaped building of connected rooms, whose doors faced a common parking lot. A brightly painted fluorescent Adirondack chair sat outside each room, facing the road. The Twin Pines featured an eye-catching colourful neon sign, still in use. Two pine trees and a black bear advertised "air conditioning." The sign was cracked and broken in the corners, the black bear missing his right hind leg, and, a few of the neon tubes burnt out, so, the sign now read: "Tin Pins Motel" and "a condition."

A decommissioned rail car served as the Red Caboose Diner; poutine its specialty. The in-ground swimming pool had seen its last poolside martini years ago. The manager's office was attached to the rooms and included a small reception area.

Dave opened the office door, a screen door affair slipping off its hinges, triggering a tired pump organ recording of the first two bars of Johnny Cash's *Ring of Fire* that in turn signalled Dave's bemused arrival.

"Hi. Reilly?" inquired Dave, from the doorway.

"That's my name, don't wear it out," said a man with his back to him, fussing with an old Seabreeze record player in the corner of the reception area. Dave thought of Kate's roof. The needle scratched through two rotations, and Glen Campbell's "Gentle on my Mind" began to play.

The man turned around from his music duties.

"Well, good morning, stranger," he said, adjusting his comb-over. "Wait, no, are you Dave?"

The Sarge's brother, Reilly, was a short, bespectacled, bald-ing man. He reminded Dave of Wally Cox—the reedy voice of *Underdog*, the animated 1960s super-hero parody cartoon—a character Dave understood all too well.

"Your brother, the Sarge, sent me," replied Dave.

"Yupper. I knew you weren't no stranger. You got some-thing theatrical about you. Yup, there's a man who works in the thee-ate-er I says to myself. And I knew the voice 'cause I heard it before."

It was as if Reilly had stepped off the set of *Hee Haw*.

"And a stranger's only a stranger until the other fella says 'good morning' back," Reilly said quickly.

Dave took his cue.

"Good morning," he said. Just how long had Reilly been living on his own?

"Good morning, my no-longer-stranger-new-friend. That's what Glen Campbell says in all his music."

"I know I've always appreciated a back door being left open for me," Dave joked.

"Oh, that's rich. Back door being left open for ya. Yup, Glen could sing it all," said Reilly, humming the chorus, now playing.

"So, Reilly, your brother mentioned that you might have a room I could rent for the next week," said Dave, redirecting the conversation.

"Yup. What you need?" said Reilly, pulling out his reserva-tions binder.

"Two single beds would be great," said Dave, trying to

decipher Reilly's upside down chicken scratch.

"Yup, I got something for you, my new thee-ate-er friend. Room Fifteen. Two singles. Air conditioning. Colour TV. Wi-Fi. Whole nine yards," fired off Reilly in rapid succession. "You can even reach Galveston."

Reilly found himself particularly funny.

"You want to see it?" he asked.

"I'm good," said Dave. "How much?"

"For you, no cost, my thee-ate-er friend," said Reilly.

"LIST!"

The ghost was back.

"LIST!"

Dave's head was instantly pounding.

"Alright, alright, I hear you, you battlement banshee," he snapped.

"Battle-ment what?" asked Reilly offended. "Now, if you're going to be rude about it, I can just as easily—"

"No, Reilly. Sorry not you," said Dave, glaring at the ceiling.

"You got Tourniquet's Syndrome?" asked Reilly.

"Something like that," said Dave. "Yes, I'd like the room but I have to pay you. I appreciate your generosity but a free room is bad luck for me."

"There's no such thing as a free lunch." He remembered his mother's words from childhood. "If it's too good to be true, it is."

"Alright," said Reilly. "A toonie a night. Each. Since you want me to charge you somethin.'"

Dave thought about Reilly's offer.

He would still be paying rent, wouldn't he?

The ghost remained silent.

"Deal," said Dave.

Reilly jotted down the reservation.

"And I'll throw in a free front-row seat cushion for any performance you like," Dave added.

"Closing night," said Reilly, closing the binder. "I like to go on closing nights. By that time, you guys have all the bugs worked out."

"Done," said Dave with a thumbs-up.

The opening violin swell of "Wichita Lineman" played as he shut the office door.

ॠ

"Hi, Mom, how are you?" Dave said in the motel parking lot, his iPhone set on speaker.

"You're alive. Not that I would know."

"It's nice to hear your voice too."

"I've left you twelve messages since yesterday." Her voice was shriller than usual.

"I'm sorry. But I don't have cell reception."

"Nice try. You just don't want to talk to your seventy-five-year-old mother."

"Stop it."

"I can cancel your car insurance."

"I'm kind of busy right now. What do you want?"

"What do you think I want?"

"I don't know."

"Yesterday morning I'm having my breakfast, and the paper arrives. I'm turning to the crossword on page twelve, and what do you think I see?"

"Your obituary."

She ignored him. "I'm turning to the crossword and I come across a headline. And what do you suppose the headline reads? Take a wild guess."

Oh boy.

"I can explain," said Dave.

"'Director's immorality blamed for cancelled Shakespeare production.'"

"It's all a misunderstanding."

"And it's my son's name in print. My son is a vulgar abuser of women and children. Well, isn't that a lovely thing for a mother to read on a summer morning. And then the neighbours start calling."

"It reads worse than it is. I'm none of those things, and you know it. The producer didn't understand the play and wanted me to make cuts that I couldn't, and wouldn't, do."

"It's you and your high-and-mighty Shakespeare again. Do you want to end up in prison?"

"No one's going to prison."

"You have asthma."

"I've got to go. I'm dealing with a recasting issue."

"Why don't you put on plays people actually want to see?"

"Mom!"

"And, for God's sake, please tell me you're not messing around with some local yokel."

"I'm not."

"I know what happens when you get stressed. Your common sense goes out the window."

"Mom, please."

"Don't let your cheese slide off the cracker."

"I have to go."

He hung up and turned off his phone. His mother would make an excellent Fury. She'd read the article. "Great," he said to the Shakespeare bobble-head doll glued to the top of his dashboard. He pulled out of the motel parking lot. "That's just great." The bobble-head nodded. "Oh shut up."

He turned on the car radio and adjusted the tuning dial. The twanging sound of a slide guitar, a country fiddle, worn brushes on a ride cymbal, and a slow tenor-singing drawl assaulted his ears. The song ended and there was an awkward pause. A voice crackled to life.

"And that was Lloyd Snow. No relation to Hank, but he's still pretty good. I'm yer host Too Tall Tim and thanks for travellin' with me down the backroads here on Kinmount Heritage Radio."

Too Tall Tim sounded about eighty-five. Dave pictured

him in horn-rimmed glasses, a straw Stetson, white shirt, and western tie hunched over a microphone with a mess of corny old jokes scrawled on his wife's recipe cards.

Tim continued: "Hey, why did the summer schoolteacher wear sunglasses?"

"Why?" Dave asked his seven-inch Shakespeare.

"Because her class was so bright."

No danger of that happening in Kinmount, Dave thought.

Tim guffawed himself into a coughing spasm. "We're broadcasting live from the truck stop so come on down 'cause I'm givin' away fly swatters and bingo dabbers. Courtesy of Bill's Butcher Block. Meat so fresh you'll wanna slap it."

Dave sighed. A sigh loud enough to get him inducted into the Hall of Sighs.

"It's another thighs-sticking-to-plastic-chairs-day, folks," announced Tim. He rang a triangle. "And it's Lola Whale's birthday!"

Dave turned up the volume.

"Sixty-five and still alive," said Tim. "Today's birthday wish comes from Flo down at the Laundry-Copy."

"Flo?!" exclaimed Dave.

"You can find Flo in Kinmount's yellow pages."

"Page," said Dave dourly.

"Now, we got a big council meeting happenin' tomorrow night," Tim continued, "about whether that out-of-town director fella has been tamperin' with ol' Shakespeare. Lola says he's added cuss words and the like. 'To be or gosh darn be.' Yup, that's what our birthday girl says. And she'll probably be there too."

"What the—?"

There was a moment of radio silence followed by the scratching sound of a needle skipping. Dave turned the radio off and turned left onto Circle Lake Road.

Twenty minutes later, he came upon the village of Literal. Population: 325. A blink and you've missed it village. The welcome sign read "WHERE EVERYBODY IS A SOMEBODY."

He drove slowly past an old barn selling antiques. A battered and faded sign on the driveway said: DEAD PEOPLE'S STUFF.

"Tradition is just peer pressure from dead people," Professor Schlosser told his first-year class. Consequently, Dave refused to buy antiques.

He noticed a tow truck parked in front of a supermarket. "Bob's Collision" painted on the side. Across the street was the volunteer fire department. Dave had images of Bob colliding into parked cars on purpose and volunteers lighting houses and barns on fire.

Could one be too literal in Literal?

FIVE

The Brewster's front yard resembled a stuffed petting zoo. Taxidermied sheep, llamas, pigs, and chickens were carefully mounted and posed as if grazing naturally. Dave half expected the pig to snort like King George and roll over in hopes of a tummy scratch. The silence was creepy.

The Brewster front porch was a veritable cornucopia of Canadian wildlife—a black bear standing on its hind legs with a dinner triangle suspended from a raised paw, a pair of bobcats perched on two rusty lawn chairs, and a moose head mounted beside the front door.

To the right of the porch was a large garage with a sign above the loading doors, boldly announcing the family taxidermy business: WE STUFF YOUR STUFF.

Dave rang the front door bell and was greeted by the sound of an electronic wolf howl.

The door opened and there stood a tall, young man with narrow, stooped shoulders, jet-black hair, and large, protruding ears. He was a human owl of sorts—with a large, flattened, disk-like face, eyes close together and facing forward, giving them the appearance of binoculars.

"C'mon in," he said quietly. "I'm Ziggy." His eyes were dark with a sadness that filled his pupils.

"What was Robert talking about?" Dave said to himself. "This guy looks like a Tim Burton version of Boo Radley."

Dave gingerly crossed the threshold. He noticed the rest of the moose was standing in the living room facing the veranda wall, its headless neck pressed firmly against the faded wallpaper. Even more disturbing was the gathering of stuffed family pets staring out the living room window in manipulated poses of patient waiting—four cats, a beagle, two labs, three hamsters, and a ferret.

"Grab a seat," said Ziggy, beckoning to a wingback chair facing a fieldstone fireplace.

Were a stuffed Rusty and Jerome lurking somewhere? Dave took a seat in direct view of a one-eyed elk head mounted above the fireplace. It looked like the victim of a wildlife mafia hit.

Just as Ziggy was sitting down on the sofa, a tiny old woman burst into the room, wiping her hands.

"You must be that director fellow," she gushed. "I'm Monika, Ziggy's grandmother. Can I get you a bite to eat?" Her apron was covered in the stains of species Dave could not hazard a guess at as to their origin.

He looked to Ziggy who silently shook his head "no."

"Thanks but no," said Dave. "I've eaten." His growling stomach begged to differ. The Sarge's breakfast had been hours ago.

"I have a batch of moose medallions just out of the oven," she said, taking relish in her dish.

"Moose medallions?" Dave asked uneasily.

"Testicles," said Ziggy.

"I'll pass," said Dave politely. He glanced at the decapitated moose, whose balls were definitely missing.

"How about some stew? Just take me a minute to heat it up." Ziggy's grandmother didn't take no for an answer.

"I'm just fine," said Dave as his stomach let out a blaring, tuba-like groan.

"Doesn't sound like you're fine to me," she said. "Be right back." She left the room before he could protest.

"I tried," Ziggy sighed. It was a long-suffering sigh. Oscar-worthy. "Why do you think I'm a vegetarian?"

Dave looked up at a snowy owl perched over the hallway entrance. Its marble-eyed glare gave him the willies. A man appeared in the entrance. He too was tall and stoop-shouldered, with dark sunken eyes but sporting a striking shock of grey hair, what Ziggy would look like in thirty years.

Ziggy's father carried something in a cloth grocery bag.

"Hope I'm not interruptin' anythin', son, but you gotta take a look at this," he said, easing a furry object out of the bag.

Dave stared in disbelief at the creature cradled in Ziggy's father's arms. It was the macabre artistry of a rogue taxidermist, hearkening back to the lows of a P.T. Barnum sideshow. Weird was an understatement.

It was a duck-billed beaver.

"Ain't she a beauty," Ziggy's father rhapsodized. "Better than anythin' ol' Captain Hunter ever discovered."

"Who?" asked Dave with a confused look to Ziggy.

"At the end of the eighteenth century, there was a guy named Captain John Hunter, and he was exploring Australia. He sent a duck-billed platypus pelt, along with a sketch of the animal, back to England," explained Ziggy.

"To a bunch of British scientists, who thought it was a hoax," continued Ziggy's father. "One of them figured that since the platypus had come by way of the Indian Ocean, the platypus was likely the invention of some Chinese taxidermist who had sewn a duck's bill onto a furry mammal's body. They took a pair of scissors to the pelt, huntin' in vain for stitches. None were found. And the platypus became a reality."

"My father thinks he can fool David Suzuki," said Ziggy.

"You betcha. Take a close look at that bill," said his father, shoving the stuffed beaver hybrid under Dave's nose. "Not a stitch in sight. Mr. Suzuki won't know what bit him."

An older version of Ziggy's father appeared in the entrance. He was dressed in denim overalls and held a bowl of stew in his left hand.

"Bandit stew for our guest," announced Ziggy's grandfather. He placed the steaming bowl on the coffee table. Dave felt nauseous.

"I was readin' about you in the paper. Got in a ruckus with Lola, did ya?" he asked.

"You could say that," Dave replied carefully, wanting to

change the subject.

"She's cuckoo," warned Ziggy's grandfather.

"You know her?" asked Dave.

"Ever been in her basement?"

"Yes."

"What did you see?"

The discovery hit Dave.

"YOU?" he said incredulously.

"That's right. I stuffed every one of those heads. It took me years. Taxidermy is serious business. You have to pay careful attention to make the dead animal look like it did in life. Now, I'm old school. I examine livin' animals in the field, studyin' the cranin' of a neck, the extension of a wing, the movement of a muscle between fur and skin. The new generation of taxidermists do it all with a computer. No artistry in that if you ask me."

Was there actually such a thing as a new generation of taxidermists?

"Did she really hunt with a crossbow?" Dave asked.

"Oh, yeah," affirmed old Mr. Brewster. "Lola would disappear every autumn for two months and come back with a new batch of heads for me to stuff and mount."

"Ever do any husbands?" Dave joked drily.

"Let's just say I wouldn't want to be the one digging up her basement."

"Did you know her daughter?"

"You better eat that stew before it gets cold," Ziggy's grandfather replied with an almost imperceptible hardness in his voice.

"Did Lola's daughter—" a screaming child running in the hallway interrupted him.

"ZIGGY! ZIGGY! ZIGGY!"

A twelve-year-old boy crashed through the entrance. He was a younger version of Ziggy.

"Stop yer shouting. What's all the commotion about, Garnett?" said the boy's father.

"I gotta speak to Ziggy," panted the panicked boy. "It's important."

"Alright, alright, son. Just don't get your paws in a trap."

"Yes, sir," gulped Garnett.

"C'mon, Pa, I'll show you the new owl-wolverine hybrid. How the feathers mask the neckline."

The two elder Brewsters left the room.

"Ziggy, I need your help," said Garnett oblivious to Dave's presence.

"What now?" Ziggy sighed again.

"Oh, Ziggy ...," stammered Garnett.

"What now?" Ziggy demanded. His impatience with his brother was clear.

"Um-hmm," his younger brother paused, stared at Dave, and then decided to continue. He broke down sobbing: "Oh, Ziggy, I killed him!

"Slow down, Garnett," said Ziggy. "Killed who?"

"Skipper!" wailed Garnett. He collapsed on the floor. "It was an accident! If Uncle Harvey finds out I poisoned Skipper, they'll have to drag the river to find my body."

"How come you poisoned Uncle Harvey's bird dog?" asked Ziggy, trying to make sense of events.

"Oh, don't say that, Ziggy. I didn't poison him. It was an accident. I was after an egg-suckin' raccoon, and Skipper just came up and snatched the poison pill."

"You know, when Uncle Harvey finds out you poisoned a five-thousand-dollar dog, he's going to have *you* stuffed," said Ziggy.

"Oh, Ziggy, he'll scream like a banshee! Quick, drag the dog out on the road! We'll run it over!"

"No, Garnett." Ziggy was firm. "I'm on probation. I can't get involved in your dog-poisoning cover-up schemes."

"All we gotta do is drag Skipper out in the road. We'll run him over with dad's Pontiac. We'll tell Uncle Harvey he got hit by a car."

"No, Garnett. Now, go over to Uncle Harvey's and explain

it was an accident. Promise to buy him a new dog," Ziggy instructed firmly.

"That'll take all my allowance for the rest of my life. I'm better off taking one of my strychnine pills."

"And no more strychnine in the house," added Ziggy sternly.

"Then there better be no more matches in the house," Garnett fired back nastily with a deliberate look at Dave. "He's an arsonist, you know."

"Get out," ordered Ziggy.

"Fire-starter."

"Now!"

"Yeah, yeah, yeah. Thanks for nothing."

The boy sulked out of the room.

"I'm so sorry about that," Ziggy apologized awkwardly. He was clearly embarrassed. "Family of oddballs."

Pets in the Brewster neighbourhood had gone missing for years.

"Is there someplace quiet we can go?" Dave asked warily, wondering why Ziggy's grandfather refused to talk about Lola's daughter. He slid the stew aside and searched the living room for an emergency exit.

SIX

Dave sat around a fire pit in the Brewster back yard surrounded by a pack of stuffed timber wolves. Ziggy was standing by the leader of the pack. He turned to face Dave and stared at him in silence. Then he slowly widened his eyes, pressed his arms tightly to his sides, and began to recite in a deep resonant voice:

"I am an orphaned taxidermied night owl,
I'm still on the wood block, ankles cuffed,
hunched, one glass eye eyeing you.

"My carcass is wood and wool but
this is my real skull—
I stand on my true legs,
wings arched, head cocked,
already in my glass box,

"I am bound to the taxidermist.

"I know his grunts, cinching up
My taut belly—oh, the buzz of a bone saw,
the click of ear openers and the
automatic awl.

"Who better understands
a gooseneck hide stretcher
and fleshing blades and fish skinning shears
and bone cutter forceps than I do?

"But he will never know what it is to be me.
(Oh jealous stitching!)
He'll never know how the wings shiver
just before they beat."

Dave was still absorbing Ziggy's audition poem. He was a weird find—to say the least.

"You wrote that?" Dave said, scrawling the words "bizarre" and "fascinating" at the top of his *Romeo and Juliet* title page.

"I like to mash up storytelling and spoken word poetry as it pertains to my life," said Ziggy. "To explore what it means to be a Brewster."

"And what *is* it like?' asked Dave, examining the wolf closest to him. It appeared ready to leap back to life.

"I don't really know," Ziggy shrugged. "All I know is that I hate taxidermy and that I'm committed to sharing stories in a different way. My mother is a great storyteller."

"Does she live with you?" Dave hadn't met her inside the house.

"No. She moved out last month. After the fire."

"Right." The fire.

"I really miss her. Want to see a pic?"

"Sure."

Ziggy passed Dave his iPhone.

Dave shielded the phone from the sun with his right hand so he could see the image. The screensaver shone with a picture of Ziggy, aged about twelve, hugging a tiny woman whose smile could unlock a door.

"She's beautiful," Dave said. How could this five-foot-tall woman have given birth to a giant like Ziggy?

"I wrote and illustrated a children's picture book in honour of her," said Ziggy, somewhat embarrassed. *Leapling the Dust Bunny*. My mother hates to clean, so we have dust bunnies the size of guinea pigs. Little eyes peering out from under my bed."

"And you can't mount a dust bunny," said Dave with an understanding nod.

"Exactly."

Dave braced himself to ask the question he knew he had to. He cleared his throat.

"Robert didn't tell me much about the arson incident. He said I should ask you."

Ziggy looked away, his stooped shoulders stooping even more.

"I was making a short viking movie on my iPhone. It was the final scene—the funeral for my hero, Kinmount Willie. I made a miniature raft out of Popsicle sticks, put it in the river outside the town limits, and lit it on fire. It floated out about twenty feet, engulfed in flames. The wind picked up. But, instead of blowing out the fire, it caused the raft to reverse direction. It floated towards a large, two-storey boathouse. I waded out to try to grab it. But, before I could get to it, the raft drifted under the boathouse doors. There must have been gas on the surface of the water. Suddenly flames were attacking the insides. A cruiser exploded. I called the volunteer fire department. By the time the fire truck arrived, the boathouse and boat were gone."

Ziggy turned back to face Dave. "The boathouse was Judge Robert's."

Dave nearly fell off his stump. Robert certainly hadn't mentioned that.

"I thought I was done for," Ziggy continued. "I burnt down the Judge's boathouse. I blew up his boat. But he didn't throw the book at me. And he could have. Instead, a suspended sentence, probation, and community service. Robert is the finest person I know. He truly saved my life. He's my hero."

"He's an inspiration to me too," said Dave.

Was Robert the reincarnation of Coeus, the titan god of intelligence and farsight? Justin (the actor formerly known as Tybalt) was certainly a latter-day Apollo. An idea struck Dave. What if mythological creatures really did once exist, but over the years, they slowly mixed in with humans. Their blood may have mostly faded away, but if you looked closely, you could still see it—the blood of fairies in the way a ballet dancer hovered mid-air before they hit the ground. The blood of dryads in hikers who never tripped over roots. The blood of sirens in people who never had a problem getting a date. The blood of mermaids in a surfer who could be tossed around underwater for a long time without drowning. The blood of the Furies in Lola, or the blood of shapeshifters in the way an actor adjusted their personality to become their character with scary accuracy, like Baldwin, and hopefully, Ziggy.

"You like comic books?" asked Ziggy shyly.

"I suppose I do," said Dave, mulling Ziggy's question over in his mind. "Aren't super heroes the Greek mythology of your generation?"

"Superman was the first nice guy I met," said Ziggy. "He grew up in a small place. He was different. He longed for something more. He lost his mother and father and was raised in another world. A bit like how I feel."

"I've never given Superman much thought," said Dave. But Ziggy had a point. Trying to figure out one's place in the world and overcoming loneliness were difficult universal experiences. Seeing Superman try to balance his personal life as Clark Kent was a heightened example of the pressures one had to deal with in real life, balancing work with family and friends, or trying to have an intimate romantic relationship when suddenly duty calls. Dave had never managed to find that balance or have a relationship last longer than six months. He was, self-admittedly, Mediocre-Man in that regard.

"How old are you?" Dave asked, intrigued by Ziggy's maturity and self-awareness.

"Nineteen." Ziggy stared up at the sun.

"Benvolio is an old soul too, and a night owl of sorts," said Dave, feeling an affinity to the strange sad lad. "Trapped in a society in which he doesn't belong."

"I understand that feeling," Ziggy shrugged again.

"I know you do," said Dave gently. "The part is yours if you want it."

Ziggy's eyes brightened then clouded over.

"Would you mind not telling the company about my probation?" he asked, staring at the fire pit. "I feel bad enough as it is."

"Sure thing," assured Dave. "Don't worry, Ziggy. It will be fine."

Dave did not recognize his own voice. Was he really saying things would be fine? Was he actually testing the waters of optimism?

SEVEN

The architecture of Kinmount's "fount of all wisdom" resembled a toilet. The council chambers were buried in the bowl. Four storeys of municipal departments were housed in the tank.

"That's why they're so full of shit," the Nurse said.

She and the rest of the company were making their way up the steps. Robert joined them, having been released from hospital earlier that afternoon. Baldwin and Justin each carried a large duffel bag. Lady Capulet was armed with a legal portfolio. Ziggy had met the company at a read-through earlier that morning.

Dave was fired up for the meeting. For justice.

The cast entered the chambers. The chamber featured a U-shaped council table for seven members, a secretarial desk in front, and a gallery. Lola was nowhere in sight. The gallery was packed with onlookers.

Had *The Kinmount Crier* article caused the turnout?

Was it Too Tall Tim's radio show?

Had the controversy Lola stirred up translated into an unruly mob wanting to witness the blood battle between political correctness and freedom of speech?

Did they want to witness Dave's crucifixion?

Alas, no.

As Dave and the company found seats, a heated debate was ensuing amongst the Mayor and the ranks of the town council regarding the overspending on a new hockey arena—two million dollars over budget to be exact.

"How could this happen?" screamed an angry taxpayer.

"So they could line their pockets with kickbacks!" yelled another.

"There has been no fraudulent activity or illegal activity associated with this overspending," assured the Mayor. He was a sunburned, stocky middle-aged man, his clothing and hair of equal unruliness: a polyester dress shirt that refused to stay tucked into the pants of his rumpled tan suit, and yellow straw hair that sprouted out defiantly in all directions like a thatched medieval roof.

"If you didn't know, then you should have known, McGee!" shouted an incensed Jimmy O'Connor from the back of the gallery. "And now you're going to make our hockey teams pay through the roof for ice time!"

A chorus of boos filled the chamber. If the Elizabethan tradition of tossing vegetables at bad acting was still on the books, then the Mayor was on his way to becoming a tossed salad.

The council secretary was transcribing at a furious pace, his tapping fingers a blur.

Baldwin and Justin jumped up, each hoisting a pair of skates over a shoulder and wielding hockey sticks.

"Mr. Mayor, I want to express my frustration with the hockey arena drought in this community," said Baldwin, having blacked out two of his front teeth.

"The what?" spluttered the Mayor, caught off guard by Baldwin's verbal slapshot.

"Every time I turn around, Kinmount is building another theatre. Or an art gallery," Baldwin complained.

"Oh, it's worse than that," Justin joined in. "Heck, ya can't even walk down Main Street without bumping into a bookstore. Or, even worse, a library."

"All this town thinks about is theatre. All this town cares about is where are the actors going to get more rehearsal space. All the groups are competing for more stage time." Baldwin was on a roll. "How can the Red Lion afford the cost of new jerseys for its Shakespeare Mechanicals bantam improvisation team?"

"My mechanical what?" shouted Jimmy O'Connor.

"Where can the actors sharpen their wit? If Too Tall Tim broadcasts one more theatre production on that radio show of his, I'm gonna break this over his head," said Justin, waving his Sherwood goalie stick.

"What are we hickey players to do?" cried out Baldwin.

"Hockey," corrected Jimmy O'Connor, ripping off his black armband.

"Hickey," Baldwin fired back. "And you know all about hickies, Jimmy."

The gallery erupted.

"How dare you, Baldwin McGregor! You are banned from my tavern for life!"

Dave feared a bench-clearing brawl.

"Order!" shouted the Mayor, slapping the council table with a freckled hand. "We have lots of arenas and outdoor rinks and you know it. Why we have more rinks than any other community in Canada relative to our population. Every merchant in Kinmount sponsors a hockey team. We would've won *Hockeyville* last year if it weren't for you two upstarts figure-skating in drag on national television. We could have had Ron McLean here in Kinmount. But, no, you hooligans ruined that hope. I have a hard time even calling you Canadians." The Mayor was verging on a seizure. "We don't have theatres! We don't have art galleries! We don't have bookstores! And we certainly don't have libraries!" He sat down in a huff.

"Exactly," said Justin.

The gallery of locals was confused.

"Mr. Mayor, you and your council think culture is something you find in the back of your fridge," stated Baldwin, sitting down.

"Art is not something you step in and wipe off your shoe," concluded Justin, sitting down.

The cast cheered. The remainder of the gallery did not.

"Your turn," Justin winked at Dave.

"Just warming them up for you," grinned Baldwin.

Dave was doomed. How could he possibly bring the Mayor and the mob on side?

"Mayor McGee," a voice pronounced from the council table.

It was the businesswoman who was part of the triumvirate that'd paid him the visit. She rose to her feet with a rigid self-imposed authority. "It has been brought to council's attention by Lola Whale that the director of our Summer in the Park production, one David Middleton, who sits before us, has added his own vulgarities to *Romeo and Juliet*. The issue needs to be addressed."

"Yes, it certainly does," said the Mayor, tucking in his shirt-tail and attempting to regain his composure.

The businesswoman looked out over the heads of the spectators. "Ms. Whale?" she announced, raising her voice.

A door opened at the rear of the gallery. A middle-aged woman appeared in formal business attire, looking smart and sophisticated. The first four notes of the Judge Judy theme song should have played her in—the four notes belonged to Beethoven's "Symphony No. 5," described by the deaf composer as "Fate knocking on your door." In Dave's case, it was Lola knocking on the door, dressed in a grey skirt suit with a white blouse and black pumps, a conservative blonde wig, carrying a structured black handbag. She walked down the aisle toward the council with a peculiar air of refinement, a delicate picture of polish and posture. She arrived at the microphone, inhaled deeply, and pursed her lips. "Your worship and council, guests and concerned citizens, ours is a family festival, and I am concerned that Mr. Middleton's additions will be inappropriate for our children." The softness of her voice coupled with her refined manner suggested royalty.

Inbreeding, Dave thought.

"Mr. Middleton," said the Mayor, "what do you have to say for yourself?"

Dave looked up and whispered to his "Uncle" Thomas, "Words don't fail me now."

He stood up slowly, scanning the crowd until he spotted Kate sitting in the back row beside Jimmy. She gave him a quick reassuring smile, while at the same time trying to calm Jimmy down and explain the definition of satire.

Dave took out his notes.

"Friends, Kinmount-ians, countrymen, lend me your ears," he began, placing his hands firmly on the guest speaker's podium. He avoided Lola's stony stare.

An awkward silence ensued.

"Mayor McGee, I want to begin by apologizing for my two cast members' Bob and Doug routine. I assure you they meant no harm. Satire is a hallmark of freedom of speech in this country. It hearkens back to the early satyr plays of ancient Greek theatre. While their manner of delivery might be offensive to some, the content they cleverly fashioned is valid. The arts do provide for the psychic wellbeing of a community."

"Did he say psychotic?" asked the taller stoner, turning to the shorter stoner.

"Hush!" whispered Lady Capulet. "He's talking about the emotional and mental wellbeing of our community."

"In balance with athletics," said Dave diplomatically. "One of the interesting things about *Romeo and Juliet* is that you're dealing with a play that everyone feels they know." He looked briefly at Lola who turned away, refusing to meet his eye. "So, there is always a concern of originality. There is an expectation that I, like many others, must have some sort of special concept or wild spin to make the play exciting again. It was my goal from the outset to avoid that pitfall, and I constantly remind myself that, though this play is well known and performed regularly, it is still as exciting and engaging as it always was without my meddling. So I found my real challenge wasn't to be original, but to tell the story as if it had never been told before, and to immerse everyone so fully into the unfolding action that they forgot they ever knew what was coming next. Now, I understand that the council has concerns about my staging of *Romeo and Juliet.* That I have been tampering with Shakespeare's language. Under no circumstances have I added a single word to Shakespeare's original text, and I intend to prove that now, if you will permit me."

"Please do," said the Mayor. "And no funny business," he added with a look to Baldwin and Justin.

"I assure you there is nothing remotely funny about my having to stand before you this evening. I believe you all know Lauren Ravenwood, former head librarian at the Kinmount Public Library."

"We do," said the Mayor uncomfortably. There were sheepish looks amongst those council members responsible for the library's closing.

"With your permission, Ms. Ravenwood is going to assist me," said Dave, channelling his best Atticus Finch. Social media had just announced that morning that *The Catcher in the Rye* had been banned in yet another American town.

"Yes, get on with it," muttered the Mayor. He hated to have to eat guilt in the evening.

"Ms. Ravenwood?" Dave said by way of formal invitation.

Lady Capulet joined him at the podium.

Dave continued: "Mayor McGee, I work from the original texts of Shakespeare. They were put together for the first time in a volume called the First Folio in 1623 by two members of his acting company. Seven years after Shakespeare's death. They are the unsung heroes of English literature. Without them, Shakespeare's works would never have survived."

"Unnecessary." Lola expelled the word across the chamber.

"Ms. Ravenwood has a facsimile of the First Folio with her tonight," Dave soldiered on, ignoring Lola's attempt to distract the council.

Lady Capulet held up the weighty tome.

"I have made photocopies of specific examples to demonstrate Shakespeare's original usage. His words, not mine."

Lady Capulet passed out the neatly stapled pages to the council, Lola, and the gallery spectators.

Dave turned to a dog-eared page in his Folio.

"I want to bring everyone's attention to example one. I believe this is the most contentious passage. In this scene Mercutio, a trickster and troubled soul, is teasing the Nurse, a woman of questionable morals. Romeo, joining in on the revelry, asks, 'What hast thou found?' Mercutio responds with a pun." Dave put on his reading glasses and read aloud:

"'No hare, sir; unless a hare, sir, in a Lenten pie,
that is something stale and hoar ere it be spent.'
Mercutio then sings:
'An old hare hoar,
And old hare hoar,
Is very good meat in lent
But a hare that is hoar,
Is too much for a score,
When it hoars ere it be spent.'"

He removed his glasses and faced the council. "Every word is Shakespeare's."

"And what does it mean?" Lola said askance.

"Something about an old rabbit before Easter," said the Mayor.

"He's calling the Easter bunny a whore," said Lola gravely.

The gallery began to murmur.

"Not exactly," said Dave. "In Shakespeare's day, you were supposed to give up meat for Lent. As a result, rotten meat baked into a pie was the only meat you could buy. Mercutio is comparing a meat pie at Lent to the Nurse's tawdry ways."

"Implying the Nurse is not fit for eating!" Lola exclaimed.

The gallery exploded.

Dave's plan had backfired.

"Answer me, Mr. Middleton. Implying the Nurse is not fit for eating!" she repeated, eager to light the match.

Dave could smell the kindling smoking.

"Yes," he said weakly.

"Your worship, I rest my case," Lola declared. "Regardless of whether Mr. Middleton wrote those disgusting lines or not, they are still unfit for the ears of the youth of our community."

"Why would anyone want to eat a nurse?" asked a twelve-year-old boy innocently. He was standing in the second row.

"Exactly," said Dave, turning to the boy. "They wouldn't, son."

"Yuck," said the boy.

Laughter filled the gallery.

"I wouldn't want to eat you, either," the taller stoner said, jabbing the Nurse.

"You wish," she fired back.

"Order!" shouted the Mayor. "Mr. Middleton?"

"Shakespeare was writing on two levels," Dave explained. "He kept the groundlings entertained with his puns and innuendos and the upper classes enthralled with his sweeping poetry. That is his brilliance. He had the ability to juggle two very different audiences at the same time. And the dirty puns went over the heads of the children—just like they do today." He referenced the boy in the second row.

Lola tapped her podium with a ruler until she had the full attention of the room.

"I'm looking at example two, Mr. Middleton," she said. "Could you tell us what a 'poperin pear' is, please?"

"LIST!" the ghost shouted in his head.

"We are waiting, Mr. Middleton."

"LIST!" the ghost shouted again.

Dave looked to Kate. She gave him an "I told you so" look.

"LIST!" the ghost screamed.

Dave gripped the podium for support. How could Lola possibly know what a "poperin pear" was slang for when she barely knew the play? He racked his brain for an answer. She had to be bluffing.

"I ask you again. Would you tell us what a 'poperin pear' is?" said Lola.

"A 'poperin pear' is ... a large pear," said Dave carefully.

"And what is it Elizabethan slang for?"

Dave felt his feet catching fire.

"It describes a human body part," he said feebly.

"What body part?"

"A body part."

"*What* body part?"

The flames were licking at his chin.

"The penis," he said inaudibly.

"I cannot hear you. Would you repeat that, please?"

"The penis," he said uneasily.

The gallery was both aghast and titillated.

"And what was it used for besides eating?"

Lola would not let the pear go.

"It was an Elizabethan dildo," said Dave with as much dignity as he could muster. Working at a Tim Horton's drive-thru might not be so bad after all.

"Pop 'er in!" shouted a groundling, getting the pun.

The gallery roared.

Dave's humiliation was complete. He'd give Justin back his money. Race out of town. Never to work again.

Robert stood up.

"Do you know what a dildo is, son?" he asked the twelve-year-old boy.

"Your worship!" screamed Lola.

"Order!" shouted the Mayor. "Judge Wyld, if you please. There are children present."

"One moment please, Mr. Mayor. I assure you their morals are not in danger. Answer my question, son. Do you know what a dildo is?"

"No sir," said the boy. "I don't."

"My mother was born there!" shouted out a landed Newfoundlander in the gallery.

Robert turned with a laugh and saw another young lad sitting beside Jimmy.

"Are you Jimmy O'Connor's grandson?" he asked kindly.

"Yes, sir," the boy replied.

"What's your name young man?" Robert asked.

"Finbar," replied the boy, standing up.

"Well, Finbar, do *you* know what a dildo is?"

"It's the name of a hobbit," replied the boy.

The gallery began to laugh.

"The name of a hobbit?" asked Robert quizzically. "How so?"

The boy looked up at his grandfather who squirmed and shook his head. "For God's sake, no," he whispered hoarsely.

"Please tell the truth, Finbar," said Robert.

"Sit down, boy," Jimmy ordered.

"He will in one moment, Mr. O'Connor. The hobbit's name, please, Finbar?"

"Dildo Baggins. He's a character in a DVD my gramps has in his office."

"And what is the name of that DVD, Finbar?" asked Robert

"*The Lord of the Cock-Ring*," Finbar answered.

"I told you to stay out of there," Jimmy blustered. All eyes were on him.

"I haven't watched it," said the boy. "I'm more of a *Star Wars* fan."

The gallery broke into hysterics.

"I'm sure you are," said Robert gently. "Your worship, you see how ridiculous this all is. Sadly, Kinmount is quite capable on its own of broadening the perspectives of our youth without any help from William Shakespeare or Lola Whale."

Lola looked at him with loathing.

The gallery roared.

"Why, it's Dildo O'Connor!" shouted out a Red Lion regular pointing a finger at Jimmy.

"Cock-a-doodle-do!" shouted another.

Jimmy's face turned redder than his tavern's moniker.

"You should change the name to the Red Dildo, Jimmy boy!" laughed a drunk in the back.

"Order!" The Mayor struggled to regain control of the proceedings. The groundlings were winning.

Robert cleared his throat.

"Your worship, with your permission, may I continue?"

"Go ahead," the Mayor sighed. The fall election had just hit the fan.

"Are you okay?" whispered Dave.

"Never felt better. Now help me over to the podium."

Dave did as he was instructed. Robert cleared his throat and addressed the gallery:

"Romeo and Juliet will open the youth of Kinmount up to the experience of live theatre. They will be rewarded with the gift that accompanies all great drama: the capacity to live on a level that non-theatregoers will never experience, and the opportunity to profit from thousands of years of wisdom."

"Years of depravity is more like it," interrupted Lola. She was losing ground and knew it.

Robert ignored her.

"Throughout history, theatre has been a primary means of teaching. Medieval theatre taught about the Bible and Christianity, Shakespeare's *Romeo and Juliet* can be seen as defending true love within a vulgar and cynical society. Not unlike our own community of Kinmount."

"Vulgar!" screeched Lola. "The town of Kinmount?!"

"I believe the souls of today's youth are screaming for meaning." Robert went on unabated. "Despite the sheer volume of information and stories we receive on a daily basis, we have lost the scale of Shakespeare. He told grand stories depicting all aspects of the human condition. *Romeo and Juliet* contains every possible human emotion: love, lust, hatred, fidelity, hope, despair, bravery, fear, friendship, honour, greed, jealousy, revenge, ambition, pride, compassion, grace, humility, and redemption."

"Lust! We all heard it! Your worship cannot allow such—"

"Please, Ms. Whale, in a moment. Continue, Judge Wyld," stammered the Mayor, his patience and armpits reaching their limit. He was drenched in sweat.

"Let me address Ms. Whale's concerns regarding the children of our community," Robert said calmly, about to deliver his verdict. All that was missing were his judge's robes. "Ms. Whale is well-intentioned, but ultimately misguided. Most of us in this room grew up reading or listening to nursery rhymes as children."

There were nods in the gallery. Dave remembered not wanting to eat pie as a boy for fear of a blackbird popping out.

"Nursery rhymes have more than ten times the number of violent scenes as *Romeo and Juliet*," Robert explained. "Most nursery rhymes contain some kind of violence, whether accidental, aggressive, or implied, from death to some very unsettling stories about gender relations. Do Little Miss Muffet or Jack and Jill or the Incy Wincy Spider need a violence rating system. As a judge, I could sentence many of the characters in nursery rhymes for their crimes: Jack the candlestick arsonist, Old Mother Hubbard for child abuse, Peter for forcible confinement of his wife, liars hanging from telephone wires. 'Ring-around-the-Rosie' is a ditty about catching the plague, and it's far more disturbing than any plague references in *Romeo and Juliet*. Yet, when we were children, it went right over our heads. The true meanings of nursery rhymes did not register until we were much older.

"Reinterpretation of ancient storytelling through modern eyes is difficult, Ms. Whale. Laying the blame on Shakespeare and Dave Middleton for exposing children to violence when watching *Romeo and Juliet* in Kinmount is simplistic. It diverts attention from vastly more complex societal problems. Our bigger task is to make sure our children and youth are supported," Robert carried on. "Instead of banning plays in Kinmount we should be addressing literacy and teen pregnancy."

Lady Capulet instigated a round of applause. Dave joined him at the podium.

"Ever think of running for Mayor?" he whispered under his breath.

"There's fire in the old woodstove yet," Robert replied with a wink. "Finish it."

"There is still the vulgarity issue, your worship," croaked Lola.

"Oh, right," sighed the Mayor, fanning himself with Dave's

Folio handouts. "Well, I guess we'll—"

"Mayor McGee, if I may," interrupted Dave cautiously. He shuffled his notes and addressed the gallery.

"My ancestor, Thomas Middleton, was a contemporary of Shakespeare's. He collaborated with Shakespeare and adapted his plays after his death. But my 'Uncle' Thomas was always overshadowed by the Bard.

"Touring entailed many problems for my uncle. There were no permanent theatres outside of London. So, although his acting troupe had a license to perform, he could be denied the right to play on the grounds that there was no suitable place, that the danger of plague was too great, or for other reasons. Upon arriving in a town, my uncle presented his credentials to the mayor, who usually requested that a performance be given before the council. If the council was pleased, it rewarded the actors with a payment from the council's funds and authorized additional performances for the public."

"I see," hummed the Mayor, getting what Dave was driving at.

"Surely your worship isn't being taken in by such historic drivel," jeered Lola.

"A brilliant turn," whispered Robert to Dave. "Bravo!"

Dave revealed the final card up his black short-sleeve t-shirt.

"In keeping with that time-honoured tradition, I invite you, Mayor McGee, and the council, to watch a run-through of *Romeo and Juliet* on Sunday evening. If you find any snippets of dialogue or stage business offensive, I will remove them before the public performances."

"Sounds fair to me," said the Mayor. "Minus the council funds, of course. All in favour?"

The council raised its hands in surprising unanimity. All eyes were on Lola.

"You are making a terrible mistake," she replied, her voice catching in her throat. "You are being conned by Mr. Middleton. Once *Romeo and Juliet* is finished, he gets to go back home to his cave to wreak havoc on some other unsuspecting community, while we in Kinmount are left to clean up his mess and pick up the pieces of our damaged children. It will be worse than Humpty-Dumpty, Judge Wyld, far, far worse. I am truly horrified by council's decision. You should all be ashamed of yourselves."

"Council's decision stands, Ms. Whale," said the Mayor, ever the politician. "Thank you for bringing forward your concerns."

She glared back at the lot of them.

"I'll be revenged on the whole pack of you!" she bellowed and stormed out, her refinement tossed to the non-existent wind.

EIGHT

Outside, on the city hall steps, the company embraced Robert.

"You idiots, what were you thinking?" Dave said to Baldwin and Justin. "Leading an arts satire charge?"

"It's all how you handle the puck," said Baldwin. "What do you call twenty hockey players on a bus?"

"A full set of teeth," said Justin.

"Jimmy's face changed colours faster than his dance floor." Baldwin stopped mid-laugh. "Oh, shit, I've got to find me a new watering hole."

"I talked to him," said Kate. "Once I explained to him that the *Romeo and Juliet* bar tab this month has paid his lease until Christmas, surprise, you're no longer banned."

"Funny that," said Dave. "Unfortunately, we are back at ground zero." He couldn't believe the small-town politics. "Right where we were when Lola kicked me out and started her vendetta. Only now I caved to censorship."

"No, you have not caved," said Robert. "You presented a strong case and you've given them the opportunity to judge for themselves."

"You did that, Robert, not me."

"Nonsense. You were reasonable. Not some crazy, mad Shakespeare director. You did more for arts education in this community than you'll ever know. That's the first time I've ever known town council to agree on anything. The windmill is tilting in our favour."

"We shall see," replied Dave, with guarded optimism. He wasn't safe from banana peels quite yet. Even though he didn't know anyone who'd actually slipped on a banana peel, save for silent movie clowns and the Friar.

"How was Lola even allowed to attend?" Miranda asked.

"She hasn't been arrested," Justin said. "John had her in for questioning this morning. But no charges have been laid yet. The investigation continues."

"Great. Well, now she's madder than a wet hen and a hornet combined. No telling what she'll do next," said Dave. He looked around the parking lot. "No sign of her Ram."

"Anyone notice a broom vapour trail in the sky?" said Baldwin.

They found themselves looking up at the sunset. Not a vapour trail in sight. Instead, a perfect blend of orange and pink hues melting into dusk. As if on cue, the crickets began to tune, their legs rubbing together in unison, an orchestra of hidden cellists on a summer's eve.

"What a beautiful concert," sighed Miranda. "They're singing."

"Stridulating," said B.J.

"What?" Baldwin said.

"The chirping cricket music. It's called stridulation," said B.J. "And the sound doesn't come from rubbing their legs together. It's their wings, actually. And only the males can create it."

"His dad's an insect genius," Miranda grinned.

"Typical," said the Nurse. "The men are playing music to seduce the females."

"Saturday night at the Red Lion," chirped in Baldwin.

"Beware of the insect Romeos, ladies," said Kate. "You'll be waiting longer for child support payments than for my daughter to finish getting ready in the morning."

An awkward silence followed.

"I wonder why a cricket chirp is used to indicate an awkward silence in a comedy?" said Robert. "It doesn't make sense. Nature is anything but quiet."

"Listen!" said Miranda. "They're harmonizing."

They listened to the slow and languid concerto. It sounded

more like a hundred smoke alarm-change-the-battery chirps to Dave's untrained ear.

"If only it could last," he mused, tongue firmly in-cheek.

The company began to disperse. Miranda and B.J. rode off on their bikes. Dave looked for Kate, but she'd already disappeared.

ৎ

Dave cautiously checked his rear-view mirror to make sure he wasn't being followed. He felt like Ichabod Crane trying to avoid the headless equestrian. An hour later, he arrived at the motel after taking a series of deliberate detours.

There was no sign of B.J.

Dave became annoyed. He felt like a parent staying up to wait for his teenage son to return home after violating an agreed upon curfew. What was he going to do? Tell B.J. the television was off limits? He'd like to ban B.J.'s turnips and weed.

Shortly after midnight, the door opened and B.J. entered in good spirits.

He smelled of sex.

Of course—it dawned on Dave. Had he actually been that stupid to believe B.J. and Miranda were only running lines for the past two weeks?

B.J. tossed his knapsack in a chair and bounced onto the other bed.

"How was the *ride*?" asked Dave curtly.

"Sure worked up a sweat," B.J. grinned, not cluing in.

"I bet," said Dave drily.

"Took the backroads. That gravel is a killer. No wonder they call this the Highlands. More hills than Rome."

"And how was the beach?"

"Good. Beautiful moon tonight," B.J. said. "And the stars. Incredible. You just can't see them like that in the city. You really see why Romeo talks of Juliet's eyes being like two of the brightest stars in all the heavens. The show's going to be magical, Dave. Like what Robert said about the theatre in his speech tonight."

"Oh, boy," Dave murmured.

"What's that?" asked B.J.

"Nothing."

Dave had to tread delicately. It really was none of his business, but he was going to make it his business. "How's Miranda doing?" he asked carefully.

"Fine."

B.J. wasn't helping the situation with his catechistic response.

"I haven't had much of a chance to talk to her, what with Apocalypse Lola," said Dave. "It's been crazy for all of us. I'm worried it might be affecting her."

"She's doing fine."

"I promised her father I'd look after her." Dave functioned best within a very small box.

"Miranda's not a child," said B.J., rolling a joint.

"But this is her first acting job after theatre school," said Dave, trying not to sound like Miranda's father.

"What are you trying to say, Dave?"

"Look, I know you guys are close ..."

"And?"

"And summer theatre has a way of—"

"We're buddies," interrupted B.J.

"Buddies with benefits, B.J.?" Dave put it out on the table.

"What?"

"Miranda is no Chickpea." It was probably the dumbest thing to come out of Dave's mouth in the last two weeks.

"We're friends," B.J. reiterated.

"It's okay, B.J. I'm not mad at you. These things happen. Just be straight with me."

"It really is none of your business."

"I'm making it my business." Dave hated to have to say it.

"It's complicated," said B.J.

"Always is," said Dave.

"Alright, we're together. Happy?"

Despite his irritable response, B.J. appeared to be relieved to not have to conceal their secret any longer.

"Since when?" asked Dave.

"I think it all started the moment Miranda tasted my turnip stew."

One in a million, thought Dave. "And then?" he asked aloud.

"At the beach. The night you were at Kate's. The night before Lola kicked us out."

"What about your girlfriend?"

"What about her?"

"Does Miranda know about her?" Dave asked.

"Of course." B.J. seem surprised Dave could even ask the question.

"Sorry, but it's—" said Dave, wishing he'd never brought the subject up.

"Yes, I've been up front about it. Miranda knows that my girlfriend and I are on the rocks."

Dave heard himself in B.J.'s rationale. "Does your girlfriend know that?" he pressed.

"You're not exactly the expert on relationships" B.J. fired back. He wished Chickpea was on-hand. Literally.

"No, I'm not," Dave pressed on. "But I don't want to see you make the same mistake I made at your age."

"No danger of that," said B.J. in Chickpea's voice.

"Be careful, B.J. You are both young," Dave implored. "Ask yourself this? Are you falling in love with Miranda or are you falling in love with Miranda as Juliet. And is she falling in love with you or you as Romeo? It's the *Romeo and Juliet* young lovers' syndrome. It has ruined more relationships than *Salt-Water Moon*."

"I've heard the stories," said B.J. "I know all about the curse. But this is different."

"Under normal circumstances, what's between you and Miranda wouldn't be any of my business. But these are not normal circumstances," said Dave. "You're a good guy, B.J. I knew that when I cast you, turnips aside. You're closest to her."

"Don't worry. I'm keeping my eye on her." B.J. retreated to the bathroom.

"And, I hope you don't mind me saying this, but your girlfriend situation isn't helping, no matter what you say," Dave shouted to be heard over the noise of the running faucet. "You tell Miranda you want to be with her, but you haven't broken it off with your girlfriend. Mixed messages, my young friend, I'm just saying."

"Okay, okay, I'll call her right now. Satisfied?" B.J. shouted back, spitting toothpaste into the sink.

Dave left the room and sat on the steps of the "Tin Pins" ancient swimming pool, giving B.J. privacy to make his phone call.

He stared up at the stars. No eyes stared back. The lonely words of Johnny Cash drifted out through the half-opened motel office window. The man in black interrupted the neon crackle of the sign.

Lonesome was right.

Dave called his ex.

NINE

Despite being up at the crack of daylight, Dave still managed to find himself stuck in rush hour traffic. He did not miss the Don Valley Parking Lot.

He pulled into the back lot of the Lorne Greene Theatre School shortly after nine. Ms. Greerson, the school's wardrobe mistress, was busy repairing doublets when he knocked on the door.

"Enter," she commanded with a voice hoarse from a two pack a day habit. Ms. Greerson had worked at the school since as long as Dave could remember. There wasn't a student who hadn't adored her fatalism and goodwill smoke handouts. But times had changed. Ms. Greerson was now the last survivor of the school's morning-and-afternoon cigarette break. The current administration respectfully turned a blind eye.

"How are you, Ms. G?" asked Dave playfully.

"David Middleton. Lovely to see you. Give this old needle and thread a hug," she exclaimed.

Dave squeezed her tight and could feel every vertebra in her tiny frame. Ms. G had aged into a miniature xylophone.

"So, you need some dresses, doublets, and hose, eh? I was just fixing these up for you. Doesn't matter what decade, young men still don't know how to hang up a costume. Where were their mothers growing up?" Ms. G shook her head. It was her personal pet peeve, a pet peeve of all costume designers, dating back to ancient Greece when chorus members' togas, after a quick change, were left littering the backstage stone floor at the Theatre of Delphi.

"I always hung mine up," said Dave with a jocular wink.

"Yes you did, my boy. The rare exception. Now, I've sorted through some of the stock. They're hanging on that rack there." She pointed to a rolling rack beside a shelf of dressmaker dummies.

"Thanks, Ms. G."

"You got measurements?" Ms. G barked, tossing Dave a measuring tape.

"Right here," replied Dave, waving a Red Lion serviette.

"Good boy."

Dave began sorting through the costumes. If he hadn't gone into directing, Dave would have been a costume designer. He loved the order, yet imaginative artistry, of design.

"Flight-in-restriction is our goal," Ms. G always said to the new recruits on day one. Costume design was, strangely enough, a mandatory first year course in the acting program at Lorne Greene. Dave was that rare male student who thrived in its fabric and assembly environment. To the astonishment of his mates, he mastered a sewing machine—cross stiches, piping stitches, and all. He'd remained a favourite of Ms. G's over the years. The feeling was mutual.

"You heard about old Hindenberg, eh?" Ms. G hacked.

Gerald Hindenberg had been the school's artistic director in the '70s and '80s. He was a self-appointed guru who believed in breaking young actors' spirits. His approach was not only abusive, but also counter-productive, as the actors in Dave's class didn't learn how to rely on themselves and their skills and abilities as creative artists.

"Vaguely," said Dave. Since moving to Birch Lake, he'd been out of the loop.

"Five former students launched a class-action lawsuit against him, documenting years of abuse and harassment, claiming he was a serial sexual predator. The lying over-privileged sack of shit."

"About time," said Dave. Gerald Hindenberg ordered students to attend his touchy-feely house parties. A dangerous combination of Twister, Spin the Bottle, and theatre history trivia ensued. The corruptive power imbalance destroyed many of his classmates' love of the theatre. The altar of spiritual creation smashed to pieces by the dirty-nailed, groping fingers of Gerald Hindenberg.

"Wrecking ball arrives on Monday," Ms. G volunteered.

What with his Kinmount fiasco, Dave had completely forgotten about the school's impending demolition. The new location would open in September in a converted department store.

"What will you do, Ms. G?" he asked.

"I'm moving in with my sister. And her five cats. I'll be fine." Ms. G coughed and hacked up a lung.

ॐ

Dave arrived back at the rehearsal site just in time for Chickpea's memorial. Baldwin and Miranda were in attendance. The Sarge and his son watched respectfully from a distance. B.J. stood under the elm tree, a melancholy figure, trying to collect himself. He held a bag of Chickpea's stuffing.

"Chickpea wasn't just any pea in a pod," he expounded. "He's the one who kept me amused with his unabashed enthusiasm, supported me with his preening, and perched upside-down when I was discouraged. He's the one who taught me that parrots can purr. Sadly, Chickpea didn't just 'hop the twig' from old age. No, he was murdered in cold purée. Goodbye, my purple pal."

After concluding his eulogy, B.J. released Chickpea's stuffing by the riverside. Miranda released freshly picked purple daisies in tandem. Before the stuffing and flowers could hit the surface, the wind changed direction. Chickpea's "ashes" whirled back towards shore. A piece of his stuffing blew into B.J.'s eye. Another piece got stuck in Miranda's lip gloss. B.J. tried to remove the piece of stuffing but it stuck to his hand. He tried to shake it off and it stuck to his jeans. He began to laugh. Miranda peeled the piece off her bottom lip and attempted to toss it back towards the river. The wind picked up. The piece of stuffing blew back into her hair. The flowers too were now swirling towards the mourning party. A purple daisy landed in Miranda's hair followed by another and then another. She began to giggle. Dave and Baldwin joined in. Chickpea the parrot was still working it as an after-puppet.

"Chickpea always had a great sense of hummus," said B.J., removing the last piece of stuffing from his mouth.

The Sarge and his son soldiered over to Dave.

"All quiet on the Highlands front," reported the Sarge. "Only one incident of note. At oh-two-hundred a large pickup pulled in, headlights off, and parked behind the old sawmill to avoid detection. Upon close inspection, the windows of said vehicle were steamed up. I had a bit of fun shining my beam in the driver's window. The commotion inside would give Tom and Jerry and Costello a run for their money. The driver's window finally descended. Pot smoke poured out. The two teenagers' eyes were perfectly narrowed and as red as the devil's butt. They scrambled to find themselves amidst their hastily adorned inside-out t-shirts. I assured them I wasn't the police and they weren't in trouble. At least not with me."

"Got that t-shirt," said Dave. As a boy, he used to sneak down to the Lake Ontario waterfront on summer nights carrying a bag of breadcrumbs. He hunted for parked cars with their windows steamed up. Crawling up beside an unsuspecting Pinto, he would toss the bread crumbs onto the windshield. Within seconds, forty or more screaming seagulls would swarm the car, something out of a Hitchcock horror film. The screams in the car were louder.

"The young lady was particularly embarrassed," said the Sarge. "'A dab of aloe vera will help with that hickey in the morning.' She thanked me, and they attempted to creep away.

He needs a new muffler."

"Sarge, you just prevented Kinmount adolescent pregnancy number three hundred and five," said Dave.

"Johnny, don't you listen to that," said the Sarge to his son, who was glued to his hip.

"Three hundred and five what?" asked Johnny, preoccupied with thinking about inside-out t-shirts.

"Exactly," said the Sarge with a wink to Dave. "Otherwise, a moored boat party at the marina. Cranking out the tunes. I thought Pat Benatar went out with the '80s."

"Most overplayed karaoke song at the Red Lion," said Baldwin. "'Hit Me with Your Best Shot' is Jimmy's signature tune for his happy-hour tequila poppers."

"What's even sadder is that the Red Lion still *has* a karaoke night," said Dave.

The rest of the company emerged.

The day was spent on costume fittings and showing Ziggy his Benvolio blocking. Dave quickly discovered Ziggy would never learn to handle a rapier and dagger. His flailing limbs and knobby knees gave him a stooped scarecrow effect. He was as awkward as a cow on a crutch. Fortunately, Ziggy's acting made up for his lack of coordination. He managed to make Benvolio a plausible peacemaker: terrified of violence, and running scared while trying to solve Romeo's problems. His cadence and rhythm of speech were unique—an intentionally created, low-pitched rural accent that treated all punctuation as optional. He noticed the unwritten nonverbal cues in the First Folio text and squinted at B.J. at the end of his speeches. In short, Ziggy brought so much of himself to the role it was near impossible to tell he was acting, save for the heightened language and baggy breeches.

Ginny's yellow highlighter could barely keep up with him.

Despite the fact that Benvolio and Romeo tried their utmost to prevent the violence from occurring, they had to face up to their responsibilities—responsibilities that could've led to Romeo being executed. Both were afraid to. When Mercutio and Tybalt were killed—the two people who wanted to fight in the first place—Benvolio and Romeo were in a lot of trouble. In a split second Benvolio made a life-altering decision. He ordered Romeo to run away, and, despite his fear, Benvolio bravely told the Prince exactly what unfolded. Benvolio did the right thing. In essence, he took the fall, moving from adolescence to manhood in the instant. Ziggy brought integrity and grief-stricken vulnerability to this watershed moment in the play, his sense memory channelling the boathouse fire.

The company responded in a clear-the-dug-out rush to embrace their new bases-loaded, home-run hitter. Adversity's solution, as is so often the case, proved to be a better fit than the original casting it remedied.

TEN

Much to Dave's chagrin, when the company retired to the Red Lion after rehearsal, it was Saturday karaoke night. To make matters worse, the Prince was the host. He lugged his equipment out of his van and began setting up on the small stage at the rear of the tavern. The Red Lion was already packed with local wannabe Whitney Houston divas and Elvis Presley pack rat country crooners.

The Prince was in his element.

"Are you ready to have some fun? Come on up and put your best 'you' in kara ... you ... ke! Only one rule at the Red Lion ... no rap."

"At least there's that," muttered Dave.

"And don't forget to tip your host," slipped in the Prince.

Dave should've gone back to the motel. Ziggy had enough common sense to go home and work on his lines. He dug his fingernails into the table. Karaoke was a minefield rife with social pitfalls and torrents of shame.

"You didn't need to come to karaoke night if it annoys you that much," said Miranda.

She promptly got up, circled a song on the request sheet on the table, delivered it to the Prince, and made her way to the bar.

If brevity really was the soul of wit and karaoke, Dave silently prayed for no one to sing "American Pie."

The taller stoner took to the stage. The opening guitar lick of "Footloose" began to play. He couldn't resist the urge to dance an awkward Kevin Bacon tribute. No one wanted to see a lone person dancing on a stage.

"Take your clothes off!" the shorter stoner catcalled.

It was sad.

And no one wanted to be sad at a bar—especially Dave.

The night wore on. Power ballads were destroyed one after the other. Bon Jovi was burning his leopard-print cowboy hat.

Dave cringed watching a tiny little mouse get onstage and squeak out Fleetwood Mac, like she was forced to do it at gunpoint.

Maybe she was.

B.J. and Miranda hit the stage. The opening bump-bah-bump of "Summer Nights" signalled the inevitable.

"Maybe they think it's cute to sing a duet, but it can only end in one of two ways," Dave whispered hoarsely to Baldwin. "Either the audience recoils at the saccharine sweetness of it, or revolts at the sounds of two terrible singers attempting harmonies. They'll be broken up before they reach the end. Their relationship will thank me," said Dave smugly.

He was wrong on both counts. The audience cheered and joined in.

Yet, Dave didn't leave. He was glued to the stage as sure as a highway driver slowing down to ogle a car wreck.

B.J. dropped the mic.

BA-BOOM!

The Prince took to the stage.

"Alriiiiight, careful with that mic, Romeo. It's the only one I own. It's last call, folks. Time for two more. But, before we do, I want to invite a special guest up on the stage. Dave Middleton, come on up."

Dave looked for the closest exit.

"Dave here is directing *Romeo and Juliet* in town, opening next Friday. Six nights from now! And we've got a bunch of the cast here tonight. He is going to sing for us in just a moment."

Dave froze. Had someone in the cast signed him up as a practical joke?

"Come on up, Dave," insisted the Prince.

Dave had no choice but to join the Prince on deck. He could see Kate laughing at him from behind the bar.

"I don't sing," he murmured uneasily, wishing he was listening to Reilly's Marty Robbins collection through the office motel window. In truth, Dave was a karaoke coward.

"As a karaoke jockey," said the Prince, putting a sweaty arm around Dave, "I've come in contact with many people like Dave Middleton, and I'm glad to say I've converted at least half of them. Karaoke is NOT a talent competition, and NO ONE expects you to have real singing talent. Karaoke is all about having fun singing the songs you like to hear."

The crowd cheered.

"It's for all us everyday Joes of Kinmount who'll never see phase one of *American Idol*. People who say they hate karaoke show up with the wrong mentality. They come expecting a concert and then ridicule people who don't measure up. When encouraged to take part the response is always, 'Oh, I can't sing.' Just like Dave here. Fortunately, once they realize that it's just fun, and after a couple of drinks, they usually get in the spirit of things. Right, Dave?"

The Prince had not forgotten Dave had cut the opening Chorus speech. He had his revenge.

"If you can't beat them ... arrange to have them beaten," Dave said. "I'm leaving my opinions to science."

The crowd laughed until they stopped.

Dave waved to Kate and sat down. The Prince was flustered but quickly recovered: "And now, Justin Reimer is going to come up."

The iconic piano opening of "Don't Stop Believing" began. Surely the Prince was joking.

Justin journeyed to the stage.

"This is for you, Dave, and the company of *Romeo and Juliet*!" he shouted.

It was going to be a tragic demise worthy of Shakespeare. Worthy of Dave's "Uncle" Thomas.

Worthy of this noble Kinmount hero's Achilles heel—kara-oke.

It was officially time to stop believing.

And then a miracle happened.

At least to Dave it was a miracle.

Justin hit the high notes. He didn't just hit them, he owned them. Singer and audience became one in a giant karaoke communion of love and fellowship. Justin had done it again. He'd out-journeyed Journey.

The Red Lion exploded in a lighter-flickering ovation. Dave finally got it. Justin was *their* Steve Perry. He was the hope of Kinmount.

Justin sat down beside Dave.

"Just keep on believing," he said. "And, don't forget, you're speaking at our service tomorrow morning."

Dave had been too preoccupied with his town council defence to give his promise a second thought.

"Of course, I didn't forget," he lied. "Can you give me directions to your church?"

"Fifteen minutes south of your motel, big frame house. You can't miss it. I'll tie a white balloon on the mailbox. Eleven o'clock. And bring your appetite."

"So, no church?" asked Dave puzzled.

"Our home is the community meeting house. We're Mennonites," smiled Justin. He paid his respects and left the bar, high-fiving patrons on the way out the back door.

The karaoke machine spewed out the final song of the night—"Sweet Caroline." The Prince led the crowd, including Dave, in a drunken chorus of Neil Diamond's bah-bah-bahs. So loud, Dave bet all of Kinmount must have heard it.

Dave waited for Kate to shut down. He'd never attended church in his life except for a brief stint as a boy dragged to Sunday school before his father died.

"Did you know Justin was a Mennonite?" he asked, connecting the dots.

"You didn't know? There's a bunch of them live south of here. A splinter group from Kitchener or something. The modern kind."

"That explains him not arriving for rehearsal in a buggy."

"I never got to hear you sing," Kate said, locking the till.

"That's a good thing. I didn't notice you grabbing the mic either."

"Nope." A moment later: "Elspeth is at a sleep over tonight."

"That's nice." Dave was too busy wondering what he was going to say at a Mennonite church service to pick up on Kate's invitation.

"Feel like joining me on my roof for a nightcap?" she tried again.

"I'd love to but ..."

Kate's timing sucked. Panic and responsibility dictated a rain check for sure this time around.

"No worries. Forget about it." She busied herself sorting empties.

"It's not that. It's just—"

"Forget it."

"I promised Justin I'd speak at his church service tomorrow morning."

"You what?" She started to laugh.

"What's so funny?"

"You're going to speak at a Mennonite service?"

"Yeah, so—" He was beginning to turn red.

"You!"

"Yes, me. I shouldn't have mentioned it," he said embarrassed. He fumbled for his car keys.

"That I'd pay admission to see."

"You want to come with me?"

"Only if you churn butter for me," she laughed, turning off the lights.

"Seriously. I could use the moral support."

"Let me sleep on it."

"Anyhow, I've got to get back to my room and figure out

what the hell I'm going to say. I haven't done an all-nighter since theatre school."

"You okay to drive?"

"I'm good."

"Have fun."

"Parting is such sweet sorrow and some other such rubbish that hack from Stratford wrote."

"Good night," she said, opening the back door.

"When we're not together, I churn for you."

"Go back to your dorm and study," she said, playfully pushing him outside to the parking lot.

"I'd totally get shunned for you!" he shouted as she returned inside.

She locked the door behind him, and Dave was on the road. Mennonites, karaoke, and Kate spun in his head. He took no notice of the headlights behind him.

ELEVEN

Dave hadn't given his faith much thought. Most of his friends were God-fearing atheists. He was more of a universal believer, a clam chowder of influences and methodologies collected, tested, and rejected over the years—a Heinz 57 bouillabaisse of questions. Like the old joke about the insomniac, dyslexic agnostic who spent nights awake wondering if there was such a thing as a Dog.

If Dave *were* a religious man, the voice of Hamlet's father's ghost would be even more troubling. Elizabethans were in the midst of a theological war as to whether ghosts were truthful liars, or the product of an enfeebled brain. Catholics tended to believe in them as special apparitions from God, Protestants to believe they were the devil or a demon, and educated skeptics to believe they were the result of a mental process of self-deception. Gut instinct was nowhere in the equation.

"I always thought Mennonites were a bunch of stiff, humourless dairy farmers who preferred to live without electricity and Walmart," Dave said to B.J. as he entered the motel room.

"And hate buttons," said B.J., holding up a large grey one. He was sitting quietly on the orange shag carpet, surrounded by sewing supplies. A cross-country ski sock was slipped over his hand in a C-shape. In his other hand, he held a marker and was in the process of making two dots above the seam for eyes.

"Buttons?" said Dave, tossing his keys on the table and latching the door.

"Most Mennonites don't wear buttons," said B.J.

"Justin does."

"I wouldn't say Justin is your typical Mennonite."

Dave put on a pot of coffee and went online. Forty-five search engines later, he found an obscure selection of nineteenth-century Mennonite poetry.

"Listen to this," he said.

B.J. put down his needle and thread.

"Oh mighty Oak stand tall against the Sun,
Endure adversity's cruel Winter snow,
Branches of Faith bend down on God's bled son,
Crucified leaves to the mighty Winds blow."

"Cool. Very elemental," said B.J. "Rather Shakespearean?"

"Exactly what I was thinking, Watson."

"Is it?"

"No, it's a translation of a German Mennonite poet. Written almost two hundred years ago."

Dave grabbed his First Folio and flipped through the comedies.

"Aha!" he exclaimed.

"What?" said B.J., attaching an eye.

"Got it."

He found his cell phone and scrolled through his contacts. He found the number he was looking for and dialled.

The phone rang five times before the other end picked up.

"Hello?" said a groggy voice on the other end.

"Hi, Will, it's Dave. Dave Middleton. Sorry to wake you—"

"Do you know what time it is?" the voice mumbled, half asleep

"I know it's late but I really need your help."

"Are you okay?" said the voice. "Have you been drinking?"

"I'm fine. But I'm speaking at a church service tomorrow and you're the Bible expert so I was wondering if ..."

"LIST!"

"What the—" said Dave.

A rock came smashing through the window.

Kate showed up at ten with two coffees in hand. She saw the broken window as she approached the door.

"Hello," she shouted through the shattered glass.

"Hey," Dave shouted back, scrambling to open the door.

"Now what's happened?" she said.

Dave shook his head. "This came crashing through the window around four this morning," he said.

"We've got a new problem," said B.J., sitting at the end of his bed, clipping his toenails. He gestured with his newly created sock puppet to a large rock on the carpet. Crudely spray-painted on it, the words, "BEWARE THE FURIES!" in red block letters.

"Not cryptic at all," Dave muttered.

"Great," said Kate. "So, now Lola knows you're here."

"We haven't touched it," said B.J. "The police can dust for fingerprints."

"Have you called them?" Kate said, taking charge.

"I called them hours ago," replied B.J. "The dispatcher told me they were dealing with an emergency and she'd send two officers by this morning to get a statement."

"We checked outside and didn't see anything," said Dave.

"Have you asked any of the other guests if they saw anything?" said Kate.

"Guy next door was woken up by the smashing glass," said Dave. "When he opened his door all he heard was a vehicle racing down the road."

"Did it sound like a truck?" asked Kate.

"He couldn't tell. He'd had a few." Dave stifled a yawn. He hadn't slept in twenty-four hours and the coffee wasn't working.

Kate strung it all together. "She could've pulled in quietly with her headlights off. Rolled down her window, threw the brick, hit the gas and been out of sight in seconds. Did the owner see or hear anything?"

"Reilly was watching TV in his office," said Dave. "Had the volume turned up. Didn't hear a thing."

"He's cutting some boards for the window right now," said B.J.

"We now live in a society where pizza gets to your house before the police," said Dave. "It's been six hours!"

Worse than trying to hail a cab on New Year's Eve," said B.J.'s sock-puppet in a high-pitched squeak.

"Try calling them again," said Kate. "This is serious."

Dave checked his watch. "We have to get to the service."

"The service can wait," she said, putting her foot down.

"No, it can't," said Dave. "B.J., can you call them again?"

"As soon as I get these eyebrows sewn on," he said, holding up a bright piece of yellow yarn.

"Boys do not grow up to become men. They just grow bigger," said Kate, her exasperation with the two of them growing.

"You've said that before," remarked Dave, grabbing his First Folio and some hastily scrawled notes. "Got any new material?" He brushed past her.

"It bears repeating, don't you think?" she snapped back. "Watch out!" Dave narrowly missed cutting his toe on a shard of glass.

He exited the motel room followed by Kate, shutting the door behind her. "Jesus, this is a serious situation and you seem to be blowing it off like it's nothing," she exclaimed.

"No, I'm not," Dave responded. "We have to go. I gave my word to Justin. B.J.'s calling the police again."

He climbed into the passenger seat of Kate's Jeep and they headed south in quest of Justin's white balloon. He didn't notice she was wearing a light blue sun dress for the occasion, preoccupied as he was with making sense of his notes.

Under normal circumstances, it could have been an idyllic summer Sunday country drive. The kind of outing Dave's grandparents enjoyed when they were courting.

The Jeep passed one farmers' field after another, each dotted with giant party sandwiches of fresh hay.

"Speaking at this church service is not in my wheelhouse," Dave said, breaking the silence of the repetitive view. "Say a prayer for me, will ya?"

"Don't mention poperin pears," Kate riposted, not taking her eyes off the road.

TWELVE

The Reimer family home was a simple white, two-storey affair. A large tree in the front yard provided shade for a long veranda that was furnished with a single white rocking chair.

"It looks like something out of *The Waltons*," said Dave as Kate parked the Jeep on the grass beside the long, winding driveway. In front of them was an assortment of pickup trucks and family minivans. He could hear children laughing and dogs barking inside. The screen door opened, and Wayne and Shuster rushed out to greet them.

Justin and an older man in comfortable summer clothes (who could easily have been a descendent of Big Joe Mufferaw) were waiting for them on the porch.

"Greetings and welcome," boomed the older man, "I'm Noah, Justin's father."

"Pleased to meet you, sir," said Dave with an awkward formality. "And this is my ... uh, friend, Kate."

"Nice to meet you, Noah," said Kate, ignoring Dave.

"Your 'friend', eh?" laughed Noah. "I'd be making preserves with her ASAP if I were you. Before someone else invites her to make a quilt. Why, I broke a commandment just meeting her."

Justin gave his father a look.

"No offence intended," he quickly said to Kate. "My son has to remind me what year it is."

"None taken." Kate said.

Noah patted the porch railing. "My father, six brothers, and

I built this from the ground up. Forty-five summers ago," he explained to Kate.

"I had no idea you were Mennonite," Dave said to Justin while scratching Shuster's ears. "Why didn't you say something earlier?"

"I had to find out what you were all about," replied Justin. "You tell most people you're a Menno and they act strange. I didn't want it to influence how you treated me or directed me."

Noah rounded up the children, who happily hung from his beard, for Sunday school.

"Over the years, there has been a lot of splintering. Groups disagreed about how to best live out our faith," said Justin.

"You mean the horse and buggy crowd," said Dave.

"Yes. We're more progressive."

"So, what's *your* history?" asked Kate, taking in the Reimer's picture-perfect red barn and matching out-buildings.

"We're of the Swiss-South-German Mennonite strain that settled in southern Ontario in the early eighteen hundreds," explained Justin. "Came up from Pennsylvania after the American Revolution. We're pacifists and didn't take sides. What's the shortest book in the world?"

"What?" Dave asked.

"*Mennonite War Heroes*," Justin grinned. "Not taking sides didn't go over so well. So, we left. Moved to St. Jacobs. Forty years ago, my grandfather was getting tired of the rigidity of the old ways. So, he packed up and we settled here. The rest of the family followed."

"How many of you are there?" asked Kate.

"Come on in and you'll see," said Justin, opening the door for Kate. "Oh, and a word of warning, my grandfather mostly speaks Plautdietsch."

"Platypus-what?" asked Dave.

"It's our native language. It's inherently funny, really. But any joke in Plautdietsch is untranslatable. Don't even try."

"I won't," said Dave, winking at Kate.

"And, don't worry. Worship usually only lasts an hour. You'll be speaking at the end of the service. I'll introduce you."

Fifty Reimers—of all ages: aunts, uncles, grandparents, children, grandchildren, nephews, nieces, and neighbours—were assembled in the large family room. Only John was missing.

"Long shift. Overnight emergency," said Justin quietly. "A wedding brawl in town."

"The bride was probably the groom's sister," Dave whispered to Kate.

After a series of warm introductions, Noah slid a sturdy coffee table against the fireplace to make room for a podium. He was the family's worship leader.

The service opened with a hymn. Dave was bowled over by the Reimers' four-part harmony.

"The Von Trapp family has some serious competition," he whispered to Kate.

The closing segment of the worship was given over to personal testimony.

"We put our emphasis on the importance of community," Justin quietly informed Dave and Kate. "It's our prophet-sharing plan."

A family neighbour from down the road got up to speak.

"That's old Abe Loeb," whispered Justin. "He's speaking about the spiritual lessons he's learned from wood."

"I look past the ugliness and wounds to the beauty inside, both in wood and in people. God does the same," Abe concluded.

It was Justin's turn.

"I want to talk about bridging the gap between Mennos and non-Mennos," he began. "Faith and art are united. We, in the Highlands, need to be inspired to do and not just observe. We need more art and culture in our community. And we need people to spark that art. And one of those individuals is Dave Middleton, who is directing *Romeo and Juliet* for Kinmount's Summer in the Park Festival next weekend. I've gotten to know Dave over the past few weeks, and he is a gifted director with a passion for Shakespeare, and is a true tonic for our community.

He's going to share a few words with us."

"Here goes nothing," Dave said to Kate, getting up.

"No pears," she said.

He joined Justin, standing before an imposing, hand-carved hutch, littered with preserves.

He could not open with a joke. "A Mennonite walks out of a bar," would not fly.

He cleared his throat.

"Thank you, Justin. And thank you to all of you for inviting me to your service today. It is indeed an honour to be with you," he said stiffly. He remembered his breathing. His mouth was dry. Justin handed him a glass of water. He took a quick sip and opened his First Folio to a bookmarked page. The entire Reimer family was staring up at him with expectant looks.

"Don't disappoint them," he said aloud. He adjusted his notes and began:

"William Shakespeare knew what it was like to protect and promote his faith within a larger society that frowned upon him. He was, in fact, a closet Catholic, forced to carefully insert his beliefs in his works to avoid persecution and imprisonment by a Protestant monarch. Yet he prevailed. Despite the odds. His faith informing his art and his art informing his faith.

"'To be or not to be: that is the question.'

"The works of Shakespeare have given us some of the most profound statements in history, many of which are part of our everyday lives.

"'To thine own self be true' for example.

"But scholars have wondered if there might be parallels between the Bard and something a bit more divine. Shakespeare had a deep knowledge of the Bible. Now, was Shakespeare involved in the most important writing project of his time, the English translation of the King James Bible? Although there is no way to verify this, at least one set of clues indicates Shakespeare probably had some involvement with at the least the Old Testament.

"My good friend, Will Crosswell, the pastor of St. Matthew's United Church in Birch Lake, is a former classical actor. He explained it to me like this. Shakespeare lived from 1564 to 1616. The creation of the King James Bible began in the year 1610, the year in which Shakespeare would have been forty-six years old."

"The Globe Theatre had just burned down and Shakespeare had retired as a result, and moved back to Stratford. It was probably too much for him to bear, his precious theatre reduced to smouldering timbers.

"Is the King James the English translation you use?" Dave asked Noah.

"It is," confirmed Noah.

"Great," said Dave. "Please turn to Psalm 46 in your bibles. Now, count exactly forty-six words into the psalm. What word do you find?"

"Shake," offered up Justin.

"Now count forty-six words back from the end of that psalm. What word appears?"

"Spear," said Abe Loeb.

"Exactly," said Dave. "It just seems too much of a coincidence to think that it was by fluke that the forty-sixth Psalm would be translated around the time of Shakespeare's forty-sixth birthday and the forty-sixth word from the start and the forty-sixth word from the end would be 'shake' and 'spear.' Reverend Will believes Shakespeare slipped in a secret byline to prove it was his handiwork."

"So, why isn't this common knowledge?" asked Justin.

"It would have caused a scandal had it become known. Shakespeare was a kind of Taylor Swift of his day. A popular entertainer, but not somebody you'd put in charge of translating the Bible."

"Are you saying that the Old Testament is the word of Shakespeare and not God?" asked Justin's mother.

"Not at all," said Dave. "Reverend Will thinks Shakespeare just changed those two words. Using synonyms."

"He's got a lot of nerve," muttered Justin's grandfather.

"And, then again, maybe it's all a coincidence," said Dave affably, avoiding a debate. He was, after all, out of his theological element. "Now, I was reading through some of Shakespeare's plays in preparation for this morning, as well as some early Mennonite poetry. I came upon this passage from *As You Like It* that stood out. The play was written in 1599, about thirty years after the founding of the Mennonite Church in Europe, if I'm not mistaken?"

Some of the older members of the family nodded.

"In the play, a group of individuals flee a corrupt court and take refuge in the forest. There they are transformed. They find love and regeneration. They also meet up with the court dictator's banished brother, Duke Senior, and his band of exiled forest lords. He is in many ways the spiritual cornerstone of the play.

"I'm going to read a brief passage. It reminds me of what Mr. Loeb shared with us earlier this morning, finding beauty in wood and such. So, here is the banished duke talking to his followers:

'Now, my co-mates and brothers in exile,
Hath not old custom made this life more sweet
Than that of painted pomp? Are not these woods
More free from peril than the envious court?
Sweet are the uses of adversity,
And this our life, exempt from public haunt,
Finds tongues in trees, books in the running brooks,
Sermons in stones, and good in everything.
I would not change it.'

"It's hard to believe it wasn't written by a Mennonite poet. And doesn't it feel a bit like what we're all sharing this morning?" Dave asked.

The assembly murmured its approval.

He sat down and joined Kate. "Mission accomplished," he whispered.

"And you avoided the pears," she whispered back.

"Maybe Shakespeare was a closet Mennonite," joked Noah,

going to the front of the room. "Now, David, don't you actor types gather together and dress up to congratulate yourselves each January at your Golden Globe Awards?"

"Hollywood does, yes," replied Dave politely. It was not the time or place for a discussion on the difference between American film acting and Canadian theatre.

"Did you know we have *our* own Golden Globe Awards?" Noah continued.

"No, I did not, sir," said Dave, giving Justin a look.

"You bet we do," beamed Noah. "To honour the best Mennonite portzelky of the new year." The gathering of Reimers laughed.

"A portzelky is a deep-fried, ball-shaped raisin fritter," said Justin to Dave. "Delicious."

"I'll take your word for it," said Dave.

"Thank you again for sharing the Bard's words with us, David," Noah concluded. "Your insights have given us food for thought, indeed. Next week, Tobi Pekovich will be our guest speaker. His topic: 'A hoof and a heart both need mending.'"

Time was then allotted for silence and reflection. Prayers for the needs of others followed.

Strangely, Dave found himself thinking of Lola. What kind of Abe Loeb wood was she? A hardwood or a soft wood? Both it seemed. Was she a birch? Impossible. The souls of deceased wise women inhabited birch trees and Lola was anything but wise. The only thing she had in common with a birch tree was her "bark." An elm, perhaps? She certainly was diseased, but Whale was not a Dutch surname. She definitely wasn't a willow—Lola made other people weep. A maple? Yes, but a Manitoba Maple, because Lola was a festering weed. She'd messed up the wiring of his life, made communication impossible, electrocuted his mind, and tried to burn down the branches of his art. With hellfire.

Was Lola the kind of control freak who created her own hells before the real one could get to her? Dave certainly understood that terrain.

He took the moment to clear his mind of hell kindling. Superstitious nonsense and fearmongering. He took a left turn. Did Lola suffer from clinical depression? In Shakespeare's day, there was another term for depression: melancholy. Elizabethans thought melancholy was brought on by too much "black bile" in the body, which caused irritability, a distorted imagination, and all kinds of unpleasant symptoms. Lola certainly had the bile department covered.

If Lola visited an Elizabethan apothecary, his cure would've been simple: "Take two leeches and call me in the morning."

If only it were that easy in the twenty-first century.

THIRTEEN

Kate was annoyed.

She hated navigating the "washboard" side road.

"A grader needs to scrape this gravel road smooth again," she remarked as a stone chipped the windshield.

They drove in silence. Again.

Dave spoke first.

"So, I was thinking the whole community could build us a house, then a barn, and we'd have twelve or fourteen kids—you know, just you and me," he joked, relieved to have the service over.

"Ha, ha. Very funny." She turned onto the paved main road. "You did well today," she said, deliberately not looking at him.

A few kilometres whizzed by.

They got caught at a train crossing. An eastbound freight train roared by with two diesel engines in the lead. Dave began counting the cars aloud.

"What are you doing?" said Kate.

"Counting," Dave replied. "Two. As a kid, I was alone a lot, so I'd count the cars to relax. Four. Railroad yoga. Six. I used to flatten pennies on the tracks. Eight. I kept them in a Gerber's baby food jar. Ten ..."

One hundred and thirty cars later and they were on their way again.

"That's the last sound I want to hear before I die," said Dave.

"Now, there's a cheerful thought," said Kate, bouncing over the tracks and impatiently passing a slow-moving tractor.

"So," said Dave, "John shared that Lola has a legitimate alibi for the night of the tent attack." John had arrived home just as his mother was serving up sandwiches for lunch. He was uncharacteristically irritable, the wedding brawl having left him with a black eye and swollen wrist.

"Really?" Kate was skeptical.

"Apparently one of her Furies stayed over. And Lola reported her truck stolen. John said they found it on a bush road just north of town. Her tires and the imprints at the site are a match."

"What do you think?" Kate asked, glancing at a gathering of Jersey cows munching in a field.

"I'm not convinced," said Dave. "She could be covering for Lola."

"My thoughts exactly. Lola is cagey. And insane. One step ahead of the law."

"We need Columbo on this case. Always trust a rumpled trench coat, a low-key apology, and a glass eye."

"Actors," sighed Kate.

They pulled into the motel parking lot.

B.J. rushed out to meet them.

"Police didn't show up until an hour ago. Apparently they were dealing with a brawl at a wedding."

"Was John here?" asked Dave, wondering why John hadn't mentioned he'd been sent to the motel after the wedding.

"No, it wasn't John. I didn't recognize him. The other one was the older guy from the night of your arrest."

"Frank?" asked Dave.

"No. The other one."

"The one who smashed my head with the door?"

"Yeah. The tall guy."

"Tall guy?"

"Yeah."

"He wasn't that tall."

"Tall enough."

"But he wasn't tall."

"Taller than me."

"Are you two finished?" said Kate.

"And no one else saw anything?" said Dave.

"The few cars that were in the lot belonged to families with small kids on vacation. And they were all asleep. The rest of the guests were out. Probably at the wedding. A lot of bruises and black eyes limping in this morning, that's for sure," said B.J.

"Not surprised," said Kate. "And now you need security for the motel. Lola isn't going to quit."

"What's wrong with that woman?!" Dave exclaimed.

"If we could find an exorcist, we could take care of her," said B.J.

"We can't afford it. They'd repossess her," quipped Dave glumly.

Reilly strolled over to join them, a Louisville Slugger casually bouncing on his left shoulder.

"Called my insurance, all good. First thing tomorrow, I'm ordering security cameras. Hook them up to the TV in the office. Get some of them motion sensor lights. I'd just like to see anyone try something now with me walking the line."

He swung the bat narrowly missing Dave's head and taking out a patio lantern.

"Easy, slugger."

FOURTEEN

"The heat was hot."

The line from "A Horse with No Name" pretty much summed it up.

Birds were about to burst into flames.

Not only was it the hottest last Sunday in July in years, but to add perspiring insult to perspiring injury, it was also the hottest time of the hottest day, three p.m.

The sunstroke hour.

In short, it was a Kinmount Farmer's Almanac sizzling prophecy. The air smelled like ironing. The Burnt River earned its name. Even the sun was looking for shade.

Beside the old sawmill were the best parking spots, gauged by shade rather than distance. Not surprising, the Prince arrived first. The voice of Too Tall Tim could be heard joking on his afternoon show on the Prince's radio,

"We've got a scorcher, folks. It so hot Mennonites are buying air conditioners. Why, it's so hot I saw a funeral procession pull through the Dairy Queen. Jake Rowsome's cows gave powdered milk this morning. Clarence Pattimore's cornfield is popping. It's so hot that—"

Ginny pulled in and turned off her ignition.

"Whew! My seatbelt buckle feels like a branding iron," she groaned. "I actually burned my hand opening the car door."

The company assembled on the grass, awaiting instructions from Dave.

"Damn you, Al Gore," yelled Baldwin, raising his fist at the sun in mock protest.

"It's so hot the trees are fighting over Wayne and Shuster," said Justin, filling two bowls with a jug of water. He gingerly placed them under the picnic table without spilling a drop.

"I took a piss behind the mill, and it evaporated before it hit the ground," said the taller stoner, joining the border collies under the picnic table.

"I washed and dried my clothes at the same time this morning," said Miranda, leaning her bike against the tree.

"My sweat is sweating," complained the Friar.

"It's so hot I'm going to water board myself," said the Sarge, pulling off his tank top.

"Me too," said his son.

"Did you see anything last night?" asked Dave.

"It was so quiet you could hear the flap of a barn owl's wings," the Sarge replied. "You ever hear a barn owl in flight?"

"No," said Dave.

"My point," said the Sarge. "Quieter than a Shenyang J-31 fifth-generation stealth multirole fighter."

"Okay ... good," said Dave whose knowledge of aircraft was limited to Air Canada Jazz Tango.

There was no need to get the company worked up about the rock incident at the motel before the run-through. He and B.J. had agreed to that on the drive in.

"Gather round!" Dave clambered on top of the picnic table. "I know it's hot. But we can use it in the run. The play is set during a blistering July heat wave. How does this affect the characters' judgments? Emotional states? Hangovers plus heat equal double dehydration. Not only for Mercutio, but also for all of you. Keep drinking water backstage. If you feel sick, we will stop. No sunstroke martyrs.

"Today is an important day. Not just for Kinmount, but for theatre everywhere. It is the battle against censorship. We are drawing a line in the sand. A line worth fighting for."

"Are we changing anything?" asked the Nurse, fanning herself. Life was imitating art again.

"No, we are not," Dave declared. "Not a single thing. Not a word, not a line, not a gesture, not a single bit of stage combat. We are going to attack the story the way we've rehearsed it, the way Shakespeare would've wanted it to be attacked. Full throttle. Making every moment count. We have persevered despite impossible obstacles."

"What about the council?" Peter shouted out.

"The council?" asked Dave rhetorically.

He looked to the blazing sun for an answer.

The sun appeared to wink back.

He squinted in understanding.

Then, as quietly as the cracked smile that now formed beneath his glistening nose, he began to recite and improvise:

"Proclaim it, Baldwin McGregor,
That he or she which have no stomach to this fight,
Let them depart; their gas tank shall be made
And toonies for convoy put into their pockets:
We would not die in that actor's company
That fears their fellowship to die with us."

"Who's going to die? What's he talking about? I'm not going to die. Fuck that," muttered the shorter stoner.

"Shut up," hissed B.J. "He's quoting *Henry the Fifth*. He's using death as a metaphor. He's boosting our morale. Listen."

Dave rallied himself. The theatrical hybrid of Winston Churchill and Kenneth Branagh bursting to life.

"This day is called the feast of Kinmount—"

"What?" The shorter stoner was confused.

"Ssshhh!" Justin gave him a look.

Dave's departure from literary tradition was an inspired variation. It was a boisterous parody so full of loving tribute that the seniors across the river, who had gathered in the heat, raised their canes and walkers; a small number were of British descent, remembering their Second World War childhoods and Laurence Olivier delivering the same inspiring speech, sans

Kinmount, during a BBC radio programme.

Dave plunged onward:

"She or he that outlives this day, and sees old age,

Will stand tiptoe when the day is named,

And rouse them at the name of Kinmount."

"Kinmount!" shouted a feisty senior, waving her box of Kleenex.

Dave waved back. He began climbing each rung of the difficult speech he'd put to memory years ago in speech class. His voice, a blast of hot air, catching fire.

"Old men forget: yet all shall be forgot,

But those here today will remember with advantages

What feats they did this day: then shall our names be as

Familiar in their mouth as household words,

Be in their flowing cups freshly remember'd:

Dave, B.J., and Miranda,

Justin and Baldwin,

Ziggy, Joan, and Lauren—"

"And me!" yelled the Prince.

"And you, oh mighty Prince!" Dave shouted.

The Prince beamed.

"And so you all!" shouted Dave with a victory cry.

He had won. Even if the council censored the production, the company had succeeded in achieving something more important—solidarity. They were applying the best of themselves to their fight for justice.

"This story shall the good parent teach their son;

And August in Kinmount shall ne'er go by,

From this day to the ending of the world,

But we in it shall be remember'd;

We few, we happy few, we band of sisters and brothers—"

Dave was in full stride, Shakespeare and Kinmount neck and neck:

"For you today who shed your sweat with me

Shall be my sister and brother—"

"I've already shedded everything!" interrupted the taller stoner.

The company roared with laughter.

"And those on council now come to judge
Shall think themselves accursed,
And hold their manhoods cheap whiles any speaks
That fought with us upon Saint Kinmount's day!"

Wayne and Shuster barked. The company cheered. The English soldiers at Agincourt would have cheered. Dave caught his breath.

"Saint Kinmount, that'll be the day," sneered the taller stoner.

"Has a nice ring to it," said Justin.

The Mayor and his council arrived a few seconds later, lawn chairs in tow. Elizabeth Mackenzie, the summer student reporter, followed.

"It's hot enough out here to breed sheep," whined the Mayor, wiping his brow. His forehead was steaming. "It's so dry we'll have to ship the fish in the Burnt River to Lake Ontario so they don't forget how to swim."

"Hotter than a firecracker lit at both ends," panted Booger. "My armpits are making their own gravy." The stains on both sides of his white shirt dripped down to his waist.

"He's wearing Crocs," said Baldwin, pointing at Booger's green plastic slip-ons.

"The holes are there to let his dignity flow out," said Dave.

"You all ready?" asked the Mayor.

Dave nodded.

"Well, let's get 'er done," said the Mayor, opening his lawn chair.

The rest of the council assembled their chairs in the shade. Elizabeth was busy taking notes.

א

"Gregory, upon my word, we'll not carry coals," exclaimed Capulet's second servant in disgust, entering from the saw mill and dropping his heavy burden—a basket filled with stage weights—with a loud thud, centre stage. Centre "grass" to be specific.

"No, for then we should be colliers," came the quick-witted response from Capulet's first servant, the shorter stoner, in hot pursuit ...

The play exploded with a fury and a focus unlikely to be seen again. Dave had never experienced anything like it. Performing as if their lives depended on it. And in a sense they did. Two hours passed in the space of a minute.

The Mayor stifled a yawn.

The company awaited his critique.

Elizabeth had two headlines ready to go. Her pen was poised.

The Mayor cleared his throat.

"Let me begin by saying ...

FIFTEEN

The Kinmount Crier

"City Council Okays *Romeo and Juliet* content"

By Elizabeth Mackenzie

KINMOUNT—Members of the Kinmount Town Council have given their enthusiastic approval to an open-air production of William Shakespeare's *Romeo and Juliet* that opens a three-day run this Friday.

Directed by Birch Lake resident David Middleton, the play makes use of a local cast and local financial support.

The production—which takes place at 8 p.m. Friday, Saturday, and Sunday in the park beside the old sawmill—has faced controversy after producer Lola Whale disassociated herself from it over her concerns about violent content.

As a result of Ms. Whale's concerns, Kinmount's Town Council viewed a dress rehearsal of the production Sunday evening and thought it was a "wonderful production," said Mayor Mike McGee.

Committee chair Tom "Booger" Lacey said he enjoyed the production very much. He admitted he was even surprised by the show's professionalism and said he would not hesitate to bring youngsters to see it.

Town councillor, Marje Galligan, who also saw Sunday's sneak preview said, "The cast was really terrific, and the river setting added a lot to the production."

Mrs. Galligan said she had no problem with the violence in the production. She felt the production was true to the time in which it was set, a time when "women were not treated very well."

Mr. Lacey agreed. He said the play does indeed include some "bawdy funny things." But he felt everything in the play was a fair depiction of what Shakespeare wrote.

Admission to Romeo and Juliet is free, with donations gratefully accepted by the cast and crew.

There is limited seating so please bring a lawn chair or blanket and bug spray.

SIXTEEN

The taste of victory was sweet.

The company celebrated at the Red Lion, Kate and Jimmy behind the bar improvising Italian shooters, a combination of Campari, extra dry vermouth, cane sugar, ground cinnamon, and, Miranda's favourite, lemon juice—the chaser. It was the ultimate party shot, dropping the Campari and vermouth into a glass of orange juice, lighting it on fire, and downing it as fast as possible. The lemon juice reluctantly followed.

It left a bad taste in Dave's mouth. "Symbolic of the Capulet-Montague feud," he said, mid-toast. He was actually thinking of his bitter feud with Lola.

"You slayed the Goliath of censorship," Robert said to Dave with a grand smile that covered his eyes. He had dropped in to mark the occasion. "With the sling of your integrity."

The Goliath of censorship. Dave liked the sound of that.

Word travelled fast.

The Peterborough Examiner, *The Lindsay Post*, and *The Whig-Standard* picked Elizabeth Mackenzie's article up the next morning. To Dave's surprise, it was the front-page headline in *The Birch Lake Beacon*. Skip left a message on his cell phone with the news.

"My mother must have phoned the editor," Dave said.

The news of the council's endorsement of Dave's vision spread like wildfire. Social media sites ate it up. Dave's friends and colleagues, his mother's Facebook group, and, a mash-up of middle-aged dog and cat lovers, liked and shared. And re-liked and re-shared.

Hashtags exploded on theatre community Twitter feeds: #UncensoredBard.

By Wednesday, the article went national.

The Globe and Mail's theatre critic called Dave for an interview.

After reading the article, a copy shop in Haliburton donated their services to the cause. The cast spent Tuesday afternoon re-postering.

Early Wednesday evening Dave conducted the technical setup. Rufus Sly, a friend of Peter the Clown, drove in from Lindsay towing a trailer of lighting and sound equipment, stands, and extension cords.

Rufus was big of beard and clad in plaid, a lumbersexual—even in summer—who had never been near a sawmill until showing up at the rehearsal site. He was a card-carrying Tinder date. He no doubt sipped craft beer at a university bar with sad eyes and a permanent unrealized dream of living in an isolated bush shack. His artfully scruffy hair was barely contained by his ridiculous woollen toque. He looked like an extra who had wandered off the *Game of Thrones* set.

There was something fundamentally wrong, Dave thought, with appearing rugged, when Rufus had probably spent twenty minutes of his morning delicately trimming his beard in a bathroom mirror.

"He's a metro-jack, I'm sure of it," said Paris to Dave, with a smirk.

"A metro-jack?" asked Dave.

"A metro-jack is a man who falls in the category between a metrosexual and lumbersexual," explained Peter.

It was all a bit much for Dave.

There was no active power source in the old sawmill. Moreover, the marina was too far away. Justin brought in a generator.

"Do you have any lavalier mics?" Dave asked Rufus, who was busy uncoiling extension cords.

"Eh?"

"Do you have any lavs?" Dave repeated.

"One sec." Rufus left his tangled mess of extension cords snaked together on the grass and hauled out a lighting stand and ladder from the back of his vintage pickup truck. "I thought you were doing the show without mics," he said, climbing up the ladder and gesturing for Dave to hand him up a Leko. "Lavs will cost you extra."

"I just need one," said Dave. He steadied the base of the ladder.

"One?" asked Rufus, puzzled. He plugged in his light and hopped down.

"It's for my Lady Capulet," explained Dave. "She's as quiet as a mouse in a grave. I would like to augment her volume so she matches the rest of the cast's voices. Feasible?"

"No problem, Davo," said Rufus, giving Dave a quick high five. "Consider it done." Rufus adjusted his fake glasses, jotted down the microphone addition in his faux-leather notebook, and lumbered over to his truck.

"Davo?" said Dave, watching Rufus wrestle with a mosquito.

"Metro-jack hipster slang," replied Peter.

"Davo" reviewed his plan with Ginny. "There's no rain in the forecast for the next five days. The show begins at eight. The lights kick in an hour later at dusk, just as Mercutio and Benvolio stumble into Capulet's orchard after the party in search of Romeo. By the time the balcony scene starts it will be a glorious summer night, the lights and the moon doing the trick to illuminate B.J. and Miranda."

"Hey," shouted the Nurse, sitting in the front seat of the Prince's van. "Too Tall Tim just announced Lola is his guest on his call-in show tomorrow afternoon."

"That I want to hear," said Baldwin, plunking himself down in the shade.

"I'd pay to be a shadfly on that wall," said the Nurse. "You should call in, Dave."

"Yeah, right," said Dave. "And after I can jump in the Burnt River."

"C'mon, share your side of things," coaxed the Nurse.

"I'm not poking that bear," said Dave. Never give a Fury a second chance.

"Tell Kinmount what really happened," said the Nurse.

"The ten people in Kinmount who can actually read a newspaper already know the truth," said Dave. "Lola is a paradox with a very short fuse. Besides, have you listened to the idiot who hosts the show? He thinks Moosehead is a misdemeanour. Leave it."

"It might help sell tickets," offered up Miranda.

"I'm not calling."

Dave returned alone to the motel. He knew Lola had to be cooking up something in that feverish brain of hers. But the "what" would have to wait.

SEVENTEEN

Thursday is nothing in itself, a Friday wannabe. And nothing screws up a Friday more than realizing it's Thursday.

It's the day named after Thor, the hammer-wielding Norse god of Marvel comics and Disney takeovers.

It's the day ruled by Hecate, the ancient Greek witch-goddess, the proper day for dark magic and spell casting.

And it was the day of Lola's live radio rodeo.

They sat at the Red Lion bar: Dave and B.J. each drinking a Keith's, Miranda sipping on pineapple juice, Baldwin nursing a hangover cure, and Kate listening to the radio. The air conditioner wheezed and rattled in a losing battle against the heatwave. It was three p.m. Two hours before their technical rehearsal.

"I hate pineapples," Baldwin growled. His head was throbbing. The basket of greasy fries and chicken fingers and glass of Coke weren't working.

"No one asked you," said Miranda, with just a trace of superiority. "I hate chicken fingers, but you don't see me volunteering my opinion without being asked."

"Freedom of speech," said Baldwin, dipping a cold fry in his plum sauce.

"Freedom to be rude," Miranda corrected him. "Polite society is a combination of manners and knowing when to speak and when not to."

"Maybe I don't want to be polite." Baldwin chewed and spewed with his mouth open. "So, my hating pineapples and voicing my opinion will lead to the fall of civilization. Is that what you're saying?"

"In a manner of speaking, yes. You should try being more like a pineapple. Stand tall, wear a crown, and be sweet on the inside. Like me." Miranda scored her point, stole a French fry, and headed for the washroom.

"It's a stupid name!" Baldwin shouted after her. "There's no pine, and there's no apple."

Kate turned up the radio. An old-time gospel hymn was winding down.

"I'm gonna have the time of my life
when the time of my life is over,
I'm gonna get carried away
when I get carried away."

"That was a big hit for the Heritage Singers back in the day. There ain't no classic like an old classic," the all too familiar voice of Too Tall Tim chimed in.

"Does everyone in Kinmount have the same DNA?" Dave said in disgust to the radio.

"I resemble that remark," said Baldwin.

"That's why the cops haven't arrested anyone yet. The DNA all matches, and there are no dental records," said Dave gloomily.

"Will you two be quiet," scolded Miranda.

The oddball sound of a slide-whistle descending in pitch cut in.

"On the weather front, there's no relief in sight," announced Too Tall Tim. "Environment Canada says we're expecting no rain from the east and the west and the south and not even a little bit from the north. Forty degrees on the thermometer I'm looking at right now through the station window. I just said that without fainting." He burst out laughing, taking Dave and the Red Lion by surprise. A howling hee-haw of horror.

"Is he having a seizure?" Baldwin snickered.

"Someone should tell him it's not his jokes people are laughing at," said B.J.

"I should call in," said Dave. "Tell him the village wants its idiot back."

"Stop being so mean. He just has a special gift that makes people laugh more than any joke could," said Miranda.

"Who's laughing?" Baldwin smirked.

"Hey, Tim," said Dave to the radio again. "Why do the geese fly over your station upside down? Because there's nothing worth crapping on."

Tim regained his on-air composure: "Heck, even the mercury is boiling. Highland farmers, a word of warning, feed your chickens crushed ice, or they'll be laying hard-boiled eggs."

"Seriously," said Dave.

"This just in." Tim rifled through a ream of papers. "There's a swarm of locusts heading our way from the prairies, but the weather folks figure the heat will kill the lot of them."

"Will someone please kill *him*," said Dave.

"Now, we all know that the heatwave is due to that global warming," said Tim. "According to a statement from Green Peas, if global warming continues, in twenty years, the only chance we'll have to see a polar bear is in a zoo. So, in other words, nothing is gonna change."

"He's got a point," said Baldwin.

"Me and Booger went out for lunch yesterday," Tim continued. "After a delicious slice of Alice's coconut cream pie, we headed back to Booger's hardware store. I needed to pick up a lawn chair for *Romeo and Juliet*. More on that coming up with our special guest, Lola Whale."

Dave sighed.

"So we're opening the door when Booger overhears his cashier telling a customer, 'We haven't had it for a while, and I doubt we'll be getting it soon.'

Booger jumps in and quickly assures the customer that he'd have whatever it was she wanted by next week. After she left, Booger reads the cashier the riot act. 'Never tell the customer that we're out of anything. Tell them we'll have it next week. Now, what did she want?'

'Rain.'"

Too Tall Tim's laughter would not, and could not, be
tamed.

"Can you put some vodka in this?" Baldwin asked Kate,
handing her his glass. Twenty years of living in Kinmount was
twenty years too many.

"And now a word from our sponsor, Acil Earp's Used Weapons," Tim announced.

A pre-recorded advertisement played.

"Does the high cost of security have you blue? If so, come
by the store and browse through our complete selection of used
guns and knives, or find what you need in our mace and tear gas
department. Now we understand that many people are hesitant
to buy used weapons, but all of Earp's used weapons are absolutely guaranteed to kill. If you find a weapon here that won't
kill, you bring it back, and we'll give you something that will. It's
our guarantee. If Earp's can't kill it, it's immortal."

"Just like Lola," said Baldwin.

"Is that guy for real?" said Dave. Four more days and he
could kiss Kinmount goodbye. Forever.

"We're at the top of the hour, and it's time for the news,"
said Tim.

There was a flustered pause.

"Now, where did it go? I had it here a minute ago."

The sound of Too Tall Tim madly sorting through papers,
banging his head on his desk, and cursing filled the airwaves.

"Where in the hell did I put them pages?" he muttered, still
on-air. "I've looked everywhere and still can't find them. Well,
I'll find them later. Anyhow, here's a quick low down. World
peace talks break down. Attack imminent."

"Brilliant," said B.J.

"Very concise," said Dave.

"Hit Kinmount first," said Baldwin.

Too Tall Tim was back at it:

"And now it's time for our main event, the ribeye of ribeyes,
our weekly afternoon call-in show *Tall Talk with Tim*. Today's

topic: 'To bard or not to bard, that is the question.' My guest today is the grand dame herself, Lola Whale. Helloooo, Lola!"

"Hang on to your hats," said Dave.

"Good afternoon, Mr. Perkins." Lola's response was calm and polite.

"I know that tone," quipped Dave, a trace of unease registering in his voice. "The lull before the storm."

"Sssshhh!" hushed Kate.

"To get our listeners up to speed, there's been a lot of controversy these past two weeks over a new play in our community. Now, it's not new in the sense of when it were written. How old is *Romeo and Juliet,* Lola?"

"Juliet is almost fourteen," said Miranda, playfully elbowing B.J.

"The play is four hundred years old, Mr. Perkins," said Lola, now a self-appointed Renaissance scholar.

"Four hundred and twenty-five years," said Dave. "She knows nothing about the bloody plot or the date it was written but, she sure knows what a poperin pear was used for."

"Four hundred years!" exclaimed Tim. "That is old. That's when rainbows were in black and white."

"Anyone got a needle," said Dave.

"Now then," said Tim, attempting a British accent, "*Romeo and Juliet* was written by Will-i-am Shake-speare."

"He's giving Keanu Reeves a run for his money," Dave quipped. Keanu set the standard for bad accents in acting when he co-starred in Coppola's *Dracula*. "Whoa, it's a vampire, dude," said Dave, imitating the *Bill & Ted* slacker star.

"Aye, but Dick van Dyke, 'e makes Keanu look like Lawrence Oliver," said B.J., putting on a terrible cockney accent.

"Hush!" Miranda scolded.

Lola was in the middle of replying to Too Tall Tim.

"Correct, Mr. Perkins," she said. "The Swan of Avon himself."

"Listen to her," said Dave. "Like she's on a first-name basis with him."

"But Shakespeare is new to Kinmount," said Tim. "This is the first time the Bard has been performed here, is it not?"

"It is," said Lola, without a trace of vitriol.

"And *Romeo and Juliet* opens tomorrow night down by the old sawmill?"

"We shall see," said Lola.

"What!?" sputtered Dave, spilling his Keith's.

"Really," said Tim. "Now, Lola, you have some issues with the production. And you quit as the show's producer?"

"That I do and did," answered Lola with a measured formality.

"Would you care to share your issues with our listeners?"

"Her issues?!" Dave fired back at the radio. "How much time have you got, Tim?"

Lola recapped her concerns.

"We in Kinmount have been duped and deceived. Mr. Middleton's perverted direction of this beautiful love story is a smut-filled, immoral, violent attack on women. It is not suitable for families or pets."

"Pets!?" Dave repeated.

"I see," replied Tim. "Now, the Mayor and town council watched a run-through on Sunday night, and it was reported in the paper on Monday that, by all accounts, they enjoyed the show. Gave it their full support. What do you say to that?"

"They are obviously mistaken," Lola replied. "Someone has to be the moral watchdog for this community."

"Ah, the pet she's talking about," said Baldwin.

"Well, we appreciate that, we surely do," said Tim, ever the likeable and diplomatic host. "Should *Romeo and Juliet* be performed this weekend? I want to give you, our loyal listeners, the opportunity to weigh in. So, if you have a question for Lola, give us a ring. The phone lines are open."

"Brace yourselves," said Dave. "She can start an argument in an empty house."

The first caller rang in.

"Hello, you're on the line," said Tim.

"Am I on?" said a voice.

There was an instantaneous burst of feedback.

"Turn your radio down!" Tim shouted. "My ears are under attack!"

"Sorry, I forgot," said the voice.

"Please!" the Red Lion blurted out.

"This is Dorothy Barker, chair of the textbooks committee at Kinmount Secondary School," said the voice.

"What's up, Mrs. Barker?" asked Tim, a trace of apprehension in his voice. Dorothy was a call-in regular.

"I agree with Lola," stated Mrs. Barker.

"Thank you, my dear," replied Lola graciously.

"Great," muttered Dave. "Any bets on whether Dorothy Barker is a book-burner?"

"And what, pray tell, is wrong with *Romeo and Juliet*?" asked Tim.

"It depicts sex among teenagers," warned Mrs. Barker. "And we're not for that, and we're certainly not going to encourage it. Furthermore, it shows a rampant disrespect for parental authority."

"You are aware that William Shakespeare wrote the play?" said Tim.

"Oh, yes we are. And I'm looking into the rest of his stuff too. He wrote *Barefoot in the Park*, didn't he?"

Dave rolled his eyes. "Listen to her." An idea hit him. "She has to be part of Lola's coven," he said. "Along with Flo, the Laundry-Copy shop owner."

"LIST!"

"Shut up," Dave whispered to himself.

"What?" Kate asked.

He pointed to his head.

Too Tall Tim answered the phone in his studio.

"You're on the air," he said broadly.

"Hey there, Tim, I just want to say how much I enjoy your program," the voice said.

"Why, thank you. And who do I have on the line?"

"Marilyn Jenkins."

"Well, if isn't our Member of Parliament. Fancy that. Are you working hard or hardly working?" Tim chortled.

"He does have the common touch," said B.J.

"You know what that idiot and your beer bottle have in *common*?" said Dave. "They're both empty from the neck up."

"Ssshhh!" Kate and Miranda hushed him in unison.

Marilyn Jenkins, a real estate lawyer by trade, was well versed in manipulating the media to her advantage.

"I'm back in the riding on summer recess and I'm looking forward to seeing all my constituents this weekend at Summer in the Park," she read off her prepared notes.

"*And* you're judging the monster truck pull at the race-track?" said Tim.

"You bet. I come from good Kinmount farming stock, Tim."

"Oh, we know you do, Marilyn. When's the last time you were in the barn loft? Just kidding." He wasn't. "So, what do you have to say to Lola?"

"Ms. Whale, I'd rather be offended by Shakespeare than censor him," Marilyn said. "If we sometimes have to take a deep breath at what we hear in Shakespeare, so be it; better a lungful of indignation than a world in which the remorseless hand of evil prevails. Shame on you, Ms. Whale, for trying to derail this cultural event in our community. I'll see everybody at opening night tomorrow. Break a leg, Mr. Middleton and team."

She hung up.

"Do you have a response to that, Lola?" said Tim.

"You bet she does," grumbled Dave.

"Quiet," said Miranda.

"Sadly, the prime minister, who, may I point out, was a drama teacher at one time, has corrupted Ms. Jenkin's values," said Lola. "Ottawa is a liberal cesspool. And Ms. Jenkin has become a part of it."

"But didn't you volunteer on Marilyn's last campaign?" said Tim.

"Good one," said Baldwin.

"A brief lapse of judgment, Mr. Perkins, and nothing more," replied Lola curtly. "I was tricked, the same way Mr. Middleton tricked me into producing *Romeo and Juliet*."

"Hear that?" sputtered Dave. "She lies better than a used-car salesman. It's pathological."

He turned his attention back to the radio.

"Alright, Lola, let's tape the cow's udder for a moment," argued Tim. "Did you not run for council a few years back on a platform to open a nudist beach?"

"She wanted it to be a family nudist beach," said Baldwin.

"Did she now?" said Dave, downing his second Keith's. "Try and stop a sixteen-year-old teenager from getting a hard-on. Behold the great crusader for children's morality. Pellet guns speak louder than words, Lola!"

"I am not here to discuss beaches," said Lola bluntly.

"Fine," said Tim. "But you did pitch your summer Shakespeare to the community committee long before any director was hired."

"I don't recollect anything of the kind." Her voice was becoming strained.

Too Tall Tim returned to the phone lines.

"Okay, caller number three, you're on. Let it all out."

"Steve Stotts, Tim."

Amplified feedback interrupted the transmission. Kate grimaced.

"Steve! Turn that radio down! Folks, you have to remember to turn your radio down when you call in, 'cause it just blows the hell out of my ears! So what about *Romeo and Juliet*?"

"Sure, let it go on. I'm calling to announce I will be a candidate for town council in this fall's election."

"Steve, we're talking Shakespeare here. Besides, you've been running for town council as long as I can remember. Why don't you just give up?"

"Now, in the past elections, my opponents have made personality a major issue. Let's face it, in a personality contest,

I'm always going to lose. I mean, I'm a dentist and I was born in Toronto, and a lot of people naturally seem to hate me."

"You're right there, Steve," Kate spoke up, addressing the radio. "Idiot."

"You know him?" said Dave, surprised.

"My ex," Kate said. "He's an experiment in Artificial Stupidity."

"Your ex is a deadbeat dentist?" said Dave, having a hard time matching the voice on the radio partnered with cool-hand Kate behind the bar.

"Skip it," she said matter-of-factly.

"BUT THIS YEAR," Steve shouted in a voice too loud for radio, "I'm injecting new and vital issues that cannot be ignored by the voters. Did you know there are thousands of Canadians who pay no taxes whatsoever?"

"Like who, Steve?" Kate said to the radio again.

"Like welfare mothers and prisoners!" said Steve by way of an unprompted response.

"They don't pay any taxes?" asked Tim.

"No! And it would be easy to tax the prisoners, 'cause everyone knows where they are."

"Well, you've got a point there, Steve, but we're talking Shakespeare with Lola Whale and—"

"And I think we should have a volunteer police department," Steve said, cutting Tim off. "I've crunched the numbers and it makes a lot of sense. We find volunteers and, as long as they own their own vehicle, we give them a badge."

"And if that doesn't work out, we can always just declare anarchy and see what happens," said Dave to the radio.

"Thanks for that, Steve. And we wish you the best of luck this time around."

"Well, you only have to win once to—"

Too Tall Tim hung up the studio phone.

"I tell you, that Steve Stotts is a man ahead of his time," laughed Tim. "Remember you heard it here first, folks. But right now we're talking Shakespeare. Ah, here's caller number four. You're on the air."

"This is Earl Patelle, Tim. I have a question for Ms. Whale."

"Yes, Mr. Patelle," said Lola.

"Who's Earl Patelle?" Dave asked.

"Publisher of the *Crier*," said Kate.

"Is creativity good for children?" asked Mr. Patelle.

"Healthy creativity is," responded Lola.

"Would you say Shakespeare was creative?"

"Of course," said Lola.

"Then why do you believe that creativity should be censored?"

"That's not what I'm—"

"Do you believe in human rights, Lola?"

"You will let me finish my sentence—" she was getting flustered.

Mr. Patelle continued to talk over her. "One of our basic rights is the right to knowledge. And Shakespeare provides knowledge. Do you disagree?"

"No, I do not disagree, but—"

"Exactly my point. In our little village of Kinmount, our town council got it right."

"Nice left-hook, Earl," observed Dave.

"Knock-out," said Baldwin.

"Good day, Ms. Whale." Mr. Patelle hung up.

Lola was incensed. "How dare you hang up on me? I will not stand for such—"

"I'm afraid you're sitting," interrupted Tim. "I'll take the next caller."

"I just want to say who cares if Shakespeare's language isn't exactly dinner-table talk," said a voice that sounded remarkably like that of the Nurse. "He wrote to entertain his audience. They were just as entertained by dirty jokes as our own audience is today—except now instead of playing on words about being 'hung,' we see Will Ferrell's ass on screen. I am pleased that the mayor and council understand that and support it. I think it's time, Lola, for you to get your head examined."

"My head examined!" screeched Lola. "I could get on your level, Joan Gallagher, but I don't like being down on my knees as much as you do."

"Watch the language there, Lola. We're a family show," jumped in Tim. "I wouldn't want to have to censor you now."

"And while you're at it, Lola, try joining the twenty-first century, you crazy witch," said the Nurse.

"Crazy witch! Mr. Perkins, are you going to let her speak to me like that!"

"Now, she's done it," said Dave. "Stop baiting her," he begged the radio. "Hang up!"

Before Tim could utter a word, the Nurse fired off another shot. "Is it true your second husband was found dead in a red bikini?"

"That is a malicious rumour, and you know it," roared Lola.

"It was a turquoise one-piece," said Baldwin to Dave.

"And aren't you under investigation for vandalism and attempted manslaughter?" enquired the Nurse.

"Oh boy," said Dave. "She's really pushing it."

"Liar!" Lola fired back. "My truck was stolen by those ne'er-do-wells who ran over their tent themselves and are framing me for it. I was nowhere near their rehearsal site. This is the kind of riffraff we have attracted to our community."

"You're the only riffraff in Kinmount, Lola," said the Nurse, hanging up.

"How dare you, Joan Gallagher!" Lola screamed.

"Well, that's all the time we have for today, folks," said Tim, trying to salvage the afternoon. "Don't forget to check out *Romeo and Juliet* this weekend and support some local acting talent."

"Are you defending Dave Middleton and his band of liars, thieves, and whores, Mr. Perkins?" Lola demanded.

"Special thanks to my guest, Lola Whale, for being with us—"

"Answer my question. Are you?!" she roared.

Tim took a deep breath and forced a friendly sign-off. "Join me next week when our guest will be, well, I'm not sure who our guest will be, but I'm sure they'll be great."

He hit the off-air button. Unbeknownst to Tim, the button stuck.

"We're off the air, Lola," said Tim. "Please, leave."

"Don't you use that tone with me," she growled. "My first husband tried that and he found himself an early grave."

Ba-bang.

"They're still on the air and that idiot doesn't know it," said Dave.

The entire village of Kinmount was glued to their radios. Cars pulled over, merchants and customers stopped mid-transaction to listen, the bank locked its doors early. It was the radio boxing match of the century.

"You evil little dwarf," Lola cried.

"There's no call for words like that," spluttered Tim.

"You will show me some respect!"

"Respect!? You're a lying hypocrite."

"Hypocrite! How dare you!"

"Would you prefer nuttier than a squirrel turd?"

"Here we go," said Dave, gripping the bar.

"If you pulled your socks up you'd be blind," Lola laughed cruelly. "Too bad the midway won't let you on the rides this weekend!"

"God only lets things grow until they're perfect!" Tim fired back. "It's always the hypocrites pointing the moral finger. Get off your high horse and take a look at yourself."

"I'll high horse you," she shouted.

"The show is over, Lola," said Tim. "Get out!"

"Come here, little man," she ordered, ignoring his appeal.

"What's she doing now?" shouted Miranda.

"She's taunting him," said Dave.

"Put down that ashtray!" shouted Tim in a panic.

"You can smoke in a radio station?" asked B.J.

"Put that ashtray down!" Tim hollered again.

"Stop me!" bellowed Lola.

A loud scream echoed across the county.

"Did she just slam it down on his head?" said Baldwin.

The radio began to chant.

"Hecate! Come owl-eye Goddess, seer, walker in the dark!"

"What are you doing, Lola?" winced Tim in pain. "Sit down!"

"Grandmother of the moon!" Lola wailed.

"What is that crazy loon doing now?" exclaimed Baldwin mid-swallow.

"Who's Hecate?" said Kate.

"She's the witch of all witches," said B.J., gripping Miranda's hand.

"Makes the Furies look like a bridge club," said Dave, beginning to sweat.

"Hold high your lantern to share your light with your Priestess!" Lola intoned.

"Lola, stop it. You're scaring me!" Tim pleaded.

"Blessed Black Bitch, I hear your hounds baying at truth!" Lola's voice rose in an incantatory tone.

A dog began to bark outside the Red Lion.

"What the fuck?" said Baldwin.

"It's a coincidence," said Dave. The hair rose on the back of his neck.

The dog barked louder. Then another.

"Make it stop!" cried Miranda.

Kate raced to the back door and fumbled with the knob.

"It won't open!" she yelled back.

"That's impossible!" Dave shouted. He stumbled to the door and pushed. The door would not budge.

"We're trapped!" screamed Miranda.

"Calm down!" Dave yelled. "B.J.!"

B.J. wrapped his arms around Miranda's shaking frame.

"There has to be a logical explanation," Dave shouted. "LIST!"

"Go away!" he screamed.

"LIST!"

"Nooooo!" He banged his head against the door in a desperate attempt to make the ghost's voice stop.

Blood splashed on the door. His blood.

"He's hurting himself!" Kate yelled. She tried to pull Dave away from the door. "Somebody help me!"

Baldwin grabbed Dave's shoulders and pulled.

"Lead me onward!" Lola shrieked across the airwaves. She was the three Furies morphed into one.

"Stop it," screamed Tim. "Put that chair down!"

The sound of crashing furniture drowned out his terrified voice.

"Your name is writ on my soul!" Lola howled.

"NO!" screamed Too Tall Tim.

And then it happened.

The sky turned black.

The heavens opened up.

Fork lightning crashed and flashed outside the windows of the Red Lion.

Peels of thunder clapped and boomed.

Rain exploded in an Old Testament cloudburst.

"Vengeance is mine!" cried Lola.

"NO!" screamed Too Tall Tim. "Don't!"

A streak of lightning filled the bar windows as if thrown by Thor himself. His hammer pounded the sky.

"NOOOOOOOO—"

The power blew.

Darkness.

The radio signal went dead.

Silence.

EIGHTEEN

So, the two dead European guys with beards, and the old dead Greek guy with a beard and toga are drunk in a bar in Athens.

A drag queen, wearing snakes, walks in.

The drag queen says, "What do you get when an English playwright, a Spanish novelist, and a Greek poet burst into flame?"

The three men reply in unison, "What?"

And the drag queen says, "A good start."

POOF!

PART FOUR: MEASURE

"We'll measure them a measure and be gone."

William Shakespeare, *Romeo and Juliet*

ONE

The world held its breath.

Silent as a country graveyard.

Then.

Sirens.

And not the mythological variety. Rather, the sirens of three emergency vehicles—a police car and two ambulances—navigating the abandoned streets, luring curious citizens to living room windows with their bewitching wails.

TWO

The storm was over as quickly as it began. The lights flickered and power was restored.

"Oh my god," said B.J., opening his eyes.

"Oh, shit," said Dave, rubbing his bleeding forehead. There was a huge gash above his right eyebrow.

"What just happened?" Miranda quivered.

"I have no idea," said Dave, sinking to the floor.

"Did Lola just do what we think she did?" Baldwin asked, pouring himself a stiff drink from behind the bar.

No one could explain the seemingly unexplainable event.

Kate inspected Dave's wound. "You need stitches," she said.

She drove him to the hospital. As they sat in emergency, the loudspeaker was abuzz with coded alerts.

Two ambulances arrived. Too Tall Tim was rolled in on a paramedic stretcher, groaning in shock and pain. A second stretcher followed. Lola was ranting and fighting against the restraints strapping her down. Officer John followed.

The evening sun drove the clouds away. The heatwave had mysteriously ended.

ॐ

The gift basket was gigantic: boxes of delicate crackers and gourmet cheeses, English wafers, Ceylon tea, brightly coloured fruits, all wrapped up in red cellophane and tied with a big red bow. It sat upon the picnic table like an IED. The red cellophane glowed under the sun's rays. To an active imagination, it appeared to be radioactive.

The company gathered around it. Wayne and Shuster sniffed it liked trained K-9s.

"What does the card say?" asked the Nurse.

Dave tore open the small sealed envelope. The card was standard florist's stock. Three red roses bedecked the right-hand corner. Dave read aloud.

"Break many legs tonight, my lovelies!"

The sender was anonymous.

"LIST!"

The ghost did not waste a second.

"Don't touch it!" Dave got between the basket and his actors. "I don't trust it."

"Hey, man," whined the taller stoner, "You don't think it came from Lola? She's locked up."

"I don't know," said Dave. "I've got a bad feeling. She could've ordered it days ago."

"I'm hungry," said the shorter stoner. "C'mon, man, it's fine."

The Sarge grabbed the basket. "I'm with Dave on this. That crazy witch could have arranged the delivery earlier in the week. Who knows what she's done to these apples?"

"I'll get the basket to my brother after the show," said Justin.

"In the meantime, we're locking it in my truck," said the Sarge. He tossed the pair of stoners a bag of potato chips. "Go crazy."

ॐ

The controversy over censorship did not seem to bother the residents of Kinmount. A packed opening-night crowd brought the old sawmill back to life. Lawn chairs stretched back to the parking lot. Picnic blankets covered the ground.

Robert volunteered to work the box office, such as it was.

He sat at a folding card table and collected the donations in a decommissioned aquarium. It had been his daughter's as a child, filled with angelfish, neon tetras, and an adventurous newt named Ralph, who died one morning after having climbed over the glass in an attempted prison break. He'd managed to crawl across the kitchen floor as far as the sink mat before drying out. But he'd left a legacy—his old underwater "home" was now filled to the brim with a different kind of "fish," the cold, hard cash variety—purple dead prime ministers and civil rights activists, and faded green queens.

The audience was filled with familiar faces—the Reimer family, Jimmy O'Connor, the Murrays, and the seniors from across the river. The Reimers sat on the ground in the front row, not wanting to spoil the view for children.

During the final scene, Jimmy's grandson, Finbar, screamed at Romeo that Juliet was faking her death. Romeo refused to listen.

The show went off without an iambic hitch, save for the actors' sweat. The stage lights coupled with the summer night created a sauna—the period costumes would have to be cleaned daily. Not surprisingly, Flo's Laundry-Copy refused to help. Dave sprayed them with vodka, an old trick he'd learned from Ms. Greerson.

ॐ

Dave's remaining days in Kinmount flew by.

He and Kate spent the Saturday afternoon before the closing night performance exploring the fairgrounds. Dave won her a stuffed pink snake at ring toss.

Too Tall Tim was back in action, his remote setup between vendors of pretzels and beavertails in front of the race track. He wore a neck brace and stuck to his usual livestock jokes. "What happened to the cow that jumped over the barbed wire fence? Udder destruction."

"Too Tall Tim makes Al Pacino look like a giant," Dave shared with Kate as she drove him back to the motel. "He's the perfect height for an armrest. He's not at all what I'd pictured in my head. Funny that." Radio personalities never matched their on-air voice.

A final packed crowd for closing. Word had spread. Theatregoers and the merely curious showed up from across eastern Ontario. Even a few die-hards made the trip from Ottawa and Toronto.

Reilly, true to his word, sat on a cushion in the front row on closing night.

"How much?" asked Dave, watching Robert and Ginny finish tabulating the final door receipts.

"Guess," she said.

"Four thousand," said Dave.

"Ten," said Robert.

"Ten thousand?" said Dave.

"Ten thousand beautiful-arts-loving-dollars!" Ginny gushed.

"Who would have thought it? In Kinmount, of all places" said Dave. He was gob smacked.

"You caught the windmill, David," Robert grinned triumphantly.

Justin was paid back in full. Dave, B.J., and Miranda received full payment. The company voted and agreed to purchase a replacement tent for Kate and a new bike for Dave. *Romeo and Juliet* still had a surplus of five thousand dollars. The rest of the cash was given to the actors and Ginny—four hundred and fifty dollars each.

The company assembled at the Red Lion to celebrate closing night. Jimmy's idea of hosting a cast party was offering two-for-one chicken wings.

Kate was busy working the bar, as per usual. B.J. had joined Miranda and her parents at a table. Baldwin was busy flirting with Miranda's younger sister.

Lady Capulet and her fiancée, Jennifer, sat at the bar sipping spritzers with Ginny.

Rufus, Peter, Paris, and the Nurse danced to the Prince's retro collection and sang karaoke alongside a legion of adoring Saturday night female fans.

"I didn't get to see it," said a middle-aged karaoke regular with pink dyed hair. "I don't understand Shakespeare. What was it about?"

The Prince gave her a squeeze. "Well, it's about this Prince."

The Friar glumly watched from the sidelines, devouring potato skins, vowing to himself to move out of Kinmount come September.

The stoner servants had a better offer—a game of Lights Out in Bobcat's basement.

Justin worked the room, making sure everyone was having a celebratory good time.

Dave's directorial disconnect had started on opening night despite acting in the show. Under normal conditions, opening night was the testing time of the whole process—there was nothing left for him to do. The performance was in the hands of the actors and technical crew. Dave preferred to watch his openings in the back of the theatre, his theory being he could make a quick getaway if necessary. He never stayed for opening night parties, much less closing night. Opening nights were akin to giving birth and then no longer being necessary. An inescapable loneliness required slipping out the back door. But Dave could not Paul Simon his way out of *Romeo and Juliet*—he was stuck playing Capulet.

He sat at a table in the back in mid-conversation.

"Can you believe that idiot misread the weather report?" he said to Ziggy and Robert. "Rain *was* in the forecast."

"Still, it was a strange coincidence," said Robert.

"Pretty random," said Ziggy.

"No," said Dave. "Wayne and Shuster were the dogs barking outside the door of the Red Lion. Justin had pulled in to warn us about the oncoming storm. So we could protect the lighting equipment. I couldn't open the back door because it had been slammed the night before by Jimmy and the dead bolt mechanism had jammed. You see? There was a perfectly logical explanation, not some far-fetched witch's spell."

"And Lola?" asked Robert.

"Admitted to the psych ward," replied Dave.

"We'll never know for certain if she caused the storm or not," said Ziggy, picking the olives off his nachos, subscribing to the belief there were more things in Heaven and Hell than dreamt of in Dave's philosophy.

"Don't let your imagination run away with you," said Dave. "At least she's off the street and in custody."

"I think it's sad," said Robert, biting into a nacho. "I still wonder what happened to her."

"I don't," said Dave. "I'm officially finished."

"What's next?" asked Robert.

"No idea," said Dave. "Back to Birch Lake and I'll see what August brings."

"What about you Ziggy?" asked Robert.

"I'm going to petition the prime minister to have the Burnt River recognized as a legal entity," Ziggy replied. "It's time to save the environment around here."

"I can tell you exactly what's going to happen," offered up Dave cynically. "The feds will rename the river Ms. Burnt River and spend hundreds of thousands of dollars on new signage, completely missing the point."

Justin sat down beside them.

"It's been a blast, Dave," he said, toasting Dave with a club soda.

"Thanks again, man," Dave said. "We couldn't've done it without you."

"People loved the show," said Justin. "You should hear the buzz on the street. Kinmount is the new Stratford."

"Hardly," Dave thought. "That's great," he said instead.

"So, I've decided to produce the Shakespeare in the Park next summer," Justin shared, full of sober exuberance. "With one condition—you return to direct."

"What?" Dave laughed. "*As You Like It* set within a nine-teenth-century Mennonite community with a few bad apples?"

"Sounds good to me," said Justin.

"Let me think on it," said Dave. "Next summer is a long way off."

Goodbyes were said. Hugs given and received. Phone numbers exchanged to be forgotten. Equipment taken away. Costumes washed and packed. B.J. got a lift home with Miranda and her parents.

ॐ

By Sunday afternoon, there was no sign the show had ever existed.

Robert sat with Dave having a farewell pint at the Red Lion.

"'Twas ever thus," he said, "the bittersweet ephemeral nature of live theatre, living on only in the memories of those happy few who partook."

"The dying breed of the twenty-first century," replied Dave sadly.

"Hey, listen to this!" exclaimed Kate from behind the bar, turning up the radio.

"Breaking news," announced Too Tall Tim. "An arrest has been made in connection with the Burnt River tent hit-and-run, the Twin Pines Motel vandalism, the gift basket apple poisoning incident, and, the real kicker, the ecology centre arson and homicide a few years back. And it's not Lola Whale, folks."

"What!?" exclaimed Dave, nearly falling off his chair.

"Nope," Tim continued. "Florence 'Flo' Moyer, owner of the Laundry-Copy, has been taken into custody. Well, shit, oops, shoot, doesn't that beat all."

Too Tall Tim and the Red Lion patrons both sat in stunned silence. Kate turned off the radio.

"The Ghost was right," said Dave as the revelation slowly dawned on him.

"Pardon me?" said Robert not comprehending.

"Long story," said Dave. "He tried to warn me during the radio call-in show. I'd just mentioned Flo's name as possibly being one of Lola's Furies."

His gut instinct had been trying to tell him the truth all along.

"There's something I have to do," he said to the two of them.

THREE

"How is she?" he asked the older volunteer at the nursing station, while discreetly reading her nametag.

"Athena," he smiled. "Nice name."

"It's Greek," she said.

"Trust me, I know," he said with a quiet little laugh. He shook his head—maybe Horatio *was* onto something.

"What's so funny?" she asked.

"Cosmic coincidence," he said. "Nothing more."

"She's heavily sedated. Don't do or say anything that might upset her."

Dave tapped on the door as he entered the room.

Lying in bed in her hospital gown, Lola was tiny and frail. She appeared far older without her wigs, costumes, and makeup.

"Lola?" he said quietly.

She rolled over in the direction of his voice. He could barely recognize the face staring up at him, eyes glazed over from sedatives. Not a Fury, but a broken, haunted lonely soul.

"We are all broken in one way or another," Dave thought aloud. "Doing the best we can."

He squeezed her hand.

FOUR

Dave pulled into his driveway shortly after noon. The tree was gone. His shade was gone.

The leftover stump served as a gravestone. Dave counted its age-defining rings. The Manitoba Maple had been cut before its time.

He unlocked and entered his tiny bungalow. The house smelt musty and unlived in, the way it always did when he returned from an out-of-town gig. He opened his fridge to grab a Keith's. It was the last of his beer and the only item in the fridge. The beer bottle felt warm to the touch. He noticed the fridge light was off. He examined the bulb. It looked fine. He flicked the light switch on in the kitchen. Nothing. He turned on the radio. Nothing. He checked the fuse box. Nothing was amiss. He flicked on his bathroom light. Nothing.

"Oh, shit," he muttered to himself. He found the unopened disconnection notice tucked inside his First Folio. He'd been using it as a bookmark. He'd have to go to the hydro office first thing in the morning. Until then, there would be no light breaking through his yonder window.

He checked his cell phone. It was half-charged. Enough juice to get him through the night.

He surveyed the latest carnage, as he always did, from his being away. His three spider plants, which sat on the windowsill over his kitchen sink, were dead; their leaves grey and yellowed, drooping sadly like three dying soldiers tangled in barbed wire. He searched under the sink for a garbage bag. He was out.

He opened his back door. The deck and walls were covered in dried-out shadflies, the last wave of the July invasion. "What would possess anyone to want to study bugs?" He set about sweeping up the carpet of stinking corpses when there was a knock on the front door.

"Now what?" he said to himself.

He opened the door. It was Skip, his neighbour, holding a stack of mail.

"Welcome back," he said. "How did it go?'

"It went," Dave said, consciously putting Kinmount in the past. It was a familiar ritual. "I survived."

"I saw the articles online. Sounds like you had quite the battle."

"I tilted at a few windmills," said Dave, being deliberately crisp so he could collect his mail and shut the door. He was in no mood for Skip's banter.

"Right, okay," said Skip. "Anyhow, here's your mail. Hydro was by a couple of times while you were gone. Cut your tree down. And they were by again yesterday. Went around to the back of the house."

The last thing Dave wanted to mention was that he was stupid enough to let his power be cut off. Skip already thought he was odd enough.

"Thanks for checking on things and cutting my lawn. I'll get that six-pack over to you tomorrow," he said, starting to shut the door.

"No worries. Hey, we still have to have you two over for a barbecue. How's Friday night?"

"Sure thing," said Dave, closing the door.

"Yesterday. Really?" he said to himself, while rummaging for emergency candles and a lighter.

The sound of a dog barking excitedly next door interrupted his search. "Hell is other people's pets," he mumbled to no one. He braced himself to deal with Ruffles when his cell phone began to ring. He checked the caller ID.

"Hi Mom," he said, taking a swig of warm beer.

"You're back," she said in her usual "why-didn't-you-call-me-the-minute you-walked-in-the-door" tone of voice.

"Yes, I'm back," he said, waiting to see where the conversation was headed. It dawned on him for the first time that his mother sounded like Lola.

He didn't mention the hydro disconnection.

"I'm glad you're back," his mother said.

"Me too." His house had its familiar empty feeling.

"There was just no way I could manage to get up there to see it," she said. "What with this bad hip and all."

His mother had been refusing to have hip replacement surgery for months, fearing the doctors would botch it and she'd be using a walker for the rest of her life.

"I understand, Mom. It went well," he said, and genuinely meant it.

"Good. No more monkey business with that producer woman?"

"No more monkey business with that producer woman," Dave repeated slowly with a serenity he wasn't accustomed to.

Lola's healing had begun, dependent on the kindness of strangers.

Aeschylus got it right. And so had Chickpea. It really *wasn't* over until the fat parakeet sang.

"Have you called your ex?"

His mother was utterly predictable.

"Yes, I called her."

"And?"

"We're meeting for coffee later in the week."

"Good. I like Rosaline."

"So do I. Look, mom, I really have to—"

"So, did you sleep with anyone down in Old McDonald farm country?"

"Mom!"

"Well, did you?" His mother was relentless.

"Stop it. It's none of your business. And, no, I did not."

"Who is she?"

"Enough! Okay, yes, I met someone, all right. But we're just friends. Her name is Kate and she's—"

"Some bar maid, no doubt."

"We are not having this conversation."

He hung up and polished off the rest of his beer.

His phone began to ring.

"Look, mom, I already told you—"

"Mr. Middleton, eh?" said a voice with a thick northern Ontario accent.

"Oh, I'm sorry," Dave apologized. "I thought it was my mother calling back. She does that. Ad infinitum"

"No problem. This is Herbert Ross callin'."

"What can I do for you, Mr. Ross?" Dave asked warily. He didn't recognize the name or the accent.

I'm callin' from Little Hawk Lake on behalf of our community centre," Herbert Ross of Little Hawk Lake began.

Dave didn't have a clue where Little Hawk Lake was.

"The folks up here have been readin' about you and that Shakespeare play you just put on. Now to be gettin' to the point of the scissors, we're startin' up a twenty-four-hour summer Shadfly Festival next year. And we want you to come on up here and put on a show. Somethin' big. With wings. Free accommodation and we'll fly ya in, the whole nine yards! So, whattya say?"

"LIST!"

"He travels best that knows when to return."

Thomas Middleton

Afterword

Kinmount

I chose the name simply because of the comic noun and verb combination. For no other reason.

I have never a directed a show in Kinmount, Ontario.

I first noticed the exit sign for Kinmount on Highway 35, over a decade ago, on my way to summer stock rehearsals in Haliburton. A few summers ago, I stopped in for a quick sight-seeing visit while driving home to North Bay from Brockville – specifically to check out the Burnt River, the Austin Sawmill, the Highlands Cinema, and the Fairgrounds.

Some historical facts in the novel regarding the fictional Kinmount are based on its real-life counterpart. The village is named after sixteenth-century Scottish border warrior Kinmount Willie and logging on the Burnt River was its primary industry.

After that, any resemblance ends.

The real-life Kinmount is a lovely spot nestled in the beautiful Ontario Highlands and home to a population of five-hundred friendly highlanders and summer cottagers.

This fact isn't in the novel - Kinmount was incorporated on April Fool's Day, 1859.

Acknowledgements

I salute all the artists still fighting the good fight in the trenches of live theatre. To all of you whom I have had the pleasure to collaborate with in those trenches (and it is a long list) I thank you.

I want to pay tribute to my mentor, Neil Freeman, for turning me on to Shakespeare and setting me on my First Folio orthographic journey at York University in 1984. You left us too soon, old friend.

I have to thank my incredible wife, Marian Robinson. From reading early drafts, supporting my long hours of writing and rewriting, and providing invaluable input, she was as important to *Kinmount*'s realization as I was.

I want to thank John Metcalf for making me a better writer. My deep thanks and respect to Mitchell Gauvin—he is the kind of incisive, insightful editor the Canadian publishing industry is lucky to have. His astute advice was always timely and spot-on. Thanks to Kevin Hoffman for the cover design.

And special thanks to Heather Campbell of Latitude 46 Publishing for her tireless vision and support of Northern Ontario writers—more trench work.

Exit pursued by bear.

About the Author

Rod's first novel, *A Matter of Will,* was a finalist for the 2018 Northern Lit Award for Fiction. His short story, "A Farewell to Steam," was featured in the non-fiction anthology, *150 Years Up North and More*, in 2018. His short story, "Botox and the Brontosaurus", appears in Volume I of the online magazine *Cloud Lake Literary*. Rod is also an award-winning director, playwright, and actor, having directed and produced over 100 theatrical productions to date, including fifteen adaptations of Shakespeare. He was the 2009 winner of TVO's Big Ideas/ Best Lecturer competition. *Kinmount* is his second novel. www. rodcarley.ca.